D0981523

PRAISE FOR
Beth Gutcheon and *Leeway Cottage*

"Often, when a novel is labeled 'ambitious,' we understand that its re-
viewer is giving the writer a polite A for effort, while silently deducting
points on literary merit and readability. What words then—important?
'unforgettable'?—to describe ambition realized, as in the case of Beth
Gutcheon's enthralling seventh novel. . . . There is wit here and an eye
for the telling detail. . . . *Leeway Cottage* is a triumphant and true love
story."                                                          —*Boston Globe*

"Incredible. . . . A remarkably rich and emotionally jarring novel filled
ultimately with hope."                                                —*Pages*

"Stirring. . . . Narrated at split-second speed. . . . The World War II saga
anchors the novel, giving it resonance beyond the family dramas
Gutcheon tells so well. Her extensive historic research . . . gives a sense
of authenticity."                                          —*Los Angeles Times*

"As few novelists could, Beth Gutcheon, author of six outstanding
books, juggles the incredible, little-known story of Denmark's citizens'
rescue of more than seven thousand Jewish compatriots with the story of
wartime America. . . . Gutcheon sees the human condition clearly and
records it with compassionate understanding. . . . *Leeway Cottage* is a gentle,
even tender book. Every reader will be wiser for it."                —*BookPage*

"A good old-fashioned, all-encompassing read, with tears and smiles guar-
anteed."                                                     —*Library Journal*

"A rich saga of an American family told with moving clarity. . . . Beth
Gutcheon's novel is a symphonic exploration of the ties that bind and
just as often rend."                                   —*Milwaukee Journal-Sentinel*

$2.05  MAY 2015

"Compelling. . . . Ambitious. . . . The author's gift for plunging readers directly into her story is evident on the first page. . . . Gutcheon's insights are . . . keen, her sympathy for all her characters . . . [is] contagious."

—*Kirkus Reviews*


"[*Leeway Cottage*] is one of those books that makes you not care if you're delayed in the airport several hours while waiting for your connecting flight. That's high praise for summer reading."

—*San Antonio Express-News*


"Charting a marriage against the backdrop of a tumultuous century, Gutcheon writes evocatively of love and war."      —*Publishers Weekly*


"Deliciously readable."                    —*San Francisco Chronicle*


"Gutcheon's tale is more than just a story of a marriage; it's a metaphor for an era."                           —*Booklist*

# LEEWAY COTTAGE

Also by Beth Gutcheon

# LEEWAY COTTAGE

Beth Gutcheon

HARPER ⬤ PERENNIAL

NEW YORK • LONDON • TORONTO • SYDNEY

HARPER ● PERENNIAL

This novel is a work of fiction. References to real people, events, establishments, organizations, and locales are intended only to convey a picture of the real world in which the fictional story takes place. All other names, characters, and places, and all dialogue and incidents portrayed in this book, are the products of the author's imagination.

A hardcover edition of this book was published in 2005 by William Morrow, an imprint of HarperCollins Publishers.

P.S.™ is a trademark of HarperCollins Publishers.

LEEWAY COTTAGE. Copyright © 2005 by Beth Gutcheon. All rights reserved. Printed in the United States of America. No part of this book may be used or reproduced in any manner whatsoever without written permission except in the case of brief quotations embodied in critical articles and reviews. For information address HarperCollins Publishers, 10 East 53rd Street, New York, NY 10022.

HarperCollins books may be purchased for educational, business, or sales promotional use. For information please write: Special Markets Department, HarperCollins Publishers, 10 East 53rd Street, New York, NY 10022.

FIRST HARPER PERENNIAL EDITION PUBLISHED 2006.

*Designed by Jeffrey Pennington*

The Library of Congress has catalogued the hardcover edition as follows:

Gutcheon, Beth Richardson.
    Leeway cottage : a novel / Beth Gutcheon.—1st ed.
        p.   cm.
    ISBN 0-06-053905-4 (hardcover : alk. paper)
        1. Married people—Fiction.    2. Summer resorts—Fiction.
3. Maine—Fiction.    I. Title.

PS3557.U844L44  2005
813'.54—dc22          2004054111

ISBN-10: 0-06-053906-2 (pbk.)
ISBN-13: 978-0-06-053906-1 (pbk.)

07 08 09 10 ❖/RRD 10 9 8 7 6 5 4

*For Frank Kelley, magister optimus*

# LEEWAY COTTAGE

The funeral is over. The ashes, in matching urns, are on the mantelpiece. There is no way to know whose last will or testament is in force, so they have decided to close the house as always, and leave it for the winter. Next summer, when the flood tides of memories and mourning currently swamping them have receded, they will be better able to cope.

They have decided that each of them will take home one thing from Leeway for the winter, for comfort. They are going through the house somberly, saying their goodbyes in their different ways, each looking for one object that will keep the dead alive and close a little longer.

In the back of a closet in the upstairs hall, Eleanor opens an ancient garment bag and finds a shapeless and tarnished handful of ribbons and tulle. She gives a shriek.

Monica and Jimmy emerge from back bedrooms. "What *is* that?"

"It's The Dress!"

"She *kept* it all these years?"

The three of them stare at it, the debutante dress of legend. It is more of a rag than the couture dream they had imagined. Eleanor puts it back on the hanger and zips it back up in its bag, where it will wait, ready to be called as evidence in a yet-to-be-settled case of outrage in which all the principal parties are now dead.

Although none of them has said so, what each of them most wants to take home is the house guestbook.

Monica finds it.

"I've decided," she calls from the dining room.

Eleanor comes in from the big living room where she has been scanning the bookshelves, and sees her sister holding the very thing she was looking for.

"Finders keepers," says Monica.

"Where was it?"

Jimmy is coming down the stairs.

"In there," says Monica, pointing to an antique tavern table their parents used as a sideboard. "In the drawer."

Jimmy walks in holding a framed picture of their father and mother sitting in the stern of *The Rolling Stone*. They are at anchor in some island cove, Burnt Coat, or Pretty Marsh. The sunset flares gold on the water behind them, and they are tanned and happy, holding cocktails and wearing sunglasses and smiles. Jimmy has been about to announce this as his choice when he sees the guest book in Monica's hand.

"I was looking for that!" he says.

"It turns out we all were," says Eleanor.

"Where was it?"

The sisters point to the tavern table.

"I say 'finders keepers,' " says Monica.

"Unless one of us owns the table." Their mother has employed her sunset years in wandering around the house promising things to people, often the same thing two or three times, and applying stickers delivering her orders from beyond the grave.

Eleanor kneels down to peer under the table. She pulls her head out and reaches for the glasses on a cord around her neck. She pokes her head under again and reads, " 'Property of James Brant Moss.' " She stands up and looks at her sister, and they both say, "Oh, surprise."

$M$ore than one person in the hundred-odd years since it was built has wished that the walls of Leeway Cottage could talk.

The house sits on the crest of a hill overlooking Great Spruce Bay in Dundee, Maine, where once Homer Carleton grazed his sheep, and before that his father, Horace, went broke trying to dam a stream and develop a waterworks. There are still rusting cables and huge blocks of dressed granite to be found at the stream or in the woods, to the delight of the summer children who arrived after the Carletons sold up and moved inland.

Before the Carletons, generations of Abenaki Indians made their winter camp in the lee of this hill, and left an important kitchen midden at the foot of the meadow. This was found and dug out in the 1920s by a local enthusiast, to the despair of scientists who came after him. (Gladdy and Tommy McClintock and Annabee Brant loved watching the Enthusiast fiddling away with his brushes and little diggers all one summer when they were children. They often pitched in with trowels and garden spades in the evening, after the man had gone back to the village for supper.) Archeologists who arrived in later decades hoped to learn the structure of the Indian shelters and their social arrangements: ephemeral truths of how lives were lived, conveyed less by the objects themselves (of which the museum at Orono already had plenty) than by their placement in their surroundings when found. Too late: what was left of the midden at Leeway Cottage was a large pit turned into an underground clubhouse by the McClintock children, and a shoe box left to the household by the happy amateur, full of useless arrowheads, shells, and bone fragments, and ever after stored under the pantry sink.

Though it has not yet been discovered, there is also a sizable cemetery under the brow of the hill, made some nine thousand years ago by an earlier people who buried their dead with red ochre. There was most likely also faith and ceremony; there may have been dancing, keening, antiphonal singing, for all we know. Of all their motion and sound and feeling about their dead, only a color remains. They had left the area so long before the Abenakis arrived that no one now can say who they were, or where they came from, or why they disappeared.

Apparently no human, from the red ochre people to the Brants and McClintocks, had failed to notice that here was a stirringly beautiful swath of God's creation. In the twentieth century, Leeway Cottage sat in a broad sweep of yellow meadow in summer, filled with wildflowers and crowned with a huge oak that many claimed was the oldest in the state. The house was a big, airy ramshackle cross between a castle and a barn, wide open and welcoming, yet with a breezy austerity, as if it dreamed it were a summer house on some Baltic island off the coast of Sweden. It was built by Ingvar Eggers, sailor and violist in the Ischl Quartet, who first came up the coast in 1882 with Herman Thiele scouting for a cool retreat like the mountain spas of Europe, as a haven for themselves and for fellow musicians escaping the heat of Boston, Philadelphia, and New York. The house Eggers had built on the lee shore of the bay for his growing brood of children ever after smelled of fir balsam and pipe smoke and summerhouse books. The main room was vast, filled with dark oak furniture and iron lamps sporting oiled-paper shades made and painted by Mrs. Eggers. It became the site for Sunday-afternoon musical gatherings of friends and colleagues who had settled near each other. When the weather was fine, and the music drifted out the windows along with the floating voile curtains, summer neighbors drew up on the lawn to listen, then ventured up to sit in comfort on the porch, and finally were welcomed inside, officially an audience.

There was a huge fireplace at one end of the hall, made of egg-smooth popple stones gathered from the beaches of certain of the outer islands. The walls of this room held books from floor to ceiling, and the window seats were filled with board games, cards, jacks, Pick-Up Sticks, poker chips, and wooden jigsaw puzzles. There were four or five bedrooms upstairs, and two full bathrooms, with cast-iron tubs on claw-feet and the flushes in separate closets in the European style. A ground-floor wing with three or four more bedrooms set off in a northerly direction beyond the kitchen. Framed on the wall of the downstairs powder room was a letter, dated November 1889, to August Dodge, the local builder. In a confident script it read: "Dear Mr. Dodge, Mrs. Eggers has had another baby. We will need two more bedrooms and a bathroom, to be ready by June 15. Yours sincerely, Ingvar Eggers." No further instructions had been given or taken, and when the family arrived they found the rooms ready and entirely to their satisfaction.

There had been fewer, over the years, who wished that the walls of The Elms could talk.

It was not that the lives lived at The Elms were less interesting than those at Leeway, but they were more formal, more public, and because lived on a scale unsustainable without a large staff, little that happened there had gone unobserved or unreported in the first place.

The Elms was built in 1889 by Mrs. James Brant, a wealthy widow from Cleveland who had been to Newport and to Bar Harbor, and knew what she wanted. This turned out to be a vast stone villa with Tudor pretensions, formal gardens, a carriage house, a boathouse, and a sort of hospital wing for the comfort of her daughter, Louisa, who had "never been right."

Annabelle Brant had a great deal of money she had not been born to or raised to handle. Her charms were many. She was good at sports and games, physically brave, fairly witty, and could be extremely generous both civically and privately. On her first visit to Dundee, she stayed at The Homestead on Carleton Point, the new boardinghouse, from which the guests took picnics to the top of Butter Hill, went bathing at the small sand beach on the Point (a rarity on these rocky shores), played cards, went to dances, and played some decorous tennis on a grass court built by a leading citizen of the town, Simon Osgood. The next year, Annabelle returned to The Homestead for the whole summer, bringing her children, two nannies, her horses and carriage, and an English coachman who by chance was also called Osgood. She loved the freedom and informality of life in the summer colony. After spending so much of her Cleveland life under the brooding cloud cover that seemed constantly to expire into the sky from Lake Erie, she loved Dundee's succession of brilliant blue and gold summer days. She especially loved the music played all around the village by those artistic people, and by the third year she had bought a beautiful stretch of this heaven just off Carleton Point and set about creating an establishment.

Simon Osgood, who was taking a flier in copper mining up the Kingdom Road in these years and planning a hotel in town for the commerce he hoped would soon be booming there, had stopped in at Gus Dodge's shop the autumn that work on The Elms began. After he studied the plans he asked, "In what sense is this a cottage?" Gus thought about it and said, "I guess because she left out the throne room."


Early in the summer of 1890, when the house was finished, Annabelle Brant gave a party. She invited the carpenters, masons, painters, and plumbers who had worked on The Elms to bring their wives and show off the magnificence they had created. She invited the local gentry insofar as she understood it. The Osgood family was there, of course. Dr. Bliss and the August Dodges came, also Phineas Treworgy and his daughter (that was rather a mistake), Captain and Mrs. Cousins, and Miss Catherine Bowey and her mother. Mrs. Amelia Smith Beedle, a successful novelist of the day who summered on the eastern side of the bay, arrived dressed entirely in lavender, including her parasol and her hose. And Mrs. Brant invited the musicians: Thaddeuzs and Lottie Hanenberger, the Eggerses, Mrs. Mabel Thomas, the Stoeckels, and the entire Ischl Quartet.

The town talked about the party for the rest of the summer. How old Mrs. Bowey, who shared a birthday with Queen Victoria and had a fixation on her, explained to Mrs. Hanenberger that this was a "cottage" because the front door opened directly into the reception hall, with no "foy-ay" (she pronounced it in the French manner), and that the Queen's Cottage in Kew Gardens was exactly the same. How Mr. Simon Osgood invaded the kitchen to see the New Process stove that was said to be so clean and efficient. (He predicted, correctly, that Florence Eaton, who was cooking for Mrs. Brant, would have a good iron woodstove back in there before the summer was over. The New Process was moved to Miss Louisa's wing, where her keeper, Miss Burns, claimed to like it.) How the carpenters' wives were made to admire the elaborate paneling, hand-carved in Florence, Italy, that their husbands had installed in the dining room, and how Mr. Leander Osgood went out to the stable to introduce himself to the English coachman, and see if they were cousins. (The coachman Osgood was scandalized at this and didn't know where to look.)

Miss Louisa, who was then twenty, wore a very pretty muslin afternoon dress and sat with Miss Burns in the Great Hall near the tea table. Miss Burns was from Glasgow. Louisa's brother, James, who had just finished his first year at Princeton, had half a dozen friends visiting, including a boy who flirted recklessly with Berthe Hanenberger in the gazebo. It was the beginning of a halcyon summer in the Carleton Point colony. Did the young ladies want to take a canoeing picnic to Beal Island? James Brant drove to Old Town and brought

back canoes. Did Miss Hanenberger play tennis? By September she
did, and by the next June there were two more grass courts in addition to the one at The Elms, one at Leeway, and one at the Thomas
cottage. One of the houseguests at The Elms brought golf clubs, and
Mrs. Brant at once ordered a slice of the lawn made into a putting
green. The guest didn't know how to use any of the clubs except the
putter, but Miss Burns did and soon there was a positive mania for
teeing up golf balls on little cones of sand and driving them into the
salt pond. By the end of the decade, a man who belonged to the
Country Club at Brookline, Massachusetts, had drawn a scheme for
a nine-hole course that would just fit on the acres between Mrs.
Brant's cottage and the causeway over the salt pond, artfully making
water hazards of the deep inlets that reached into the rock shoreline
and then withdrew every six hours, like the fluid fingers of a tidal
hand. Mrs. Brant organized an association of summer sportsmen and
donated the land to this newly formed Dundee Golf Association. By
the next season the course was ready for play.

In Dundee, Annabelle Brant had found the perfect theater for the
performance she'd been giving in Cleveland to insufficient notice,
for her taste. It was just the right size, big enough for the scope she
required, but not so big that she was likely to be upstaged or out-
classed. A summer had the same magical sheen as a play or ballet, exactly because it was not year-round, like real life; it existed only in a
single known and idyllic season each year. In every June arrival,
one's first spicy draft of the fir-scented air upon stepping from the
Boston packet onto Carleton Point Landing contained the knowledge of September, that what began would end. Because it would
end, one was free to be transported, as at a performance or in a ship-
board romance. And for the duration of its annual run, Annabelle
Brant could take the stage confident that everyone, from her many
guests to the rudest mechanical in the village, was taking in every
gesture. On the Cleveland stage there were too many other players.
And the audience knew too much about her, and she about them, for
either to fully enjoy the experience.

The role she had chosen for herself was a mixture of Lady Boun-
tiful and the Queen of Sheba, occasionally (and sometimes jarringly)

interrupted by portrayals of the Blessed Virgin in devotions to her sacred child. Although it was her son, James, whom she loved with a passion that was slightly unhinged, these maternal displays usually involved Louisa in the supporting role, a part gentle, stunted Louisa played nearly perfectly. There are worse things that can happen to some mothers than to have a child trapped in childhood, as long as the trap is sprung after continence has been achieved and before the onset of adolescent rebellion, and in Louisa's case it had been. Miss Burns kept Louisa clean and groomed and prevented her doing anything unseemly in public, and Louisa's own gentleness kept the illusion attractive.

While Louisa played the changeless tot, her brother, James, was cast as the love interest in the family drama. The Victorian Age was one that so romanticized the bond between mother and children that this did not appear as grotesque as it might have to another era. Annabelle didn't like a lot of surprises. It seemed natural for her to have all the important roles played by people who were dependent on her, financially or otherwise, and she was a woman of appetites, fun-loving and not yet old. James was a delightful young man, and he was hers; why wouldn't she dote on him? For one thing, James took after her late husband. He was almost handsome, with a square-jawed open face, sleek dark hair, and a ready smile. He was gregarious and full of goodwill; he expected to be loved and approved of and he pretty universally had been. James had a dim understanding that his mother packed some big guns, with which she occasionally mowed down menials who displeased her, but as she had never turned her firepower on him, he didn't concern himself. Instead he thought of her as a delightful eccentric, an attitude that charmed her, as most of his attitudes did. She enjoyed the tacit assumption that he was the love of her life and she was his, for twenty-eight years, right up to the moment he announced he had fallen in love with Berthe Hanenberger.

It was a shock to both their systems. James was a rising young man of business in Cleveland by that time. He'd been a favorite beau to the city's debutantes for a decade, as well as an invaluable escort and bridge-whist partner to his mother. Though he had his own social life, James took dinner with Annabelle several nights a week and every Sunday noon after church. He was available to take his sister for drives out to the Shaker Lakes, and to go to the theater. He joined Annabelle at The Elms for several weeks every summer and filled the house with friends and amusements. Annabelle expected he would marry someday, and she sometimes pictured planning a wedding with the grateful parents of some charming and biddable Cleveland bride. It would be another delightful entertainment, starring herself and her James. There was no room in this scenario for his loving the likes of Berthe Hanenberger.

The entry in the Leeway Cottage Guest Book for the Sunday it started was in Ingvar's handwriting.

> *Very hot—most of the audience sat on the porch and listened at the windows. Two of Herman's students played the new "Dolly Suite" of Gabriel Fauré, for piano à quatre mains. Extremely charming. Berthe Hanenberger is home from Germany and gave us some Brahms lieder. Mother served more than two gallons of lemonade and we ran out of ice. Thunderstorm after supper.*

A house's guest book is a public document, while falling in love, though it often happens in public, is a private cataclysm. It happened to James when young Berthe happened to catch his eyes with hers and hold them a moment as she sang. He was one of the few sitting inside, steaming in white linen trousers and shirtsleeves. He hadn't seen Berthe in years. He remembered her fondly, the shy girl with the charming giggle who'd just put up her hair and gone into long skirts when they first came to the Point, and Bud Harbison made such a play for her. She'd been game and sweet and a great addition to their bunch that year. But now here she was all grown-up and apparently effortlessly making this astonishing sound. This young woman was *alive,* she had a whole vibrant universe inside her, and suddenly he saw his true home. He had been born to share that universe with her, to nurture and protect it, and to know that when she sang, no matter how many people heard her, he was her true audience.

It took him the rest of the summer to make her see what had to happen next. She returned his feelings fast enough, once she realized how serious he was. Who wouldn't? He was a sweet and lucky and happy man. They spent every minute together that they could. They took her younger brothers and sisters, along with several of the Leeway children, on picnics to the top of Butter Hill. She came to The Elms to sing for Louisa and Miss Burns; he borrowed the carriage from Osgood and drove her, with her parents, to Schoodic Point, which the Hanenbergers had always wanted to visit, and then to a tearoom where they had popovers and homemade jam. They gathered blueberries and played golf in full view of Annabelle and her set, maintaining cheerful decorum for all to see, while aching for each other. Once they dared to go out for a moonlight sail, just the two of them. The water was like melted silver and the stars seemed closer to earth than they had ever been. James asked Berthe to sing for him, and she did, her voice pure and gleaming; he felt it darting into the night sky as if it could sew the stars together, making a net that would suspend them together forever. After that, the thought of parting was unbearable. James proposed marriage. Berthe's soft brown eyes filled with tantalized hope, while her mouth said, But, but, but . . . Her father's plans for her. What she owed him. James said, "You are my life." She said miserably, "I love you. But there are other people in the world . . ." She meant in her world. People she also loved, to whom she had obligations. He, elated, said, "But you love me."

James went home and told his mother he was going to marry Berthe Hanenberger, half expecting congratulations. Annabelle said terrible and unjust things about foreigners in general and the Hanenbergers in particular. (One might know them socially, these were modern times, but to marry out of one's class and culture . . . James managed not to point out that his father had done just that when he married *her,* but holding his tongue made him nearly as miserable as speaking out would have.)

Berthe told *her* mother that they were terribly in love, hoping for an ally, but found none. Her parents wanted her to marry someone worldly, mature, highly cultured—these Brants, they were from *Ohio,* they hadn't traveled, they spoke no languages, they were grocers or something, weren't they? . . . The Hanenbergers belonged to an aristocracy of talent and accomplishment recognized the world over, while Annabelle Brant with her purchased grandeur was a comic figure. "You have a gift from God," her father announced. "You can't build a *career* amid *burghers* in *Cleveland* . . ."

It was terrible. James and Berthe suffered at their separate dinner tables the layered pain of having upset people they loved, and of being bereft themselves. They escaped from their houses and met in secret, in one of the changing cabins at the bathing beach where nobody went in the evenings. The cabins were made of wood, painted on the outside but unfinished inside, and they smelled strongly of pine sap and towels and damp bathing shoes. In Mrs. Eggers's cabin, where the children had made a row of sea urchin shells and sand dollars along the two-by-fours that braced the walls, they agreed that the furor they had caused was intolerable. They would part forever. They held each other, eyes brimming, the decision made. James touched her cheek with one finger, causing her tears to spill, as he murmured, "So beautiful . . ." Berthe turned away. His heart broke with love for every move she made, as she took one of the sand dollars from the shelf and slipped it into her pocket before she opened the door and walked away from him into the lavender twilight without looking back. James could see her shoulders shaking, and knew that she wept as she went. He stood looking out at the water, paralyzed with longing, thinking of what it meant, that she couldn't leave him without taking that sand dollar to keep. They endured exactly six days without seeing or talking to each other. On the morning of the seventh day they were married in Union by a justice of the peace, and then they were gone.

The newly minted Mr. and Mrs. Brant went to Europe for the fall. Berthe had to see her teacher in Germany, to explain, to pack up her

belongings. These they left in storage in Munich until they knew
where they would settle. They traveled for the rest of the autumn,
and by Christmas, as James hoped would happen, Annabelle was
ready to welcome them at home and present her new daughter-in-
law to Cleveland society. After Christmas in Ohio they went to
Boston for the New Year and received the sorrowful blessing of
Lottie and Thaddeuzs. Eventually they settled in New York, where
Berthe resumed her studies and in time made her performance debut,
and James went into business in the New York office of a Cleveland
firm. They had ten years together; then, Berthe died.


"But how?" Annabee asked her grandmother. This was in 1924,
when James Brant's only child was five, and old Annabelle was in
the last summer of her life. The child had come up to her grandmother's bedroom at The Elms, where Annabelle spent most of her
days on a chaise longue by the window, playing intricate solitaires
and talking on the telephone.

The day was bright, and sheer curtains blew at the open windows overlooking the inner harbor. It was dry weather under a high
mackerel sky, and Annabee's mother, Candace, had taken the machine and gone to Bar Harbor for the day. Annabee had pulled an
album from the shelf, hoping it held gramophone records. Instead
she found pictures of her father in his golden youth, and all manner
of other mementos. She carried it to her grandmother for decon-
struction. There were yellowed cuttings from newspapers, pressed
leaves or flowers from corsages, dance cards, a four-leaf clover. Then
they came to a studio portrait of her father, young, with a lady
Annabee had never seen before.

It was taken in the autumn after James and Berthe were married.
Berthe was smiling, her large expressive eyes wide, her beautiful
dark hair piled on her head. James had one arm around Berthe's
waist, a gesture of pride and protection. "This is your daddy's first
wife, who died," Annabelle said, touching the photograph with a
lumpen finger. She knew perfectly well that the dread Candace had

forbidden to have her daughter told that there had ever been another Mrs. James Brant. "Isn't her dress pretty? She had it made on their honeymoon in Paris, which is in France."

Annabee was electrified. The dress looked fussily old-fashioned to her, but the news that Daddy had had a wife before her mother trumped all thoughts of personal style. "Why did she die?"

"She died having a baby," said Annabelle.

"Why?"

"I'm not sure, I wasn't there."

"Where was she?"

"In New York. Where they lived."

"What was her name?"

"Berthe." Annabelle made it sound as exotic as she could, and assumed a once-upon-a-time voice. "She was a beautiful girl, an opera singer. She gave concerts people paid money to go to. And she spoke many foreign languages. German and French. Italian. They met right here in Dundee, you know."

Annabee knew no such thing. This was absolutely the first she'd heard that her father hadn't been born the day he married her mother.

"Look," said Annabelle, turning the page. "Here's an article in the paper about one of her concerts. Here is her name . . ." She tapped each *b* as she pronounced, "Berthe Brant."

"What does it say about her?"

"That she sang very beautifully, and everyone clapped and clapped and clapped," said Annabelle, sighing at the wonder of it. It didn't actually say that, Annabelle could no longer read newsprint without a magnifying glass and she didn't know what it said. But little Annabee got the picture.

Old Annabelle died in Cleveland in the spring of 1925, of pneumonia. She was buried in Lakeview Cemetery. Annabee was impressed at the depth of her father's sorrow, and with the fact that before they left for the funeral, he had fastened around her neck a locket that her grandmother used to wear, with "Annabelle" engraved upon it. He also showed her the beautiful triple rope of pearls with a diamond clasp that her grandmother wore in the evenings. He said he would put the necklace in a safe-deposit box for her until she was older. Her mother, Candace, had pearls, but these were bigger and there were a lot more of them.

Annabee had known she was special to her grandmother, and was very sorry she was gone, but didn't realize that meant gone forever. She could see she was gone from Cleveland; her bedroom was empty, all the medicines were thrown out, and the steam apparatus was put away. But she didn't entirely understand that she would also be gone from The Elms next summer and from everywhere, for all the years to come. Also church had been long and she was glad to be outdoors in the warm sun, and her father was standing apart from her, accepting condolences at the graveside. She began to relieve her boredom by seeing what she could make of the writing on the big stones. She could see that the one at the top of the hole that Granabelle's big fancy box had gone into said ANNABELLE BRANT APRIL 3, 1838—which she could read because it was her own name. The one beside it was just the same size with the same kind of writing. It said something with a juh, *j*, that she knew stood for "James," and then some numbers and then big words. (In fact, it read, JOHN SYDNEY BRANT, OCT. 1, 1835–MAR. 28, 1878. TO EVERYTHING THERE IS A SEASON AND A TIME TO EVERY PURPOSE UNDER HEAVEN. Annabelle, knowing she would not remarry, had had her own stone cut at the same time she ordered her husband's.)

Annabee next went to work at a stone a step or two away, that had two big *b*'s in the name. Brant was easy, her name again. She was working on the first name, sounding the letters quietly in sequence as her nurse had taught her, when her mother arrived beside her. Candace paused for a moment, then picked her daughter up, and kissed her on the cheek. Candace was pretty, with pillowy bosoms and hips, and she knew she made a touching tableau with sturdy small Annabee in her arms. Slowly, as if her feet were bound by sorrow, she stepped away from the watching mourners.

"I was reading," Annabee said. She kept her voice quiet, she knew they shouldn't be talking.

"I thought you were, lovey. My smart girl."

"I could read 'Brant' on that one . . ."

"Yes, they all say 'Brant.' It's the family plot. There is Grandfather, and Granabelle, and Auntie Louisa, with the picture of an angel." Candace pointed to each grave. Louisa had died of the influenza the year Annabee was born. Annabee looked at the one she hadn't pointed at.

"The first name was a buh. *B.*"

Candace gave it a minute. "Oh," she said, as if it had just come to her, "that must be poor Berthe. She was married to your daddy for a little while, a long time ago."

Aha. So it was true! Annabee had tried this topic last summer and it had not gone well, but this time Mummy herself had brought it up.

"I saw a picture of her, in Maine."

"She was awfully pretty," said Candace.

"Did you know her?"

"No, not at all, she was much older than I am. She was very vain, poor thing, and she laced her corsets so tight when she was having a baby that she punctured something and died."

"What are corsets?"

"Something ladies wore in the olden days to make them curvy."

"Did you?"

"No."

"Because you're already curvy?"

"Because your daddy likes me just the way I am." She smiled, so Annabee did too.


It wasn't actually true, though. Candace was not an easy person to like, and James didn't, much.

Watching Candace Brant arrive at The Elms in the summer of 1926 was like watching the *Aquitania* dock. She had refused to go to Dundee for more than a week each summer while old Annabelle was alive. Now, however, she gathered Annabee and the nanny, sent the cook, the waitress, and the housemaid ahead by train, and even so took so much luggage that two separate automobiles were required. The social secretary, Miss Somerville, drove Candace and Annabee, and Osgood followed with Lizzie and the trunks. Osgood drove so slowly now that it took him an extra day to get there, but he had been recently widowed and James wouldn't allow Candace to fire him. She wanted to. She preferred to staff the whole house with colored, whom her mother in Knoxville found for her and sent north.

Poor Auntie Louisa's wing at The Elms, with its separate kitchen and rooms for nursing staff, had been closed since her death. Candace ordered it opened and prepared as a nursery wing for Nurse Lizzie and Annabee.

"It will be so much better for Lizzie and Velma, Jimmy," Candace explained. Velma, the cook, found a thousand ways to make her displeasure felt at home when Lizzie used "her" kitchen to prepare the nursery's meals. Nurse Lizzie was what Candace called a "high yellow," and the rest of the staff resented her.

"But we'll never see Annabee if she's way over there. I like having her right down the hall."

"It won't make any difference if she's down the hall or not. Could we just live like grown-ups for a couple of months a year? Do you think?"

When James arrived to join his family at The Elms, he found all the bedrooms on the second floor of the main house had been "freshened up" by a decorator from Knoxville he didn't remember being asked about. A great deal of chintz and chenille was involved. James walked from one to the next—this one in blues, mostly aquamarine, the next in shades of intense yellow, the wallpaper a mass of buttercups.

"Now when we have guests there will be at least a minimum of comfort," Candace said.

"When was there ever not?" James countered, but at once regretted it. Candace gave him The Look.

"I couldn't invite my family, with the rooms the way they were."

"I see," said James. "I think I'll go down now and see how Osgood is getting along." He did the rest of his tour of inspection at another time, and by himself. He said nothing about the changes except to order that a leather chair that had been his father's, which Candace had sent to the servants' sitting room on the third floor, be brought back to his study.

"I've asked Lizzie to bring Anna in to say good night, before we go out to dinner," said Candace that evening. He'd been there for some six hours and still hadn't been given a chance to see his daughter.

"Who is Anna?"

"Your little girl, my silly."

"Annabee?"

"Do you know that that woman at the post office with the *grande poitrine* is known as Nellabee to one and all?"

"Nella B. Foss?"

"Yes."

"Yes, I know it. I've known her for donkey's years. And . . . ?"

"Doesn't it strike you that the 'Annabee' business is a little . . ."

"What?"

"Could you help me with my little pearls, please, lovey? The catch is hard, it's so tiny."

He put on his glasses and went to her at her dressing table. "The 'Annabee' business is a little . . . ?" He wanted to hear her finish the sentence. She wanted him to read her mind and agree with her. He fastened the clasp at the back of her neck in silence.

"Oh . . . is a little . . . common."

James didn't say anything. He stood behind her and met her eyes in the mirror of the dressing table.

"Not the *person,* I mean. Mrs. Foss is a lovely *person,* all wool and a yard wide, as my daddy would say. I just mean the name."

There was a long pause. "Where is it we're going for dinner?"

"The McClintocks," said Candace.

"Thank God," said James.

"Why?"

"Because it's a house where you can still be sure of getting a drink."

There was a polite knock, and Lizzie opened the door. Annabee, pink from a bath and wearing a long linen nightgown and matching robe and slippers, bolted for her father.

"Annabee!"

"Daddybee!"

James scooped her up and swung her around and around. After they kissed each other they buzzed, zzzzz, zzzz, at each other and laughed.

"Jimmy, she just had supper . . . if you twirl her around, she'll up-chuck."

"No she won't, not my honeybee." He put her down, but didn't stop smiling and didn't let go of her hand. "Look how brown you are!"

"Gladdy and Tom and I are going to be Indians when we grow up!"

"That's a *wonderful* plan."

"I have three arrowheads in my room, I found them!"

"Yes, there's a shell heap full of arrowheads on the McClintocks' land, you'll hear all about it. It's so interesting," said Candace. "Anna, do you want to put on perfume with Mummy?"

Annabee shouted, "Yes!" and Candace looked at Lizzie and made a small gesture, as if the noise had hurt her ears, couldn't Lizzie teach this child to behave like a lady?

"Come here then, dear. We'll use this one tonight, now you— No! Oh, for heaven's sake, no, you don't just *douse* yourself . . ."

Annabee had eagerly seized the intended bottle, pointed at herself, and squeezed the atomizer bulb. Now she looked dismayed, and her mother softened. "You do it like this, watch Mummy." Candace stood and sprayed the scent into the air before her and then stepped forward, with her eyes closed. She inhaled and opened them. "You see? You spray, then step into it, spray and step into it . . ." She pantomimed this action several more times, as if demonstrating a maneuver of daunting complexity. "That way the scent breathes around you all evening." Finally she handed the bottle back to her daughter, who tried her best to imitate her mother this time. "Very good, now that's enough, though, lovey, it's very expensive . . ."

And had mostly wound up on the rug. But Annabee quivered like a puppy, hoping her mother was now pleased with her.


Candace and James were either out or entertaining every night of James's stay that summer. They gave one large dinner, with dancing afterward, while Candace's mother and sister (with family) were staying, and people drove over from Mount Desert for it. James ran into old Gus Dodge at Abbott's the next day.

"Heard you had quite a wingding out to your house last night," Gus said to him.

"We did."

"Heard it was some fancy."

"It was so fancy I didn't know half the people there," said James. Gus laughed. "Not your idea of rusticating?"

"If I'd wanted to spend every night in a dinner jacket I could have stayed in Cleveland," James said.

Gus gathered his purchases and counted his change. "Let me know if you want to come in for a hand of poker down to the fire-house. Thursday nights, it's come-as-you-are."

"Thank you, Gus. There's nothing I'd like better. I trust you'll come around and explain where I'll be to Mrs. Brant?" Gus laughed, and so did Max Abbott behind the counter. After James had gone out, Max said, "I'll look forward to that, Gus."

"To what?"

"Hearing you explain to Mrs. Brant that he'll be down at the fire-house playing poker."

"I'll save you a ringside seat," said Gus.


James was, at least, allowed to spend his afternoons with Annabee. They went sailing in one of the yacht club's small tubby sailboats, aptly named Brutal Beasts. Annabee loved it when the boat tipped, and adored the peaceful hours of sun and high blue sky alone with her father. They went swimming at the bathing beach if the tide was in, otherwise they went over to the salt pond and swam from the dock that had once belonged to the cellist from the Ischl Quartet, now owned by a family named Cluett. One day, when Kermit Horton announced the mackerel were running, James hired a fisherman named Tom Crocker to take them out trolling. It was pouring rain, but not cold. James and Annabee stood in their yellow oilskins and baited hooks with bacon. They had five lines with multiple hooks off the stern of the Ruth E, and once the mackerel struck, they hit so fast and furiously that two people couldn't pull the lines in fast enough. Rain dripped from their sou'westers down their necks as they dumped the wriggling fish into a bucket, where they gawped their mouths and flopped until more came in on top of them. James and Annabee laughed with delight, and the rainwater ran into their mouths, as they rebaited the hooks and pulled in the lines hand over fist until they had filled two buckets.

"Had enough?" their boatman asked.

"I think we've got all we can handle, Captain Crocker. Annabee never eats more than two buckets of fish at a sitting." Annabee giggled, giddy. Tom Crocker turned the boat around, heading back through the sheets of rain and slate-gray seas for the inner harbor. James stood in the stern cleaning mackerel on a blood-scarred board, throwing the guts to the seagulls, who screeched and cried and wheeled overhead, until they filled the air above the boat's wake in a great noisy cloud. At the wheel, Tom Crocker stared straight ahead, and now and then took a pull from a flask he kept in the bib pocket of his oilskins and called his "hired man."

Until she was an old lady, Annabee remembered that day as one of the happiest of her life. She and her daddy went in by the kitchen porch when they got home, since Candace had turned the family mudroom into a swagged and carpeted "ladies' cloakroom."

They left their wet slickers on the kitchen porch and were bundled into towels by Maudie, the upstairs maid, and led up the back stairs to take hot showers without disturbing Candace's bridge party. When they were dry and dressed, they went to the kitchen where Velma had soaked the mackerel in milk. Annabee sat with her daddy and watched as Velma dredged the fish in cornmeal and fried it in a huge iron spider. They ate at the kitchen table until they couldn't eat another bite. Annabee, who never actually liked fish much in later life, remembered that meal as ambrosial.

"You should just taste it once!" said Annabee, when she was brought in to say good night, wanting her mother to share the joy of the afternoon.

"Lovey, that is *trash* fish," said her mother.

"You're missing something," said James. "Fresh caught . . ." But he didn't push it. Candace had turned from her dressing table to give him The Look. Which meant, in this case, One more word, and I will tell you in front of this child what I think of you for deigning to put that cat food in your mouth.

Full or not, James was required to climb into his dinner clothes and go out to an evening party. The party was an "all-talky" as Candace archly called entertainments that didn't include contract bridge, at which she excelled. At the party, Candace apologized all through the meal for her husband's rudeness in eating so little; the rest of the mackerel was ordered fed to the servants.

James had protested, when Candace announced she was bringing her own household help with her instead of hiring locals, as his mother had done, that they would be lonely, Negro servants on the coast of Maine. Candace shrugged and said, "They'll survive." Her own staff knew how she liked to be served, and it made it easier for her. She didn't add that if they had to keep to themselves, she'd be just as happy. She didn't like to find herself dealing with people at Abbott's who knew all the backstairs chat from her household.

But it turned out James was wrong about the servants being lonely. There were a number of other households in the colony with colored help, and more in adjoining villages up the coast. When Candace gave her dancing party she had borrowed staff from her new friends to help serve refreshments and midnight supper; as a result her servants made backdoor friends with the servants from other houses and had quite a social life of their own. Mr. Britton's driver Zeke began beauing Maudie; he took her on a picnic up Butter Hill on her day out, which Candace thought simply too droll. And on a Thursday night in August, the entire domestic staff of The Elms went off with Zeke in Mr. Britton's big Packard car to the Colored Owl's Ball in Orland. This was no inconvenience, as Candace was going out to play bridge that evening, and Peggy Somerville, the social secretary, who really *was* lonely, said she'd be glad to take care of Anna.

When Candace arrived home at ten, Miss Somerville heard the car in the drive and hurried over from the nursery wing.

"Good evening, Peg. Was she a trial?" Candace gathered her gloves and bag from the car and got out, leaving it in the driveway for Osgood to put away. The two women walked into the main house.

"I'm afraid she wet the bed, I'm so sorry." Miss Somerville brought some anxiety to this confession.

"Didn't you make sure she 'went' before you put her to bed?"

"Yes, I *did,* and I asked her again after I read her a story. She *swore* she didn't have to."

Candace stared at her. Her eyes were cold and her nostrils fluttered, a bad sign with Candace. Miss Somerville stood her ground, but blinked like a pigeon.

Finally Candace said, "I *thought* we were through with that."

Miss Somerville said nothing.

"Well," said Candace. She strode off toward the scene of the disaster. Miss Somerville bobbed along behind her, trying not to wring her hands or twitter.

When Candace arrived in Annabee's room, the child was asleep. Her mother yanked the door open with a sound like a rifle shot. Annabee snapped awake and sat up, confused and staring, all in one motion. Her mother clicked on the overhead lights, which washed out the comforting circle of yellow night-light on her bedside table, cast by a small bulb like an egg held in the paw of a painted wooden bunny rabbit.

Candace looked at her daughter and Annabee looked back. Actually, Candace did not see a child before her. She saw a humanoid being made of an uncontrolled and uncontrollable substance, the only thing in her life, now that her mother-in-law was dead, that couldn't be compelled to behave in the way she required. You could give it orders, but it still shouted when it should speak normally, upchucked, ran fevers, ran when it should walk, broke things, sat with its knees splayed like a boy, soiled its underpants, lost its new shoes, and wet the bed.

Candace stared down. Annabee met her eyes as much as she could, trying to guess if defiance or apology would help, and if not, would anything?

Candace hurtled off into the bathroom and returned with the laundry hamper. She pulled out a wet sheet and stood holding it, looking down. To Annabee she looked nine feet tall. Without a word, but with a gesture of distaste, Candace let the sheet drop back into the hamper. She strode to Annabee's dressing table for the broad-backed hairbrush. She strode back to the bed and jerked the clean covers off Annabee; taking her arm, she flipped her over onto her stomach. She pulled up the cotton-knit nightgown with pink satin bows threaded into the hem. She pulled down the little cotton underpants, not so easy to do, since Annabee now had her legs rigid and clamped together, all her muscles tensed tight against what was coming. Candace spanked her as hard as she could, blow after blow with the back of the hairbrush. Miss Somerville counted the slapping sounds from out in the hall.

And events proved that Candace had done quite right that evening, as Annabee never wet her bed again, for as long as she had the use of her wits. (When she lost these, she became suddenly and spectacularly incontinent, but that was many years in the future, when everyone who might have made some sense out of the way her life began and the way it finished was long since unable to testify on the subject, including herself.)

For Christmas in 1926 James gave Annabee her own Brutal Beast, painted yellow and named *Honeybee.* It was bobbing on its mooring when she arrived at The Elms the summer of 1927. Tom and Gladdy McClintock appeared within minutes to crow over her return and the new boat. They were off in it at once to sail to town for ice-cream cones and after that were out on the water almost every fine day. They sailed to the yacht club, around to the east side of the bay to visit the Maitlands, even out to Beal Island to poke around the abandoned houses. Business was booming and times were good; James also bought himself a sloop called *Toccata,* but the first time he took Candace out sailing, the wind came up, the boat tipped, she was splashed, and her hat blew off. She was filled with satirical remarks the rest of the summer about Some People's ideas of pleasure. Then the children began winning sailing races. Candace, who liked winners, became sorry she couldn't go out to watch. She demanded that James commission a motor launch for her, like the mahogany lake boats she had envied in her childhood. James ignored the fact that the boat she wanted was utterly inappropriate for tidal waters. He wrote to John Alden in Boston and commissioned one. When it arrived the next summer, the boat was noisy, very wet in any kind of chop, and wildly difficult for the boatman to get into and out of when the boat was on the mooring, but no one said a word to Candace about that, for fear she would start complaining about the tides, which no amount of money could correct.

James hired young Harry Allen as boatman for the launch and provided him with a dashing uniform. This was necessary, since the Maitlands had in the bay a hundred-foot yacht with several dozen in crew who lived aboard and never were seen out of their crisp blue jerseys and spotless white trousers, with the yacht's name embroidered on every garment. Bess Maitland reported that the laundry for the crew alone was simply staggering, and claimed she wished her husband would buy a sweet little boat like *Toccata* that they could sail by themselves, but of course her husband didn't do anything of the kind, and a standard had been set.

Annabee was skippering *Honeybee* this year, with Gladdy as crew. In July little Elise Maitland had won almost every race, but by August Annabee started to beat her, and once that happened, Candace was out every race day, sitting grandly in the forward compartment of her launch wearing a linen duster and carrying a parasol, being driven from mark to mark as if in a limousine. When Annabee won, her mother came to the tea at the yacht club following the race. When she lost, Candace went straight home.

There was a wide group of children who sailed together, raced against each other, holed up at Leeway on rainy days, playing charades, or mah-jongg, or invading the kitchen to make fudge. Gladdy McClintock's birthday became a favorite summer holiday. One year, Professor McClintock turned their whole living room into a spiderweb, and twenty children shrieked and laughed, tumbling over each other, trying to untangle it, each following her own string to a prize hidden behind books or under the window-seat cushions. Another year, there was a treasure hunt that took bands of children all over the Point deciphering clues, and yet another year, a scavenger hunt, during which they could walk, sail, paddle, or row but were not allowed to ride in anything with a motor. Even so, one team (Elise Maitland's) succeeded in bringing in every item on the list, including a live goat.

There was a maiden lady from Bryn Mawr named Violet Holmes on the Point who was raising her three orphaned nieces, Andie, Betty, and Lucie Cochran. Her cottage, Sherlock Holmes, was built right on the ledge overhanging the harbor, with porches wrapping around three sides, and heart-stopping views of the sunset. All the children on the Point called her "Aunt Violet," and loved her. Every August, Aunt Violet had a "measuring party." Each child stood against the porch wall to have her height marked on the shingles with her name and the date. The child who had grown the most since the year before won a prize. Once it was Annabee; often it was Lucie Cochran or willowy Elise Maitland and once it was Tom McClintock. It was never Gladdy. Gladdy was built like a fire-plug. She had a quiet but bubbling sense of humor, and a gentle-ness that was universally felt and loved; physical beauty would never be among her personal glories, but no one ever born noticed that less than Gladdy. Of all Annabee's friends, in Cleveland and Dundee, Gladdy was the one who made her feel completely loved for herself, not her boat or the size of her house or her father's money. Most of all it was Gladdy who provided a counterbalance against the bewildering fact that Annabee's mother so patently dis-liked her.

Annabee's summer crowd grew older. By 1931, they still hiked and picnicked and sailed together during the golden days, but at night, the older ones took to dancing to Victrola records and began to fall in and out of love with each other. A shy, rather strange boy named Homer Gantry was given a Model T which he drove to an evening party at Sherlock Holmes. He left it quivering and burping in the driveway rather than turn it off, as getting it started again without the help of the chauffeur was not a trick he had fully mas-tered. When he finally managed to herd some of the gang outside to marvel, the car was gone. He raised a hue and cry that it had been stolen, until Andie Cochran gently pointed out the dark bulk of the car in the bay, where it had evidently driven itself; the running lights could be seen still glowing beneath the water. Gladdy and Annabee weren't there, but they heard about it. Everybody heard about it. Poor Homer.

The same year, 1931, a trim young German named Werner Best signaled his ambitions for advancement within his political party, the National Socialists, by writing a policy paper. He urged that Communists and Social Democrats should be "reeducated" in concentration camps. Jews should be deprived of the legal protection of the state. They should be forbidden to buy flour or medicine, or to use the telephone, or to travel on public transportation. Leadership of the party was not yet clearly established; perhaps Dr. Best thought this would make him a candidate.

Dickie Britton and some of the racier boys in the Dundee summer colony started running with a couple of the Eaton boys from the town. One night four of them were coming down Great Spruce Bay in the Brittons' motorboat, having been all the way to Canada, when a launch full of revenue officers came booming out of March Cove on Beal Island. Before the chase boat reached them the boys had to drop an entire case of Canadian rye whiskey overboard. There was much laughter the rest of the summer about the fact that they'd dumped it in the very deepest channel of the bay, where it remains.

By January of 1933, leadership of the National Socialists was firmly in the hands of Adolf Hitler, and it wasn't only the party that was taking him seriously. In Berlin, elderly President Hindenberg was forced, unhappily, to invite Herr Hitler to become chancellor of Germany and form a government.

In the summer of 1933, when Gladdy and Annabee were fourteen, the McClintocks celebrated The Gladys Birthday by taking the whole bunch out to Beal Island for an evening lobster picnic. They hit the beach in a flotilla of motorboats, sailboats, and canoes. The girls gathered driftwood for the fire while the boys helped Dr. and Mrs. McClintock off-load bushels of corn and steamer clams and dozens of live lobsters packed in seaweed. The young roamed in groups, gathering berries and playing sardines while the food was being cooked. They ate sitting on the rocks, using stones to pound open the lobster claws, and throwing the empty shells into the sea to be carried out on the tide. When supper was over and the daylight almost gone, the grown-ups packed up their gear and pushed off home, leaving the young to come later, after moonrise.

They built up the fire and cuddled around it, watching lights of the night sky on the water. Annabee had a crush on Tom McClintock that year, but he was hopelessly smitten with Elise. Somebody's houseguest had a flask of bootleg rum which they poured into the punch after the grown-ups left. Elise and Tom drew back from the circle of firelight so they could neck. Homer Gantry got completely drunk and threw up on his pants. One of the boys had a ukulele and could play a little. The Cochran girls sang beautifully, but nobody sang as beautifully as Annabee. When it was nearly time to pack up and start back, Annabee (who had not been drinking) started to cry.

Gladdy and several others formed a circle around her.

"It's all right . . . it'll be all right," Gladdy said in distress, not that she had any idea what was making her friend so sad. She stroked Annabee's arms and back. "Do you want me to call Tom?" Annabee shook her head violently. Of course, it was nothing to do with Tom.

"Can you tell me?" Gladdy was trying to imagine what, besides heartache, could cause such a storm of grief to a girl like Annabee.

"I just don't want to go home," Annabee managed to say.

"You don't?" Gladdy couldn't imagine this. She loved home.

"Do you want to spend the night out here?" asked Lucie Cochran, kindly.

"Yes, do you?" Others around the fire chimed in, quite liking the idea. "We could all stay, and watch the sunrise . . ." Annabee was shaking her head.

"That won't help . . ." She was getting control of herself, slowly. "I mean to Cleveland. All my happy times are here."

Gladdy thought about this for a long moment. She could think of false comforts to give but it wasn't in her nature to utter them. So she stroked Annabee's back, and said, "Oh, honey."


In Germany, by 1936, things were going pretty well for the chancellor. There were some civil-liberty issues that were unattractive, but he'd gotten the country back to full employment while the rest of the world was in a depression; it was better than the guy in the White House had done. A lot of the employment was involved in rearming the military, creating an air force, things Germany wasn't supposed to do, but Hitler claimed that France and Britain had never disarmed to the level they were supposed to, either, under the Treaty of Versailles. He was just keeping things fair. It was humiliating, the Versailles Treaty. There were maybe parts of it that hadn't been such a good idea in the first place. Take the Rhineland. Sure, you can see why France wants a buffer zone, but the Rhine is German, and the Rhineland is German. How would it feel if they said, "Okay, from now on the Mississippi is French? You can't do anything east of the Mississippi that France doesn't like"? In March of 1936, Hitler took the Rhineland back. He marched his troops into it and there he was. Everybody said, "Now what?"


Annabee's father was a good deal older than her mother. In 1936, he was sixty-three, overweight, and smoking two packs of Camels a day. During Prohibition he'd started to drink too much, almost as a matter of principle. When it ended, he saw no reason to modify the habit. In Cleveland he continued to go to an office in the Arcade during the day, but he didn't do much but manage his investments, and his days generally included long lunches at the Tavern Club, drinking martinis and playing backgammon. He played a little golf on weekends. He continued to serve on charitable boards and to play very good bridge in the evenings. On all-talky evenings at home he would often be struck, after a couple of what he called "stumplifters" at the cocktail hour and wine with dinner, with the desire for an audience. He would lean back in his chair a little, and spread his arms benevolently, and start prying open canned stories, to see if anyone would eat them. If there were guests (and they would only be old friends at this point), they would fall quiet and wait for the oft-told punch line. If there were no guests, Annabee tried to supply the lack; Candace didn't bother.

James and Candace had kept separate bedrooms for years, as when he was drunk, he snored. One morning in the spring of that year, after Annabee had left for school but before Candace was up, James slipped in his shower and broke his hip, and wasn't found until water overflowed the shower stall, where his body blocked the drain, and ran out under the door and into the hallway. He never recovered; Annabee was to see him only once more, in the hospital, so full of dope he was barely awake. He died alone, at three o'clock the following morning.

Annabee was devastated. The house was soon crammed with people and flowers. She sat in mortified silence as her mother said to her circle that Maude was upstairs packing up Jimmy's clothes—she had given the lot to the gardener, who was almost the right size.

"Candace—hadn't you better wait a little while?" Bud Harbison asked. He had recently been widowed himself.

Candace tapped a cigarette out of her case and lit it crisply.

"Why?" Blue smoke came out of her nose and mouth.

"There's no rush. Annabee might like to go through them first."

"Anna? *She* can't use them . . ."

"No, but he was her father."

Candace looked over at Annabee, who was staring at her shoes. After a pause she said, "Well, I don't want her going all to pieces."

"No. But still. It can wait a week or two."

Annabee's classmates from Hathaway Brown came to pay their sympathy calls. They came with their mothers, dressed as for church.

Annabee had the sense that the mothers viewed this as a teaching opportunity, rather than an action intended to produce solace. This is the way we pay a Sympathy Call. They sat together stiffly and said things about how terrible they would feel if their own fathers died. None of them had known James at his best.

The one thing that taught Annabee anything about true kindness was that Gladdy came from Philadelphia to the funeral. When Annabee telephoned her, weeping, Gladdy said, "Oh, no!" and burst into tears herself. Then called back, and asked if she could be met at the Terminal station at eight-fifteen the next morning. She came without proper mourning clothes, though her mother had lent her a black shawl to wear over her Sunday-school dress. At the funeral, Gladdy walked with the family, and at the graveside, she held Annabee's hand as the huge mahogany casket was lowered into the ground, while the sun shone and birds sang and the cemetery bloomed with dogwood.

Candace had had James's grave dug at the left side of the plot, beside his long-dead father, leaving a blank space on the right between old Annabelle and the marooned remains of Berthe Hanenberger Brant.

"But now there's no room for your mother beside your father," Gladdy said.

"She doesn't plan to die," said Annabee.


She was Anna after that, to everyone except her oldest friends. She and her mother both went into mourning, but for six months only. They didn't go to Dundee at all that summer; instead, they went abroad.

"A complete change; we both need it," Candace announced. "You haven't been anywhere except Cleveland and Dundee." Candace and her Jimmy had done a great deal of traveling early in their marriage. In Annabee's bedroom at The Elms she had a shelf full of nasty little dolls they had brought her, which you could only look at, not play with, in native costumes of Wales, Scotland, Norway, Sweden, Holland, France, Germany, Italy, Spain, and Greece. "Where would you like to go most?" Candace asked now.

"Paris," said Anna.

"You'll be going to Paris your whole life," said her mother. They went to Egypt. They sailed the middle of June on the *Rex,* of the Italian Line, and played bridge all the way across. The surprise to Candace was that Annabee played well from the beginning and got better and better. By the time they toured the Alameda Gardens in Gibraltar, they were arm in arm, laughing together more than they had in their lives.

From Gibraltar they sailed for Tangiers and went on to Rabat and to Fez, where they bought rugs. After Morocco, they sailed for Port Said and from there went by train to Cairo. Tommy, Gladdy, Elise, and the others got postcards and letters all summer, with pictures of pyramids, of their hotels, of the S.S. *Egypt* on which they went up the Nile, of their private car and dragoman, of themselves attending a camel race, of Candace riding a camel. Annabee was homesick. Candace bought her a beautiful gray star sapphire and, when they got home, had it set in a dinner ring for her to commemorate the trip.

"Better than a doll in a burnoose," Annabee wrote to Elise.

Mother and daughter put off their mourning right after Thanksgiving; in spite of black clothes and the veil she wore in public, Candace's social life was already back at full throttle. She played bridge several times a week, in the afternoons with her lady friends, sitting at card tables in someone's living room, with crystal ashtrays and monogrammed lighters on little glass-topped tables at their elbows. At evening parties she played with Bernard Christie, the Brant family lawyer, a confirmed bachelor with soft hands and very pink cheeks. Mr. Christie became her escort for dinners and theater as well. He tried to interest her in opera, although she warned him she was allergic to singing. After two acts of *Tosca* she had to be taken home.

"It's so *affected,*" she said in the car.

"All right, you tried it. If you don't like it, you don't."

"I get enough of that at the house, with Anna carrying on like Galli-Curci . . ."

"She has a voice, you know, *ma belle.*"

"I *know* she has a voice, believe me. When she sings on the third floor, you can hear her in the kitchen."

"I think you should let her take lessons."

Candace rolled her eyes.

The week Candace and Annabee put off their mourning clothes, as the first Christmas cards of the season began to appear in the mail, they both received thick cream-colored envelopes bearing the following invitation.

MR. AND MRS. ORVILLE BROWN TALBOT
REQUEST THE PLEASURE OF YOUR COMPANY
AT A SMALL DANCE IN HONOUR OF THEIR DAUGHTER
ALICE ST. JOHN
DECEMBER TWENTY-EIGHTH,
AT TEN O'CLOCK
THE MAYFIELD CLUB

Et cetera, et cetera. Alice Talbot was a grade ahead of Annabee at school, but her twin brother, Toby, was a sort of friend of Annabee's. They had danced together at dancing school and once won a silver dollar which he had let her keep.

"Wasn't that kind of Polly to include you," said Candace.

"But I'm not out yet."

"No, you're not, but *almost* . . ."

"You mean, I can go?"

"Oh, why not?" Candace looked up and smiled. "You won't wear a long dress, of course. Polly was devoted to your father, you know."

Annabee did know, and it mattered to her. There were not so many who had remained devoted to him.

Of course she had nothing to wear to Alice's party. They went shopping. First to Halle Brothers, where Candace had a favorite

saleswoman. Annabee stood in her best silk underwear in the dressing room, surrounded by mirrors, while Candace sat in a plush chair
and smoked Old Golds. Mrs. McCall ran in and out with dresses
gathered from every department. Everything Mrs. McCall could find
was either too poufy, or too décolleté, or not suitable for dancing. At
the end of the day, they put two dresses on hold, and went downstairs to salvage the expedition by buying Annabee's first long white
kid gloves.

"Oh, dear," said Annabee as they settled into the backseat of the
car. Osgood had finally been retired and Candace was driven now
by a patient colored man from New Orleans named Ralph. It was beginning to snow, and the streetlights were already on.

"Don't worry. Tomorrow we'll go to the Band Box. Yvonne will
have something, she always does." The Band Box! Yvonne was from
Paris and so were the clothes, and if she couldn't suit you, she'd have
something made up. Annabee might wear a dress from Paris, like
Berthe, the lost love of her father's life.

At the Band Box, Annabee stood in the middle of the room,
while Yvonne walked around her as if examining a horse. She used
her hands to pull Annabee's shoulders back, then with one finger
caused her to lift her chin, as if she'd forgotten Annabee was alive
and a speaker of English. She gazed thoughtfully, then cried, "Ah!,"
and left the room in a rush.

Candace sat as if at a performance. Yvonne reappeared at the
door to her atelier and said, "I have it, mam'zelle, come with me," and
Annabee did.

When she reappeared, Annabee was wearing a swirl of royal
blue taffeta, with draped shoulders, a V-neckline, and a very small
waist.

Candace stubbed out her cigarette and sat up straight. "Yvonne!"

Yvonne used her hands to cause Annabee to rotate slowly. "Ooh
la la, non?" she said to Candace, complacently.

"Anna, you look simply marvelous."

Annabee blushed. While she had been tucking and pinning her
in, Yvonne had rattled off names like Schiaparelli and Lanvin;

Annabee wasn't sure that one of them had actually made this dress, but she knew it was *très chic,* and it certainly might have been made for *her.*

"We just have to take it in here, and here." Yvonne touched the waist in the back and the shoulders. "And of course she needs a little . . ." She touched Annabee's tummy.

Candace chuckled. "Yes, I see she does."

"What?" asked Annabee. She couldn't see that she needed anything else if she had this dress.

"A little corseting, lovey. Should we take care of that before you do the fitting, Yvonne?"

"No, *pas du tout.* We can fit her now."

"I suppose I don't dare ask what this will cost?"

Yvonne laughed merrily. "No, I wouldn't, madame. You can see the dress is perfect for her, *par-faite,* so what can you do?"

"Not a thing," said Candace, exhaling a stream of smoke, and Yvonne called toward the atelier for a seamstress.


When the dress arrived at the house, in a huge box as full of cushioning tissue paper as if the dress were made of glass, Candace and Annabee retired at once to Candace's dressing room for a viewing. Annabee had on her girdle, her first, and satin slippers dyed to match the blue taffeta. With the dress on, she turned this way and that before the full-length mirror as her mother stood in the doorway.

"You know," Candace said, "it's too bad you can't put your hair up."

Annabee took her hair in her hand and twisted it up onto her head. Suddenly she looked years older, and terribly sophisticated.

"Can I not?"

"Not until you're out, but it's too bad. What jewelry do you think of wearing?"

Annabee hadn't thought of any jewelry; she was thinking that if Tyrone Power happened to be at the party, even *he* would fall in love with her.

She mostly had costume jewelry, except for a ring with her birthstone her father had given her, and the locket that said "Annabelle."

"We might try my coral beads, but the color is risky . . . you know what I'd like to see? I'd like to see you try your grandmother's pearls."

The pearls! Annabee turned from the mirror to look at her mother, eyes shining. "Could I?" She had thought she'd have to be ancient as Granabelle before she could wear those pearls.

"Of course you can. Just call Mr. Christie and he'll get them out of the vault for you."

Oh! Imagine this dress, and those pearls! She'd be stunning, she'd be like her grandmother, she'd walk into the room and all heads would turn!

"They may not suit, you can't tell till you try," said Candace. "Would you like me to call him for you?"


The afternoon of the party it snowed without ceasing, but the snow stopped toward evening. Annabee put on her dress at last and went to join her mother. Candace was wearing a long strapless gown of bottle green velvet. Annabee helped with her last hooks and eyes. Together they chose evening bags and perfume; together they sprayed the air before them and then stepped into the cloud of fragrance. When Mr. Christie finally arrived, on the dot of eight, they were ready and waiting.

"Ask him to come up, Maudie," Candace called down the stairs, when she heard the male voice in the hall. Mr. Christie duly appeared, his cheeks pinker than ever. "Good evening, ladies. Oh, my, I'll be the envy of the town."

Annabee had stood, to honor her elder, but also to show her dress to full advantage. "You are a vision," he said to her, bowing. "Your pearls, madam." He took a long narrow case of green kid from an inside pocket of his coat and handed it to her.

Annabee opened the case. The pearls were larger than she remembered, and the color even warmer.

"Well," said Candace. "Let's have the full effect . . ."

Watching herself in the mirror, Annabee lifted the pearls and fastened them around her neck.

She looked at herself. She stood, she turned. Mr. Christie took a step back and cocked his head. No one spoke. Annabee walked into the dressing room and looked in the full-length mirror. She came back out.

"The length is just wrong, isn't it."

It was. All three knew it; the bottom of the rope hit the neckline in a way that hid rather than enhanced the effect. She took off the pearls, before anyone told her to, feeling very mature. There would be other evenings, and other dresses.

Candace went to her jewel box, took out the string of coral beads, and tried them around Annabee's neck. They hung perfectly, framed by the V of the neckline.

"The color is wonderful . . ." said Mr. Christie, doubtfully.

"Wait," said Candace. She took back the coral beads and produced instead a pair of diamond clips. She clipped them to the sides of Annabee's neckline. "There! Now that's better—now the jewel you see is the girl herself!"

"Candace, you're a witch," said Bernard. "It's quite, quite perfect." And Annabee could see that it was. She began to smile. Diamonds! And before she was out!

"All right, ladies? Shall we be off?"

"Yes, just a minute, what am I going to wear?" said Candace. "I'm going to be completely upstaged by my daughter." She sounded pleased about it.

"Mother, you wear the pearls."

Candace turned from her jewel case to look at Annabee.

"You wear them. They'll be perfect. It's a shame to have them out of the vault and not use them."

Candace looked as if she had never been more pleased with her child than she was at that moment.

"Well, thank you, lovey." She had the pearls on in an instant and didn't need a mirror to tell her how they looked. Mother and daughter beheld each other, smiling.

"Well!" said Bernard. "Ladies—your chariot awaits."

They had dinner downtown at a new French restaurant. It began to snow again as Mr. Christie drove them toward the Mayfield Club, but nothing happened to prevent their arrival, and finally, there they were in the receiving line, moving toward Mr. and Mrs. Talbot, who stood with Alice between them, all smiling and shaking hands.


The ballroom was hung with dark green swags and fairy lights. The room was filled with girls in long gowns, boys in white tie, talking, flirting, drinking champagne. Annabee sat with her mother and Mr. Christie at a table where they would have a view of the dancing. At midnight, Alice came in with her father, and the orchestra began "The Most Beautiful Girl in the World" as they waltzed alone on the floor. Annabee suddenly was near tears. All the years ahead of her, of missing *her* father. He couldn't see her in her dress from Paris, at her first ball. He would never dance the first waltz with her at her own debut, or walk her down any aisle.

Mr. Christie was standing before her. "May *I* dance with the most beautiful girl in the world?" She looked at her mother, who was lighting a cigarette and nodding.

Mr. Christie was about the same height as her father, and he danced very smoothly. In a moment Toby Talbot cut in, and Annabee's evening began.

She danced far more than she sat out, in spite of her mother's warnings to expect to be a wallflower. Champagne had made her cheeks bright, and unlike her dancing-school partners, these boys were taller than she, and held her close enough that she could follow. She might not be Miss Popularity at Hathaway Brown, but boys got a look at her bustline, and maybe her diamonds, and trotted right over. This confused and surprised her, but appeared to get her mother's attention. Annabee was sorry when supper was over and her mother announced it was time to go home.

"Next year, you can stay till dawn," said her mother.

Annabee slept almost to noon the next morning. When she came downstairs, she found that a boy from the party had sent her flowers, with an invitation to the club dance on New Year's Eve. Her mother was vastly amused. "You made your first conquest, my dear," she said. Then instructed her how to word her regret.

## 1937

Unfortunately, the Christmas brightness did not survive the New Year, and it was a long sad winter for Annabee. She ached for her father, and her mother didn't want to hear about it. A girl in her class whom she thought was a friend had turned against her; she had no idea why. She took up smoking and for a while she was welcomed by the popular girls who talked slang and accepted car rides from boys. She carried a stash of matches and Tangee lipstick in her purse, and hoped, daily, that she'd be given the nod when the group decided where they were meeting to light up after school. But then she won a part in the spring musical, which the popular girls thought was hopelessly SS & G, and there were no more whispered messages or notes slipped into her desk. Her new ex-friends went out the side door, laughing, as Annabee reported to the gym to rehearse.

"Sweet, simple, and girlish, oh, lord," said Candace. The girls of her youth who'd been branded that were pretty tragic, and she wasn't one of those mothers who blamed the crowd who ostracized her child. Candace identified with the ostracizers. She, too, thought all these rehearsals and gingham costumes were fairly wet. It would be one thing if Annabee wanted the part because there were boys in the play, which there were, but that had nothing to do with it. Annabee wanted the part because she wanted to sing. (Candace rolled her eyes, and the word "showoff" could be overheard in her supposedly sotto voce conversations with friends.) Gone was Annabee's hope that she'd finally gained a mother.

Tech and dress rehearsals ran quite late the week before the performances. ("Two whole performances! My," Candace said.) The Hawken boy playing the lead kept going up in his lines, and a doltish girl from the freshman class could not hit her marks and kept delivering her big number from the dark next to the spotlight.

"I'm sorry, Ralph," said Annabee, when she found him asleep in the car waiting for her.

"That's all right, Miss Anna. I have to go fetch your mother later anyway."

"Do you? Where is she?"

"At the Playhouse. There's some big do there."

Annabee made herself a cup of cocoa in the kitchen, then settled down in the den to wait for her mother. Both of them coming in late from their busy lives involved with the theater.

When Candace walked in, she saw the light in the den and came to the door. There was her daughter, half asleep, with a mug in her hand, wearing pancake makeup with painted freckles and a cocoa mustache.

Annabee looked up. Before her stood her richly upholstered mother, with her ermine capelet over her arm, wearing a long dress of ice blue peau de soie and the triple rope of Grannabee's pearls.

"You're up late," Candace said.

"Long rehearsal," said Annabee.

"What are you looking at? Is something showing?" Candace felt for the shoulders of the gown to see if a lingerie strap had escaped.

"No."

"Oh." She then laughed trippingly, as if it had just this moment come to her. "The pearls. They're perfect with this dress, aren't they?"

"Yes, but . . ."

"Yes?"

"I thought you would ask me."

"Did you? Why?"

"Well, because . . ."

"You didn't need them yourself tonight, did you? They don't really go with your getup . . ." When Annabee still didn't speak, Candace said, in a brisk and dismissive tone, "But if you want pearls so badly, of course you can have them."

"My father gave them to me."

"All *right,* Anna. Good night."

Candace turned and disappeared. Annabee could hear her open and close the door of the downstairs closet. She heard her mother climb the front stairs, go into her room, and close the door. Annabee was wretched.

She went through the next day feeling sick. The final dress rehearsal was a disaster. At home she couldn't rest or eat. Her mother wasn't home and would be out for dinner, Velma said.

Annabee lay in her room angry and jumpy and growing more wound up by the minute. Finally she got up and crept to her mother's door. She stood listening hard. Then she turned the knob and went in, half expecting to find Candace on the chaise longue lying in wait for her.

The room was empty. Annabee went to the dressing room and stood facing the jewel case. She listened to her blood pound through her heart, expecting her mother to spring at her from somewhere.

The case wasn't locked.

She had the lid up. Annabee looked at the little plush compartments full of gold and silver, onyx and pearl, topaz and sapphire.

She lifted the top tray out. Underneath was a shallow compartment with necklaces, amber and jet and garnet, old-fashioned and rarely worn.

She opened the drawers. There were jewelers' pouches and bags of softest suede; she went through them all. No pearls.

At a noise in the hall her heart nearly stopped.

"Oh, it's you, Miss Anna," said Maudie in the doorway. "I saw the light in here and I thought, Now who is in there?"

"Sorry—I must have scared you."

"That's all right."

Annabee walked past Maudie and went back to her room without explaining herself.


The opening night was a triumph. Annabee was surrounded afterward by parents of girls who barely talked to her, saying how wonderful she'd been. Her teachers said the same. One said Annabee should go to New York and study, she really should. Annabee said thank you, thank you, thank you. She felt a distance away from herself the whole night.

When she got home, her mother was in the library. "I'm in here, lovey," she called.

Annabee went to the door.

"How did everything go?"

"It went well."

"I'm so glad to hear it. I'll be there tomorrow, with bells on, so will Bernard."

"Okay."

"Are you going straight to bed?"

"I guess so."

"Sleep well, then."

Annabee went up to her room. When she turned on the light, the first thing she saw, lying on her dresser, seeming to pulsate, was the green kid necklace case.

She nearly wept with relief. She went to it. She stroked it. She pushed the round gold hook of the case clasp out of its eye, then pushed it back. She kissed a finger and tapped the case with it. Hello, Granabelle. Hello, Daddy. She put the case into her drawer under her sweaters, and noticed she was famished. She went down the back stairs to the kitchen and made an enormous sandwich from the cold chicken left from the supper she hadn't touched.


The performance Saturday evening was almost as good as the first. Mr. Christie was wildly enthusiastic.

"You have star quality, young lady. When you held that high note, I felt chills up my spine. I did. You could be on Broadway."

Annabee wriggled with pleasure.

"I'd like to try classical," she said shyly.

"Even better!" cried Mr. Christie. "The Juilliard School! You're a shoo-in—"

"Bernard, don't give her mad ideas. You were just fine, lovey. Much better than the lead, really."

"Thank you, Mother." She wished that in her mother's world success didn't require someone else's defeat, but still. She was here. She hadn't said anything mean. She'd returned the pearls.

There was a cast party, at which Annabee was not a wallflower. There was euphoria. For some there was also letdown, especially for the boy who learned he had played the whole last act with his fly open. But not for Annabee; she had a beautiful green kid case in her drawer and inside it the most beautiful pearls in the world. From her grandmother, who had loved her, from her father, whom she adored, and now, too, from her mother. They were hers, her heritage, they were love.

That night, after a hot bath, wearing a clean nightgown, she climbed into bed. In her hand she had the green leather necklace case. She waited a long moment, thinking of her grandmother, her father, and of her mother down the hall. Then she opened the case.

Inside was the single string of pearls Candace had resented all these years, since the moment James gave the heirloom pearls to Annabee.

⌒

"My father gave those pearls to me when Granabelle died. To *me!*" Annabee was standing in the door of the sun porch where her mother was eating breakfast and reading her mail.

"You're much too young for pearls like that. Where would you wear them?" Candace didn't look at her daughter. She swallowed a bite of soft-boiled egg and took up another letter.

"He gave them to *me*. You were right there, you heard him."

Candace finally looked up. "You know, Anna, your father wasn't at all well, those last years."

She returned to the egg in her egg cup, scooping at it daintily with a tiny silver spoon.

Annabee had a tight knot of rage and tears in her throat, and it ached. With her face flaming, she stormed back upstairs.


On Monday morning she took the Rapid to Public Square to see Mr. Christie. He met her at the door of his office, all hail-fellow-well-met.

"You're looking lovely, Anna." He took her elbow and guided her to his inner office. "Are you sure you won't let me give you lunch?"

She shook her head and took the chair she'd been steered to.

She didn't know how to begin. Mr. Christie assumed a blank, pleasant expression. She could see in his eyes that he would be entirely pleasant and correct, but not helpful. He was her lawyer and trustee, the only one she had, but she was not his only client.

"When my grandmother died, my father gave me her pearls. That you brought me the night of the dance."

"Did he?"

"Didn't you know that?"

Mr. Christie steepled his fingers.

"Just a moment." He rang a bell, and a secretary appeared. "Mrs. Doughty, will you bring me Mrs. Annabelle Brant's will? And Mr. James Brant's. Thank you."

"He gave them to me the morning of the funeral. My mother saw him."

The wills were brought in and laid on his desk. He turned to glance at one, then the other.

"For such a large estate, your grandmother's will was quite simple," he said. "She set up an education trust for you when you were born, but everything else, except for the usual bequests to servants and charities, was left to your father. Cash, securities, all real and personal property."

Annabee looked at him. She could see how this was going to play out, and she longed to slap his cute pink cheeks.

"So the pearls were my father's that morning, and he gave them to me."

"So you say."

"He *gave* them to me! He did and *she* knows he did!"

"Anna, Anna."

"Do you think I'm a liar?" She couldn't keep the ugly word from popping out like a toad, because someone here *was* a liar.

"I have no idea. I wasn't there."

She shouldn't have said that word. If he had liked or felt kindly toward her up to now, he did no longer.

"Your father's will . . ." He turned to it and gave himself some time to turn the pages. Then put it down, folded his hands, and met her eyes. "Is equally straightforward. Half the value of his estate is yours outright when you turn eighteen. The other half, including all real and personal property, is your mother's for her lifetime, with the balance to go to you at her death."

"I see. And her half. She can do whatever she wants to? Give it to the poor, spend it on her nephews in Knoxville, throw it out the windows?"

"She can do anything she wants with the income, which is not small, including throw it out the windows. With the principal she can do what she needs to do for her reasonable maintenance."

"And who decides what is reasonable?"

"The bank and the trustee."

"And the trustee is . . . ?"

"I."

Of course. There was a long silence in which they looked at each other. At least he didn't smirk.

"And the real property?"

"The house in Dundee is hers for her lifetime, but not to sell unless you agree. The Cleveland house is hers outright, with all contents."

"All."

"Yes." He stood up. "You should be aware that I tried many times, over the years, to get your father to revise his will. It is simply good practice. But in his later years, business was not . . . his main interest."

Oh, thank you for reminding me, Annabee thought, wishing she could plunge his antique letter opener into his high round little tummy.

"Goodbye," she said.

"Goodbye. Come in anytime you have questions."

Annabee was mad at everyone when she got to Dundee that summer. She was furious at her father for falling into a gin bottle and hardly bothering to flap his flabby arms as he went under. It never occurred to him that he had a daughter? That she was defenseless against this awful Mother person without him? She was furious that Leeway Cottage was rented this summer to some strangers from Buffalo. Tom McClintock was living at home selling men's dry goods at a department store in Philadelphia. Gladdy was a counselor at a girl's camp on Lake Winnipesaukee. Except for Elise Maitland, who was in Europe seeing all the sights Annabee hadn't gotten to see, the Depression had finally gotten to almost everybody; even the younger crowd was depleted, with most of the girls busy babysitting and waiting on tables, anything for a little pin money. The only person who could crew for Annabee was poor tragic Homer Gantry, *God,* he was stupid. She won every race, but so what, they were racing against twelve-year-olds. Just when it seemed things couldn't get any worse, *Mister Christie* came for two weeks, with a whole trunkful of sporty little play clothes and straw hats and it was *Candace* this and *Candace* that, morning, noon, and night. Annabee spent a lot of time by herself smoking Chesterfields in the shadow of the bridge at the reversing falls, God, it was boring. *Mister Christie* thought the house enchanting but just a little, you know . . .

"Dowdy?" Candace supplied.

"Well, you said it, not me," he trilled, and they both laughed wickedly.

"Everything was *perfect* in Annabelle's day, *nothing* could be touched . . ."

"Oh, I know, believe me. You know what would be really smart, though."

"Tell me."

"I mean, I'm just thinking out loud—"

"*Ber*-nard . . ."

"Well, what would be really *smart* would be to get rid of all this chintz, just *get* rid of it, and do the whole place over in black and gold, with mirrors."

Candace stared at him.

"You hate it. Never mind, I was just thinking out loud . . ."

"Brilliant."

"You think so?"

"Brilliant . . . it's *just* what it needs!"

Candace was like a pointer quivering in the presence of a bevy of quail. So much to demolish! So much to buy! So much to spend!


Annabee was so angry at both of them she was barely civil. She was so mad that when poor tragic Homer Gantry invited her to a student concert of chamber music at the Ischl Hall summer school, she went. And that was a revelation. Her Dundee world had always seemed to her like theater-in-the-round, with the bowl of the summer people around the bay, with their houses and cars and yachts and parties as the performance. Suddenly she learned that there were multiple stages. There were whole other worlds here, full of color and drama and incident, people making friends, making art, finding God, where no one knew what went on on the Point or cared. Here were people no older than herself, who had spent their golden hours in passionate study, their bodies pulsing with music that coursed out of private inner places and into the hall, causing everyone to see that they were beings apart, they were artists! When she saw a girl her age, no older, with a violin at her chin, give a tiny sign to her colleagues that caused all four, at precisely the second chosen by her, to commence the most gorgeous torrent of sound, she thought she would die of want.

Here was a world. Of union, of beauty, of belonging. Such as she'd begun to fear didn't exist.

At the intermission, Homer turned to her and said, "I thought they took the Haydn a little fast, didn't you?"

"A little," she said. Which had been the Haydn?

"Would you like some lemonade?"

Actually, what she wanted was to go home and find her piano music and begin the hours of practice she had balked at when she was ten. She followed Homer out of the hall, where old photographs of the Ischl Quartet and Fritz Kreisler, Ossip Gabrilowitsch, Leo-pold Auer, Efrem Zimbalist, were hung under the gaze of a stuffed moose head. Outside in the sun, young music students sold punch and cookies. Homer walked up to the girl who had led the string quartet.

"Ho, there, Homer," she said.

"Hello. Took the Haydn a little fast, I thought."

"Did you? That's what Sasha thought too. Well, come back Sunday, maybe you'll like it better."

"I will. Zondra, this is my friend Annabee Brant."

The goddess of music gave Annabee a smile. "How do you do? Did *you* think the Haydn was too fast?"

Before Annabee had to answer, another of the musicians came up and announced that a party was leaving to swim. Did they want to come? Zondra did. Homer said no, they wanted to hear the rest of the program.

"All right," said Zondra. "Are you coming tonight?"

"To what?"

"Cookout. At the Obers' camp on Third Pond."

Homer looked at Annabee. Did she want to go? She did. And she would be welcome among these superior beings? Apparently.

"Good," said Zondra. "Can you give Elsie and me a ride?"

On the way to pick up Zondra and Elsie, Annabee said to Homer, "I'm changing my name."

"Okay. Which one?"

"I want to be called Sydney."

"Annabee Sydney?"

"Sydney Brant."

"Okay. Why?"

"I'm just done. I'm done being Annabee. Sydney is my middle name. I'll be A. Sydney."

"Okay."


Annabee was completely astonished to find that for the rest of the summer she was doing something that resembled keeping company with Homer. Who dutifully struggled to call her Sydney when he remembered. The music students were lively, welcoming, serious about music but otherwise playful. They were snobs about nothing except talent. Annabee could understand not more than half of the musical banter, the teasing of the pair suspected of hanging the sign in the hall that said "Exit here in case of Brahms," the ones who loved Schoenberg, the ones who loathed him, the gossip about the faculty, who couldn't play anymore, who pinched the girls. At home, when no one could hear, she did go back to playing the piano. One afternoon at the hall she was asked to turn pages for a handsome boy called Josef who was playing a Schubert fantasy for a master class. She was as thrilled as if she'd been asked to play the piece herself.

She loved that they didn't know where she lived, she loved that they assumed she had been living and breathing music since toddler-hood, they thought everybody had. Homer wanted her to give a party at The Elms for them all, but she wouldn't even talk about it. She didn't want them meeting Candace, she didn't want Candace meeting them. And she knew that if they saw her in that pompous house it would change everything.


"And how is your daughter's school year going?" asked Candace's dinner partner over the consommé at a party in Hunting Valley that October.

"It's a bit of a mess," said Candace.

The man, who she believed was named Bill, was mildly startled, as in his experience mothers could be counted upon to have nothing but exceptional children. He'd forgotten the daughter's name but had expected to hear Mrs. Brant drone on about her through the soup course, which would leave him free to eat.

"Ah?"

"First she decides to change her name. Now she thinks she wants to go to college. It's ridiculous. What good does it do those girls? They just come home and turn into the kind of female who's always running around asking people to give money to things. It's not as if Anna were an intellectual."

"I see."

"I think she should take a lovely finishing year in Florence or somewhere. Then if she wants to do something useful before she gets married she can join the Junior League. But no. You'll never believe what she said to me this morning. She said, 'Mother, I'd like to learn to cook.' " Candace did a very good Annabee imitation.

"Cook?"

"That's what I said. I said, 'Cook? What on earth do you want to learn to cook for?' And she said she'd been to a picnic or hoedown or something this summer where the family lived in a cabin and the mother did the cooking. Can you imagine the sort of thing?"

He could, actually.

"I said, 'Fine, but what kitchen do you plan on using?' She said, 'This one.' I said, 'Velma's kitchen, you mean? And when she quits, are you going to do the interviewing and hiring, and firing when the new ones turn out to be drunk or pregnant?' "

"Or—"

"Yes, not know how to turn on the stove . . . Children have no idea, do they? The cook I had before Velma couldn't cook but she could eat—she was so fat she broke the toilet seat in the servants' bathroom. And before that—oh, before that was the one who got drunk during Anna's birthday party. Here I am, trying to give her a perfect day, with thirty little children all washed and starched and waiting for their creamed chicken, waiting and *waiting*, and when I

went to the kitchen, the cook was com-*pletely* drunk, in tears because
I didn't love her."

The dinner partner started to laugh.

"You laugh—that wasn't the worst, the worst was that she was
sitting on the birthday cake at the time."

He laughed louder.

"She was—I had ordered one from the baker to save her trouble,
'Happy Birthday, Annabee,' it said, with an elaborate picture of a
merry-go-round in icing. Anna was mad for carnival rides of all sorts
at the time. The chauffeur had left it on the kitchen bench and this
creature was *sitting* on it. Too fat to notice."

The dinner partner was laughing so much the hostess looked
down the table to see what was happening. Bill for his part was extremely sorry when the next course was served and he had to turn to
the partner on his left. He thought Mrs. Brant was delightful.


Annabee couldn't see how she was going to get out of the box she
was in. She wanted her mother's respect. She couldn't imagine making life plans without her blessing. And yet everything her mother
pictured for her future struck Annabee with horror. To go to Europe to be "finished"? Then loll around Cleveland waiting for some
booby to marry her? There had to be something better than that. Yet
whom could she talk to? Elise was going to Vassar, but Elise was
brilliant. And Elise's mother *was* "one of those females who serve on
boards and run around asking people to give money to things."
Gladdy was going to be finished, and she thought that was fine. Her
father couldn't afford four years of college for her. She felt lucky that
she'd have the year in Rome.

College? As a matter of fact Annabee *wasn't* an intellectual;
higher math was agony for her and she hadn't a very large curiosity.
She didn't even much like to read. She couldn't think of a time since
her father died when she'd been as happy as she was onstage. She'd
been more than herself, something great, something good, then. Life
was rich when you had a passion. The young musicians she'd met
knew who they were and what they wanted to do with every spare

minute. Annabee wanted that. She wanted to cook wonderful food and grow beautiful flowers and get better and better at something besides bridge.

And in this state of suspension and confusion, she got up every morning, went through the day in her saddle shoes and brown blazer, doing what was expected of her, exactly as if she wanted nothing more than this life, forever, nothing more than being an inferior version of her mother, for that was certainly all she would attain to, if she held to the current plan. And would that have pleased Candace? Possibly.

After Christmas, Candace began talking of giving Anna a ball of her own in June. It wasn't much done, the private parties, in these economic times. All the more reason to give everyone a treat, said Candace. "If Jimmy were alive, he'd insist," said Candace. (Since his death, Annabee noticed her mother had acquired the ability to read her father's mind, speak for him, and be his interpreter on earth.) "You can invite your friends from Dundee and have a house party."


The party was to be in early June, at the Kirtland Club. Several families planned dinners beforehand, and all the girls in Annabee's class, including the ones who had not concealed the fact that they couldn't stand her, were now bubbly, thrilled at the fun of a party on the grand scale, as it used to be done. Several of the girls had been allowed to buy new dresses for it, which Yvonne at the Band Box was pleased about. But when it came to dressing Anna, Candace decided that this time, Cleveland was too small for her. Over the Easter break, she and Annabee took the train to New York and checked in at the Waldorf.

They had a lovely week. Annabee spent most of the time with Elise Maitland, and Gladdy came up from Philadelphia for two nights. Elise and a friend from her Chapin days showed Annabee Greenwich Village, and they went to the opera one afternoon while the mothers played bridge. It was a first for Annabee. She couldn't decide—did she want to be Elise, suavely hailing a cab and insisting politely at the box office that she preferred the dress circle, center, to a box with partial view? (What did it mean?) Or the soprano, in her

majestic magenta nightgown, dying at the top of her lungs throughout the final act? One morning she even went off by herself (on the
subway!) to meet Zondra at the Mannes School. The hubbub of
music making, the dissonant noises from the practice rooms, the
laughter and confident chat in the halls seemed a vision of heaven to
Sydney, as Zondra called her.

There were the mornings at Saks and at Bergdorf's, and finally a
dress of ivory satin with a dropped waist and a tulle overskirt that
all agreed emphasized Anna's best points and was made for dancing.
She could hardly believe her mother was saying yes. "It's *so* expensive, for a dress I'll wear once . . ."

"You like it, don't you?"

"I love it."

"Well, then. You could add a train and some lace and wear it to
be married in."

"Yes, indeed you could," said the saleswoman, hardly believing
her luck.


By the time they boarded the train home, Annabee felt as if her blood
had turned into light. She was shining. She and her mother played
honeymoon bridge as the train rattled west in the dark night.

Gradually through the wet weeks of May, Annabee felt herself
floating on emotional thermals that seemed always to buoy her upward. Candace was always at Annabee's side, consulting her about
the dance band, the silver printing on the matchbook covers for the
party, the menu for supper, the decorations, whether to serve coffee
and bouillon at the door as guests waited for their cars, or just let
them drive home drunk. Mr. Christie suggested champagne glasses
with Annabee's monogram for the guests to take home. Candace
thought this, too, was a marvelous idea.

Annabee was almost sick with anticipation the day of the party.
She was terrified of not having fun, or of having fun and being punished for it. But Gladdy was full of happy confidence and Annabee
tried to imitate her. At a lunch party, while Annabee could hear in her

head what slightly malicious thing Candace would say afterward about the food, or the decorations, there before her was kind, whole-hearted Gladdy saying, "How *delicious*! Thank you so much, I never *had* a better time," and meaning it. If Gladdy and Annabee stood at the top of a staircase, Gladdy was filled with anticipation of the pleasure awaiting below, while Annabee was filled with the knowledge that she would probably trip on the way down, and that Candace would not be a bit surprised.

To the Talbot family's dinner for the debutantes before the dance, Annabee wore a short dress and the sapphire dinner ring from Egypt, and Gladdy, dressed in the only evening dress she had, said she'd never seen a human being look prettier than Annabee. There were toasts and good cheer and even Annabee began to forget to be nervous. This wasn't so bad. The moon was full, she was over her period and would not bleed on her clothes, and it seemed possible that nothing would go wrong after all. Toby Talbot and Tom McClintock were her escorts. Tom looked piercingly handsome, and even Homer Gantry was look-ing pretty good; he called her Sydney, he had a tall silk opera hat, and kept doing a rather funny imitation of Bertie Wooster.

When the dinner was almost over, Ralph came to the door to drive Annabee to the club to change for the dance. At the last minute darling Gladdy went along to help.

In the room Candace had taken for Anna to change in, Maudie had laid out everything she needed, before rushing off to dress Mrs. Brant. There were her new long gloves, her new ivory shoes, extra silk stockings, the long silk petticoat, and the ivory dress, the beauti-ful dress, with its deeply scooped neck and its shimmering skirt.

They got her out of her dinner dress without getting any lipstick or powder on it. They got her into her shoes and petticoat. Annabee puffed herself with powder and flapped her arms to be sure she was dry in the armpits. Gladdy held up The Dress, and Annabee stepped into it. She watched herself in the mirror as Gladdy hooked her up and she and the dress became one.

"Annabee! *Look* at you!" Gladdy cried, straightening.

Annabee smiled. Yes, indeed. Her hair, which had been done that afternoon, was swept up onto her head and gleaming. The dress made her neck look like a swan's.

Maudie hurried in.

"I'm sorry, Miss Anna." She was supposed to help Annabee dress, but Candace had suddenly needed her instead.

"It's all right. Gladdy's here."

"Hey, that looks pretty good on you!"

"Pretty good! She's a goddess!" said Gladdy.

"Could you do this necklace for me, Maudie?" She was wearing her mother's pearls. She had not made a peep about them. Let her mother wear Granabelle's pearls; let her be buried in them. Annabee was young and looked wonderful. That was enough.

They freshened their lipstick, they powdered their noses. They squirted their clouds of perfume and stepped into them.

"Ready?"

"Ready."

"Should we go down, is Mother ready?"

"She's just getting her face on," said Maudie. "Go ahead."

They could hear the orchestra as they descended the staircase. Tommy McClintock and Toby Talbot were waiting in the hall, and Annabee could see in their faces how pretty she looked. Herbie Calhoun was waiting for Gladdy, and waiters were gliding around with trays of champagne in monogrammed glasses.

"A bit of all right!" cried Homer Gantry, in full Bertie Wooster mode.

"Where will you receive?" Tommy asked.

"We'll ask Mother, she'll be right down." The hall was beginning to fill with boys in black tie, and girls in strapless gowns that made them look like groups of tulips.

Annabee was looking toward the ballroom, like a Thoroughbred in the starting gate. She was ready, she was fit, she was finally eager to run. This was going to be a night to remember.

She saw a look of surprise on the upturned faces of several girls who were facing the staircase. She saw the expression spread to their escorts. She saw Mr. Harbison come to the door of the ballroom as if to be sure of what he was seeing. This moment took less than a second, before Annabee turned around, but in memory it seemed to last an hour. What on earth?

Mr. Christie was now in the hall, at the foot of the stairs, impeccable in his tailcoat. Annabee looked up the stairs.

Her mother was on her way down, her carriage and pace majestic. Except for a slightly rosier tinge to the satin encasing the dramatically cantilevered bosom, Candace and her daughter were wearing the same dress.

"Oh, honey . . ." Gladdy whispered, close at Annabee's side. She put her gloved hand on her friend's naked back.

What happened next was that, of course, Annabee put herself entirely and egregiously in the wrong for the rest of the evening, at least to Candace's satisfaction. She turned on her heel, took a glass of champagne in one hand and Tommy's hand in the other and went into the ballroom where she insisted he dance with her, and he did.

Mr. Christie came and tried to cut in; Annabee wouldn't let go of Tommy. Mr. Christie followed the waltzing pair around the dance floor insisting she stop and come out and receive with her mother.

"No," Annabee said. She put her empty glass on a passing tray and took another one. In the outer rooms, no one knew what to do. After a while the young gave up and went in to join the party. Annabee happened to be dancing with Homer when Candace herself hove into the room and bore down on Annabee like a steamer running down a wayward dinghy.

"I've never seen anything like this behavior, Anna."

"Don't talk to me."

"It's completely ridiculous. Our figures are entirely different, no one but you even sees a resemblance . . ."

Annabee took over the lead in the dance and clumped off with Homer to another part of the dance floor.

*    *    *

When the houseguests were finally all gone, having had the time of their lives, and Annabee had nearly recovered from her hangover, she took the Rapid to Mr. Christie's office again.

"I am eighteen now," she said.

"I know you are."

"You said when I was eighteen I could have my money."

"I believe, if he had known he would not be here to guide you, your father might have provided for a longer-running trust—"

"But he didn't."

". . . but he didn't. As I was about to say. He didn't, and control of it is yours now, if you want it. I take it you do?"

"I do. Where is it?"

"It's at the Cleveland Trust, of course. If you will calm yourself."

"I'm perfectly calm."

He looked at her, with an eyebrow cocked. It was really just as well, he thought, that he'd never had children.

He pushed a button summoning Miss Doughty.

"Miss Doughty, would you please bring in Miss Brant's trust agreements, and her latest statement?"

When Miss Doughty delivered them, he handed them to Annabee.

"The first is the trust your grandmother set up to pay for college."

"What if I don't want to go to college?"

"Read the language of the trust. If you make the case to the trustees of an educational purpose—"

"And the trustees are?"

"Your father was one. In his absence, Mr. Watson, and I—"

"What if I want to study music?" she interrupted. Again.

"As it happens, my dear, I have always believed that you should be allowed to study music."

"Oh."

After that she listened quietly as he explained that the education trust was to continue for her children. The other, much larger account was hers outright, though he strongly advised her to confine herself to spending the income and leave the principal where it was. That was all. He leaned back in his chair and looked at her, as if he had done his duty and had no intention of doing more. If she wanted to go off and run through it like a dose of salts, that was her affair.

She paid a visit to Mr. Watson, the family banker, and arranged to have income checks delivered on a monthly basis to a bank she would name as soon as she was settled. She demanded a large amount of cash which Mr. Watson begged her to put into traveler's checks. Then she went to the station and left for New York. Her mother found out she was gone when Maudie informed her a suit-case was missing and the bed hadn't been slept in.

1938

"What'll it be, gents?"

"Do you have any Danish beer?"

"Whaddya think, this is a beer garden. Of course we got Danish beer. Also Dutch, German, Austrian, Czech . . ."

"Carlsberg?"

"Two of those?"

The waiter hustled off into the smoke and racket.

"Homesick?"

"I must be," Laurus said. "What did you think of the violist?"

"Fair."

"Why?"

Imre settled his violin case between his feet where he was sure nobody in lederhosen would step on it. He turned his palms up and shrugged.

"Very correct. But not enough . . . chutzpah. *Brillo*. Something."

"You never like the violists."

"Just because I said they're the idiot children of chamber music?"

They were slowly divesting themselves of their gloves and mufflers. Laurus wore knit gloves inside leather mittens to protect his hands, while Imre lavished all his protection on Beatrice the fiddle, which was after all 175 years older than he was and by a factor of several hundred the most valuable thing he owned.

"I heard her do a lovely *Harold in Italy.*"

"I'm happy for you. What do you hear from home?"

"They're worried about *der Führer.*"

"Are you taking any home leave this winter?"

"I wish I could get my parents to come to New York; they've never been here. But they won't. Everyone's busy. Nobody likes a winter crossing."

"Will they come next summer, then?"

"They pretend they will. But in the summer they love their nights by the sea. Those endless twilights."

"I don't blame them."

There was a silence while they thought of summer and home. Outside, the wind on West Fifty-seventh Street blew the last of the October leaves, and with a rattle as of buckshot thrown against the windowpanes, the rain began. The waiter came, with brimming pilsner glasses on a tray balanced on his back-bent hand. He swooped this onto the table in a graceful motion that ended with the tray under his arm and his pad and pencil in his hands held before his chest. He looked at them over his glasses with the air of a man who has only a two-bar rest before the music will carry him off again, and hopes his partners haven't lost their places in the dance. The young friends ordered bratwurst and sauerkraut, cheap and filling, and more beer.

"Skål."

"Skål. What are you working on?"

"The Diabelli Variations," Laurus said. "Some Chopin, some Ravel. And of course I have to do the Grieg in January . . ."

"You can do that in your sleep."

"That's a problem in itself. How are things at school?"

"I have three students of real talent, and ten who should be violists. At least they work like animals. Oh!"

"What?"

Their hot food had arrived and someone in the bar had turned up the recording of the oompah band.

"I should have mentioned this when I called, Clara asked me to. There is a vocal student preparing her first recital. She needs an accompanist. It would be a lot of work . . . but easy money, and no traveling."

Laurus had just discovered he was famished.

"Tell me about her."

"She has a voice, I'm told. No technique."

"Uh-oh. Pretty?"

Imre considered. "More handsome than pretty. She moves badly. In that way of American girls, as if they are on the hockey field."

"What is she preparing?"

"Of course, a Schubertiade."

"I might rather enjoy that. And she can pay?"

"It seems so."

Laurus Moss first laid eyes on Sydney Brant in a practice room at the Mannes School of Music. She was very nervous. She was taller than he, with dark hair she wore piled on her head, which gave her an old-fashioned serious look. She had a streak of white at her temple, though she was very young. Her eyes were red, as if she had been crying (she had, but they did not speak of it), and in spite of the fact that she was neatly dressed and appeared clean, he could smell the sweat of nervous fear on her skin. Poor beast. He sincerely hoped she had at least a thimbleful of talent.

They shook hands. Sydney saw a neat man, compact and vaguely foreign, with short brown hair and pale blue eyes. He was very well trimmed, somehow. She especially noticed his hands, which were small, with wide palms and short strong fingers. His manner was kind, a quality she was desperate for. Her German pronunciation was atrocious and she had just come from a diction class in which her classmates had not been gentle.

"Where shall we begin?" Laurus seated himself at the piano and played a series of arpeggios.

"Perhaps here," said Sydney. She opened her music to *Meeres Stille,* and placed it before him.

He knew the song. He knew, too, that whatever they started with would be something she thought she did well.

"How do you like to take it?"

She gave him the count with her hand, and he began. She did not. They both laughed, he kindly, she embarrassed.

"Are you ready? All right, again."

This time she sang. The song was low, mournful, and the sound she produced was cellolike. But he could see that she was working so hard to remember her breath, her diction, her acting, all the thousands of things a singer must be master of, that he couldn't tell if she had any musical intelligence at all. When the song was finished there was an uncomfortable pause.

Laurus said, "Before we go on, would you do me a favor?"

"What?"

He knew she was waiting to be told something about her performance, but there was nothing he could say about it that would help.

"Sing something for me in English."

"Oh, I—haven't prepared anything, I don't know the—"

"Anything. A folk song. Something from the radio."

"Really?"

"Please."

She stood for a moment. Then she began to sing the first thing that came to her, which turned out to be "Falling in Love with Love." She addressed the song to a far corner of the practice room.

When she finished and looked at Laurus, she blushed because of the way he was smiling.

"Thank you."

"You're welcome."

"Tricky intervals," he added by way of praise.

They were both embarrassed for a moment; he because he knew so much that she did not, and yet was not here for the purpose of teaching her. She, because the situation was utterly alien to her, and she felt, as she had about a dozen times a day since she arrived in New York, that she had no idea who she was. Princess, frog, master, servant, artist, or joke person. It was amazing how much emotional dissonance one could experience and continue to function.

"Shall we go on?"

"All right."

"*Meeres Stille* again?" When she hesitated, he knew that she knew it had not been good.

"What about *Gretchen am Spinnrade*? I assume you will try that one . . ." Anything to get her to make a fresh start.

She turned to the page and he began. She sang this time with a self-forgetting that let the music flow a little better.

When it was over, he said, "*That* was fun. Let's do it again."


After the first week, feeling guilty (though grateful) for the amount she was paying him, he invited her out for coffee.

"Your English is so good," she said, when they had hot mugs and a small plate of cakes between them. They were in a tea shop in the basement of a brownstone just off Madison. Outside the day was bright and cold, with a smell of snow in the air.

"I come from a small country; nobody learns Danish. It is the same with the Dutch. We have to learn everyone else's languages early."

"Do you?"

"Have you never been to Europe?" he asked, marveling at how disconnected these Americans were from the rest of the world.

Sydney explained about the trip to Egypt.

"This mother is formidable, then."

"She's a horror," said Sydney. And saw that she had shocked him. "To me, anyway. The world is filled with people who think she's a wonderful woman."

"Your brothers and sisters? What do they say?"

"I'm an only child."

"Ah."

"I take it your mother isn't a horror?"

"Oh, no. She is a joy. She has no faults at all except that she is too plump, and she refuses to learn to ride a bicycle." He was smiling without knowing it, and this made Sydney smile, too.

"So your father. Is *he* a horror?"

"Parents are not allowed to be horrors in Denmark. He's like a sprite. He is small and lively and he has a great sweetness. And it's his fault that my mother is plump, because his hobby is baking. At weekends he smells of almonds and usually has powdered sugar all over his clothes. Sometimes in his hair."

"And he can ride a bicycle?"

"All Danes can ride bicycles. Except my mother."

A pause.

"Brothers and sisters?" Sydney asked.

"One of each. My brother Kaj just finished his medical studies. He's a young toad, of course," he said happily.

"Kye?"

"Yes. *K-a-j*. My little sister is Nina. She's at university."

A pause.

"Are you the only musician in the family?"

"My mother performed when young. She teaches now. And my aunt Tofa. Mor plays piano, Tofa plays violin."

"Do you miss them very much?"

"I do."

There was a silence. Sydney looked sad.

"Where is this formidable Mama, then?" Laurus asked.

"Ohio."

"And that's where you live?"

"It's where *she* lives. I live here."

This had the feeling of a statement that was true, but concealing more than it said.

"But if someone asked you, where is home?"

"Oh! I would say 'Dundee, Maine.' "

"Dundee, Maine! You are from *there*?"

"Have you heard of it?"

"Of course I have heard of it! Home of the Ischl Quartet, of the Thieles and the Eggerses and the Hanenbergers! Everyone who plays chamber music knows Dundee, Maine."

Sydney said, "My father was married to Berthe Hanenberger, Thaddeusz's daughter."

"Really!" He sat back in his chair.

"Before I was born. She was a singer. Have you heard of her?"

"No. But her father . . . My mother spoke of hearing him. She said he played like a god."

"Did you always know you would be a musician?" Sydney asked. She hoped he would say no, as she was always looking for clues that there were others with this vocation who began as late as she.

"Oh, yes. My mother began to teach me when I was very small."

"And then . . ."

"And then, when I was older she arranged for me to play for some important people, who sponsored me for conservatory train-ing. When I was seventeen I won a competition and went to Vienna to study, and after that, touring. You know the sort of thing."

She didn't. She had no idea how real musicians made livings, but then she had little idea how any working people made their livings. She nodded and smiled.


The coffee after her practice hour became a ritual, at least on days when Sydney's lessons were over and Laurus had no rehearsals. They talked of pianos; Laurus's mother had a beautiful Hornung & Møller grand in a walnut case. It was the piano he learned on and the one against which he measured all others. His earliest memory was of his mother at that piano playing Chopin, with morning light pouring into the room over her shoulder. Sydney knew only Ameri-can pianos. Her grandmother had a square Steinway grand at The Elms which was used at parties. Sydney had a Mason and Hamlin upright now.

"You live in a flat by yourself?" Laurus lived in a tiny studio he sublet from another musician who was in Australia for the year. It was crammed with the books and clothes and boxes of music of both of them. He pictured Sydney in a similar place.

What he pictured wasn't so far wrong, as pictures go, but it lacked completely all the background detail that would clarify what the foreground meant. Girl alone in New York apartment, sitting at piano dreaming of the concert stage. Up to a point.

When the newly created Sydney first arrived in the city she had gone to a hotel for single women. There were people to talk to at meals and there were curfews, and rules, as in a girls' dormitory. It was home to many girls just out of college, in first jobs or at secretarial school. Also to older ladies in reduced circumstances who discreetly sold antiques or jewelry on Madison Avenue, who moved among the young ones like living reminders of the way big dreams could go wrong.

Sydney had hoped to find a congenial group at this hotel with whom to go to the movies, or maybe out dancing. But she couldn't seem to find her way into their lives. Whether she didn't listen well, or she laughed too loud or at the wrong times, or something else, she never knew. She concluded that these girls were too frivolous for her. She was deadly serious about an image of a girl in an old-fashioned dress in Paris on her honeymoon, a girl who spun art out of her very body and made people stop and stare with her voice. None of the other girls at the hotel seemed to be fighting for their lives. So she thought it would be better to live alone in an artist's garret if she could find one. She couldn't, especially as she'd been misled as to what a garret should look like by the set design of the Met's *La Bohème*. But she did find a one-bedroom apartment in a brownstone owned by a woman who was nearly deaf and didn't mind her practicing.

All through Sydney's first breathtakingly hot summer in New York, Candace was up at The Elms, holding forth. There was a widower on the Point who was paying her attentions and who played excellent bridge. She had written to Sydney once, inviting her to come up for a weekend at least, but Sydney hadn't answered. When old friends asked if she would appear at all that summer, Candace answered with a superior smile and a merry twinkle, "Anna's terribly busy *expressing* herself."

Though herself was the last thing she was expressing. She felt like a worm caught out on a lawn when the early birds began arriving, lost and exposed, trying desperately to find her way out of danger in a world she could barely recognize. She had to work for hours a day at the piano. Not that she would ever play well enough to accompany herself, but (as her vocal teacher said) she had to train her ear. She gathered that if her ear had been a child it would be on its way to reform school. It needed discipline, it needed guidance, it needed years of remedial work to teach it to coordinate the notes on a page with a sound imagined in the brain. And the brain, ah! The *brain,* before she could sing a note, had to be taught to make an *image* of the sound she wished to produce, which would involve *color,* and *timbre,* and speaking of that, she had to learn all about the mechanics of *making* that sound, to learn to envision the vocal cords running from front to back, not up and down, to understand where the breath went, how the larynx moved, how the lips and the tongue and the opening of the mouth shaped the tones that she produced, she felt she might as well have signed up to learn how to build a pipe organ from scratch, it would have been easier. And then the physique, oh, well, to learn to support the sound from the soles of her feet upward, who knew how essential was the abdomen to the art? And then, languages! In addition to the hours a day of sight-reading Clementi at the piano and pieces that Mozart wrote when he was six, and the exercise of Hanon, she needed total immersion in German. (A private tutor was engaged, a fusspot named Frau Blucher, who was augmenting her income teaching in a girls' school where fewer and fewer wanted to speak anything but French.) Sydney needed Italian and French as well, and as soon as possible, but she already had more hours of work scheduled in each day than she could actually do in a week.

And where in all this was the music? When did the nightingale sing? When she had prepared her song, the way a painter prepares a house that hasn't been painted in forty years. First there was patching and puttying, scraping and sanding, then a coat of primer, then more sanding, fifty hours of that before one hour of applying color. Her vocal teacher, a vast Romanian woman named Madame Dumitrescu, looked at her with scorn when she expressed disappointment. What did you think, little polliwog, we get to stand on a stage before discerning multitudes by having *fun*?

When she was finally given her first song, it was not to sing it, it was to translate.

"Yes? What did you think? You could sing a song you didn't understand? Translate it. Yourself. And check the pronunciation of every syllable; Thursday you will recite it for me from memory in German and in English."

So, on Thursday did she sing? No. On Thursday she memorized the rhythm of the poem without words or notes. Laaa-lalala laah-lalala laah laah. When she could say the words on one note perfectly in the rhythm of the music, with a metronome, she was allowed to learn the pitches. Over and over, with one finger, she played the notes in order. She was not allowed to sing along, no, no, no, what a stupid suggestion. Sing? No.

She must play the notes, hearing the intervals until she could hear the notes without playing them *and* form a mental image of the sound she would produce for each one. (That again. An image of a sound. Yes, of course, did she not even speak English?) When she could do all that, and only then, might she stand with the music in her hand and with the metronome, very slowly, sing the *notes* in rhythm, lalalala. That of course was an appalling moment, after all that work and all that waiting, as the difference between the sounds she heard in her head and what came out of her mouth was so terrible. Next, she sang the *words* in rhythm but on one pitch. Then she had to put the song away for several hours. And after all that, she was allowed to think of it as a song, and try to *sing* it.

Sydney worked and worked through October. The landlady downstairs slipped in the tub and broke her wrist. She took to waiting in the hall for Sydney to come down on her way out to class, with her list of necessities for the day. Sydney found herself trudging in cold wet weather from stationer to grocer to pharmacy in search of things she had never heard of. Cocomalt Powder. Saraka granules for constipation. One windy evening she delivered to the landlady her bag of oranges and the jar of Vicks VapoRub she had asked for; she stayed to listen to the new Stromberg-Carlson that had been delivered that morning. The first news out of it was that soldiers in Berlin had attacked the Jewish neighborhood and broken everyone's windows. The news was all so awful all the time now. Sydney climbed the stairs to her apartment. Maybe she ought to get a cat. Or a boyfriend.

Once at school she casually asked another student, a Danish flautist, "Is Laurus a common name in Denmark?"

"Not at all," said the girl. "Laurus Moss is the only one I know of. Have you met him?" Sydney, mortified, blushed and said it was only an idle question.

"Oh. Well, Lauritz is the common name. Like Melchior, the tenor. Laurus is a family name."

"Have *you* met him?"

"Of course," said the girl. She was tall and lanky, with honey-colored hair and a beautiful accent.

November passed. Sydney thought maybe her mother would want her to come home for Thanksgiving, but neither of them made the first move. She spent Thanksgiving Day with the Maitlands, who lived on Park Avenue in a duplex apartment as big as a house. It was like visiting a foreign country; she'd been in the land of starving students so long she was half surprised it could be done without a passport. At least when she asked the Maitlands to call her "Sydney" henceforth, they said, "Of course, dear," and did it.

In December she began work on *An die Nachtigall.* "Die Nachtigall," trilled Madame Dumitrescu, "that is the masterpiece. So simple, but profound, that last line, the way the piano *melts* into the inversion of the major chord, under the high G . . ."

Sydney tried to look as if she had been just about to mention that very thing. Madame Dumitrescu pounced down at the piano and plunged in at the last line of the song, a strange event, like coming upon a severed limb that pranced, unaware it had no body. " 'Sing mir den Amor . . .' " She blared it out in her meaty mezzo as the piano demonstrated the *melting* business. Sydney struggled to appear to understand.

Madame Dumitrescu looked at her with demented eyes, aswoon in Schubert. Sydney meanwhile was in the grip of terror. She had picked this song because it looked easy and was short. The last thing she wanted on earth was to be stepping up to a masterpiece, beloved of Madame.

"Now, then," cried Madame. She closed her eyes and played the lilting first measures of the song, swaying with the music. When Sydney began to sing, Madame's eyes snapped open and the music stopped.

"He lies sleeping upon my heart! He lies sleeping upon your *heart*, he didn't hand you a tub of lard! 'He lies sleeping upon my heart . . .' " She sang the line her way. Sydney knew this was going to be a long hour.

He lies sleeping upon my heart, my guardian spirit sang him to sleep.

She sat at the piano while night fell and an east wind blew in from the river, turning their street into a rattling canyon. She realized she had nothing in the apartment for dinner but a can of hash. Ugh. She played the melody of the "Nightingale" over and over again. She pictured herself, outdoors in summer, with a beloved man asleep in her arms, asleep because he is so safe in her presence and protected by her love that he has let down his guard all the way to the ground. And she is safe from him too; a man asleep is a man one is free to love without defenses, unlikely in that state to find fault or turn satiric or even to say merely, "No, that's not what I meant."

She stopped playing. She sat in her catless, plantless apartment and pictured a young woman, perhaps Berthe Hanenberger, with her heart full and her love asleep in her arms, somewhere in the world where there are nightingales. She felt what that would feel like. A young man, kind, handsome, asleep and in love . . . who? Laurus Moss? Were there nightingales where he came from?

It had to be somebody. She closed her eyes and imagined herself, beloved, the guardian spirit of a dear sleeper, herself awake to the beauty of the world, and speaking the language of the nightingale. And what sound would you make to represent that feeling? She closed her eyes and sang the song.

When Laurus arrived the next day to accompany her practice, a complicated thing had become simple. For the first time since she began her training, she could forget it and sing. Laurus played. She pictured the feeling. Her throat made the sounds. As she sang, her eyes turned to him. In fact, what she was seeing was inner entirely, but her eyes moved to Laurus's face, and in surprise, when she hit the G, he turned to her and their eyes briefly locked.

When the song was over they were both silent. Then slowly, both began to smile.

"Well!" he said. "That was fun—let's do it again."

But they didn't begin again immediately. For a while both of them just smiled. She could sing. Sydney could sing. The girl could sing.

And had he fallen in love with her when their eyes locked? Sydney always thought so. For the rest of their lives, though she never asked him, she believed that. The day she really sang, and he suddenly saw her.

But actually, for Laurus, it happened differently. The "Nightingale" afternoon was for him only the moment he stopped feeling sorry for her and began to take a genuine interest. When they went out for coffee after their session he joked with her in a new way. She felt the difference and it made her looser, warmer, and easier to be with.

He asked her what she was doing about Christmas. She said she had no plans, except to work. He said, as he never would have before this afternoon, that well then—perhaps she would like to come with him to a party on Christmas Eve. Some musicians, all far from home. They would have a real Scandinavian Yule celebration. Her eyes shone. She hoped more than ever that Candace would write or call, to know when she would be home. Maybe never, she could now say.

There was another week and a half until the school closed for Christmas break. Laurus canceled one practice hour because it was the first night of Hanukkah. Sydney pretended she knew all about that, and wondered if he was Jewish. She rather hoped so, as she hadn't found the nest of Christians she'd been raised in all that warm and cozy and was interested in exploring other options. But maybe he was just a citizen of the world, as so many musicians, and New Yorkers, seemed to be. She bought a balsam wreath for her door, and another for her landlady. She was invited to go caroling with some of the music students one Sunday evening and afterward they all ate cheese fondue at a restaurant called Chalet Suisse, and laughed and sang some more, and if you lost your bread in the stiffening melted cheese, someone kissed you.

She was oddly happy. Having braced herself to be stunned with loneliness, she was instead luxuriating in an aloneness that had its own advantages. She enjoyed the crowds of shoppers on the streets of Midtown. She took herself to see the Christmas windows of the stores, and even went to watch the children sitting on Santa's knee in the toy department at Macy's. As she watched the children squirming with pleasure and whispering their desires into his big pink ear (and also the confident ones in velvet clothes who had memorized their lists and recited them as if placing an order), she thought about going as a child with her father to see Santa at the May Company. Afterward she was allowed to choose one toy right then, whatever she wanted, and her father bought it for her. She remembered the year she chose a little shaving kit, with a soap brush and shaving soap and little toy razor so she could cover her face with lather and then peel it back off in neat strips along with Daddy as he stood in the bathroom in his trousers and undershirt in the mornings. She remembered Candace's scornful laughter when they got home. She was very little, and didn't understand what was wrong with it. She remembered the year her father had made her what he called an Advent stocking—a stocking with twenty-four tiny presents, all wrapped, so she could open one every day until Christmas morning and that would help her wait for the great day. And of how livid Candace had been when she found that Annabee, who hadn't really understood the Advent concept either, had opened all the little packages the first morning.

On Christmas Eve day, in the early dusk, Laurus arrived to take her to the party. It was just cold enough for snow and big soft perfect flakes had started around noon. They were going to Greenwich Village, and though Sydney could easily afford a taxi, Laurus led her as a matter of course to the subway, although it took three different trains and at that, they didn't get very close. It was fun to make their way through the throngs at Grand Central as they ran for the shuttle to the West Side, and then again in the dirty and cavernous catacomb under Times Square, full of buskers making Christmas music and passing hats.

The apartment on Downing Street was up a narrow flight of stairs, uneven and sporting a carpet runner that was already soaked with slush. On the landing before the door of the party was a pile of wet galoshes. Inside people crowded together, drinking punch, talking and laughing. Laurus led Sydney in her stocking feet to meet their hostess. Gudrun was slim and blond with bright cheeks and eyes, perhaps the most beautiful flesh-and-blood woman Sydney had ever seen. She was assembling a large platter of gravlax, scattered with dill and capers. She kissed Laurus, wished Sydney a happy Christmas, and handed her the platter. "Here, you can pass this. Laurus, take the toasts."

The two of them made their way through the party with the platter. Imre Benko greeted Sydney warmly and took her by the elbow, explaining that it was the Swedish custom to shake hands and introduce yourself to every person in the room, and though neither he nor she was Swedish, he wanted to be sure she behaved herself.

There was a small tree in one corner with ribbons and carved and painted decorations. There were candles everywhere; *The Messiah* was playing on the record player, and something very warming and delightful was in the punch. This was Sydney's dream of a party, with everyone jammed together, and no servants passing things or washing up in the kitchen. There were many small presents under the tree and pinned to the tree itself. Someone arrived with a homemade *bûche de Noël,* and someone else with caviar. Someone put out a Stilton cheese and Gudrun's husband, Eric, appeared from the kitchen with a huge pot of meatballs he had been cooking since morning. Soon a cloud of dishes emerged from the tiny kitchen and spread out to cover the dining table, like a swarm of bees that looks so much bigger than the hive it came from as it fans out against the sky. People circled the table, filling their plates, and then sat, if they could find a seat, and if not stood eating with their bottles and glasses balanced on a mantelpiece or bookshelf nearby. An immensely tall redheaded Scotsman began to flirt with Sydney, especially after the *bûche de Noël* had been served, and champagne poured, and someone called for Christmas carols. A plump girl named Myrna played the piano; everyone sang. Often during the evening, Sydney felt Laurus watching her, happy that she was enjoying herself. He himself, easy and merry, was in his element.

A few couples said their good-nights, as they were going on to other parties. One or two had to get home to relieve a babysitter and one had a toddler with them who had fallen asleep on top of the coats. When the group was of a size to fit into the dining room, Gudrun emerged from the kitchen with a charlotte mold upside down on a plate. When she lifted the mold, she revealed a tightly packed cake made of dry flour. As everyone crowded around the dining room table, Gudrun carefully set her wedding ring on the center of the cake. The attentive Scotsman took a seat beside Sydney and explained the game to her.

"It's like musical chairs," said the Scotsman. "We go in turn around the table, cutting away the flour. You can take as much or as little as you like, but the person who makes the ring fall has to pick it up with his lips."

Myrna began with a bold slice. The flour cake stood firm, revealing only a slightly crumbled surface like a wall of shale. Imre cut a whisper of flour. Then Gudrun, and so on, with much teasing and calling to each other. Sydney was terrified she'd destroy the thing when it came to her, but she didn't. The Scotsman, showing off, took rather a large cut. Myrna declared she was going to make Eric go into the flour but Eric survived. People began to undercut the remaining pillar holding up the ring, and Laurus teased the Scotsman that he was going to have flour all through his beard. When it was Sydney's turn she took the tiniest sliver and for a trembling moment it seemed sure that Laurus was right—the Scotsman was done for. Then, as a cry went up from the table, the pillar collapsed. Sydney's eyes widened, and her cheeks turned red. But after only a second's hesitation she put her hands behind her back and went snout down into the plate of flour. When she came up laughing with the ring between her lips, with flour all over her face, even in her eyebrows, Laurus looked across the table at her elated and comical face, and saw something he thought he recognized, that filled him with delight. And he fell in love.

"How do you do, Mr. Moss?"

"Very well, thank you, Mrs. Brant," said Laurus cheerfully.

"You could call him Laurus, Mother," said Sydney. Considering that she'd given her mother plenty of reason to guess that they'd come home to announce to her their engagement.

Candace said serenely, "Thank you, dear," and ignored the suggestion.

They were standing in the reception hall at The Elms. It was August of 1939, the first time Candace and Sydney had been face-to-face since the previous June, and if Sydney had had any hopes that her absence had made her mother fonder of her, she was over it by the time she and Laurus had tramped across the room to where Candace stood in full regalia, including a silk morning dress and a pair of large gray pearl earrings.

What Candace saw: her daughter, dressed in some, she supposed, Bohemian getup, a long skirt and sandals, with her dark hair uncut and worn in a bun. She had dimly hoped that a year in New York would have taught "Sydney" something about style, but . . . no. It had rather, apparently, encouraged those qualities in her daughter she found least attractive. Exactly as she had told Bernard it would.

And here on her daughter's arm, or at her side anyway, was her idea of a beau, a Jew from Europe who played the piano for a living.

At least he didn't look Jewish. Trim brown hair, blue eyes, small-ish nose, very tidily dressed, and speaking English.

"Wait till you see Elise Maitland" (pause . . . ) "Sydney. She's come back from Paris dressed in Mainbocher. Really marvelous." (She pronounced it *man-bo-shay,* as if it were French. Laurus hap-pened to know that it was German, and pronounced *mane-bocker,* but felt he shouldn't mind if Herr Mainbocher didn't.)

"How nice for her. Where would you like us to go, Mother?"

She meant what rooms. They were still standing in their traveling clothes, after a very long trip by train to Union and a rather hot drive out to the coast. She was ashamed of this welcome.

"You're in the room next to mine, upstairs, and your friend is out in the, you know, in poor Aunt Louisa's wing."

In the nursery. *Quelle surprise.* In the nanny's room? Or her old bedroom with the folklorica dolls? In any case, virtually in a separate building.

"I'm in the blue room?"

"The—what we called the blue room, yes. And your old room is all done over. Mr. Moss will be perfectly comfortable. I'll get Ralph to show him."

"I'll show him," said Sydney. She left her suitcase by the door and led Laurus out.

As they walked together along the swept path, fragrant with pine needles and lined with blooming white *Rosa rugosa* bushes, Sydney felt like Gretel leading Hansel toward the cottage of the witch. Since the first night Laurus kissed her on Christmas Eve, she had feared this moment, which would follow if their happiness together contin-ued to bloom as it had so suddenly and thrillingly. She had been se-cretly frantic to guess what exactly he saw in her. She had adopted the ways of the other music students, wearing what they wore, eat-ing where they ate, buying standing-room tickets at the symphony and opera, dreading the moment Laurus would learn she was rich and either be horrified or entirely too pleased.

She watched him from the corner of her eye as they walked, waiting to learn what would change now.

The answer was, nothing. If the house was grand, he didn't seem to notice. He merely looked at her with a slightly wicked smile and said, "Very handsome, the formidable Mama."

When they came to the door of Poor Auntie Louisa's wing, he put his valise and raincoat down and walked past it down the lawn to where he could see an open sweep of the inner harbor, with the high August sky arching and fishing boats and sailboats bobbing on their moorings.

"Isn't it beautiful?"

"It's so like home!" he said, turning to her.

"Really?"

"I didn't know anything in America looked like this. Whose boat is that?"

"Mine."

"Can we go sailing?"

"Right now?"

"Yes, I want to see everything. All at the same time."

They hurried back to the house, Sydney humming with relief and happiness. So that was that. There were all kinds of wealth in this world, and Laurus's was his talent and his merry spirit, and she never saw any sign in his long life that he envied anybody a material thing, or made distinctions among people based on anything but their moral grace. This, she was beginning to realize, was one very unusual man.

Laurus was installed in Sydney's childhood room, which had been "all redone" in the sense of repainted, and was now yellow instead of pink. The dolls were still where they'd always been. The bedside light was still a painted bunny holding a painted egg. Her stuffed animals were piled on her canopy bed.

"In case you forgot to bring your own teddy bear," said Sydney. Really, it was masterful. Would Candace put Mr. Christie in this room?

Laurus said, "This was your room? I am so glad. When I go to sleep I will have your dreams."

"I hope the Doll League of Nations doesn't give you nightmares."

He looked up at them. The German doll was very cheery and blond and Bavarian.

"Is there a Czech one?" he asked.

"I don't think so. Why, were you going to hide it from Brunhilde up there?"

"Yes. One does what one can."

He turned to a picture in a painted frame, of a plump little girl in a very short dress, her sash practically at her armpits, her hair caught back in barrettes in a way Sydney always hated. She was wearing Mary Janes and little white socks and had an enormous scab on her knee. The nurse had taken this picture with her box Brownie, one day when Sydney—Annabee—had been dressed up for a birthday party.

"Is this you?" He turned to her, smiling.

"You can see why 'The Ugly Duckling' was my favorite story."

Laurus laughed. "It's everyone's favorite story. But not all of us turn out to be swans."

Sydney blushed.


Sydney herself was installed in the room next to her mother's, but there was certainly no point in calling it the "blue room." It was starkly black and white lacquer with a lot of aluminum tubing to the furniture, the last word in moderne.

Sydney changed into shorts and a blouse and went down to tell her mother they were going sailing.

"How do you like your room?" Candace asked.

"Lovely," said Sydney, who detested it. "What happened in here?" They were in her father's den, but the walls of mahogany bookshelves were gone, and something terrible had happened to the remaining woodwork.

"Isn't it charming? I had the wood pickled."

"Oh. Good. Well, we'll see you later."

"Fine," said Candace.

When they came in from sailing, Candace was sitting in the Great Hall with a laden teatable before her.

"There you are, lovey. Bring Mr. Moss in for a cup of tea, won't you?"

Sydney glanced at him sideways. She had been hoping they could slip out to the kitchen and make some coffee for themselves. But Laurus marched right over, wished Candace good afternoon, and took a chair next to her.

"Cream or lemon?"

"Lemon, two sugars, please."

"*Sydney?*"

"Just plain. Strong."

"Did you have a nice sail, Mr. Moss?"

"Blissful. It reminds me so much of home."

"And I hope you'll have a sugar cookie. It's Velma's specialty. Perhaps you won't like them, you're used to such elaborate pastries at home, are you not?" Candace offered the silver-rimmed plate, piled with paper-thin cookies on a doily.

Sydney saw the yawning pit open up between her mother and Laurus and prayed that he would see it and avoid it. But Laurus said, "Yes, but isn't it funny, the whole world calls them Danish pastries, while we call them Vienna bread."

"Are you sure?"

"Very sure. My father's father was a baker."

Crash. There he went, headfirst into the trap. Now he was at the bottom of a pit with Candace towering over it, looking down.

"Really!"

"Yes, he made an almond bread you could not get anywhere else in Copenhagen. I miss it terribly. But these are delicious, he would have loved them."

"Have another."

"Thank you."

"Your grandfather was a baker." Candace pronounced this casually but it accompanied a steady gaze at Sydney, a look that said, Oh, of course, a *baker*. We entertain tradesmen all the time here at The

Elms, by all means bring home a butcher or candlestick maker next. "And your father . . . is a teacher, I believe?"

"Yes, he teaches history and geography at *gymnasium.* You would say 'high school.' " Sydney was grateful that he had no way of knowing that her mother would not esteem this calling very much higher than baking. One might know a college professor, but schoolteachers were more like domestic servants.

"And your mother is a—hausfrau? Is that what you call it?"

"*Husmoder,* we would say. She keeps the house also but she's a musician. A beautiful pianist."

"Ah. More tea, Sydney?"

Sydney shook her head. She didn't know how to tell Laurus this whole meal was a trap, that they were in as much danger as the children in *Hansel and Gretel* who ate the magic food and were turned into gingerbread. How soon could they get out of here?

Laurus took more tea and Candace added hot water to her own cup as she said, "And you play the piano, too."

"Yes."

"And what kind of music do you play?"

"Do you like classical music?" he asked, smiling.

"Not very much," she said, returning the smile.

"Then," he said with great sweetness, "you wouldn't like it."


When they rose to leave her, Candace said airily, "Oh, and I've invited a few people in to dinner to meet Mr. Moss."

Sydney was dismayed. "*Tonight . . . ?*"

"Everyone is so eager to meet your . . . friend."

"You might have asked me."

"It will be very simple. The McClintocks, the Brittons, the Maitlands, and old Mrs. Smith Beedle. You'll like her, Mr. Moss, she's artistic too. Elise is coming, Sydney."

Oh, good. In her Man-bo-shay clothes, no doubt. "Are Gladdy and Tom?"

"No, they're not here. Just a family party, Mr. Moss. Don't dress."

*    *    *

Sydney had suffered torments of anxiety and stage fright before her recital in May, but what she suffered as she took her bath and dressed for dinner that night was not a great deal less. Laurus would be humiliated and want nothing more to do with her. There had been no way to tell him that when her mother said, "Don't dress," what she meant was "Black tie, not white." Sydney had no idea what clothes Laurus had with him but except when he was onstage, the only suit she'd seen him in was the one he'd worn on Christmas Eve and that was heavy wool. This would be a nightmare, he would blame her for it. He would leave. Her mother had planned this, to demonstrate how entirely ridiculous it was to expect refined people to socialize with foreign Jewish bakers' families.

They shouldn't have come. She should have just stayed away from Dundee until Candace died. But there was no way to explain to Laurus why, and besides, she was such a moron she kept hoping one day something would change and she'd have a mother after all, so here they were.

When she came downstairs at quarter to eight, she saw it was worse than she'd expected. Her mother was wearing her tiara.

Sydney was wearing a long black silk skirt and a white silk blouse, the clothes in which she'd given her recital. She and her mother looked dressed for different parties. For different epochs, really. (The rest of Candace's costume was lilac charmeuse, very soignée, and not at all appropriate for a matron's figure.) Sydney indicated the tiara. "Is that what you mean by not dressing?"

"Oh, you look fine, dear. No one will notice."

Before Sydney could answer, the Brittons arrived, and right behind them the Maitlands and the McClintocks came in together.

"Don't you look lovely," said Bess Maitland to Candace, barely having looked at her. She turned to Sydney and folded her in an embrace. "Darling girl! We've missed you! You haven't been to see us in months!"

Elise, who did indeed look very stylish, came to hug her next.

"Bonsoir, chérie, mais comme tu es belle!"

"Really?"

"You are *blooming.* Can you come to lunch tomorrow? I have ten million things to ask and tell."

"You know I have a . . . friend . . . with me?"

"Of course, I want both of you."

But Sydney's eyes were on the door. Here was Laurus, having had a nap, with his hair still wet from the shower . . . perfectly turned out in a dinner jacket and black tie. Sydney felt a wave of astonishment. Was he some sort of magician? That he was at home in any situation? She watched as he came straight to his hostess and greeted her, and it seemed to Sydney that her mother was nonplussed. Bakers' children who traveled with proper dinner clothes? Rather well tailored at that?

Before she could say anything, Bess Maitland went to him. She took his hand in both of hers and said, "But aren't you Laurus Moss?"

He smiled and gave a small bow.

"We heard you play this winter in New York! Gordon, look, it's Laurus Moss! Sydney, dear, is *this* the friend you've brought us? What an amazing girl you are." Now Gordon Maitland was shaking his hand and mentioning the Grieg concerto and Elise had joined them. Bess had taken her houseguest right away from Candace and was telling the McClintocks what luck it was to have him here, when Mrs. Amelia Smith Beedle arrived.

Candace went to meet her guest of honor, who was in her late eighties and tonight dressed entirely in mint green, including a dirty feather boa. She was carrying a very small dachshund which she handed to Candace.

"How good of you to come, Mrs. Beedle."

"Thank you for saying so. Now which of these ladies is my hostess?" Mrs. Beedle steamed past her and into the fray. "Good evening, so nice to see you, Amelia Smith Beedle."

"It's Bess Maitland, Amelia, you remember we had lunch together yesterday."

"We did?"

"Yes."

"What did we have?"

"Lobster Newburg. You remember Gordon . . ."

Bess took her on around the circle helping her to greet the other guests. It was apparent that she had gone well beyond "artistic" into another state altogether and that her presence at the table was not likely to be quite the social coup Candace had planned.

The final guest arrived: Candace's Bachelor Beau, Norris Cummings.

"You're looking lovely as ever, dear lady," he said to Candace. She thanked him, desperate to get this evening back on track, and hustled him toward the group. As he joined the others, Candace handed the dachshund to the waitress and said, "Will you please take this to the kitchen and feed it or something, and tell Cook we are ready to go in."

"Yes, ma'am."

The second waitress came forward with a small sherry glass on a tray, with a linen napkin.

"Your usual, Mr. Cummings."

"Thank you, Brenda."

He took a sip to make sure it was mostly gin, then gave her a wink. He went on toward the rest of the guests.

Elise came forward and greeted him. Dr. McClintock patted his shoulder and said, "That was a good match this afternoon. You gave me a run for my money."

"Good evening, Colin. So nice to see you, Molly."

Mrs. Beedle, who was sitting in a chair now and fretfully looking for something, looked up at Norris Cummings making toward her and exclaimed loudly, "Why, here's old Flannel Mouth!"

Norris stopped in his tracks, his hand extended. Candace whisked in. "Mrs. Beedle, I believe we are served, if you're ready. Dr. M., would you take Mrs. Beedle in?" She was suddenly very cross that she hadn't placed Mrs. Beedle beside Mr. Moss, but she hadn't and now it was too late. Very unfortunately, she now saw, she had put her at the foot of the table between Colin McClintock and Norris Cummings. Who was probably in for a very long evening.

* . * . *

Laurus talked over the vichyssoise to Candace. She inquired in tedious detail about the trip from New York: Was he fond of train
travel? Yes. Was she? Not very much. Did he enjoy the scenery? It
was very interesting. Was she fond of scenery? She felt it was better
seen from an automobile. Did he drive? Yes.

When the fillet of sole was served, he was able to turn to Mrs.
Maitland.

"You're from Denmark, Mr. Moss?"

"Please call me Laurus, Mrs. Maitland."

"Thank you, I'd like to, and I am Bess. Now please tell me, I'm so
distressed about Czechoslovakia. Do you know Prague?"

"Very well. I love it."

"I do too, I think it's as beautiful as Paris. How can President
Hacha have signed away his lovely country?"

"I'm told Hitler demanded they meet at one in the morning," Laurus said.

"Not really."

"Knowing Hacha is an old man, with a heart condition. They
gave him the papers dissolving the country and told him they'd keep
him there until he signed. If he didn't, they'd begin bombing Prague
at dawn."

Bess sat back in her chair. "Thugs."

"Yes."

"Howard—did you hear what Laurus is telling me?"

Howard Britton, on the other side of Candace, broke off his conversation with her to answer, which gave Candace no choice but to
join in as well. Trying to find a way to be part of it, she found an
opening in which to say, "You must be awfully glad you're over here
just now, Mr. Moss. I've heard your people are having a terrible time
in Austria."

There was a pause. Your people. Well, there weren't any Danes,
or pianists as a group, being stripped or beaten or otherwise abused
in Austria at the moment, so it was hard to avoid inferring whom
she considered "his people" to be. Finally he said, "No one likes to be

far from home when home is in trouble, Mrs. Brant. I wish I were closer to my parents."

"They are in Copenhagen?" Bess asked.

"Yes. I offered to go back but they wouldn't hear of it, and my father says there's no need for Danes to be frightened."

"He thinks Hitler will respect the pact?"

"It is a hope. Denmark is his breadbasket after all. Well, his pork and butter basket."

"Many believe," said Candace, "that really, he just wants the traditional German peoples united again. And that's not unreasonable."

"If you're right, Candace, we should be worried that he'll take Milwaukee," said Howard Britton.

Laurus said, "There's a story told that before the pact, Hitler said to our king that the Danes and the Germans had always been such good friends, they should really be under one ruler. King Christian said, 'You'll have to talk to my son about that, I am much too old to govern so many people.' "

Even Candace laughed. Privately Laurus doubted his king would have spoken to Herr Hitler on any subject, but when true in spirit, apocryphal stories have their uses.

There was no doubt that the dinner was a great success, at least at Laurus's end of the table. At the other end, Sydney and Elise struggled to aid Dr. McClintock while Mrs. McClintock chattered to Norris Cummings. But Mrs. Beedle grew more and more fretful, poor old lady, and finally burst out, "I had my reticule! I gave it to *her,* and I want it now, please!" What could be in it? Medicine? Toothpicks? Something important evidently.

The outburst even interrupted things at the far end of the table and Candace halted the conversation there to listen.

"Whom did you give it to, Mrs. Beedle? To Mrs. Brant?"

"Which one is she?"

"At the head of the table."

"I can't see that far, I gave it to the one in the nightgown."

Candace got up and walked to Mrs. Beedle. She bent over her and spoke softly.

"What did you give me, Mrs. Beedle? How can I help?"

"My reticule. I handed it over when I came in and I want it, please."

There was a pause. "Mrs. Beedle, dear, I'm afraid you gave me your little dog."

"But . . . I need my bag. Bring it, please," she said.

"I'm afraid we don't have it. When you came in, you were carrying your little dog."

Mrs. Beedle looked into Candace's eyes. Into her expression slowly began to leak fear and confusion.

"I was?" She looked suddenly a hundred years old, mortified and distressed.

"Is there something in the bag that you needed? That I might supply?"

"It doesn't matter," said Mrs. Beedle, looking like an actor who had gone up in her lines and couldn't figure out how to get off the stage to safety.

Candace rang the silver bell standing on the sideboard and said, "Brenda, could you bring Mrs. Beedle's dog, please?"

"No, ma'am," she said.

"Excuse me?" This was all Candace needed.

"It didn't like Velma, ma'am. It went under the stove and won't come out. It's growling."

Laurus rose from the table and disappeared toward the kitchen. The dining room was silent and then everyone began talking at once.

"Is your driver here, Mrs. Beedle?" Gordon Maitland asked.

"I don't know."

Sydney got up and hurried to the front door to see if a car and driver were waiting. Meanwhile Bess filled a lot of space with What a heavenly party, and Thank you so much, and So nice to meet, and We really must soon. Molly McClintock talked softly to Mrs. Beedle, and Norris Cummings the Bachelor Beau said sotto voce to Florence Britton that he loathed dachshunds and if *he* caught it he'd rip its little head off.

Laurus emerged from the kitchen with the dog cupped against his chest. Its eyes were popping out of its head and it shook with fright.

"Here we are, Mrs. Beedle. Safe and sound." It began to keen and squirm with longing when it saw her. Laurus placed the dog in Mrs. Beedle's arms. Its nerves were shot by whatever it had been through in the kitchen.

"There," said Mrs. Beedle, "there . . ." as confused as the dog.

"We'll take you home now, Mrs. Beedle. Are you ready?" said Bess. Gordon had gone for the car.

"Thank you so much," said the McClintocks, when the first group had gone.

"But didn't you come with the Maitlands?" Candace asked.

"I'll take you home," said Norris Cummings.

"Thank you, but we're glad to walk. It's a glorious night."

"All right," said the Bachelor Beau. "Good night, Candace."

"I'm sorry about the dachshund," she said, since she couldn't very well apologize that her guest of honor had kept calling him Old Flannel Mouth.

"Nasty little German beast," he said, and went out. (And that was the end of that courtship.)

When the guests were gone, Laurus said, "Thank you for a memorable evening, Mrs. Brant."

"They never even served the baked Alaska."

"I love baked Alaska! Let's have it now!"

Candace looked at him, as if he were altogether a surprise to her.

"Yes, why not," she said. She rang for Brenda and had the dessert served, with elaborate ceremony, to the three of them.

THE LEEWAY COTTAGE GUEST BOOK

Friday, September 1, 1939

*Hitler began bombing Poland today,* wrote Colin McClintock. *It is the end of hope for the world we knew. A sorry way to finish the summer. Cruise canceled; too much fog.*

It was Labor Day weekend. The state fair had opened at the Union fairgrounds, and Sydney was showing Laurus the midway. They were strolling, eating fried potatoes with salt and vinegar, as the news began to spread. They heard it from Al Pease, a boy of the town who hailed them as they were heading for the 4-H tent. (This had been happening to Sydney all summer, town people whose faces she'd seen all her life and whose names she had never known hailing Laurus like old friends.)

"Oh, no," said Laurus. "Oh, no." His face looked pale around the lips and eyes, despite his suntan.

"What does it mean?"

"It's begun. It will be like the last time. Or worse."

Around them colored lights blazed in the gray day. To Laurus they looked suddenly like the grins of a clown at the birthday party of an unhappy child. The music from the Ferris wheel and carousel burbled merrily. Sydney didn't know what to do, burst into tears or suggest a turn in the bumper cars.

"I have to get to a radio," Laurus said. "Do you mind?"

"Of course not." They were hurrying toward the gate when they met the Cochran girls coming in, laughing. Sydney cut their greetings short. "We have to get to a radio. Warsaw has been bombed, you know."

"Oh," said the Cochran girls, and watched as Sydney rushed Laurus off.


All during the weekend they listened to the news. They listened mostly at Leeway, as Candace was hosting a bridge tournament at The Elms. Gladdy McClintock was home at last, with an amazingly attractive beau from California. Laurus and Sydney sat with them and listened to the wireless in the big room where there had been so much music, so many games, so much fun. Dr. McClintock fed the fire in the big stone fireplace. Mrs. McClintock sat with her sewing basket in a pool of yellow lamplight, mending socks stretched over a smooth wooden darning egg. There was a tired crease between her eyes and she kept pursing her lips in an anxious tic she was unaware of.

Dr. McClintock watched his wife from behind his book. He knew she was thinking of Tommy. No mother with a son that age could help it, even if America didn't get into it.

Gladdy and her handsome friend sat on the window seats in the corner overlooking the fog-muffled lawn and played hearts. By Sunday morning it was midday in Europe, and France and England were both at war. Neville Chamberlain came on the air to say that everything he had believed in during his public life had crashed in ruins. Dr. McClintock stood up and walked around the room as if he couldn't listen to this sitting down, but Chamberlain's personal despair moved Sydney; she thought suddenly of her father. King George made a speech they heard at noon and President Roosevelt talked to them in the evening.

There were no more entries in the Leeway Guest Book that summer. By Tuesday they knew that Warsaw was in flames.

"My mother studied in Warsaw," said Laurus, as they walked back to The Elms that evening. "She has lifelong friends there."

"Call her," said Sydney.

Laurus was shocked. It was insanely expensive, and the radio signal very hit-or-miss. No one called long-distance. They wrote letters or sent a telegram.

"Laurus, you have to hear her voice. She has to hear yours."

"It's the middle of the night there."

"So? What time do they get up?"

"Six-thirty. Seven o'clock."

"We'll book a call for then."

When they got home, they built a fire in the den where the telephone was, and settled down to play backgammon. "You're a very kind person, Sydney," said Laurus a little after midnight.

"Thank you." She liked compliments. She hadn't had all that many in her life.

"Are you sure you don't want to go to bed?"

"I'm sure."

They played on.

"Unless you want to be alone?" she said at about one-thirty.

"No."

When it was finally morning in Denmark, his call came through.

When she heard Laurus's voice in her kitchen in Copenhagen, his mother burst into tears. At once he said, "I am coming home, Mama."

"No," she said.

Fortunately for Sydney, he was speaking in Danish, or she would have cried, No! as well.

"You're going to need me."

"We don't. Kaj and Nina are right here."

"Kaj can't remember where he left his housekeys. Nina's a child."

"I'm putting your papa on."

Almost instantly his father was on the line.

"What time is it there?" he wanted to know.

"Late. Papa, I think I should come home."

"I forbid it," his father said. Laurus was taken aback; this was not the way they talked to each other. He could picture them standing at the phone on the wall by the door, his mother in her blue sweater pulled on over her nightdress, his father in his slippers.

"I should be there. We don't know what's going to happen."

"Nobody needs you here, don't talk nonsense. We need you right where you are."

"This is a nightmare."

"Fine. When we all wake up, then you can come. How's your girl?"

"Fine, but—"

"*Kaere,* we're all right here. Denmark isn't Poland. The sun is shining and your mother is making coffee. Don't worry. Live your life." At least Laurus thought that's what he said; some words were lost in static.

They had asked the operator to ring back with the charges for the call. The amount was staggering. Laurus and Sydney counted it out to the penny and put it in an envelope with the date. Candace had a great dislike of finding guests' charges on her phone bill.

*    *    *

Back in New York that fall, Laurus and Sydney spent their evenings
with Laurus's friends, many of whom came from Europe or had family there. They talked constantly of Danzig and Memel and the Polish Corridor, and not just as places on a map. It was irritating to hear
New Yorkers on the street chatting about trivia, as if they'd forgotten what was happening.

Imre Benko disappeared. Gudrun and Eric believed he was on his
way to France and would make his way to Hungary. He had a fi-
ancée in Budapest and sisters.

Laurus played the piano. He played obsessively, like a man taking
a drug. He played Chopin for several weeks, as if he could defend
Poland with music.

One evening, when Sydney came to his studio after classes, as
she often did, she heard his piano as she came up the stairs. Now he
was playing Schumann, the *Abschied* from the *Waldzenen*. She stood
outside and listened for several minutes. The beauty of his playing
was unearthly.

When she knocked, the music stopped.

"Come! It's open."

As she came in, he whirled around on his piano stool.

He said, "I made a vow that I wouldn't play German music. But I
can't help it. It's so beautiful. It makes me furious."

She went to him and put her arms around him.

"It's so hard not to do anything."

"I know," she said. "And remember the good Germans. This can't
go on, someone will find a way to stop the Nazis."

"I want to go to Canada," he said.

To enlist? Sydney had been about to suggest they go to the bistro
down the street for dinner. She was dumbstruck.

Fortunately for her, staying silent was the best thing she could
have done, for it left Laurus to imagine her thoughts, fierce and
courageous like his.

"But I don't want to leave you," he added.

On the morning of Tuesday, April 9, 1940, Nina Moss is asleep in the small room behind the kitchen in the apartment around the corner from Vester Voldgade. She sleeps in a discarded shirt of her brother Laurus, buttery soft, with frayed cuffs and collar. Her middle brother, Kaj, is not at home; he is on call this week, and is sleeping at the hospital where he works. It is very early morning, and Nina is dreaming that she is outside the bakery on the next street, and the baker's boy is inside, where he inhabits a bright yellow hive of light in a dark world, filled with the scents of butter and marzipan. She is trying to get the boy to sell her kringles out the back door, although the shop isn't open yet.

Then the sound of the low-flying aircraft gets into the dream. Then she is awake and the dream is gone, leaving the sounds of the planes behind, loud and close over the city. She wants the dream back but has lost all but a sense of the color of the sky outside the bakery, a blue that is almost black like the June sky at midnight. Now it is gone, diluted to invisibility by the colorless light of morning, and the metal-gray burr of airplane noise.

What planes? Danish? British? Nina gets up and goes to the sink to wash her face. Maybe France or England has decided that declaring war means something. The Soviets finally smothered little Finland, though it took all winter, and so far no one has lifted a finger. No wonder she wants her dream back.

She can hear her mother in the kitchen. She goes out, still wearing only Laurus's shirt, which reaches almost to her knees. In the kitchen, her mother, wearing her wrapper over her long blue nightgown, has opened the window and put her head outside. The fresh-washed smell of April morning is in the room, mixed with the tang of the earth in the window boxes on the sill outside.

"Can you see them, Mama? What is it?"

Ditte pulls her head in and turns around. "Germans," she says.

Nina takes her place at the window. There are people in the street now, standing in little clumps, looking upward. Nina can hear the inhuman buzz of the machines in the distant sky to the north. Now it again grows louder, coming toward the city. Now very loud. Two boys in the street point upward. Nina looks, and sees. Black crosses. Swastikas. A great flock of leaflets explode from the plane, swirl madly in its tailwind, then settle into a gentle mess of drift to the streets below. Nina watches people stoop to pick up leaflets, or stretch to catch them as they fall. While they read, they stand as if wired to their spots. Some then look to each other and speak, others walk off, carrying the paper, some throw the thing back onto the ground and leave it there. Since throwing things into the street is a very un-Danish thing to do, Nina knows this last response is very angry. She pulls herself inside and shuts the window. She and her mother stare at each other.

It is a terrible day. By the time Nina makes her way to the university, German soldiers are in the street, strutting in their green uniforms in a high straight-legged gait that is boastfulness in motion.

Nina finds her friend Harry and his girl-of-the-moment. The girl, who takes her cues from Harry, is in tears of rage. They sit over coffee at a student bar that serves coffee in the morning and beer anytime, surrounded by dark wood and tobacco smoke. From the state radio come instructions from the king and the government to accept the presence of their neighbors from the south; they are here to protect Danish borders from English aggression. There will be, no doubt, some installations to guard the west coast of Jutland, so vulnerable and open to the North Sea, and naturally, some good efficient German attention to the airport at Aalborg, so necessary for refueling German planes en route to Norway. The king will continue to be in his counting house, the government will go on sitting, the civil service will carry on, Danish as usual. To the students, who are young and have shorter memories than their elders, the humiliation of this is scalding. Denmark has fallen with almost no struggle. Thirteen dead, thirteen and it's over. They are no longer a free people. Norway is fighting on, and Harry feels betrayed by everybody. Hitler. Their elders. Themselves. Nina hotly repeats a little of this to her parents at dinner that night. Her father is content, as the table is loaded with nutty rye bread in thin slices and black bread and Danish butter and plate after plate of fish paste and sausage and cheese and herring and bottles of beer. "It's good to listen carefully," he says. "We weren't wrong to stay out of the last war."

"We lost plenty in the peace," Nina retorts. The students have talked all afternoon of Germany, Denmark's ancient enemy.

"Others lost much more," says her father, and passes her the liver paste. "We're a small country."

"Hitler isn't Bismarck," says Nina.

"We're still a small country," says her father, and her mother touches Nina's shoulder gently as she sets a last plate down on the table. She sits down across from Nina and meets her daughter's unhappy eyes as she reaches to put a hand over her husband's. We will not quarrel about this. The young are holy fools, she will tell Henrik later, in their room. They will know that themselves someday, but when they do, they'll be our age and we'll be dead. Henrik, soothed by his after-dinner pipe, already agrees with her. They will not quarrel with the children about this, although there will be times of division ahead; harmony and contentment are precious and they will need their creature comforts.

On April 22, 1940, a Monday, Annabelle Sydney Brant and Laurus Moss were married in New York City, at the Municipal Building

across from City Hall. Many years later, recapturing the day (as well
as he ever could), Laurus would remember only a feeling of unbearable homesickness and impotence, an inchoate sense that he had to
do *something*. This was something he could do. Eric and Gudrun
were their witnesses, and took them afterward for a wedding lunch
at a place near the courthouse with candles in Chianti bottles on
checked tablecloths. Laurus made a courtly toast to his bride. Eric
claimed to feel like Cousin Feenix in *Dombey and Son,* who is so
proud to be a witness at a wedding that he "puts his noble name into
a wrong place, and enrols himself as having been born that morning."

Laurus wrote a full account of the day to his family, telling them
that they would all share the joy of it when they were together again.
He said they were going to love Sydney, and she them. It had been
very strange to stand in a dingy room in New York City and pledge
to honor and protect a woman his family didn't even know. He had
always thought that when he married, Kaj would be his best man.
That little Nina, with her big wide-set eyes, would be standing beside his bride, holding her flowers. Putting this expectation aside
proved more disorienting than he had thought it could be.

In the evening, at Laurus's urging, Sydney called her mother.

"She's just going out for dinner," said Maudie, "do you want me
to catch her?"

"Please, Maudie."

When Candace came on the line, she said, "Yes, dear?," instead
of hello, indicating she had time for about one sentence.

"I wanted to tell you that Laurus and I were married this morning."

There was a silence. Then, "Well, dear. I wish you every happiness." She sounded as if she'd just bitten into a quince. Oh, of course.
Of course, Sydney thought. This doesn't mean a fine man loves your
daughter, it means you didn't get to plan the wedding. "Would you
like to speak to Laurus?" she asked, and handed the phone to him.

"Hello, Mother Brant," he said pleasantly.

"Hello, Laurus. I understand congratulations are in order."

"Thank you very much. I wanted to tell you I mean to take very
good care of your daughter."

"I'm sure you do. Congratulations. Thank you so much for calling. This is very exciting but I'm afraid I must run."

For a wedding present she sent them Annabelle Brant's six-hundred-piece monogrammed silver service. It was Victorian, not Candace's taste; she ordered a new service in a moderne design from Tiffany for herself. She also sent Sydney a letter, saying she must explain to Laurus that he could not call her "Mother." She said she was sorry to have to be that way, but it made her sick to her stomach.

The war news grew worse and worse as the spring progressed, until the Germans reached the English Channel and the British forces had to be taken off the mainland from the beach at Dunkirk, France, and carried to safety in workboats and pleasure boats. In the pictures in *Life* magazine, the escape fleet looked more like vessels for an oddly sorted yacht club cruise than a military flotilla. Holland and Belgium surrendered, France was invaded, and by mid-June, the Nazis were in Paris.

Paris. Which Sydney had still never seen and now maybe never would. Who knew what would happen to it now?

In July, Gladys McClintock and her handsome Californian, Neville Crane, were married in Dundee by the Reverend Davidson in the living room at Leeway Cottage. Happiness shone from these two, both so young and kind and hopeful as they said their vows before the fireplace, between two large potted palms. Laurus played Bach, a transcription of "Sheep May Safely Graze," on the McClintocks' grand piano before the ceremony and a Schubert impromptu after. Sydney and Elise Maitland gave a reception for them at the Country Club. The McClintocks' finances had never recovered from the punishment of the Depression, and Mrs. McClintock hadn't been well. Sydney, the old hand at marriage, was everywhere at the reception, in and out of the kitchen, directing how the food should be presented, and where Glad and Neville should stand to receive, and where the flowers should be and when to cut the cake.

She had made a wonderful discovery: if you're busy running things you don't have to stop and be civil to anyone you don't want to, like your mother.

The party was a great success. There was dancing to a gramophone, and a wedding cake baked by the Maitlands' cook, covered in coconut, Gladdy's favorite. When the champagne was poured, Dr. McClintock offered a toast to Neville. "I'd thought the expression about gaining a son was just politeness, but today it states exactly what we feel," he said. Neville stood very straight with tears in his eyes, and Mrs. McClintock smiled her gentle smile and put her hand to her heart, meaning that her husband spoke for both of them. Gladdy toasted her parents for all their love for her all her life, and her friends Elise and Sydney for the beautiful party. Then Neville thrilled everyone by going to the piano. He played and sang in a warm sweet baritone to a hushed room. I'll be loving you always. With a love that's true, always. "Not for just an hour, not for just a day, not for just a year, but always," he sang, with his eyes on his bride's. Then he stood and raised his glass to her, and all over the room, people cheered and wiped their eyes and blew their noses.

"Who'd have thought it," Elise whispered to Sydney. "The Prince of Princeton, and he has the sense to choose plain little Gladdy." Elise looked as proud of Gladdy as if *she* were the mother of the bride. Sydney was trying impatiently to catch the maid's eye; they were supposed to be pouring more champagne.

Candace came late and left early. While she was there she stayed quietly at the edge of things, watching her daughter, the happy wife, the gracious hostess, bustle about. She had that silly Mr. Christie with her again.

## The Leeway Cottage Guest Book

July 20, 1940

Saturday. Gladdy and Neville Crane were married here today. A cold day but it went without a hitch. Molly feeling better and got through it well. Tom arrived last night and stays over Sunday. A

*happy event for our last summer here. Mr. and Mrs.
Crane off to honeymoon at a secret location; drove out
of town in Homer Gantry's Model A. Everyone
hopes they aren't planning to go far.*

That visit was as much as Sydney could stand of being under her
mother's roof that summer. She and Laurus spent the rest of it in
New York, listening to the news of the Battle of Britain on the radio.
Laurus was preparing for a concert tour of the Midwest in the fall
and Sydney was furnishing their new apartment on Perry Street in
the Village. It was a ground-level floor-through with a sunny front
room for the grand piano Sydney gave Laurus for a wedding present,
and had a tiny shade garden off the kitchen in back. Sydney was
learning to cook, *frikadeller* and buttermilk soup and cauliflower in
shrimp and dill sauce, recipes sent by Laurus's mother, and meat loaf
and applesauce from *The Joy of Cooking*. In the evenings, she and Laurus would sit outside after supper, grateful as cool air began to stir at
last against their bare arms and the city recovered from the baking
day. There were nights when it was too hot to sleep, when Sydney
thought of cool fir-scented nights in Dundee, of fires on the beach
and the stars seeming to curve so close overhead you could touch
them. Laurus talked in the dark about his childhood summers in Nyborg, on the island of Fyn. The little house was right across a quiet
road from the beach. You could see the sea from the little parlor, and
upstairs there was one little bathroom, added long after the house
was built. Each bedroom had a pitcher and basin for face washing
and tooth brushing. For breakfast every morning they had a rich
plate of clotted milk with bread crumbs and brown sugar on top—he
could taste it, just thinking of it. He told her how the summer twilight would linger almost until midnight and then it was only full
dark for a couple of hours. One slept much less, he said. It was too
hard to say good night to the light; instead, you soaked the colors
into all your cells to illuminate the dark season that was coming.

He pictured his mother, playing her beloved Brahms in the front
room, watching the endless evening light making the sea a glittering
mauve, shading to gray-black as night finally fell. He pictured his

father, reading in the lamplight and smoking his pipe. Laurus could smell the sweet tobacco scent of his father kissing him good night when he was little.

It was August. Kaj would be working at the hospital in Copenhagen and Nina had a summer job in Jutland, taking care of some small children, but probably they got to Fyn for some weekends. Probably Aunt Tofa was there too, mending socks or knitting someone a jumper. After breakfast his mother and Aunt Tofa played four hands on the piano. It was a favorite morning sound, Aunt Tofa crying "Halt!" as she missed a trill or got tangled in her fingering, and the sound of the two sisters laughing.

And were there Germans in their pompous uniforms passing on the road outside? He didn't want to picture it, but he did.

Denmark was too small, and had allowed itself to be swallowed too quietly, to garner much attention in the American news, and even if you could get them there was no point reading Danish papers, which were censored. But once in a while an intrepid traveler would bring Laurus a newspaper from Stockholm, or better yet, the anti-appeasement *Handels- och Sjöfartstidning* from Göteborg which would carry Danish news. Apparently many Swedes expected that the Germans were going to win in the end, and were striving to like it. From Swedish accounts it seemed that most Danes, or very many, were thinking the same way. The papers did report that the Danes had perfected a technique called the "cold shoulder." He pictured everyone, from the king to his gentle father, with his love of puns and his courtly manners, pretending not to see the Germans so they didn't have to bow or nod. It hurt Laurus just to think about it. What must it cost to do it?

In November, Elise Maitland, in town for Thanksgiving, told Sydney and Laurus that Mrs. McClintock was dying. Neville and Glad had moved back to Philadelphia to be near her and to help Gladdy's father.

\* \* \*

*The life here is at an end,* Professor McClintock wrote in the guest book, when he closed Leeway Cottage in September. He had to carry his wife to the car, when the time came to go home, and he knew she would never be back. Getting her home was like transporting a cracked egg. He had her wrapped and bolstered into the front seat, and with every mile he feared that some bump or curve taken too fast would break her open, and the creeping poisoned larvae that were hatching all over her insides would cascade out loose in the car. When he got home, he wrote to Gertrude Abbott, the town realtor, to put Leeway on the market. That was like a death before the death. The McClintocks had hoped their grandchildren would grow up there. But they couldn't afford the house and the illness too, and the children could not yet afford to take it over. Neville Crane was just starting architecture school and neither Gladys nor her brother, Tom, had any money of their own.

But it's an ill wind that blows nobody good. Sydney Brant Moss had never had an unhappy moment at Leeway Cottage. When they heard that the house was for sale, she barely stopped to talk it over with Laurus before she bought it.

## THE LEEWAY COTTAGE GUEST BOOK

### July 10, 1941. Thursday

> *A new life here begins,* wrote Sydney ceremoniously. She had green ink in her pen to mark the change from Dr. McClintock's desolate last entry. *We stopped on the way to drive up Mt. Washington. The summit was in clouds. Laurus drove up, and I drove down. Made the rest of the trip in sunlight. The house looks perfect. Just the same. Portia and Ellen left the supper on the stove; hash and green beans and strawberry pie for dessert. Lovely to be here.*

In fact, it was thoroughly strange to be there, not as a child and a guest of the house but as the mistress of it. As was the custom in the summer colony, the house had changed hands with all of its furnishings, in fact with virtually all of its contents. No one in the McClintock family had been able to bear to go in to harvest personal belongings. The McClintocks' sheets were on the beds. Their books were on the shelves, their games in the sea chests and window seats. Tommy McClintock's red and black plaid lumber jacket hung in the downstairs closet. He had worn that jacket all the summer that he was in love with Elise Maitland, and Sydney was in love with him. There were old slickers in various sizes with the yellow rubber flaking off, a dozen tennis rackets, untold pairs of sneakers, and a Cornell letter sweater of Dr. McClintock's that Gladdy used to wear. Even Portia and Ellen Chatto, sisters who had "done" for the McClintocks for years, had chosen to stay on at Leeway.

Mrs. McClintock had died in the spring. Her monogrammed towels were in the bathrooms, and a cardigan sweater Sydney had seen her wear a hundred times lay folded on a shelf in the bedroom closet. When Sydney lifted it down there was a whisper of her scent, something like lemon verbena. A rumpled handkerchief was in the pocket. Her most intimate things, underwear and so forth, had been removed by Portia, but there were cast-off bits of her outer shell everywhere. She had been the kind of mother who extended her cheerful love to shelter any number of young friends of her children or children of her friends, who found their way to her eaves and porches like starving birds in the snow to a cache of suet and sunflower seeds.

Sydney realized as she walked through the rooms of Leeway that her own mother had never been able to stand Molly McClintock. How interesting that she hadn't seen that until now, from here. Candace, with her jewels and her servants and her big bazoom, had been jealous of the dumpy impecunious professor's wife who had loved so many people.

Sydney was standing in the big front bedroom, Dr. and Mrs. McClintock's room, with the four-poster double bed (no Hays Office twin beds here) and the sleeping porch beyond. From downstairs she heard Laurus begin to play the piano. It was the Romanze of Brahms; she'd never heard him play it before, though she had tried it herself, at least the easy part in F major. Sydney stood listening, looking down the lawn and over the trees to the wide blue water. Her heart was full. To live in such peace and beauty, and with such music!

Laurus looked up as he was finishing the piece to see his wife standing in the doorway of the great room. The fading light was behind her, outlining her strong figure, her dark hair half falling down from where she had pinned it.

He got up. "Tomorrow, the piano tuner. What are you smiling at?"

"I just realized," she said. "This is what it feels like to have a happy family."


Nineteen forty-one was Laurus's first full summer in Dundee. He made the village his own as if overnight. He taught piano at Ischl Hall, coached a chamber group, and performed at concerts on Sunday afternoons. He soon had friends among the musicians and among the music lovers. But he equally relished the local men he met in the post office or at the garage, taciturn men with droll wits and immense competence in the physical universe. His proudest moment in the summer was the day Kermit Horton asked him to join the volunteer fire department.

Knowing Laurus would be busy at the hall much of the time, Sydney had pledged to herself that she would spend the summer working on her keyboard skills and practicing new repertoire. If she didn't begin to prepare another recital, Madame Dumitrescu was going to stop taking her seriously. But as the days unfolded so did another, as yet unsuspected, aspect of her personality, like a ball of paper, crumpled under kindling, that suddenly opens up and spreads itself when it catches fire.

She owned a house! It was hers! She could do whatever she wanted to it! She could care for it and alter it, change its shapes and colors, and every single thing she did would say to people, This *is what Sydney is like,* This *is what Sydney likes,* This *is what Sydney can do!* When she walked into the den and looked at the wallpaper, really looked at it, she could barely restrain herself from peeling it off. She pictured clean paint, a pale blue, for this room, with white on all the moldings. She'd go into the kitchen looking for a palette knife or spatula with which to start prying off wallpaper, and become transfixed, planning how much better *this* room would look if you took out the wall dividing the pantry from the kitchen and moved the stove over *there,* and then . . .

She spent so much time at the hardware store and the lumberyard that she was on a first-name basis with all the clerks. She bought drop cloths and paint buckets, brushes and hammers, putty knives and sandpaper. She was often seen downtown wearing painter's overalls with scrapers and rags sticking out of her many pockets, and her hair in a bandana. Sydney, talking on the street corner with this or that tradesman, quizzing Mutt Dodge about how to strip the paint off a door or Maynard Pease about how to fix the sink in the powder room. The first time she was discovered in this happy occupation by her mother, who was walking with Mr. Christie from the post office to Abbott's grocery (about the longest distance Mr. Christie was willing to travel on foot), all her mother could say to her was, "Oh, for *heaven's* sake."

As for Laurus, the more Dundee felt like home, the more he saw Germans all over it. His body was in America, and he was too polite to impose his own preoccupations on others, but as he came and went in this peaceful village, he never ceased to be a man whose homeland had been invaded.

When he stood in the cool dark reading room of the library, and the front door opened, letting a sudden square of sunlight fall into the room between two walls of books, he helplessly imagined soldiers in uniform, black shapes in the doorway, wearing their heavy-browed helmets and big boots that made their feet seem like weapons. What if he turned and they were there, letting the door close behind them, as they advanced on Mrs. Pease at the circulation desk? All these people in the room are pretending not to notice them. The small boy and girl, sitting cross-legged in the children's book section, go on reading *The 500 Hats of Bartholomew Cubbins,* or *Kabumpo in Oz.* The cellist from down the Neck goes on reading the Boston newspaper. Mrs. Pease, though, will have to speak to them. Will she smile, as she does to everyone else? Or will she pretend that she cannot help them? And if she pretends that and they don't believe her, what do they do? How do they show their displeasure?

When he came out of Abbott's store he noticed the small group of teenagers sitting on the steps of the town hall across the street. They were always there, they or others like them. They were smoking cigarettes and lounging, filling idle hours by trying to look dangerous. Dundee was dead as a doornail in the summer if you weren't rich, or unusually smart, or old enough for a better job than raking blueberries. (Which aren't in until August anyway.) He watched their expressions as a large new convertible, a Packard, made the turn from the Carleton Point Road and headed through town toward the yacht club. It was filled with kids from away, summering in the colony, driving Daddy's fancy car probably to go sailing on someone's yacht. He saw the flat look in the eyes of the boys on the steps. What would happen to those boys, with their disappointments and their understandable resentment, when the Germans arrived with their uniforms and their big cars and their conviction that they deserve to rule the world? Would those boys find pride in themselves and outlets for anger in sabotaging the big German cars, in making the invaders' lives miserable and their work impossible? Or would they find pride in themselves and outlets for their anger in also donning uniforms, and the big shiny boots? In demanding respect from those who owed them none? Could he see those boys smiling and blocking the sidewalk as students from the Hall, carrying instrument cases, tried to make their way to the drugstore for a soda or back to their boardinghouses? Students whom even some of the nicest of the old-timers, who appeared to think they were merely noticing and embracing exotics, called "the fiddling Jews."

Everyone said the war would never reach these shores, no such thing could ever happen here. But that was irrelevant. It could happen, period. It *was* happening. What did his father do if invaders gave him an order or asked a question? Pretend not to speak German? Or smile kindly? His father who believed if you treat all human beings exactly the same, with respect and love, they will be incapable of returning you something else. What did Kaj do if they came to him in their green uniforms to have their wounds dressed, their upset stomachs cured? What did Nina do when they smiled at her in the street?

Norway's reward for having resisted the Germans was that the Norwegian Nazi panderer Quisling now ran their country. At least in Denmark the government was Danish. King Christian was in Copenhagen, riding out on horseback most days to greet his people. His brother, King Haakon of Norway, had to flee to London with his family and the entire legal government. Denmark's reward, in turn, for having rolled right over when the Wehrmacht came goosestepping over the border was to be bragged of as a "model protectorate"—the proof that Hitler was really easy to get along with if only you tried.

It wasn't Laurus's way to talk about how this made him feel. Fear and sorrow and panic could all be pumped up and made worse and then spread, like influenza, and what good did it do? You just end up like Tante Rachel who made an aria of everything, from a spider in the kitchen to a lump in the armpit, and as far as he could tell she was never calm, never well, and never much use to anybody. Better to do something practical.

Sydney found him in the kitchen one morning with Ellen Chatto, with flour, yeast, eggs, sugar, and butter all over the place. Ellen was rolling out pastry while Laurus coached her.

"Perfect—stop," he ordered, and slapped a slab of butter down in the center of the pastry. "Now, observe . . ."

He folded the pastry sheet over the butter.

"Now you," he said. Ellen followed instructions while he coached and nodded. "Now, again," he said. Sydney stood with her hands on her hips, watching, and finally went out the back door, looking for sticks with which to stir paint on the side porch.

At eleven Laurus called, "Sydney! Portia! Come to the kitchen, please, we need you!" When they arrived, mistress in paint-smeared overalls, maid in crisp uniform, they found coffee perked and the oil-cloth table spread with mugs, sugar, cream in a jug, and a plate of pastries, rather misshapen, but glistening with sugar and smelling heavenly.

"We need rabbits. Test pigs," said Laurus. "Sit, sit." He passed each one a plate with a pastry. They were still hot.

"Guinea pigs," said Sydney.

Portia giggled and tried a bite. Ellen watched. Then she tried hers.

"What's in this?" Portia asked.

"It's called *remonce.*"

"That doesn't sound very Danish."

"It is, though."

"Whatever it is," said Portia, "I'd like to eat a tub of it right now."

Portia and Sydney ate greedily, but Laurus and Ellen studied the flavors and textures in their mouths like two surgeons, bent over a patient whose innards were not conforming to the expectations they had formed before they cut him open.

Laurus said, "Not flaky enough. And not enough nuts."

"I don't think we rolled it thin enough to start with," said Ellen.

"Let's try again. All right, pigs, you can go."

This went on well into August, when Ellen had mastered the pastry and Farfar's famous fillings, marzipan, custard, chocolate, rum, and marmalade. They had branched out into kringles and braids, crescents, fans, and horn shapes, and Ellen had invented her own blueberry filling.

"I'm going to enter these at the fair this year," said Ellen, and Laurus smiled with pride. In fact she became famous throughout the county for her Danishes, and into her oldest age was begged to make them for church suppers and bake sales. The one thing she would never do was give the secret recipe for the almond ones.

If you had asked Sydney and Laurus to describe that summer for posterity, the newlyweds themselves would have been most surprised at the contrast. For Sydney it was the beginning of the happiest years of her life. For Laurus every day was a golden cloth shot through with poison threads. He had left many hostages to fortune when he left Europe. His mother's family was large, and Jewish. After Kristallnacht, who knew what might be coming? There could be pogroms, a phenomenon that had only recently seemed as distant to Western Europe as Custer's Last Stand seemed to modern New York. His poor beloved little country. When Sydney told people how happy and lucky they were that Laurus was safe in America, he felt slightly sick.

Not that he contradicted her. His task was to love her and she'd had contradiction enough in her life. But keeping one's counsel and picking one's fights is one thing when you are moving around in the world on your own as a single being. It's another in a marriage, which is a closed system. If one partner stays small and quiet in one area of the universe of two, the other one may (or must) expand to fill the void. Such at least was the action of the system inhabiting Leeway Cottage that summer, and so a pattern for the marriage was created.


One night in August, at a picnic on the bathing beach given by the Golf Association, now grandly called the Dundee Country Club, Laurus was sitting apart on a rock, watching the small children playing in the sand at the water's edge, while the older ones swam to the float, and splashed and flirted with each other. Sydney was busy arranging the picnic tables with bowls of potato chips and Ellen Chatto's coleslaw while the men grilled hot dogs and hamburgers. Deep in thoughts of another beach and a different shade of twilight, Laurus was surprised when Gordon Maitland, carrying two cold bottles of beer, came to sit beside him. Gordon Maitland was the kind of big, rich, sporty American man most foreign to him. It was not a type they bred in Europe, though they saw a lot of the American variety in the summertime, arriving at the best hotels with their excited wives and overweight children, guidebooks stretching their pockets out of shape and their wallets full of American Express checks. Laurus accepted the offered beer, and Mr. Maitland settled down on his rock. After he'd drunk half his beer, gazing peacefully at the tranquil dusk on the bay, he asked, "How are you holding up?"

"So far, so good," Laurus said.

"I'm afraid I'd be homesick as hell, if I were you."

Laurus took a long swallow of beer, and nodded.

"Do you know Tommy McClintock?"

"I only met him."

"Nice young man. He came to see me a month or two ago, about getting over to England. Wants to find something useful to do."

"Like what?"

"Well, that's what he wanted to find out. I asked him how his German was."

"And?"

Gordon Maitland smiled. "He said he can sing 'O Tannenbaum.' How's yours?"

"My German?"

"Yes."

"Good."

Maitland nodded. "French?"

"Also good."

"Any others?"

"Norwegian and Swedish, of course. Dutch. The Dutch is not perfect, though."

"Interesting," said Gordon Maitland.

It was their first serious argument. Not that it looked like an argument, since Laurus elected to tell Sydney in a public place. They were at dinner at a bistro on Hudson Street where they especially liked the coq au vin, their "special occasion" place. Sydney had dressed up, in a new suit with big shoulders, and a little matching hat.

Now she had her elbows on the table, her hands steepled over her nose and mouth, to hide the unattractive way her mouth twisted when she cried. Laurus looked at his plate. He shifted in his chair, threw one arm over the back, looked at the far wall. Then he faced himself forward again, and stretched a hand to his wife.

"Sydney."

She inhaled, trying to compose herself, and the sound of her stifled intake revealed that she needed a handkerchief. He took the square from his breast pocket and her face disappeared behind it. After miserable blowing and mopping, she reemerged. Her eyes were swimming, and her sultry lipstick was bitten half off. He reached across to touch her wet cheekbone, and said softly, "So beautiful." His touch caused more tears to spill and slide down the wet cheek.

"When I cry? Thanks a lot," said Sydney.

An approaching waiter with a bread basket saw her face and turned away to attend to another table. Laurus reached for her hand again, and was grateful that she let him take it.

"We've been so happy." Her voice embarrassed her, squeezed up into her highest register by tears.

"It's true."

"For the first time in my life," Sydney added.

"I too," said Laurus, which wasn't true, as he'd always been happy. He meant, I'm with you, we are one. Which wasn't true either, although he meant it.

"Why didn't you tell me? Why didn't we talk about it?"

"It wouldn't have made any difference. I have no choice."

"How could there be *nothing* I could say that would make any difference?"

He heard a subtle shift in her tone, a sharp edge sliding a little way out of the deck and into view. He thought carefully before he answered. He hadn't discussed his decision because there was no way she could understand (which he couldn't say). She had seen too little, there were too many holes in her picture of his world.

"Because I already know you are brave, and would insist I do the right thing." In her turn, Sydney heard a subtle change in *his* voice, a cooling, a flatness. Don't disappoint me. And certainly don't make a scene.

She didn't want him to grow quiet and turn away from her. She wanted him to go on noticing that she was beautiful when she cried. Her weapon slipped silently back and disappeared from view.

"I'll come with you," she said.

At that, he smiled. "That makes no sense. What would you do? You'd know nobody."

"Be with you."

"But you wouldn't be. My time won't be my own. There's much more you can do here."

"Like what?"

He picked up his fork. "Be here for me to come home to." Sydney picked up her fork, too, but put it down again. She wanted him with her. She wanted to keep *him* safe. The dangerous Atlantic. The U-boats. The bombs when he got there. Though it was true, he'd been battering himself against the walls of his cage, so desperate was he to find some way to fight. She suddenly saw a danger closer in; if he didn't go, he'd see *her* as the cage. She began to cry again.

By November of 1941, Laurus was in England, in the uniform of the Buffs. His last sight of Sydney was her figure at the pier beside the Hudson, in a long tweed coat with a silk scarf over her hair. It was a glowering day, threatening rain.

When Sydney heard the mooing of the foghorns as the tugs pulled the ship out into the current and Laurus could no longer see her bravely waving, she had walked the cold blocks to the subway station, desolate as the brown leaves blowing in the street. When she was back in their apartment, warm with yellow lamplight, she lit a fire, turned on the radio, and settled down to knit a sweater for him, for the day he came home.

As she was casting on stitches, Laurus was turning from his last sight for many years of the Statue of Liberty. The troubled slate gray ocean spread around him, heaving and opaque. He went below, to the tiny cabin he would share with three other men, and sat, rather stunned, on his narrow bunk. Now instead of growing together, twining around each other and learning to fill each other's crooks and hollows, he and his young wife would have to grow straight while they were apart, so they would still fit together when they had each other back again. And how long in the future would that be? Would it ever be?

By Christmas, the United States was at war, and Sydney knew for sure she was pregnant. Her tears had stopped as she settled in to make the most of this time in neutral, her time of waiting. She was oddly not frightened for Laurus now that he had survived the cross-ing. Nor was she sorry for herself, though she was passionately, per-sonally angry at Hitler. Being alone was easier since Pearl Harbor, since all the young husbands were going now, or gone. It was less as if Laurus had left her when he really didn't have to.

She kept Christmas Eve quietly in their little apartment on Perry Street, where it was apparent that she had a sort of genius for nest-building. She had spent the time since Laurus left learning to use a sewing machine. She'd remade curtains and bedclothes and even re-upholstered two chairs with fabrics bought cheap on Orchard Street. On Christmas morning there was a telegram from Laurus, wishing her happy Christmas and telling her to look in the top shelf of his closet, behind his box of sheet music, for her present. (In London, over a hot English breakfast with his fellow trainees, all reminiscing and missing their families, Laurus remarked that his was the only bride in New York who wanted a power sander for Christmas.) Sitting by herself in their little sitting room, with a mug of coffee beside her and Christmas carols on the radio, Sydney opened the box he had wrapped in green tissue in October, and was excited and happy, at the present, and at being known and loved. For her next project she was planning to build shelves for toys and books in what would become the baby's room. (If anyone raised the question of her music studies, she said she'd get back to that as soon as she had a minute.)

She had Christmas lunch with the Maitlands, which was festive and sad, because Elise had just gotten engaged. Her fiancé was leaving immediately for the air force. Gordon Maitland found a minute to take Sydney aside to say that Laurus was doing important work and she should be proud of him. And she *was* proud of him. Languages were hard for her and she was amazed at the effortless way he moved from one to the next when they were with their musician friends. She could see it must be very useful now. But it filled her with longing for him, to see Elise and her Christopher holding hands under the table. These days were full of wrenching partings.

Later in the afternoon, Candace called Perry Street.

"Merry Christmas, dear," she said cheerily when Sydney answered.

"Merry Christmas, Mother."

"Thank you so much for the scarf and gloves. They're very charming."

"You're welcome. Thank you for the fruitcake."

"Did Laurus like his necktie?"

"I'm sure he did."

"Your father always liked the neckties I chose for him."

"Yes, I know. He always said so."

There was a little silence.

"I have some other news, dear."

"Do you?"

"Yes. I want you to be the first to know that Mr. Bernard Christie and I were married last night. In a civil ceremony just like yours, dear, except ours was here at home with the Talbots as our witnesses."

After a pause, Sydney said, "Well, then I'm not the first to know, am I?"

Another pause. "Excuse me?"

"Congratulations, Mother," said Sydney, rather loudly.

"Well, darling, you don't say that to the bride. You extend best wishes or something of the sort. You congratulate the groom on his conquest."

"Okay," said Sydney. "Put him on."

This was not what Candace expected.

After a lot of rustling of the receiver being held against a skirt or palm, Mr. Christie came on the line.

"Merry Christmas, Annabelle."

"Congratulations, Mr. Christie."

"Thank you. I hope you will call me 'Bernard.' "

After a longer pause, Sydney said, "You're welcome. I hope you will call me 'Sydney.' "

"I'll give you back to your mother."

"Best wishes, Mother," said Sydney, when she heard her mother take the receiver.

"Thank you, Anna. I'm sure you mean that more warmly than you said it."

"You know best," said Sydney, and hung up.

She sat for some time in a ruck of feeling. Then she launched herself toward the bedroom, got out of her Christmas clothes and into overalls and shut herself in the spare bedroom. Soon the only sound in the apartment was the muffled scream of her new power sander.

Christmas night, 1941. Laurus and his commander are at an airstrip serving the RAF base at Stradishall. A converted Whitley bomber waits on the tarmac; pilot, copilot, gunner, and dispatcher are ready to go. Commander Hollingworth talks with the pilots, as Laurus and his countrymen, Carl Johan Bruhn and Mogens Hammer, stand together, edgy and restless. Above them a cloud cover as thick as a quilt has entirely stolen the moon and stars.

In the weeks they've been training together, Laurus has come to regard Bruhn with profound affection. He's a small man in his mid-thirties, a gentleman, which matters to the British, quiet, intense, and sometimes droll, which matters to Laurus. Laurus is sorry he is not going home himself, but he understands why Bruhn is the linchpin of London's plans for a Danish resistance. He has a quality you can't mistake, and he is young enough for the physical dangers of the work ahead, old enough to command respect, the right man at the right time. It will be up to Bruhn to identify trustworthy candidates for the work within Denmark, to create cells of partisans, to set up communications among them and back to the Danish Section of Churchill's Special Operations Executive, and to invent invisible

methods of funneling money into the country to support their activities, hoping they will soon be effective and many.

It was Bruhn's hope to be dropped into Zealand on Christmas
night, when the Germans' guard would be down. But as he stands in
the cold wind, holding his cigarette in a cupped hand, from time to
time exhaling smoke through his nose, he and Laurus can see from
the way the pilot looks at the sky, the way he turns to Hollingworth
with his mouth pinched, that they can't fly tonight. Hammer, half
a head taller than Bruhn, stands patiently watching too, and from
time to time stamps his feet to keep them warm. He's an engineer
with the merchant marine by training, and most important, a radio
operator.

Laurus waits with Bruhn and Hammer most of the next day,
going over plans, what they will do if this happens, what if that.
There will be no reception committee for them on the ground, so
they are going into the Haslev area where Bruhn knows the landscape and has contacts. They will go to a particular farmer and claim
that an encounter with the Gestapo has forced them to go underground. Bruhn believes the farmer will help them get false identity
papers. Then they will make their way to Copenhagen, to some edi-
tors and others known to be resistance-minded. Once they find a
safe place to live, Bruhn will begin his work; Hammer will get a job
in a bicycle shop in Vesterport, where the owner also fixes radios.
From there, they hope he will be able to transmit to England without
attracting notice. If this fails and they can't communicate directly,
they will place a classified ad in the newspaper.

"What should it say?" Hammer asks.

Laurus picks up a copy of the *Telegraph* and turns to the ad pages.

"Here. 'Lost lady's handbag. Piccadilly Circus.' "

"Yes," says Bruhn in a cockney accent, "I 'ave lost me 'andbag,
and I was that fond of it . . ."

"Which one did you lose, darlin'?" asks Laurus.

"Me green one."

"Oh, that is too bad, I liked your green one. Where? In case there
are green handbags lost all over Copenhagen."

"I lost me green lady's handbag, Vesterbrogade or Gyldenløves-gade."

"I used to go to a dentist in Gyldenløvesgade," says Hammer.

"Lost green handbag means you are both safe but you've lost the radio," says Laurus. "Broken strap means Hammer is injured, broken clasp means Bruhn is injured. My brother is a doctor. If you need him, tell him you come with a message from Gunga Din." He told them how to find Kaj at home or at the hospital. Bruhn and Hammer memorized the addresses.

"He'll know Gunga Din is you?"

"I certainly hope so."

"When we meet again, be sure to explain that to me," says Bruhn.

"And missing strap or clasp means one of you is dead," says Laurus.

"Aren't you just a ray of sunshine?" says Bruhn, smiling.

They get the signal that the mission is on, at last, toward the evening of December 27. Bruhn just has time to say a goodbye (again) to his wife. Hammer is ready. To minimize danger, in case one of them is captured, only Bruhn has been fully briefed with names of the Danish intelligence officers covertly working with SOE, and a courier link to the journalist Ebbe Munck in Stockholm, their conduit to the outside world. Hammer and Bruhn have been briefed together by a recent Danish arrival on the latest gossip and jokes inside the country, so they can slip unnoticed into the stream of daily life.

The plane will pick its way over the North Sea, across blacked-out Southern Jutland, then south of Fyn toward the bridge that connects the north end of Falster Island with the southern tip of Zealand. There it will bomb the Masnedø power station, then make for Haslev. The pilots will descend to five hundred feet as they circle the drop zone, and the dispatcher, in the roaring belly of the plane, will signal Bruhn and Hammer to jump, then send out after them a large metal container of arms and explosives, with its own parachute. Because Bruhn is smaller and lighter than Hammer, it is he who will jump with the radio.

When the plane finally lifts off into the night sky, after so many hours of waiting, Laurus feels an out-of-body elation. It has begun. They will have their direct contact into the heart of Copenhagen within a day, two at the most. And they will have in charge a man of brains and unusual courage who is mercifully free of troubling ego. That was a rarity in someone willing to take epic risks, and it could make all the difference to what they hoped to accomplish.

*Darling girl,* Laurus writes,

*I've thought so much about you this week, our first Christmas apart. If I live to a hundred I will cherish my image of you with cake flour in your eyebrows and the gold ring in your lips. How did you celebrate this year? I'm sure the season is muted, now that you are at war. I suppose you are blacked out now, as here. It is rather bleak outdoors when night falls, and it falls early.*

*We had a service of carols on Christmas Eve that made me miss your voice beside me. Otherwise it was quiet, the weather very gray and threatening snow but not delivering.*

*I hope you continue to feel as well as you claim in your last letter. I wish I could play for you and the baby. Do you suppose he can hear in there? There is a piano here, but it is not a good one and no one left about knows how to tune it. If you can send me a package, could you put in my Brahms? There's a passage of the Romanze that's gone from my memory and it irks me, as I like to play it and picture you listening. There's no other news here, but please write and tell me all of yours. And send me a picture of yourself with our son. Tonight I am quite sure it's a boy and I plan to name him Gaylord Trousers. Will you like that? (Who is Gaylord Hauser?)*

*Much love, my swan*

He writes this sitting on his bed, leaning his writing tablet against a copy of the evening paper which reports that the Japanese have completed their occupation of the fallen British fortress of Hong Kong. And all the time, his heart is over Denmark in the dark, traveling with Bruhn and Hammer. They should be making their jump any time now, assuming they managed to cross the German installations in Jutland without trouble.

As Laurus is cleaning his teeth with baking soda, having been unable to find proper tooth powder, Mogens Hammer is in the dark on the ground in Zealand. The sound of the Whitley on its way back toward the North Sea has died away to the west. It's a thrill to know he's on Danish soil, but there is snow on the ground and he knows that with every step he takes he's leaving a trail of footsteps proclaiming, We fell from the sky. We are enemies and we're here, but he doesn't know what to do, he can't find Bruhn. His own parachute is balled up and hidden, but the adventure can't begin until he has the radio in his arms. He wouldn't mind finding himself in a nice warm barn about now either, but first, they'll have to find the canister full of guns and explosives and hide it. It takes two of them to carry, and where will they hide it, when they're leaving tracks like this? And where is Bruhn?

As Laurus is sliding into a narrow bed between sheets so cold they feel damp, wishing for the warm solid body of his wife, Hammer finds his answer. He steps on something resilient in the dark and almost falls. He steps back, then crouches. The stars sing in the cold overhead as he touches what he stepped on: Bruhn's hand. It is attached to the rest of him, but by something more like a narrow bag of broken sticks than an arm. He may have extended it before him, the last instinct he would ever feel as if he were in a fall that could be broken instead of breaking him. Bruhn has slammed into the ground as if he were himself a bomb. His parachute is still on his mangled back, neatly packed. The radio is smashed beneath him.

As Laurus finally drifts into sleep, Hammer, too shocked to weep, is cutting the boots off his dead friend's feet. He knows there are no incriminating papers on the body but he's had to search it anyway, to find out where Bruhn was carrying their Danish money.

Sydney is fast asleep in New York on the first night of the new year, content and convinced that the baby she is carrying will be a girl. She's had her palm read by a tipsy violinist at a New Year's Eve

party. In England, it's the morning of January 2, when Laurus's growing disquiet over the silence from Denmark is resolved into knowledge. A wire is brought to him from Ebbe Munck in Stockholm. It
reads: 1 JANUARY: LOST, A GREEN LADY'S HANDBAG WITH MISS-
ING CLASP IN VESTERBROGADE OR GYLDENLØVESGADE. REWARD.
APPLY K.520 POLITIKEN.

Laurus stares at it. At first he feels nothing. Then there is a
buzzing in his ears and he wonders if he's going to faint. When he is
sure he is not, he takes the wire and goes to look for Hollingworth.

Kaj Moss has always suffered somewhat from being the second son. He is plump like his mother, but it is not he who inherited her musical gift. He has been quiet where Laurus is merry. He has doubted himself, where Laurus meets the world with the sunny expectation of delight. Kaj hangs back and waits to be sure it is safe to advance. He has his father's hands. His hands are like smart animals; they can make sense out of anything physical. He is training to be a surgeon.

Which is all very well, but the future has been elbowed aside by the present for him, as for many of Denmark's young people at the start of 1942. They have been arguing back and forth since the occupation began. Shouldn't Denmark have done as Norway did? Maybe, but how? They are much smaller. They have no mountains or deep forests in which they could hope for local advantage in battle. Denmark has farmland, open as a dinner plate. But shouldn't they be resisting? Yes, of course. The poet-priest Kaj Munk has said, disgusted, that Danes will put up with anything as long as they have plenty to eat, and this seems shamefully true. Life is too normal. And the German soldiers are not without honor. There is a difference between a career army German and a Nazi, a confusing truth they wouldn't have to consider if everything were not so chummy. What to do?

Kaj knows of a Copenhagen bookstore with printing presses in the basement. Some of his friends from student days spend a good deal of time there. No one can say that Danes don't have a sense of humor; this store is directly across the street from the Hotel d'Angleterre, where the German chiefs are living. In the bookstore basement they print an illegal paper, with news from the occupied countries. It is known, now, what is happening in Poland, eastern Germany, and Czechoslovakia. How the Jewish Problem is being solved. With every new issue, the horror grows here in the Model Protectorate. What can be done, what can be done, what can be done?

Arguments are endless at the university as well. Nina tells Kaj it goes this way: What would you do if Gestapo men broke in and announced they would kill your mother? Would you kill them first? The most common answer, pained and impassioned, is, "No. I would cover her body with mine. I would not kill, but I would give my life to protect another."

"But you are young, she is old. She wouldn't choose that."

"But I choose it. Resistance is necessary. Sacrifice is a necessary response to evil. You can shame evil by showing it honor."

"Nonsense. If you won't kill the murderers, they will kill others."

Then the argument starts at the beginning.

At the hospital the conversation is slightly different. What do you do when a Nazi comes to you to have his leg set, his wound dressed, his burst appendix removed? You treat him. You have to, you took an oath. But if he then threatens to kill your Jewish patients, can you shoot him? So far, there has been no need to make such decisions, but there are those who fear that this could change.

An anti-Semitic rag called *Kamptegnet* is being published by Danish Nazis, claiming that Jews are behind all resistance activities, that Jews control the press in Denmark as elsewhere, that true Danes, like Czechs and Poles, long to throw off their Jewish masters. The fact that the claims about Danish Jews are untrue matters less to the

Danes than it offends their sense of who they themselves are. A Danish consciousness is a democratic consciousness. It is repellent to hear Jewish Danes described as a group that can be separated from other Danes. This is a matter of national identity. Even the all too accommodating government has remained firm on this one point.

The doctors of Copenhagen dare to circulate a petition, knowing that the Germans can't shut down the whole Danish medical profession. Germans get sick, too, and besides, it would look bad. Of the seventy-five doctors on staff at Kaj's hospital who see it, sixty-four sign the petition, although they do not know what risk they may be running to do so. It is the same across the city. The doctors will support their own government, the petition says, and continue to work as healers, as long as there is no move of any kind to curtail the rights and freedoms of Denmark's Jews. It's a warning shot fired across the bow of the Model Protectors.

The German plenipotentiary is a man named von Renthe-Fink. He is a pudgy fellow with thick glasses, a career diplomat rather than a fervent Nazi. He is quite aware that the average Dane will not stand to be told that Denmark has a Jewish Problem. He has repeatedly told Berlin that if they test this, they will upset a very comfortable applecart. Berlin is bewildered. But the matter can wait. The United States is in the war now. Rommel has his hands full in Libya. Nobody wants to have to pull troops out of Russia to deal with a temper tantrum in Denmark. Leave them alone and keep the butter and cheese and sausage coming, and the shipworks cranking out German U-boats. There will be time to deal with Denmark.

The truth was, once America was in it, Sydney enjoyed the war. She hated being without her husband and she hated the sad things that happened to people, but there was plenty to like.

The war for her was like being in the spring musical, except it ran for more than two nights. It was intense. It was full of drama. People who had always seemed to have everything were suddenly undone by grief. People no one ever appreciated, like herself, or like Homer Gantry, had exciting new roles to play; they had new jobs or appeared in crisp uniforms and made gallant jokes about the uncertain future. She enjoyed the world of women banding together with new time for each other now that their men were away. And while Laurus was safe in London translating things and playing the piano, Sydney was the hero in the family; she was having a baby.

She was one of those women who seemed to have been born to be pregnant. She'd had one week of morning sickness, and that was that. She ate well and slept well. Finally, something she was better at than her mother.

She met her mother, Mrs. Christie, in Abbott's grocery in
Dundee in late June of 1942. It surprised them both, to find themselves face-to-face at the turning of the canned-goods aisle, each
clutching her ration book.

"Sydney!"

"Lucky guess?"

"You're up early this year, dear," said Candace as they brushed
their jawbones against each other.

"So are you. Mother, this is my friend Gudrun Ostlund. My
mother, Mrs. Christie."

Candace accepted Gudrun's outstretched hand. Gudrun was tall,
blond, with a long-limbed, slim-hipped grace, and something sad
around the eyes. Terribly pretty, Candace would tell Bernard, a classic Norwegian. Gudrun told her what a pleasure it was to meet her.
Candace herself looked weary, almost for the first time Sydney
could remember.

"When did you get here?" Sydney asked.

"Last night."

"Is . . . your husband with you?" She couldn't make herself say
"Bernard."

"Yes, but he's having a quiet morning. You're looking well, dear."

"Thank you."

Candace appeared quite struck, in fact, at the sight of her daughter. Here she was, trying to understand, was a can of peaches *worth*
twelve ration points? Did Bernard like them enough? Yet here
was Sydney, confidently pushing a cart loaded with things like
Spam, with a wedding ring on her finger, a high round belly proud
under her blouse, and a lovely friend with a charming accent. Almost
as if this were a version of a daughter she could take an interest in.
"And you're feeling well?" she asked, gesturing vaguely at Sydney's
middle.

"Happy as a pig in slops," boomed Sydney, for the pleasure of
watching her mother flinch.

*     *     *

"She hated being pregnant," Sydney told Gudrun, a little more audibly than Gudrun would have spoken in public, when Candace had wheeled her cart off toward the dairy case.

"Did she?"

"Claims she threw up every day for eight months. Loved to tell people that in front of me. We always wanted more children but she had herself fixed."

This startled Gudrun. Fixed? We?

"My father wanted more children. He wanted six. And I wanted sisters in the worst way."

"I see." Candace the unloving. Too selfish to have children. Candace, prepare to be shamed by your daughter, the earth mother.

Candace appeared again.

"Excuse me . . ."

"Yes?"

"I'm supposed to get oleomargarine . . ." She pronounced it "margareen."

"That's what you have in your hand."

"But it's white. I don't think Bernard can eat that."

"The color is inside the package, Mrs. Christie," Gudrun said.

Candace turned the package in her hand, baffled.

"There's a tube of yellow dye inside. You squeeze it into the bag with the oleo and squish it until the yellow is all through. It's rather fun," Gudrun added. "Children love to do it."

Candace looked as if she didn't think, somehow, that her daughter was going to be over to help her squish her margareen. She thanked them and left again.


"I don't think she's shopped for her own groceries in her life," Sydney remarked as they pedaled toward Carleton Point with their bike baskets loaded. "The cook always did the marketing." Now, though, many of the servants were working in factories for better pay and the pride of the war effort. Portia Chatto, for instance, was canning fish in Belfast. Even if Velma was at The Elms, Candace wouldn't have the gasoline to send her to town separately with the chauffeur, when Candace had errands in town herself. Rationing was a great leveler.

## THE LEEWAY COTTAGE GUEST BOOK

July 30, 1942

*It's been a heavenly month,* Gudrun wrote in her small, precise hand.

It had been a month of real peace for her in the midst of a very sad year; her husband's country was conquered, her own (it was felt) helplessly compromised, and she had lost the baby she was carrying the week after Erik left for induction into the U.S. Army.

Dundee reminded her piercingly of Dalarö, where she had spent her Swedish summers. In Leeway Cottage there were Swedish books on shelves in the guest rooms left by the Eggers family, including copies of books she had loved when she was a little girl. Sydney was in some ways a mystery, robust and loud and amazingly ignorant of any history but her own, but perhaps that was simply American. It was so uncomplicated to come from such a young country, with no ancient quarrels with the universe. They sailed. They picked blueberries. They went to concerts. They sat on the covered porches with an odd gaggle of women from the town whom Sydney had gathered to knit for the war effort. Gudrun read *Lorna Doone* aloud to them as their needles clacked and summer rain dripped from the eaves and weighed down the hollyhocks and dahlias in the beds below.

Laurus has asked again and again to be allowed to go into Denmark to join Hammer. Again and again the answer was no. He could not melt unseen into the population; a person known in music circles all over Europe cannot drop from the sky with a cover story that will fool anybody. The enemy knows entirely too much already about SOE's damaged plan; the tale was told quite fully by Bruhn's body and the smashed radio and the footprints drawing a picture of Hammer's confusion and distress. The Germans haven't found Hammer himself, but they want him badly and are vigilant in an entirely new way.

Without explosives from England it takes a home-grown saboteur hundreds of pounds of materiel to make a bomb. There are ways to annoy the enemy; you can punch a hole in a gas tank, then light the resulting fuel puddle and torch the odd motorcycle or staff car. But it's hardly worth the risk. Without help, home-grown resisters can't accomplish much, and if they can't accomplish much how do they make themselves known, to London or each other? And in London, SOE is so stunned by losing Bruhn that their whole plan for Denmark is stymied. Their only important collaborators inside Denmark are some Danish military intelligence officers code-named the

Princes, and they have a different vision from the Bruhn plan. They don't want sabotage. They want somnolent quiet, so they can build an underground army under the Germans' noses. When the time comes, cunningly dozy disarmed Denmark will rise up under the Princes' command and smite everybody. This plan has the advantage, for the Princes, of accruing maximum control and ultimately power to them. Otherwise, it's quite a gamble. Where is the proof that the Princes *can* build an underground army? If they're wrong and Danes don't flock to them, as they are certainly not doing at present, it will be impossible to tell until it's too late.

Still. In the spring of 1942, the Princes' plan is the plan. Meanwhile Hammer has been doing what he can on the ground. One result of his work is that a leading Danish politician, Christmas Møller, has taken the great risk of fleeing the country with his wife and family via Sweden to Scotland to London, where he expects to become the de facto leader of the Free Danes. He expects, with reason, that he will be advising on military and political matters and leading the Danish Council. Unfortunately, the Princes have briefed Møller misleadingly on SOE's plans and their own, causing him to put his feet wrong all over town in his first months in London. SOE is dismayed; they don't like to work with people they haven't trained themselves, and they find him ill-prepared for the work; he was the best man available for the job, but he is not the man SOE wanted. Møller, a true patriot who wants passionately to be useful, is instead largely sidelined and passionately furious. And Laurus, who also wants passionately to be useful and further thinks the Princes' plan will fail, is assigned the task of managing Møller.

For this, he is missing the birth of his first child. And he cannot tell any of it to Sydney.

$\mathcal{B}$ABY GIRL MOSS BORN 3:14 AM STOP.
8 POUNDS 2 OZ. ALL WELL STOP GLADDY.

Gladdy sent this wire to Laurus in London.

Sydney gave birth on August 8, 1942, at Seaside Memorial Hospital in Dundee. The labor was fast and furious and unremembered by Sydney afterward, as it was the age of "twilight sleep," an amnesiac drug mixed with morphine given to laboring mothers that did not so much ease the pain of childbirth as erase the memory of it afterward. The labor rooms were well away from the waiting area in any well-run hospital, so although there was much howling, those who waited for news heard none of it.

Gladdy, in spite of the extreme strangeness of being a guest in what had been her own house, had come up from steaming Philadelphia to wait with Sydney for the birth, and she arrived not a moment too soon. Sydney summoned her from sleep near midnight on the second night of her visit. Gladdy pulled on clothes, snatched up Sydney's little satchel packed for the hospital, and drove through the blacked-out village with Sydney panting with pain on the seat beside her. Her friend waddled away through two swinging doors between two nurses, and Gladdy settled down anxiously, and missed her mother.

There was only one other person waiting with her, an older woman across the room, wearing a housedress and a hairnet, who alternately dozed and smoked, taking deep anxious drags on Chesterfield cigarettes and blowing the smoke out through her nose. There were no young fathers here, and no young male doctors either. Gladdy and the older woman both sat up straight, blinking stinging eyes, whenever someone appeared through the double doors. When the nurse-midwife finally poked her head into the waiting room and said "Mrs. Crane?" Gladdy, who had been dozing with eyes open, thought for a brief excited moment between dreams and waking that she had had a baby herself.

After sending the telegram and getting a very few hours' sleep in her old bedroom at Leeway, Gladdy rode her bike in the morning light back to the hospital to sit with Sydney. She brought the *Bangor Daily* and read aloud. She witnessed the first scandalized skirmish between the nurses and Sydney, whom they caught walking to the bathroom by herself.

"Mrs. Moss!" Thulia Carter scolded. "You could hemorrhage!" Normally, mothers stayed in the hospital for two weeks after a birth. For the first week they lay on their backs and waited for the "twilight sleep" to get out of their systems. At the beginning of the second, they were allowed to sit up and dangle their feet down over the edge of the bed.

"Such baloney," said Sydney as they captured her and put her back in bed.

Gladdy was sitting in the hall knitting when Candace and Bernard arrived, emerging from the hospital elevator with flowers, an enormous plush elephant (where had that come from—luxury fabrics were all disappearing into the maw of the war effort) and a large box from Halle Brothers, Cleveland, that they must have brought with them in June.

Candace embraced Gladdy. "We simply couldn't wait to see our first grandchild." There was a note of eagerness in the voice. "How are they?"

"Blooming. Sydney is feeding her now, but we can go in as soon as they're finished. The baby looks like you, Mrs. Christie."

"Does she really?" Again, the pleasure, the warmth.

"You'll see. Especially around the mouth. She's a very pretty baby." Gladdy told Candace all about the birth, how brave Sydney had been, and how fast the labor. Bernard sat with his hat on his knee and looked down the hall into the distance.

The nurse came out of Sydney's room with the bundled child.

"Mrs. Carter?" Gladdy called. "The baby's grandmother . . ."

Thulia Carter stopped and displayed the baby's face and the one tightly curled hand that lay near her cheek. Candace put her hand to her mouth, gazing.

"*So* tiny . . ."

"We can go down to the nursery after. They'll let you hold her. But come in and see Sydney."


"Mother!"

"Hello, darling!"

Sydney looked actually pleased to see her. "Hello, Bernard. Did you see the baby?"

"She is *simply* cunning." Candace ventured close to the bed and put down her package at Sydney's feet. "Have you chosen a name?"

"Eleanor."

"Eleanor!" said Candace.

"I wanted to name her Tofa, for Laurus's favorite aunt, but Jews don't name babies for relatives who are alive. So we named her for Mrs. Roosevelt."

Mr. and Mrs. Christie took this speech quite well, for anti-Semitic Republicans.

"The flowers are beautiful," Sydney added.

"I'll get a vase from the nurses," said Gladdy. She went off with the flowers.

"I brought this for the baby," Bernard said, thrusting the elephant at Sydney. "Babar."

"Thank you."

So far, everyone was still beaming. Sydney admired the big Babar from every angle, then tucked him into bed beside her, and Bernard looked pleased.

"And this is for you." Candace handed over the big box.

"Presents!" said Sydney. "How nice, Mother!" She undid the ribbon and paused with pleasure over the tissue paper, enjoying the moment. This felt wonderful. A baby in the nursery, her mother here and not being a bitch, and expensive presents.

She folded back the tissue paper. There lay a gleaming lavender satin nightgown, with ecru lace around the neckline and the wrists. Sydney lifted it out and put the satin to her cheek. "Mother! It's just gorgeous!"

"There's a bed jacket too ..." There was. In matching satin, quilted, with ribbons at the neck, and tiny mother-of-pearl buttons.

"Do you want to put them on? We'll turn our backs."

"I'll put on the jacket. I can't use the nightgown for now, but I will when I—"

"Why can't you, dearie? Don't save it ... you deserve it now!"

"No, I mean, I can't while I'm nursing. I have to be able to open down the front."

Bernard suddenly turned and went to the window. This was not a conversation he could be privy to. The pictures it brought to mind!

"While you're ... what?"

Gladdy came back with the lilies and foxgloves in a vase. "Aren't they splendid?"

"Nursing. Breast-feeding."

"What, like a ..."

Sydney waited. Like a ... peasant? Immigrant? Negro?

Gladdy had put the vase on the bed table and grasped the situation. She said, "It's very modern, Mrs. Christie. It's natural."

"So is giving birth in the field!"

"And better for the baby. In Europe it's very common."

Sydney was working her way into her satin bed jacket. This was

all getting too female for Bernard. "I think I'll nip down to the cafe-
teria for a bun," he said.

Nobody said a word to stop him.

"It was a very nice thought, Mother, and I'll save the nightgown
for when Laurus comes home."

"Yes. That will be nice." Relief. New topic. "And when will
that be?"

Gladdy was placing a chair for her near Sydney's bed. Candace
sat down in it while Gladdy brought another for herself from the
hallway. This was Sydney's first two-visitor event.

"No way to tell."

"And what do you hear from him?"

"He dreams of fresh oranges."

"We'll have to get some for him when he's home."

"Yes."

"And he's safe, do you think?"

"Unless a bomb falls on him. He mostly gives lunchtime concerts
at the National Gallery."

"It's very good, they at least let him use his talents. You know the
Toogood boy, Arthur . . ."

"No, I don't, but go on."

"Yes you do, dear, they live out in Hunting Valley, his father's
the—"

"I never met him, but please go on."

"Well. He is a doctor, he was one term from finishing at Western
Reserve. He enlisted, and they put him to work in the *kitchen* on a
submarine, did you ever?"

"No."

"Peeling carrots. A doctor!"

Sydney looked out the window. It was always like this. Her
mother started to talk about her world as if it were Sydney's, as if
Sydney didn't exist except when she was in Candace's line of sight.
She hadn't moved to New York, or married a Dane or had a baby,
she was still right there in Ohio, knowing what Candace knew, seeing what Candace saw, as if they were sharing a brain.

There was a silence. Candace tried to start over.

"I'd like to go down and see the little one in just a minute, but I want you to know how thrilled I am . . . Sydney. Your father would be so proud of you."

"Thank you, Mother."

"And you're quite well? No ill effects?"

"My stitches hurt like hell when I pee, but that's all."

Candace flinched as if a bedpan had been emptied over her head.

"Nobody warns you about that." Sydney pressed her advantage. "Did that happen to you?"

"I'm afraid I don't remember." Candace looked at her hands in her lap. Was there no safe ground between them? Then she thought of something.

"Oh, and darling! I've enrolled her at the Madeira School."

"You've done *what!*"

Now Sydney was sitting straight up, her eyes fixed on her mother like flamethrowers. Candace didn't know what she'd done this time. But here they were again. Where they always were.

"Oh, for heaven's *sake,* Mother."

Sydney turned to stare out the window again.

After a silence, Candace said, "Well—look at the time. I better run."

When she was gone, Sydney said defiantly to Gladdy, "See? It's her baby, not mine. *The Madeira School!*" She imitated her mother's accent.

In the Danish summer of 1942, it is more and more obvious, even to those who don't wish to see it, that an occupied country is in no sense "neutral." Danish shipyards are repairing and building German ships. Danish workers are sent to Germany to free German workers for the Führer's army. Danish industries are supplying German needs, military and domestic; Denmark is a regular bastion of support and comfort to the Reich.

Danes who had at first acquiesced to the occupation begin to wonder where to go, whom to speak to about resisting. The underground presses are underground, how do you find them? Illegal leaflets simply arrive in workplaces, drop through mail slots, or explode from some window above a busy street, shot by catapults triggered with slow-burning fuses after the "publishers" were long gone. Perfecting the cold shoulder or wearing RAF colors on pins and beanies seems pretty mild, when factory workers come home from stints in Munich or Hamburg knowing that the Nazi idea of Germans unfit to live include even veterans who had lost arms or legs in the Great War.

Pacifists in the underground wonder, Can remaining passive be justified? When the leaflets bring news of a tremendous Nazi push this autumn to speed boxcars loaded with unfit humans from all over Europe toward their Final Solution before winter makes the job of transport harder?

Things were different for Norway and France and other conquered nations; they had free governments in England to express their disgust for the Nazi agenda. Denmark's ambassador to Washington, Henrik Kauffman, has on his own initiative handed over Iceland to the United States for fueling and weather stations, but the legal government, sitting in Copenhagen, officially resents it. Actions of individual Danes abroad *suggest* that Danes are not merely Germans in human form. Danish merchant ships at sea in April of 1940 had made for Allied ports, and thousands of Danish merchant seamen had gone straight to England to enlist in the British Navy and RAF. There are in England people like Laurus, working for a Danish resistance. But compared to Allied interest in aiding partisans in conquered countries, and especially after the loss of Bruhn, Denmark is at the bottom of the priority list at SOE in Baker Street, and elsewhere in London.

But if London sees Denmark as useless or even pro-German, Hitler is growing increasingly touchy on the subject of his Model Protectorate. Its king, for instance, who the Führer thinks should regard him as a brother royal. Christian X is seventy-one years old. Although in less than perfect health, he rides horseback through the streets of Copenhagen day after day, and when he appears, his subjects swarm around him, smiling, reaching to touch his horse, to shake his hand, to cheer. If the king keeps his back to the Germans when he enters a room, and passes them in the street as if they didn't exist, what are his people to do? It is this sort of thing that led to the Incident of the Telegram.

The king celebrates his birthday on September 26. The Leader of the Aryan Peoples sends him fulsome greetings, and looks forward to some royal bowing and scraping in reply. The king of Denmark sends this telegram:

MY UTMOST THANKS. CHRISTIAN REX.

People have said that the king expressed himself perfectly properly. People have said that Hitler sometimes actually foamed at the mouth when he was angry, or fell down and chewed on the carpet. In this case, whether or not offense was meant, offense is taken. Hitler recalls his plenipotentiary, von Renthe-Fink, from Copenhagen. He sends home Denmark's representative in Berlin. He summons the Danes' foreign minister, Scavenius, and reads him a riot act about the deference he wants to see from the Danes if the country's charmed life is to continue.

Now it's a Sunday in October 1942. It has been a beautiful day in Copenhagen; Kaj has been sailing in the harbor all afternoon with his cousins Kjeld and Margrete Bing and a girl named Ebba, who has brown eyes the color of buttered toast. Kaj thinks Ebba was flirting with him. He hopes so.

It is a little before full dark; the nights are drawing in. In the streets there is the scent of woodsmoke, and yellow leaves from the linden trees are skittering underfoot and beginning to collect in the gutters. Kaj is carrying his valise; he will sleep at the hospital for the next few nights. When he left home, his mother was just setting the table for Sunday supper and his father was reading the paper by the kitchen window, wearing his slippers. The kitchen smelled of rye bread and beer. Nina came in as Kaj was leaving. She'd been outdoors all day as well; they all knew it might be the last mild day of autumn. She and her friend had ridden bicycles all the way to Greve Stand, she said. Her cheeks were glowing.

Kaj is almost at the hospital, passing a café, surprised to see lights still on inside. The door opens and a woman he knows by sight, the proprietress perhaps, steps out and puts a hand to him, as if to say, There you are, can you stop a minute? Surprised, he stops. She looks up and down the street. Two Germans soldiers walk on the other side, in the other direction. The woman greets Kaj as if they were friends. (Who knows who else may be watching?)

"I was hoping I'd catch you," she says. "Please come in."

Kaj doesn't like sudden changes of plan. He wants to get settled into his room before his shift begins. But she does what she does so firmly that he finds himself responding as if performing a part in a play he doesn't remember learning. He smiles at the woman. She holds the door open for him and he goes in. Promptly, but without hurry, she closes the shop door and locks it, then pulls down the shades of the windows that front the street.

When that is done her manner changes. "Follow me, please," she says, and hurries past the counter toward the back of the shop. Kaj follows her into the kitchen. There is a large young man sitting in a chair near the stove, his skin a clammy gray. He is about Kaj's age, big, with thick blond hair soaked with sweat under his workman's cap, and his entire midriff soaked with blood. Several white aprons have been strapped tightly around his stomach.

"He took a cab as close as he dared to the hospital," said the woman.

Kaj is kneeling beside the man, feeling for his pulse. "What happened?" Kaj asks him, as much to learn if he can talk as anything.

"My mates and I were trying to bomb Burmeister and Wain. I was the lookout. Some Germans arrived and I told them they'd have to shoot me to get past me. So they did." He started to chuckle but pain broke up his smile, like a hammer crushing a walnut.

Kaj glances at the woman. How did she choose him? What made her think he was safe? She could be on her way to Vestre prison if he turned her in.

"How many bullets hit you? Do you know?"

"Two, I think." His voice was a whisper, made with breath from the upper chest.

"Did your mates get away?"

"Yes. The ones inside got away, and I got away when they chased the others. All clear . . ."

So far, thought Kaj, who still had to get him to the hospital, and do it before he bled to death. "I'm not going to risk touching this tourniquet." To the woman: "Can I get into the alley behind the hospital kitchen from here?"

"Yes. Out that way."

To the man: "Can you stand?"

"Let's find out."

They get the man onto his feet and his face goes paper white.

"Are you going to faint?" The woman steps quickly to support him on the right; Kaj has him on the left.

For a minute the eyes swim as if they're going to roll up inside his head. Then he vomits down Kaj's sleeve and onto his shoes and the floor. He stays conscious, however.

"Can you stand it?" Kaj asks. The woman is on her knees before them with a wet tea towel, sponging away the worst of the mess.

"Better now," says the man. Meaning, vomiting doesn't feel good.

"I believe you," said Kaj. "Here we go, then." And they begin, like large children in a very slow three-legged race. Kaj suspects strongly that one of the bullets has hit the hip or pelvis. With the heroism of this man's walk, the war begins for Kaj.

Twenty-three minutes later he and the senior surgeon are in the operating theater. It takes them over an hour to find both bullets and stop all the bleeding in the abdomen. Kaj is right; the pelvis is chipped very near the hip socket. These are the first gunshot wounds Kaj has worked on. When they are finally cleaned and closed, the nurse hands the senior surgeon a patient chart to fill out. Kaj watches him name the man Svend Olesen. He pauses for a moment at the space for diagnosis, then writes "perforated ulcer." This is true, as it happens. They had found quite a large one near the site of the second bullet, and repaired it. No doubt the patient's brand of factory work was stressful.

The next morning, lest he be traced by the cab driver or other bad luck, the man is transferred to another hospital under yet another name. Kaj never does learn his real one. His story will eventually reach London, though, in a coded letter from Kaj to Laurus. Laurus has by now told Kaj and Nina how to evade the censors. This particular letter will be in a batch collected in the bookshop across from the D'Angleterre, then given to a girl whose brother works a fishing boat between Dragør and Malmö, Sweden. From the docks in Malmö, the sack is taken by a Lithuanian Jewish Swede to the train station. There it is left at the feet of a certain passenger waiting for the train to Stockholm. From Stockholm, where Allied countries still have consulates, the letters go out in diplomatic pouches to the Allied world.

In November of 1942, when Eleanor Moss is three months old, Norway's Jewish Problem is suddenly addressed. Several hundred Jews are deported from Norway to Auschwitz. From exile in London, Norway's King Haakon has begged Sweden to offer them sanctuary, but Germany forbade it. In Copenhagen the illegal presses slam and grumble out the news of the deportations, and it has an inflammatory effect on the Danish people. The blacked-out winter nights in Copenhagen seem particularly long this year as people come and go in darkness from three in the afternoon until late the next morning.

By the time Eleanor is six months old (she can smile; she can turn over by herself!), Hitler's General Paulus has surrendered the Sixth Army at Stalingrad, and become the first field marshal in German history to be taken prisoner. (Hitler had recently promoted him, evidently hoping, to no avail, to inspire him either to fight to the last man or fall on his sword.) It is Hitler's second important defeat, following Rommel's at El Alamein, and it does not have a good effect on the mood in Berlin. When Eleanor is nine months old, the remaining Jews still trapped in Norway are ensnared and sent south. Of 530 deported, only 30 will survive the war.

Soon it will be time to turn attention to the Jews of Denmark. According to *Kamptegnet*, it's a turn of events the great majority of Danes long for. Since the Nazis not only want to do what they want to do, but also want to be thanked for doing it, they allow general elections to be held in March of 1943, to give this majority of Danes a chance to express their appreciation. As a public relations gambit, this is ill-advised. The election proves only that the Danish Nazi party is much smaller than Berlin thought possible, and despised.

In place of Plenipotentiary von Renthe-Fink, gone from Copenhagen since the Telegram Incident, has come the career Nazi Werner Best. He is a small neat man in a long leather coat, with a cold smile. He is complicated, ambitious, and not especially sane. It will be up to Best to deal with the growing disrespect, and worse, that will be shown to his people in the cities and towns of Denmark as the days grow longer in the spring of 1943. Although the Germans have declared that the Jews are behind the unrest, the election that was supposed to clear the way for the boxcars has instead emboldened even surprisingly Aryan folk to do the most inflammatory things.

Eleanor Moss has arrived for her first July at Leeway Cottage when the Allies invade Sicily. Finally, the Allies' offensive begins on European soil. On July 25, Mussolini, who invented that snappy fascist goose step the Italians and Germans do, the only thing Hitler still likes about his Mediterranean ally, is overthrown. He has started blaming his losses on the Italian people, and comparing himself to Jesus Christ.

In Denmark, the resistance has grown in strength and so, finally, has the support it needs from outside. Danes trained in sabotage in England are dropped into the country to organize and train others. All over Denmark, in farms and cottages, manor houses and churches, teachers and pastors and housewives and students learn to signal in code with flashlights to RAF planes circling in the night. With the parachutists come weapons, explosives, and money. In Jutland in the north, the materiel is collected at an inn run by the Fiil family. On Lolland in the south, it is dropped into the lake at Maribo with floating markers attached, to be retrieved later and hidden at the manor house at Egestofte, or buried in the pastor's woods. Half the village is in on it, the minister, the local Communists. The lady of the manor herself, Baroness Wichfeld, often gets up in the middle of the night to row guns and explosives across the lake to her Resistance colleagues. When her husband wonders why her hands are covered in calluses, she says, Oh, it's so hard to get good hand cream during the war.

In Copenhagen, Nina Moss is watching a German film with her friend Harry and his girl-of-the-moment when someone in the film raises a Union Jack. A boy in front of her starts clapping. There is a frightened silence, then people around him start clapping too. Nina joins them. Soon the whole audience is clapping and the manager of the theater raises the houselights and stops the film until they promise to be quiet.

Nina Moss is a luscious girl, the darling of her family. She has a laugh that starts in her chest and bubbles up as if her throat were a glass overflowing. She has sleek tawny hair, and brown eyes so light they look yellow in some lights. She danced with the Royal Danish Ballet when she was small; her musicality is all physical, and she has been a sprite, a gingerbread child, and a sugarplum fairy more times than she can count. Even now that she thinks of becoming a doctor, like Kaj, it is Laurus, the musician brother, whom she idolizes. She especially loves jazz, and spends many hours at the nightclub Blue Heaven with her friends, soaking up Dixieland, ragtime, and swing. She misses the American musicians who used to come.

The other thing she minds, not for herself but for her parents, are the shortages. They are less bad here than most places in Europe, but more and more Danish produce goes now to feed the Wehrmacht. Her mother misses coffee; she and her father miss Virginia tobacco. Denmark can grow tobacco of its own, but it is hot and harsh. Power, too, is rationed, and every household is cautious about using heat and lights. Many have no hot water; they boil water on the stove for dishwashing once a day, and wash themselves at the public baths once a week. Her parents have such a talent for enjoying simple things that it hurts Nina to see them go without. For Ditte's birthday in May, Nina got her aunts and cousins to pool their ration tickets to buy flour and sugar, almonds and cream, to make her mother a birthday cake. It was a surprise, and her mother wept. That day was a happy one, like before the war except that Laurus wasn't there. But there are few days like that anymore.

Nina and her friends are restless and angry. They have all read contraband copies of *The Moon Is Down,* by the American writer John Steinbeck, about a little northern town under occupation by armies of an unnamed country; the book calls the invaders "herd men," people who never learn the lessons of the past because they follow orders instead of thinking. The young Danes feel that he wrote it for them. Nina and Harry and his girl-of-the-moment believe in literature; Harry has a Danish name but no one has used it since he played Henry V in school. They are all now intensely moved that someone so far away and unknown to them as Steinbeck has been able to imagine what this feels like. Since it is forbidden to own and read the book, they must make their own copies to pass on, but mimeo stencils wear out. So far the girl-of-the-moment has typed the novel in its entirety onto fresh stencils three times.

A boy from Nina's philosophy section at university spat at a German soldier and was beaten and sent to Horserød, a prison near Helsingør where Danish Communists are interned along with others the Germans consider malcontents. He was there for weeks. When they can now, they put things into the gas tanks of the Germans' cars, slash their tires, bump into them in the streets. There are more attacks on factories doing German war work. There are bars and restaurants that the Germans are simply ordered not to patronize, as their presence would antagonize the patrons to a point the Germans want to avoid. A girl Nina knows from the children's corps de ballet, last seen in the role of a dancing mouse, is observed holding hands with a German soldier. He is handsome, and all the Germans are lonely. The girl is caught later in a stairwell at school and, as three boys hold her, her hair is cut off. Nina is there. She doesn't help, but she doesn't try to stop it. She is changing. She is angry all the time. They all are. Things can't go on this way.

Laurus is sometimes sorry he didn't let Sydney come to London with him when she offered. London is full of girls doing useful work: nursing, driving ambulances, and crowding into Quaglino's and the Café de Paris at the end of the workday. But it is chilling to pick up the papers day after day and read the obituaries. All those civilians who "died very suddenly," which means killed by a bomb. If she'd come and had the baby here, he'd be going mad trying to get her out and home, frightened if he succeeded, since Allied ships and passenger planes are all targets now, and terrified if he failed or she wouldn't go. And knowing her, he believed she wouldn't have. She had taken on a new aspect in his mind, as he imagined and reimagined her, so gradually that he didn't see her changing; she became strong, wise, unselfish, loving, and steady, everything he missed. And the more he missed her, the more he felt farther from her than three thousand miles. Since the summer of 1940, when Londoners grew accustomed to a certain manic community, as night after night the tube stations became giant bomb shelters with no place for reserve or privacy, there were and are many, especially the young, who are in some way thriving on the shared danger, the altered sense of time, living intensely for the present in case there is no future. There will be no way to describe this later, and none of them knows yet that when it is over, they will miss it.

In the spring of 1943, Laurus is restless and frustrated at SOE. They have finally dropped into Denmark a group trained to sabotage the ferries, which are so important to a nation of islands, but the group's equipment was lost. They have gotten some radios and operators in, but German trucks with better and better tracking equipment roam the Danish streets like ironclad dinosaurs, and last September, a man Laurus particularly liked was killed in the middle of transmitting from Copenhagen. Three weeks later the Copenhagen safe house of Michael Rottbøll, whom they trained for months to replace Carl Bruhn, was betrayed, and Rottbøll was killed by Danish police. Mogens Hammer was compromised, escaped to Sweden by kayak, and made his way back to London. With almost senseless heroism he agreed to be dropped back into the country to take Rottbøll's place as temporary leader of Operation Tabletop, never mind that there is almost nothing organized enough to lead. Laurus is deeply stung by the contempt the English rarely hide for Denmark's showing in this war, even while he sometimes shares it. He feels starved for something other than failure: for fresh fruit, for strong coffee, for that moment when you sit poised, hardly breathing, with other musicians, before the flash of joy as five of you hit your opening notes at the same instant.

One night Laurus goes with some other Danes to Rainbow Corner, where the GIs drink and dance. It's friendly and loud, and visiting American movie stars stop in, as they go to and from entertaining the troops. Laurus's friend Kjeld is convinced that if they go there enough they'll get to meet Rita Hayworth.

They don't, but there are cheerful Dutch and English girls who like to dance and can hold their beer, and there's an American nurse called Libby who talks to Laurus about Copenhagen, where she'd been enchanted by the Tivoli Gardens. She isn't truly pretty; her head is too long, her face too narrow, but she's beautiful when she smiles. Those full lips, those perfect American teeth. She is from Oklahoma. The only thing Laurus knows about Oklahoma is *The Wizard of Oz*, but Libby points out he's thinking of Kansas. She has a brother in the navy, and she's seen things in the wards that she'll never talk about when she goes home, but here, for as long as it lasts, nobody has to be told, and they're all in it together. One night, when her girlfriends are already dancing, she turns to Laurus and says, "Shall we?"

"He can't dance," says Kjeld.

"He can't dance, don't ask him," sings an American second lieutenant, as Laurus blushes.

"Why not?" Libby looks under the table. "He's got two feet, I counted them."

"Married," says Laurus, exhibiting his wedding band.

"Oh," says Libby sadly.

"Not everyone thinks it matters," says the lieutenant.

"But you do?" says Libby to Laurus.

Laurus nods.

"Lucky wife," says Libby.

When the music stops, and the other girls come back to the table, Libby says to Laurus, "Well, if you can't dance, I don't suppose you can play the piano," and Kjeld guffaws.

"Does that mean he can?"

"It does," says Laurus. "Why did you ask?"

"Because I can sing," says Libby.

"Can you really?"

"Sing 'White Christmas'!" demands the lieutenant. He calls for more beer.

"Jimmy, it's April."

"I know, but I love that song. 'I'mmm dreeeeaming . . .' "

To stop him, Laurus goes to the piano and plays the first chords, looking over his shoulder at Libby. Come on, I dare you. A great clamor breaks out at their table and soon Libby is on her feet beside the piano, wiggling as she pulls her slip down under her skirt. She is deliciously unself-conscious.

"Can you really sing?" Laurus asks.

"No," says Libby, "but there's a war on."

"This key all right?"

She drapes herself against the piano, lights a cigarette, and nods to him to begin. She really can't sing, but her imitation of a chanteuse is so amusing that she gets wild applause.

"Miss Peggy Lee, eat your heart out!" calls the lieutenant.

On the evenings Laurus and Libby meet at Rainbow Corner, they get into the habit of walking together through the blacked-out streets, back to the nurses' residence hall, sometimes with the other girls, sometimes alone.

One night, taking a deep breath of the soft London darkness, Libby asks him, "What do you miss most about springtime at home?"

"The first strawberries," he says, and is surprised to find that in answering he has thought of home as Denmark, not New York. "What do you?"

"American birds. There were always nests in the trees outside my window. I could watch the babies hatch out and the parents feeding them. And the first asparagus, my mother grows it. And then the tree peepers on summer nights."

"Are tree peepers birds?"

"No, they're little frogs."

"That live in trees?"

"Of course."

"What a strange country. What kind of trees do you have out your window?"

"Enormous maples that my grandfather planted. He was a Sooner. And in the spring you could take the pods that fell and split the seed end, and inside there was stickum so you could stick the pod on your little nose. We all went around with little green Pinocchio noses. Oh, and the smell of the grass the first time it's cut in the spring! That smell, coming through the classroom window while you waited for recess! And jumping rope! Do Danish girls jump-rope?"

She is enchanting. Guileless, warmhearted, like somebody's sister. Like *his* sister. She has four brothers, whom she obviously adores. He makes her tell him about the Sooners, and she makes him tell her about *smørrebrød*, and makes him laugh, trying to pronounce *"rødgrød med fløde,"* and he invites her to lunch the next day at a café serving Scandinavian food around the corner from the Danish Freedom Council.

At lunch, when their plates arrive, featuring dense bread and several kinds of toppings, she points at them one at a time and makes him tell what they are called in Danish and English.

"These pink ones?"

"They are made with fish roe, but we don't call it that."

"What do you call it?"

"Squished elevator man."

She laughs, a wonderful deep rippling sound.

"We don't have many elevator men, but when we have them, they wear red jackets."

"What's this one called?" She points to a grayish liver paste.

"That one is very bad. That one is called 'squished Negro.' "

"That is bad. I didn't think you had Negroes in Denmark."

"We have a few, mostly artists and musicians. Danes are mad for American jazz."

"I love jazz."

"Do you? Have you heard Art Tatum?"

"Nope. Is he the greatest?"

"Yep. Well, skål."

"Skål," she says, and takes a sip of beer, while studying the plate, to decide what to eat first.

"No, no," says Laurus. "You must look at me as we raise our glasses to each other, and keep looking as we drink. Then we raise our glasses to each other again. Then you can look away."

She does as instructed, and as he looks into her night-brown eyes, he feels something go through him to the pit of his stomach. Suddenly he is surprised that people do this intensely intimate thing so constantly and casually at home. Libby's cheeks are about eight shades pinker, and she seems not to know where to look. They begin eating, and talking with false gaiety about the food.

She goes every night after that to the Rainbow Corner but it's more than a week before Laurus turns up with Kjeld and a couple of others. He looks around the room, telling himself he's making sure she isn't there. When he sees that she is, he feels a hot wash of happiness.

Libby is dancing with a GI who appears to be seven feet tall,

with the biggest hands and feet Laurus ever saw. She waves from behind the giant's back, and Laurus, while pretending to attend to the
conversation at their table, orders a beer and then is surprised when
one arrives, drinks it without tasting it, and waits for the music to
stop or the giant to relinquish Libby. Not that it's anything to him,
but just to see if she will or will not then come to his table.

The music does not stop, and the giant turns out to do a mean
Lindy Hop. Laurus can't take his eyes off them.

When the music shifts to a fox-trot, Laurus, with no memory of
crossing the floor, finds himself tapping the giant on the shoulder.

He is a pleasant giant, with a wide face and an easy smile. He lets
Libby go with a bow, and she turns to Laurus the same smile of welcome she has just given in farewell. And Laurus finds himself absolutely tongue-tied. When they have chattered with ease for hours
all spring.

He remembers that he doesn't dance except with his wife. He
prays she won't mention it. He wonders if the giant is someone special to her. He has no idea how to ask. She holds him and follows effortlessly. Finally he frames a sentence.

"You're a wonderful dancer."

"Thank you. That's why I offered to dance before I offered to
sing."

He chuckles appreciatively. He feels as if his bowels might let go,
he is so flooded with emotion.

They dance until the end of the song, and then another, and then
the music breaks off at last. As he leads her to their table, he sees
Kjeld looking at him quizzically.

He orders two beers, and when they come, looks anywhere but
at her. If she offers to skål, he doesn't know what he may do afterward. When the music starts again, he gets up and holds his hand to
her. She takes it and rises to follow him. The song is "I'll Be Seeing
You." Her skin smells lemony.

"No moon tonight," Libby says at last.

"I know."

"I used to love the full moon at home. Now I wonder if I'll ever
feel safe again when there's a moon."

The full moon brings the bombers. He wonders the same thing.

In the dark of that night he walks her home. The air is warm and smells of fruit trees in bloom. What cars are in the streets have their headlights taped down to slits and they creep along, picking their way with blades of light in the thick spring dark.

At the corner of her block, Libby stops and turns to him. She knows their relationship is about to change, and she wants to be away from the coming and going of others at the door of her building.

They look at each other in silence. Then he says her name softly, and she stands immobile, waiting. He kisses her. First with his lips, then somehow their arms, their bodies, their tongues, are all part of it.

He steps away a little and then comes right back into her arms and they kiss again. Finally, he puts his hands on her elbows and holds her gently away from him. A large car with curtained windows makes its way down the street and past them, like a huge animal tiptoeing.

"And now?" she says finally.

"And now . . . we say goodbye."

A long pause. She had expected this, though hoped for something else.

"A clean cut," he says.

They stand on the edge of tears for more ticking seconds. Then he kisses his fingertips and touches them to her forehead. He says, "Always."

"Always," she whispers.

She turns and walks away from him. She has a long strong neck and perfect posture. She is wearing a light-colored dress—he wishes he noticed such things, he wishes he'd committed everything about this moment to memory, there were sprigs of some little purple flower printed on the dress, he thinks. Her dark hair swings loose at her shoulders. Feminine, capable, gentle, brave, his brain says to him. Are you mad to let that walk out of your life?

As she reaches the door of the nurses' house, she stops and turns. There is just enough light from the edge of the blackout curtain at the adjacent window for him to see her face. She kisses one finger and turns it to him, sending the kiss to him. Then she tries to smile and fails; and then she is gone. Although she goes back to the Rainbow Corner often for the remainder of the war, she never sees him there again.

*Darling,*

*I wish you could see Eleanor . . . she's like a little marshmallow girl, all soft and pink and gurgly. She's outside on her blanket under the oak tree with Sandra. I'm enclosing some snapshots I took at the bathing beach last week. I'll take more when I can get the film. You'll love so much giving her a bath. She opens her little hands like pink starfishes and slaps the water, then she clutches her hands together and laughs and laughs at the splashes. Then she does it again.*

*And you should hear the way she laughs when you make an oompah noise against her tummy. I hope you'll get to see her while she's little and cuddly like this . . .*

*Gladys is coming this week to stay with us. Her baby's due at Christmas. It will be fun to have her here, and she can borrow my maternity clothes. Neville is in the Pacific somewhere. Oh, I suppose I wasn't supposed to say that. I hope Tojo doesn't read this letter.*

*I'm enjoying my milk route. I know all the village gossip, and we talk it all over when my ladies come here to knit Tuesday and Thursday afternoons. It's such a funny group, everyone from Mrs. Sherman who sells crabmeat on the Kingdom Road to Auntie Violet Holmes. We have a new member, a niece of Dr. Carey. She went to Vassar College, and had a job in New York, in publishing, but she's been sent here to "get over something." No one is saying what. You've never seen anything like her. She has black eyes and brown hair that's almost black and she wears it very short, like a boy's. And she wears men's trousers! And in the rain, she wears a fedora! And she's really very good-looking! Her name is Anselma and her mother is Italian. If she showed up in Cleveland dressed like that, I don't know what would happen, but here, nobody turns a hair. They're used to Miss Leaf,* and those two ladies who run the pottery. It's too small a place for people not to get along.

Uh-oh. I hear Eleanor. More later.

Now it's Sunday. Sorry for the long delay. Sandra was stung by a bee, and made a colossal fuss. She's so good with the baby, I forget she's just fourteen. Onward—I have a classic Candace story for you. I happened to be at The Elms one afternoon when Ralph was getting ready to go to the dump. I saw him carry a box of old books out, and thank God I caught him—Mother was throwing out my grandmother's Line-a-Day diaries. Can you imagine? Forty years of Granabelle's life, and she was throwing them out. Without asking me. She said, Well, what are you going to do with them, read them? I said, Yes, that's exactly what I'm going to do. The next time I saw her, she asked me with that prune smile how I was getting along in the Line-a-Days. So I went home and sat down with one of them, and they're fascinating. (I don't know why they're called Line-a-Days—they're four lines a day.) I started with 1909. They seemed to spend all their time sewing and reading aloud to each other. The dressmaker would come for a week a couple of times a year and Granabelle would sew along with her, for days. Also, she always noted when she washed her hair. I counted and found she only did it about five times a year! It took two people and took all day to dry afterward. Her hair was long enough to sit on.

So I get to the page for May 18, 1910, and here's what it says: "Terrible news—Berthe Brant has shot herself!"

Shot herself! Mother always said she died from lacing her corsets too tight when she was pregnant! I went straight to The Elms with the book, and asked Candace if she knew what really happened, and she said vaguely, Oh, yes, she thought she had known that. Well, then why on earth would she say that Berthe had died of lacing her stays too tight? She said that she guessed suicide was too shameful to talk about.

What kind of people would tell a story like that, about a poor dead woman? Plus, I don't even know if Candace made it up to make Berthe seem like a fool, or if my father and Granabelle did, and the whole family agreed to tell this awful story?

And why did Berthe shoot herself?

There's no point asking Candace any more about it. She gave that horrible little barking laugh which means nothing is funny and she wishes she were allowed to hit me, and said, It never fails, Sydney, you are drawn like a magnet to the commonest things. Don't you love people who smile when they're angry?

All for now, I've got to get this in the mail. Gladdy comes tomorrow. Write! Baby and I love your letters. I'll write again as soon as I can. I love you ten bushels and three pecks.

Your
Swan

PS Forgot the best part. Now Mother is keeping a Line-a-Day. "For Eleanor," she says.

Throughout August of 1943, unraveling civil order in Denmark is infuriating to Dr. Best. In Kaj and Nina's world, Best is an archvillain. But they differ about Scavenius, their own prime minister. Kaj thinks Scavenius has saved Denmark the humiliation, the Quisling government, the disaster to their Jews that Norway has suffered. Nina says Scavenius is a Nazi sympathizer. She says she wants to shoot Hitler herself.

"But you're a pacifist," says Kaj.

"I make an exception in his case," says Nina.

Both would be surprised to learn how much Werner Best himself wants the present unrest to abate, how little he wants to have to retaliate. This is not because he is a warm and gentle person in spite of his smirk and his Nazi strut; it's for his own political survival. He is now identified with the policy of allowing Denmark relative normalcy (far more normalcy than exists in Germany anymore) in exchange for its workers and its goods. He is jockeying for the approval of the Führer. Best's competition is the dark and meaty General von Hanneken, now commanding the Wehrmacht in Denmark. Von Hanneken believes he was sent to turn Denmark into a German province. He views Werner Best as a fly in his ointment.

The Third Reich likes to give contrary orders to its subordinates; it keeps them off balance, out of league with each other, and perpetually striving for preference.

At the beginning of August, as Sydney and Gladdy are putting up as many jars of raspberry jam as their sugar rations allow, Sweden finally cancels the right of transit across its borders for German troops. Lines drawn in sand in 1940 are being kicked apart. In quiet little Odense, a town best known as the birthplace of Hans Christian Andersen, Danish strikers have badly beaten at least one German officer and refused to go back to work, no matter who begs them. All over the country the streets are full of SS troops, firing guns and threatening troublemakers. With more German troops in the country, more public and private buildings are taken over for housing and training them, increasing Danish irritation. Copenhagen's largest exhibition hall, the Forum, an extravaganza of steel and glass, is for instance being turned into a German barracks. On August 24 the militant underground delivers beer in wooden cases to the Forum, where it is happily accepted. Each has a layer of Tuborg beer bottles on its top rack and is stuffed with explosive beneath. The Forum blows up in broad daylight, without a shot fired or a Resistance fighter lost. Der Führer is furious.

Best writes to Berlin that a new situation has arisen. Berlin, however, already knows. Von Hanneken is complaining angrily that Best's experiment has failed. Best is called to Berlin to have his ears scorched off, by Himmler, as Hitler is too angry to see him. The Führer does not, as Best has suggested, think that the solution to this situation is to make Werner Best de facto ruler of Denmark. Instead, on August 28, General von Hanneken orders the Danish government to announce the following:

*There is an official state of Emergency.*

*Public gatherings of more than five people are now forbidden.*

*Strikes are forbidden.*

*Giving money or other assistance to strikers is forbidden.*

*Harassing Danes who cooperate with Germans is forbidden.*

*Censorship of the press will now be overseen by Germans.*

*All explosives and firearms must be turned in by September 1.*

*A special tribunal will be set up to judge and punish any who disobey these regulations.*

*Carrying arms or contributing to sabotage in any way is to be punished by death.*

This is the end. The government refuses to announce these ultimata, and the cabinet resigns. The king applauds.

In the small hours of Sunday morning, in dark and rain, Nina wakes, alone in the apartment, to sounds of weapon fire. Hanneken has begun his assault. Danish military installations all over the country are being seized. Officers and soldiers will be interned; weapons and materiel captured. What Nina hears is the attack on the Royal Navy in Copenhagen Harbor. Admiral Vedel, at the opening shot, has ordered the fleet to make for Sweden, or if unable to escape, to scuttle. By full day, twenty-nine Danish Navy ships have gone to the bottom of the harbor. The rest have crossed the Øresund to Swedish waters.

Dawn finds Wehrmacht soldiers posted outside government buildings everywhere, including the palaces. The king declares himself a prisoner of war, and is henceforth under house arrest.

Werner Best calls for the press and gives a manly speech declaring that "this ridiculous little country has inoculated its people with the idea that Germany is weak . . ."

In spite of Best's bluster, it is now General von Hanneken whose state of emergency regulations are posted on Sunday and broadcast throughout the day. There are tears of grief and rage all over the ridiculous little country.

Everyone has felt a crisis coming, felt it must come, thought it should come. But now that it is here, there is a terrible dread. Henrik and Ditte, at their summer cottage in Nyborg, are frightened and anxious and want to be with their children. They spend the day packing, cleaning out the icebox, draining the pipes. There are Wehrmacht soldiers and SS troops seemingly everywhere as they make their way, laden with luggage, onto the ferry and then the train to Copenhagen. It's a somber journey. They arrive at Central Station at nine-thirty in the evening. There are many other travelers at the station, but the streets outside are weirdly quiet. After a long wait, they secure a ride in a Falck ambulance, sharing it with a young mother and two very tired children who are going in their direction.

Three blocks from the station, two German soldiers stand in the middle of the street holding machine guns across their chests. They signal the driver to the curb.

Inside, Henrik, who is in front with the driver, turns around to give his wife a long look. The young mother, sitting with Ditte, seems to have stopped breathing. One of her children, the boy, raises his eyes, frightened. All these eyes, plus the driver's, are fixed on the soldier who signals Henrik to roll down his window.

The soldier leans on his folded arms with his head in the window. He takes in each of the passengers in turn, inhaling their fear. Finally he says, in German, "And what do you think you are doing?"

Henrik answers, his German hesitant but his voice steady, "We are going home."

"You didn't hear there's a state of emergency?"

"Yes, but—"

"You thought it didn't apply to you?"

"We thought we ought to go home."

"Papers, please."

Henrik and Ditte hunt for their identity cards. The young mother looks at Ditte, her eyes glassy with panic. The driver sits immobile, hands on the wheel, looking straight ahead.

The soldier looks at the papers Henrik and Ditte give him. He says, "What about you?" to the young woman, who whispers to Ditte, "Jeg taler ikke tysk . . ."

"And you." The driver takes his papers from a breast pocket and holds them out without taking his eyes from the street before him.

"It's after curfew," says the soldier to Henrik. He has all their papers in his hands.

"We are just trying to get home. We were in Nyborg. You see our address in Copenhagen. Our son and daughter are there alone."

The soldier has had his fun and it is beginning to repeat itself.

"And you're all together?"

"Yes," says Henrik. He doesn't know what's going on in the back but his instinct is to keep this simple.

The soldier hands the papers to Henrik. "You need permission to be out after curfew. Don't do this again."

"Thank you. We won't."

The soldier steps back from the car and says something to his companion. As the driver pulls away from the curb, the soldiers are laughing.

"Oh, my god," says the young woman. "Oh, my god."

"Yes," says Ditte. Henrik had now turned around to them. "You didn't have your papers?" he asks the young woman.

"She doesn't speak German," says Ditte.

But she had understood what was wanted. "I have them," she says, "but we're Jewish. I thought they were going to take us." Her accent is foreign, perhaps Russian.

"Oh, we're Jewish, too," said Henrik, although he in fact is not. "We'd have gone together." Somehow his native amusement has reasserted itself; since danger has passed, maybe there really was none in the first place. It isn't rational, it's his relentlessly optimistic temperament.

"Do you have someone waiting for you at home?" Ditte asks kindly. "A husband?"

"No, he is in the north, in Jutland, with the chalutzim. They are training to be farmers in Palestine. Who is it who calls children hostages to fortune?" She is trying not to cry. She puts her nose to the hair of her sleeping baby daughter and breathes as if praying.

"Shakespeare," says Ditte.

"Not Shakespeare," says Henrik. "Someone else. Raleigh? Bacon?"

"I'd go to Sweden tonight if I could . . ." says the miserable young mother. It's as if she suddenly believes that Ditte and Henrik will tell her how.

All this time, in spite of their fear, they have kept their voices level enough that they haven't alarmed the children. The little girl hasn't even wakened. The driver stops before the young woman's apartment building. Henrik gets out to see her to her door, but she says they must go on; they might be stopped again. Henrik shakes her hand and wishes her Godspeed, and they watch, with the driver, until she is inside the building.

Alone now with the driver, Henrik and Ditte are silent as they drive on through the long summer twilight. They would go to Sweden themselves tonight if they could. But Sweden would send them back. It has been tried. They feel as if they are in the bottom of a deep dark pocket, and the malignant giant from whose belt they swing is about to get to his feet and saunter off with them.

In Dundee that Sunday, Gladdy woke up from a long afternoon nap, thoroughly confused to be in her childhood bedroom at Leeway. She lay under her soft cotton comforter and breathed in the smells of the house, as she gradually adjusted to being not a child, but a wife, and six months pregnant, and alone.

She rolled onto her side and looked at the armchair in the corner as she let go of the last wisps of whatever she had been dreaming. The chair had a blue slipcover showing scenes from *Robinson Crusoe;* she remembered her mother sewing it. The chair had been in Tommy's room, but Gladdy liked it so much that the summer she was ten he gave it to her for her birthday. Tommy was at sea, and hadn't been heard from in weeks. Neville was in the Pacific, too, but she'd had a night letter from him only two days ago.

She felt the baby kick.

The house seemed utterly quiet. It was midafternoon; she'd slept a long time. The August sun was golden, filtered through the leaves of the giant oak tree whose branches stretched almost to her window. Sandra and baby Eleanor were most likely down at the bathing beach. Sydney had said at lunch that she and some friend from the knitting group were going to take their scarves and socks into the village to Dot Sylvester, who was in charge of sorting and packing them and taking them over to Union to the train. Was that what she said? Or had she said she was going to play golf? The house ticked quietly, as it had in her earliest childhood. The safest coziest place in the world, this house, with its musty summer-house smells.

The Robinson Crusoe chair reminded her of a blue lambswool blanket with a satin binding she had loved as a child, trailing around with it, rubbing the binding until it was tattered. Later it hung over the back of her mother's chaise longue in her bedroom. It was a crib blanket but Molly had kept it near her long after Tom and Gladdy had outgrown it, to remember the days of baby powder and midnight feedings, and sweet-smelling toddlers fresh from their baths. She would rub little pink dancing Gladdy dry before the bedroom heater and then wrap her in the blue blanket and tell her to run quick to get her jammies, and then back quick for a story. Where was it now, that blanket?

Gladdy got up and went into the bathroom between her room and Tommy's. It had a pedestal sink, with a rust stain from where the faucet dripped, and a flush with the water tank well above the commode, and a chain, a pull-and-pray. There was a stall shower, rather than a tub, which is why they had bathed in their parents' bathroom when they were small. When she had washed her face and put herself to rights, she went out to the back hall to look in the linen closet.

There were many towels and facecloths, mostly with ragged edges and her mother's monogram, and some blankets she remembered from sleepaway camp. But the blue blanket wasn't there. It must be in the window seat in her mother's room. She would love to have it to wrap her own baby in.

She crossed the silent hallway and opened the door to the big bedroom. Two figures, dark against the bright window, jumped apart as she stepped in, and three people began talking at once.

"Oh, my word, I'm so sorry," said Gladdy.

"Uh, oh, oh!" said Sydney. "You scared me! You're awake, darling, I was just going to knock on your door to be sure you—"

"I was just showing Sydney—" said Anselma.

Then they all fell silent.

Then Sydney and Gladys spoke again at the same time: "Did you—"

"I should have—"

Finally Sydney said, "Did you have a good nap? We were trying to be so quiet . . ."

By now Anselma was over by the chaise, studying something out the window.

"Yes, a lovely nap," said Gladdy with brainless enthusiasm. "Thank you so much. I sleep better here than anywhere in the *world.*"

"I'm *so* glad," said Sydney. "Well, we had a great adventure downtown, we . . . Would you like some iced tea? I would!"

"Yes, I'd love some!"

"Anselma?"

"Yes, thanks. That sounds fine." And the three of them went downstairs to the kitchen, talking slightly frantically. By the time Gladdy remembered she wanted to look for the blanket, she was on the train back to Philadelphia.


Nine days after the fall of the Danish government, on September 8, Werner Best telegraphs Berlin that he would like ships and troops and Gestapo details as soon as possible; that the convenient state of emergency in Denmark presents an ideal time to solve the Danes' Jewish Problem.

In London, at Churchill's Special Operations Executive, there is fierce satisfaction in September of 1943. Finally Denmark is boiling. Now the illusion of neutrality is behind them. This is good. At least, according to the Resistance.

For Laurus things are both better and worse.

For two years he has translated news for the underground presses, communiqués from SOE to the Resistance cells, instructions for handling bombs and weapons. He has helped with strategies, geography, and contacts; he has friends all over the country, musicians he has played with, friends he has made on tour. He knows a great deal about storage in various auditoriums and concert halls; he knows who has access to the stage doors and loading docks, places where caches of arms and explosives can be moved in and out undetected along with a grand piano or a set of drums. He knows also that Nina, his adored little sister, has been working for the student underground for a year.

The awkwardness is this. Laurus knows that if the Germans decide to move against the Danish Jews, the organized Resistance (stronger every week) is under orders to stay out of it. It is essential that the Resistance not draw down vengeance on the Jews, and similarly essential that protecting the Jews not endanger the work of the Resistance, compromising the intelligence and escape routes they need for their own work. If the worst happens, Laurus won't be able to lift a finger to protect his family.

Just after Labor Day in 1943, Bernard Christie underwent hemorrhoid surgery at the Cleveland Clinic. Most of the young doctors had gone to war, and the surgery was done by gentle old Dr. Southworth, who had come out of retirement to fill in. This was probably a mistake. Like many men of his generation he enjoyed his cocktails, and like many doctors he enjoyed his access to the medicine cabinet. More so lately, since there was no reason not to enjoy a soothing buzz in the sunshine as well as by lamplight, when all he was likely to cut was deadheads from the roses. Bernard's surgery was not complex but there are always ways for such things to go wrong and this one did. The patient failed to thrive, complained a great deal, and refused to sit up even on his rubber doughnut, even after the hospital said he could go home. At home, he was eventually found by Maudie unconscious on his bed of pain in a pool of fresh blood. His face was a greenish color and even his gums were white. He was rushed back to the hospital in an ambulance where he had many transfusions and the chief of surgery had to be called in to sew him a new anal orifice.

Candace's difficulties in explaining all this to Sydney on the phone were epic. It was a minefield of forbidden images and vocabulary, and yet she was alone in a big house with her husband in pain and possibly dying, and she didn't know what was going to happen and she wanted her daughter with her, she really did. Brash noisy Sydney, brimming with health and confidence these days, was just what she wanted. Or thought she wanted.

On her end of the phone, in her apartment in New York, Sydney heard something in Candace's voice that was new, and it touched her. Her mother was getting old. Her mother was looking into a future in which frightening and disgusting things could happen that she was helpless to intimidate or banish.

"Would you like us to come out for a day or two?" she astonished herself by asking.

"Well . . . yes, dear, I really would. If you thought you could do that."

Sydney packed up her own clothes, and the baby's diapers and equipment, and with a fair mountain of luggage, she took a taxi to Grand Central Station and boarded the overnight train for Cleveland. (IS THIS TRIP NECESSARY? asked signs from the station walls.) Travel was terrible these days, with trains crowded with soldiers and constantly sidetracked to make way for other trains on war business. With that on their minds, both Sydney and Candace had forgotten for the moment that her mother didn't really like small children.

What Sydney never forgot was that to walk into her mother's house, to have the smell of it swamping her senses as she stepped into the front hall, lily of the valley perfume, furniture polish, her mother's cigarettes, was to be assaulted with a densely layered reexperience of misery that she feared as others fear physical pain. But here it came. She was her father's daughter, and a soldier's wife, and it was the right thing to do and she was on her way to do it.

On September 17, 1943, as Bernard Christie is nearly bleeding to death in Cleveland, Nils Svenningsen, director of the Danish Foreign Ministry (or who would have been if there were still a legal Danish government), goes to see Werner Best in Dagmarhus. He is kept waiting, but only briefly. The plenipotentiary greets him politely and offers him tea.

"It's real," Best says proudly, of the tea.

Svenningsen declines. "Your people have broken into the offices of a Danish social organization and stolen files," he says.

"Really?" Dr. Best is, rather fussily, warming his teapot with boiling water and measuring out his precious oolong.

"The Jewish Community Center. They made a mess and took away lists of the members' names and addresses."

"I believe I heard about that."

"They were heard speaking German and seen leaving the premises."

"Not in uniform, were they?" asks Best. He carries the tea tray to his desk and sits down. To Svenningsen the tea smells of culture, of ancient civility, of parties his piano teacher gave after recitals when

Svenningsen was small, with pitchers of thick cream and pastries piled on plates. Best does not repeat his offer to share it.

"Not in uniform, no, but they certainly were German soldiers."

"Well, they're far from home. They get up to things when they're off duty. I wouldn't say it meant anything."

Werner Best looks calmly at Svenningsen over the rim of his teacup. Svenningsen stares at him. "This is not the start of an action against Danish Jews?"

"I assure you, it is not. There are no plans for any such action."


Nina knocks on the door of a house near Marmorkirken. She is still tan from summer sun and her hair has streaks that are almost white. A girl she knows from school opens the door and smiles her in. When the street door closes behind them, they hurry through the parlor to the kitchen, and down the cellar stairs.

In the basement, by the light of a bare bulb, a young man types a mimeo stencil on a portable typewriter, a rare object these days. Three young women are collating pages while a boy runs the mimeo machine. There is a Webly pistol lying on a shelf above him; the mimeo boy is also the guard.

Their paper is hardly more than a flyer but it has a wide readership; nobody knows how many because each copy is passed from hand to hand. The paper changes locations every week or so. *Free Denmark,* a monthly with a much bigger circulation, is being composed at present in a dental clinic, where trays of type are concealed by day in the medical cabinets and can be hidden at a moment's notice. Some mornings the dentist and his assistant have to clear cigar ash off the spit basin and check the tray of dental tools for wayward type slugs.

Nina picks up one of the sheets now running from the mimeo machine. She stares at it, then looks up at the boy turning the crank. He looks furious. She takes the page and sits down with it in the corner.

A saboteur has been sentenced to death and executed. Executed! This is the first instance of capital punishment in Denmark since . . . Nina reads the story again and again.

There is a change in the weather in the underground after this execution. A fiercer resolve, a cold settled hatred.

Hans Hedtoft is the leader of the Social Democratic Party, unemployed since parliament resigned, or rather, employed in meeting with his colleagues to figure out how to lead or serve when your government doesn't exist. On the evening of September 28, 1943, he is at such a meeting at an assembly hall on Roemer Street when a tall handsome German named George Duckwitz comes looking for him. Duckwitz had lived five years in Copenhagen as a young man, importing coffee. He came back to Denmark in 1939 to a job in the German embassy as a shipping expert. He has the confidence of Werner Best. But with his Danish friends he takes the role of the Good German, whose loyalty is to his country, not to the Nazis. Hans Hedtoft knows him fairly well, well enough to have asked him more than once what is the Reich's true intention toward Denmark's Jews.

Duckwitz arrives at the hall, looking spooked, to call Hedtoft out of the meeting. What he has to say is that Hedtoft was right in his fear; transport ships will be in the harbor by morning. The raids will begin after sundown on Friday, when Jews will be trapped at home around their Sabbath tables or later in their beds. Before Hedtoft can say more than "thank you," Duckwitz is gone.

Hedtoft calls three others out of the meeting and they make a plan. One knows someone on the police force who can provide cars with gas in the tanks. It's illegal, but it is arranged. These four set off in different directions with only a few hours to maneuver before curfew. Hedtoft goes to C. B. Henriques, a banker and scion of an old Danish Jewish family, who is respected by all. Hedtoft tells Henriques what he knows, and how he knows it.

Henriques replies, "That can't be true."

Hedtoft had expected dismay, fear, and a lot of logistical questions, but not this.

Henriques says, "These rumors have been in the air for weeks. I've already talked to Director Svenningsen. You are trying to panic a fragile and frightened group of people."

"A man I trust has risked his life to give us warning."

"A German?"

"Yes . . ."

"Then perhaps it is he who enjoys frightening innocent people."

Hedtoft rushes back to the Social Democrats. What now? They have little time left before curfew, but they set off again.

September 29 is a Wednesday. When Rabbi Marcus Melchior greets his congregation he finds more than a minyan, because it is the day before Rosh Hashanah. Melchior is in street clothes, and he has not come to begin the service. After initial shock and denial at the news he has brought them, the congregants leave with it, to spread it as far as it can be, as fast as it can be without using telephones or telegraphs, which they must assume will be monitored. Rabbi Melchior is left to wonder where he can safely store the congregation's Torah, the silver candlesticks, the prayer books. And where is he himself to go with a wife and five children?

Within hours the holy objects are secured in the basement of a Lutheran church. The Melchior family is on its way to Orslev, to the home of another pastor who will hide them until . . . until what?

In fact the trains are packed in the next few days with families heading for the seacoast. Neither the Danish police nor the German soldiers seem to notice a thing. (Later it will be known that General von Hanneken has refused to order his troops to help with Best's roundup. This is not proper work for soldiers, he declares, perhaps especially meaning soldiers whose commander sees the plenipotentiary as his chief rival.)

All day on September 29 Jews warn other Jews, and turn to their Christian friends for help. Some with no Christian friends turn to strangers. The friends and strangers, furious that it has come to this, take up the message, offering hiding places, money, whatever is needed, while passing the word to anyone who should flee, or can help. Every time one Dane turns to another and dares to repeat the warning, he puts himself in danger as well. There *are* anti-Semites in Denmark, and there are Danish Nazis, and there are people with private grudges. There are even a not-insignificant number of German and Austrian children, orphaned by World War I, who were adopted by Danes, and are grown now with complicated allegiances. Nevertheless Danes turn from one to the next, handing on this fragile, potentially deadly sac of information, knowing that it could burst and spatter all over the lives of everyone nearby, children, spouses, unlucky bystanders. They do it by the hundreds, then thousands.

Nina is in class when someone passes her a note late Wednesday morning. She walks straight out in the middle of a lecture, handing the note to Professor Rosenbaum as she passes. She runs to the café where she and her cohort often meet or leave messages for each other. There she finds three of her friends with a map of the city assigning neighborhoods to everyone who comes in. "Go to every Jew you know. Don't trust the phones, go to their homes. When you're done, go to the streets and shops. Spread the word as fast as you can." Students scatter through the city.

Kaj is at the hospital; he's been in surgery since lunch. He is consulting with his chief surgeon and looking forward to a nice cup of sugar-beet coffee when they are interrupted by one of their drivers. The driver comes in from the ambulance bay in a rush, with his cap in his hand; he tells the doctors what he has learned.

Kaj's surgery patient, who has just been relieved of her gallbladder, is Jewish. Kaj can't warn or hide her; she isn't even out of the anesthesia yet.

The chief surgeon says, "Discharge her. Readmit her as Karen Jensen." He asks a nurse to get him a list of every patient in the hospital.

"Dr. Rafelsen . . ." says the ambulance driver, who is still standing there. "Could you come . . ." He leads him and Kaj out to the emergency waiting room.

There are nine people there. Some are dressed as for the office, some for housework. Several are wearing two coats and have suitcases. One small elderly lady is in her bedroom slippers; when she couldn't be made to understand what was wrong, her daughter and the driver had simply wrapped her up and carried her down the stairs to the ambulance.

All these faces look from Kaj to Dr. Rafelsen and back to Kaj. This is their worst nightmare. These are mostly the newest of Jewish Danes, refugees who have already fled from somewhere else, whose Danish is not perfect, who see no reason Danes should help them when Poles or Ukrainians have been all too ready to join or lead the pogrom. They don't have Christian friends to turn to. They have cyanide pills they will take before they go much farther. Their own fear is as dangerous to them at this point as the Gestapo.

"What the hell is this?" asks the chief surgeon.

"Well, they're Jews," says the driver.

"But how did they get here? Have you been scooping them off the streets?"

"No, I took a telephone book and began knocking on doors of families with Jewish names."

After a pause, Rafelsen says, "I guess we better get them admitted." He shakes the hand of the gentleman nearest him. "How do you do, Mr. Nielsen. I'm sorry you're not feeling well." The Jews in the group who speak Danish try to explain what is happening to those who don't.

Kaj says, "Doctor, I have to go home for a few hours." Dr. Rafelsen turns to him. "My parents are not feeling well either."

"Ah," says Rafelsen. "Knudsen, can you take him?" As they leave, Dr. Rafelsen and his nurse are leading the band of Jews toward the maternity ward, where there are the most free beds, where they will be checked in as Nielsens and Møllers and Henningsens.

It's a mess. There is no organization, no one knows what to do besides get the Jews out of sight. Jews in Copenhagen with friends in Helsingør are rushing north. Jews in Helsingør with friends in Copenhagen are passing them going the other way. Jews who don't know where to go are paralyzed, praying, or else simply heading for the woods. If the news they've heard is true they have two days in which to disappear. Old ones, sick ones, mothers with young babies. And there are many who still believe it's a big If.

Nina is already at the apartment when Kaj arrives on Wednesday afternoon. She is sitting at the kitchen table with her parents. Neither of them is dressed for the street. Nina's arms are extended across the table toward them, palms up, as Kaj walks in. She is pleading with them.

All three turn to Kaj.

Nina says, "You heard?"

"Yes . . ."

"They won't listen."

"How do we know this is true?" Ditte asks her son. "There have been rumors all summer and nothing happens."

"Papa . . ." says Kaj.

"All I'm asking is, how do you know?" said Ditte.

"Your mother is my wife. She goes to church at Christmas and Easter. The Bings have lived in Denmark for two hundred years."

"I won't go anywhere without your father," says Ditte.

Kaj hears the chink in this wall. She didn't say she wouldn't go anywhere period. "What about Tofa?" Kaj says to Henrik.

"Tofa? Tofa is a Bing."

"Tofa is a Jew. So is Mama."

"So are you, then. Are you going somewhere?"

There is another pause.

"Maybe we are," said Nina. "Right now, we have work to do."

"What do you mean you have work to do? *You* can study any-where."

Henrik is joking, reflexively, because he can't think. But Kaj is lis-tening. He looks at Nina, and suddenly understands what work she means. Shy little Nina has done more than talk; she is working for the underground. It figures. The students all think they're immortal.

There is another pause.

Kaj goes to the phone.

"Aunt Tofa? . . . Fine, thanks, but Mama isn't feeling well . . . That's all I can say right now, but I'm worried that you will not be well either. Do you understand? Can you come right over? . . . Yes. Good. As soon as you can."

Then there is silence in the kitchen.

"I'm not going anywhere without your father," says Ditte again. "We'll be all right here."

"If you won't leave without him, he'll go with you."

Kaj looks at Nina and adds, "Kjeld Bing has a sailboat . . ." He is thinking of Sweden. If he can get his aunt and his parents out of the house and hide them for now, they could sail to Malmö tonight. They must know someone who would take them in, hide them from the Swedish police. (But who? And how to arrange it? And what if they're arrested there and sent back? That would be worse than if they just stayed here.)

Kaj and Nina turn and look at Henrik. They know how pro-foundly he is a creature of habit. They know what comfort he takes in doing familiar things in the same way he always has. He gets up in the morning, he puts on the same slippers and sweater. He puts the same kettle on the same stove. His whole day is like that. It's a joke in the family that Ditte can't get him to go anywhere except the cot-tage in Nyborg. Where he has another sweater and pair of slippers.

"We'll discuss it at dinner," he says.

*       *       *

That same Wednesday evening, Niels Bohr, the physicist, takes a postprandial stroll with his wife. They walk leisurely east from home toward a part of the Sydhavn where all the streets are named for musicians. A comfortable pair in their early sixties, they make their way along a colony of kitchen gardens where city people grow flowers and vegetables. Then, from an ordinary couple enjoying an evening walk, they quietly but suddenly become instead a pair of middle-aged refugees hiding in a garden shed full of spades and trowels and manure. At this juncture no one, including Bohr himself, is entirely sure if he has seen a way to make atoms do something that could change this war and all future wars, but very many people in the world of physics believe he is close. The British have gone to elaborate lengths to get word to him that they would move heaven and earth to get him out of Denmark if he would consent to go. He would not, however.

Bohr is well aware that the Germans have left him unusual freedom to work up to now, for their own reasons, and that sooner or later he would probably be in special danger for those same reasons. He has thought that a moment might come when his presence would be useful to Denmark. And now perhaps it has. He and his wife, thus, wait in the dark and chill and the smell of soil for the others whom the Resistance will try to smuggle out of the country tonight.

When the rest have come and it is full dark, these twelve or so, all in danger because of their brains or their politics or whom they are related to, are led from these garden sheds to the harbor's edge. They are made to crawl on hands and knees part of the way to stay out of sight. They board a little fishing boat, which, once they are safe below, slips north in the darkness through the narrow inner harbor, past Amalienborg and Langelinie and finally out onto the Øresund. After an hour, in midsound, the passengers are transferred to a Swedish trawler. In the small hours of Thursday morning they arrive in Limhamn harbor in Sweden and are taken to spend the rest of the night in the best-defended place their handlers could think of in Malmö: the cells at the police station. Bohr is out of Denmark but by no means safe. The Germans will know in short order that he has escaped, and would certainly rather have him dead than working for the Allies.

\*     \*     \*

On Thursday morning, Henrik and Ditte Moss and Tofa Bing agree that they might consider sailing off to Sweden with Kjeld Bing, but it is too late. The Germans have ordered all pleasure boats out of the water. Even rowboats are to be carried one thousand feet inland and left there. They wish they had listened to the children the night before. Frightened and chastened, they are listening now.

In the seaside village of Hornbæk, on the northeast shore of Zealand, above Helsingør, there is a beautiful beach of powder sand. Parts of the coast there are not at all unlike Dundee, Maine, with fishermen's cottages and a small white church, and grander houses belonging to summer visitors discreetly ranked among dunes and under great shade trees. One of these summer houses belongs to a family called Bennike, great music lovers from Copenhagen. They once gave a memorable party to introduce the young pianist Laurus Moss to the cognoscenti. Laurus played a Chopin Ballade, the fourth, and people talked about it for years, the colors in his pianissimo. Later, Kaj Moss was briefly an unsuccessful suitor of the daughter of the house. On Thursday morning, September 30, Kaj pays a call at their flat in Copenhagen. Kaj has no idea in what regard the family holds him since Elisabeth made it clear that her affections lay elsewhere. This is not a comfortable visit for him to make, on any level. Still.

Later in the morning, but while there is still a sheen of normality on the Copenhagen day, Henrik and Ditte Moss and Tofa Bing, dressed for travel and each with a small suitcase, board a train for Helsingør. There are German soldiers in the station, and on the train, but nothing happens that hasn't happened a hundred times since the occupation began. Ditte and Henrik hold hands, and Tofa looks out the window, memorizing the landscape.

Her sister, who can sometimes read her mind, touches her and says, "We'll be home on Monday."

They arrive uneventfully, and as they've been told to, find a certain café near the Helsingør train station, and order their lunch. There have been quite a number of families on the train north, for a Thursday, many with dark hair and clothes and anxious expressions, and through the café windows these can be seen passing, looking lost.

There were taxis at the station, but Kaj had warned them not to take one; they don't want to be traced to where they were going. This was after Kaj had subdued Henrik's insurrection in which he decided they should go back to Nyborg instead.

"The cottage is on the sea. If we have to we'll leave from there."

"Papa—it's the wrong direction. You're not going toward Germany, you're going toward Sweden. Period."

"But—"

"No."

They have finished eating and paid their bill, and are wondering how long they can sit without attracting attention, when a tall young man with long brown hair, none too clean, and a remarkably prominent Adam's apple, approaches with a jaunty air.

"Henrik Moss?" he says. "I'm Per." They shake hands all around. This is the eccentric oldest son of the Bennike family, whom none of them had met. He'd been in France "pretending to be a painter" (Elisabeth's phrase) before the war. He came home when Poland was invaded, talking vaguely of joining the navy, but he'd dithered; then Denmark was occupied and the military idled. Per had hung about Copenhagen rather enjoying life until his father quarreled with him about it; then he departed for Hornbæk and the empty summer house. He said he would write a novel.

Per has made many useful friends and acquaintances in cafés and bars from Gilleleje to Helsingør, while he waited for inspiration. He has a car waiting for them in an alley behind the restaurant.

"You have gasoline?" Henrik asks in surprise.

"No. A friend helped me convert it. It runs on hay."

It does not run very fast. But it does run, and in a half hour's time they arrive in Hornbæk, at the back door of a handsome summer house on a lane on the inland side of the beach road. The houses on either side of it are shut for the season. Nevertheless, Per urges his

guests to stay inside. He installs them in adjoining upstairs bedrooms, takes their ration books, and goes out to buy groceries.


In Sweden, this Thursday, Niels Bohr arrives in Stockholm. He is
met by an intelligence officer of the Swedish General Staff and by
Volmer Gyth, a Danish intelligence officer working with SOE, one
of the Princes. Gyth and his colleagues escaped when the government fell, to continue their work from Sweden. Now Gyth's special
charge from London is to get Bohr to England. He announces that an
unarmed RAF Mosquito bomber will be in Stockholm Friday morning to take Bohr to safety.

Bohr says, "No," politely but firmly. He is happy to be out of
Denmark himself, but that is hardly the end of the matter. What will
happen to the rest of Denmark's Jews? He isn't going anywhere until
Sweden agrees to offer them all sanctuary.

Gyth, heart in mouth, takes Bohr to the home of some friends
where he can spend the night. He installs one policeman inside the
house, another outside the door, and a third patrolling up and down
on the street beyond. He hopes it's enough.


In Hornbæk, in the house in the lane Granvaenget, the evening
passes in quiet discomfort. Per cooks supper, and after they eat, they
all listen to the BBC broadcast on the radio in his room. Everyone
goes to bed early, and no one sleeps very well.

Friday morning Per is already gone when Ditte and Henrik get
up. Tofa is in the kitchen assembling breakfast. When Per comes
back, he has two more families with him.

"Mr. and Mrs. Moss, Miss Bing—this is the family Roth and the
family Saloman. You'll have to introduce yourselves."

Mr. and Mrs. Roth are Orthodox Jews. Mr. Roth wears a full
beard; Mrs. Roth's hair is covered with a wig. The children, three
girls and a boy, are wide-eyed and quiet, though they shake hands
politely. They have spent the night in St. Olaf's Domkirke in Helsingør, and have had nothing to eat since they left Copenhagen. Mr.

Saloman is a classics teacher; his wife is a dentist. Their children are identical twin girls named Hanne and Inge. They are blond and extremely pretty and seem to speak only to each other.

In Sweden, on this Friday morning, October 1, Bohr is ushered in to see Ernst Gunther, Sweden's foreign minister. Minister Gunther expresses how glad he is that the famous Dane is on his way to safety and Bohr expresses that he isn't going anywhere until Sweden has promised to open its doors to the Danish Jews.

Gunther says, Well, of course, they could do that, if the Germans say it's all right. He will telegraph to Berlin for permission. It is very important that Sweden preserve her neutrality, which she cannot do while working one side against the other. This must be clear to Bohr . . .

When they've been ushered out, the handlers say, "Well now," to Dr. Bohr. "London?"

Bohr is angry. He says no. Asking if it would be all right with the Reich if they rescue seven thousand Danish Jews is not what Bohr is asking for.

(Oddly enough, Minister Gunther never does get a reply from Berlin on this matter.)

No. No London. Aha. Then . . . what?

Bohr wants to see the king. And anyone else who can do something useful.

Oh. He wants to see the king. Meanwhile, there are plenty of German agents in Stockholm, and the longer he is here, the more people will know it.

After Per has sorted out where everyone will sleep—there is a sort of children's dormitory on the third floor where all the girls can go, and the Roth boy will sleep with his father—the morning passes tensely but rather pleasantly. The Roth children are fascinated by the house, and shyly thrilled when Per urges them to explore at will. They go in and out of closets, they emerge wearing Mr. Bennike's hats and shoes. Per goes out for more groceries; this takes time, as he has to go to several different stores, so it will not be so obvious that he is feeding so many. Mr. Roth (they pronounce their name Rote, with a long *o* and a slight burr at the *t*) is rather frightened about Per, who seems to him blithe and feckless for one who holds their lives in his hands.

When Per comes in at lunchtime, he has fresh eggs from a neighbor's hens, among other things. Sylvie Roth looks as if she might cry at the sight. Per asks Henrik to come outside with him while the women make smørrebrød. He tells Henrik that there are strangers arriving on every train, but Gestapo Juhl, a detested Nazi from southern Jutland, has also arrived in Helsingør. "I have keys to other summer houses; I look after them for our friends. I think we should open them, don't you?" Henrik does. He says, "I'll go with you."

While Per and Henrik are turning the summer houses into hideouts, in Stockholm, Niels Bohr is with the king.

King Gustav is glad to meet with Dr. Bohr. He is sympathetic with Bohr's position. Absolutely.

Will his country, then, take in Denmark's Jews? House them, employ them, feed them, school them for the duration? Which might be forever, of course, if Germany wins the war? It is the king's turn to be angry. Well, heavens. King Gustav will let him know.

"London?" ask the handlers afterward, without much hope.

## Friday evening, October 1, 1943. Copenhagen.

Hilde Hansen has had her supper. She is listening to Rossini on the record player and drinking a small glass of beer before bed.

It is about eleven o'clock. She hears something in the hall. Footsteps. Then knocking. It's not at her door, though. It's a loud thumping across the hall.

Hilde sips her beer and enjoys her music.

Across the hall, the knocking has turned to pounding. Hilde gets up reluctantly and goes to her record player, where she lifts the needle from the groove with great care, and sets it gently on its bracket while the turntable spins out silence. If she's going to open the door to these hounds, she doesn't want Rossini to sweep out and get mixed up with them.

In the hall, two men in Gestapo uniform are standing angrily, staring at the door they've been hammering. When her door opens, they wheel on Hilde. One has a machine gun.

Hilde stands at the door of her now silent apartment. "What is this noise about?" she asks.

"We are looking for Miss Tofa Bing," says the shorter of the men.

"She's not at home," says Hilde.

"We can break the door down," says the taller one. Both men speak in German.

Hilde shrugs. "What good would that do?"

"Where has she gone?"

"Away."

The shorter one swears. They have a list. There are seven thousand Jews in Denmark, give or take. They have been at this for two hours. They have not found one Jew at home.

They look angrily at Hilde who suddenly gives them a pleasant smile. It is like a slap, and they would like to slap her back. Hilde turns and closes her door. There is silence in the hall; then she hears the footsteps clumping furiously toward the stairs, heading up to the next floor. Crossing her room, Hilde pauses to say a word of comfort to Miss Bing's cat. She goes to her turntable. She lifts the arm and blows imaginary lint from the needle, then lowers it gently back onto the record of her beloved *Petite Messe Solennelle*.

Friday evening passes quietly in the house in Hornbæk. Mrs. Roth has managed to bake a challah, which seems like a proof of God's grace, and the household shares a Sabbath supper by candlelight.

The Roth children are tired out, as they spent the afternoon on the beach running and playing, wearing the Bennike family's summer clothes. Per gave them all new names and taught them to cry "I am Per Bennike's cousin from Alborg here for a visit!" They hear no news of what is passing in the south. The phones are dead.

Stockholm doesn't know the details of what is happening across the water, because the Copenhagen telephone exchange has been shut down, to prevent the quarry from summoning help, or devising escape. But there are illegal radios, a few, sending the news, and there have been terrible things to see and hear. An eighty-four-year-old woman, deaf and blind, who refused to hide because even the Nazis couldn't be so silly as to think she threatened their racial purity, has been dragged from her home and down to the harbor. Children have been slapped, threatened, and carried from home, screaming in fear. Families have been separated, a Jewish father hauled to the harbor while his Christian wife and children beg and weep. People have been shot trying to flee or hide, people have been frightened literally to death by the pounding on the door in the middle of the night. There have been heart attacks, and there have been suicides by people who would rather die at home than let the Germans torture and kill them in camps.

In Stockholm, Bohr survives the night. And blessedly, Saturday morning brings him the king's answer. Sweden will take Denmark's Jews. A very great thing has been accomplished and everyone on this side of the sound is showing well. Bohr can leave for safety.

But he won't. It is now the second day of the pogrom. Those Danish Jews who are not already onboard the *Wartheland* and the *Donau,* or dead, are in hiding, out of reach. What good does it do to open the door, if the people forced against the wall don't know it has opened? Bohr demands that this offer of refuge be made on the front page of the newspapers. He wants to hear it broadcast on Sveriges Radio.

\*       \*       \*

Saturday morning, Hornbæk learns what the night has wrought. Per goes into Helsingør early and comes back shaken. The grapevine carries terrible news, and Mrs. Saloman puts her hands to her mouth as she listens, then starts to cry.

"Samuel," Per says to Mr. Roth, "you have to shave that beard."

"I can't."

"I'm sorry, you must," says Per. "You might as well go out wearing a yarmulke."

"It is not permitted. I'll stay inside."

"You'll shave the beard. I'll lend you a razor."

"No, I'll have to go back to Copenhagen to get one."

"What are you *thinking*?"

Mr. Roth explains that it is forbidden to shave the beard, though it can be cut. He knows an Orthodox man who has an electric razor.

"And that *cuts*?"

"Yes," says Roth, stubbornly.

Per stands staring. Finally he says, "Stay here. Promise me. Don't leave this house. *None* of you," and goes off.

What would they do if he never came back? Or if he is growing tired of this circus and turns them in?

Per is gone for several hours. He has been to Helsingør to try to buy an electric razor, without hope and without luck. Finally the pastor in Gilleleje has turned one up, and told him several other useful things in the bargain.

While Mr. Roth is dealing with his beard, Per tells Henrik and Ditte, "A friend of ours in Frederiksværk has a boatyard—he's got a German patrol boat in the shop. He was told they won't need it until Tuesday—there's nothing wrong with it. He could use it to take you across to Sweden after dark." Clearly this scheme amuses him.

Ditte and Tofa look at each other. To them it sounds too clever. It could be a trap by the Germans, and if it isn't, what if when they get there they are simply arrested? They have no exit permits. Can Per get them exit visas? Maybe just the forms for them to fill out? If he can, will it help? It is sickening trying to make decisions without enough information, decisions that can kill you if you get them wrong.

Per shrugs. It would have been fun, when this is over, to tell people about the patrol boat. He goes off again. Have they tried his patience too far *this* time?

Mr. Roth comes downstairs clean-shaven and his wife gives a scream. She has never seen him like this; she isn't sure she recognizes him. The newly exposed skin is a ghastly white with very many red spots, outraged at what it's just been through. His upper lip is longer than she thought it was, his chin a little weaker. His children come to the door to look at him and then run away and are heard giggling in the next room. Mr. Roth sits down heavily and won't talk to anyone.

There are people in all the houses on the lane now, crouching behind curtains. Per and others, the pastor, three schoolteachers, and the veterinarian, are engaged in buying and making food and trying to get exit permit forms, in case. Inside the Bennike house, however, they know nothing of the others, and feel alone. They have not been outside for twenty-four hours. They have seen German soldiers patrolling the roads and beaches. At one point in the afternoon a knocking at the kitchen door frightens them rigid. In minutes everyone is out of sight except Henrik, the children in closets, the adults in the basement, which is unpleasantly dank.

Henrik looks out the window before opening the door. There is a young woman waiting; her bicycle leans against a tree.

"Is Per at home?" she asks.

"No, he is not, at the moment. I am his uncle Henrik from Aalborg."

"I'm glad to meet you. Will you tell Per, please, that Anka was here? Tell him I think I found the rucksack he was looking for. It's quite a big one, with eight apples in it."

"I'd be glad to—would you like to write him a note?"

"No, no. No. But please remember the message exactly. I need to know when he can pick it up."

"I'll tell him."

*   *   *

It was many hours before Per came back. The children have been fed a cold supper and sent to bed; one of the Roth children has a fever, and everyone is on edge. They are in Per's bedroom, gathered around his radio for the BBC broadcast when the announcement is made: Sweden has offered refuge to the Jews of Denmark. It is all they can do to keep from shouting. Mrs. Saloman begins to cry again and the Roths to pray aloud their gratitude.

Per comes back exhausted. He knows, though he does not tell them, that there are now Jews hidden in haylofts, attics, boathouses, and basements all along the coast. Best is furious. The Gestapo is furious. Per has his shoes off, a cheese sandwich in one hand and a beer in the other, when Henrik remembers Anka's message from the afternoon.

"Brava!" shouts Per. He wolfs the rest of his supper and struggles back into his shoes. "She's found a boat! The fisherman wants eight hundred kroner apiece . . . how much money do you have?"

The Mosses and Tofa have enough. The Roths do not. But Mr. Saloman will pay for them. Per is off again. The children are awakened and dressed. Then everybody waits.

When Per comes back, cold and wet and almost too tired to speak, it is to tell them that the boat has already gone. There will be no more crossings tonight. They are glad finally to go to bed, but very frightened at what the morning will bring. Now that the Germans know every Jew left in Denmark will be trying to cross the sound, they will make an impenetrable net waiting to catch them. Won't they?

Sunday morning, October 3. A letter from the Lutheran bishops of Denmark is read from virtually every pulpit in the country. It denounces the action against the Jews, and declares that whoever protects them follows the laws of God, not of man.

The Germans, embarrassed and angry, are circling and baying throughout the country like a pack of hounds that have treed a fox but can't shake it down. There are thousands of cornered Jews under their noses. But where?

Adolf Eichmann, with his ice-cold eyes, arrives in Copenhagen.

An offer is made to General Goetz of the Danish Army and

Admiral Vedel of the navy. The Germans know that most Danes long to be *Judenrein,* Jew-free, like Aryans everywhere; they offer to exchange the Danish soldiers and sailors they interned when the government fell, for Jews. The reply comes: "There is no point in exchanging one Dane for another Dane."

The *Wartheland* leaves Copenhagen with not thousands of captives, but 202. The *Donau* leaves empty.

Sunday morning the promise Niels Bohr extracted is in the Swedish papers, and has been announced through official channels. The hand has been forced, by Bohr and by the Swedish people themselves, who are already giving shelter to the trickle of refugees who have made it across the sound since Wednesday. Some have come in the night by small boat or kayak. Some have been rowed the two-plus miles from Helsingør or Snekkersten to Helsingborg, where the distance is narrowest, by Danes young and old whose palms are skinless and bloody by the time they get home.

$S$ydney stayed in Cleveland for two weeks. It was the longest time she'd ever passed under her mother's roof without hostilities. Bernard was home again and recovering, slowly. He spent most of his time sitting in the library with a plaid rug across his knees. The unexpected event of the visit was that Bernard had fallen in love with Eleanor. She was a calm, bright, sunny child. Sydney could put the baby down on her blanket with a few rattles and Bernard would watch her for hours as she gurgled and chewed on things. She liked to crawl over to his chair and pull herself up to a standing position, holding on to his finger, and it was in that little room with Bernard that she took her first steps entirely on her own. You'd have thought Bernard and Eleanor had invented the whole proposition of upright ambulation themselves, he was so excited.

"The most *enchanting* child," he would cry to visitors. Naturally, Sydney was softening toward him. Meanwhile she was free to accompany her mother on her rounds, while Bernard and Maudie managed the baby. It was rather pleasant.

One day far in the future, Eleanor herself, with her daughters, would read Candace's Line-a-Day journal for the weekend of Denmark's dark struggle.

This is what they found:

> *Thursday, Sept. 30, 1943. Went to Dr. Stephan's at 11. Several dental casualties this summer. Went to opening meeting of Women's Com. of the Orchestra with Mabel— Mrs. Clark presided charmingly. Mr. Leinsdorf spoke—(the new 32-yr-old conductor)—hope he conducts better than he speaks. Lunch and bridge after.*
>
> *Fri., October 1. To market. It is slow work these days— Had my hair done at 12:30. Mabel here for dinner and a short eve—very pleasant. Naples has fallen to the Allies. The Germans have destroyed all harbor facilities but it is a great victory.*
>
> *St., Oct. 2. To market and bot a pound of butter!—12 pts now, but will be 16 Mon.—a wk's ration. Eleanor cried a great deal at dinner. To Dr. Stephan's in AM—toothache.*
>
> *Sun., Oct. 3. World Wide Communion at many churches. Walked to church—40 joined today. Had a roast of beef for dinner—Maudie and Velma gave me all their pts which ex-pired yest.*

So much for brave little Denmark. And "Eleanor cried a great deal" was virtually the only time her grandchild was mentioned. "Horrible Old Trout" is how Sydney taught Eleanor to speak of her grandmother.

Sunday morning, while Per is out and many Danes are at church, there comes a rapping on the door of the cottage in Hornbæk, the front door facing the lane, which hasn't been used since they arrived. Ditte and Tofa grab for each other's hands. Mrs. Roth pulls her youngest child to her and puts her hands over his mouth. Mr. Roth and Mr. Saloman leap to their feet and start herding people toward the basement. The rapping is repeated. In under a minute, only Henrik is left. He walks very slowly toward the front door. Before he can reach it, the door opens. (Unlocked! How could that be? Who had unlocked it? The children . . . ?)

A man in a rumpled suit, slightly bent, with large strong hands that dangle from his sleeves and a large asymmetrical head, stands on the step. What hair he has is white. His blue eyes meet Henrik's. Then he steps inside and says loudly, "I'm looking for the family Roth. Are they here?"

Henrik is dumbfounded. "I am—alone, at the moment. I am Per Bennike's uncle, from Aarhus." The moment it was out of his mouth he felt his pulse rate rise to 1000. Aalborg! Not Aarhus! What if everyone knows the Bennikes have no relatives in Aarhus?

The man with the head is looking at the kitchen table. There are dominoes laid out in a half-finished game the Saloman girls had been playing.

"I am looking for Samuel Roth," says the man again, loudly. Suddenly to his further horror Henrik hears Samuel cry from the basement, "We are here!"

There are rapid footsteps on the stairs from below and Samuel Roth bursts into the kitchen.

"Mr. Kjaer!"

"Is that you, Samuel?" asks the man with the head. "What *happened* to you?"

"This is Mr. Kjaer!" Samuel cries to Henrik. "Sylvia! Come! It's Mr. Kjaer!" Now there are more footsteps hurrying up the basement stairs. "This was my employer when we first came to Denmark!"

"Oh! You shaved your beard. Good morning, Mrs. Roth."

"How did you find us?" Now the rest of the Roths, followed by the Salomans and Ditte and Tofa, are crowding into the kitchen.

"My wife heard you'd spent the night at the Domkirke. At the church they thought you had gone with someone from Hornbæk so I started knocking on doors."

"You mean . . . you walked here from Helsingør?" The man is at least seventy.

"I rode my bike. Mrs. Kjaer is expecting you."

When Mr. Kjaer has ridden off to borrow a car from his friend, a veterinary surgeon, the Roths explain that Kjaer owned a transport firm where Samuel worked as a bookkeeper. "He's been retired five years, he moved to Saunte, I haven't seen him . . ."

Shortly after lunch Mr. Kjaer returns with the car, and departs again with Mrs. Roth sitting beside him and the rest of the family crouched under blankets behind the front seat. When Per comes back, he seems delighted with the tale. He immediately leaves again, to return with an elderly couple who had been jammed into an attic room down the street with eight others. "And I've found a boat. You leave tonight," he announces.

They all crowd around him. When? How? "Anka will bring the details this evening," he says.

It starts to rain in the afternoon. It is a bleak day. Ditte finds herself longing to play the Bennikes' piano, which is under a sheet in the living room, but does not dare. The hours drag. Hanne and Inge have finally begun to talk to Henrik. Henrik plays Hanne in dominoes, then Inge plays the winner. (Hanne beats them both. They are very smart, these quiet pretty girls.) By teatime Henrik has them both laughing. Their nerves are so taut they would sing like harp strings if you blew across them.

At six o'clock, Anka arrives. This time Henrik introduces her to the others. She is wet with rain. "The boat will leave at *exactly* nine o'clock," she says. "Per will take you to the beach when it's time." She collects their passage money for the fisherman. They press her to stay to get dry, as it doesn't take a doctor to see she has a hard cold. But she is off again.

They wait.

At eight-thirty, Per arrives. A good deal of his jaunty manner has worn off in the last two days. He looks drawn and weary. "Did you eat?" Mrs. Saloman asks.

"I don't remember," Per says, Mrs. Saloman hands him the packet of cheese and rye bread they have packed for the journey. Per shakes his head and Mrs. Saloman puts it into his pocket. "Please," she says. "I'm a mother."

Per lets it stay. They will not all fit in the hay burner, so the Salomans go first. It is necessary for one more person to go, and the elderly couple won't be separated. Henrik volunteers. That leaves Ditte and Tofa and the old ones sitting in silence. Twenty minutes go by. Ditte looks at her watch. The girl said nine o'clock *exactly*. She made a point of it. What if it leaves without them? What if Henrik goes on board and then they miss the boat?

Per reappears. He is chewing the cheese and rye bread. He leads them out through the rain and into the car, then sets off without his headlights. This is terrifying. What if something comes along and hits them?

They pass no cars, and Per turns down a small lane to a beach. He turns the engine off and carries the old couple's bag for them. With their coats over their heads, they hurry behind him through the rain toward a small shed that proves to be full of sail bags, oars, and other boat tackle. Here the Salomans and Henrik sit huddled along with three other forlorn people, a couple with their teenaged son.

"Has Anka come?"

They all shake their heads. No. It is well after nine o'clock.

At ten past ten, Anka walks up from the beach. She has come on the fishing boat, which is offshore; it took on passengers near Villengebaek first and there were more people there than expected. Anka guided the fisherman to this spot, and rowed ashore, but it is to tell them that the boat is full. They cannot go tonight.

She can feel the courage draining out of the group in the shed. They knew it, really. They are not going to get away. It will be like all the stories they have heard. It will be the way it has been everywhere else. They will end in the camps.

"What about the rowboat?" asks Mr. Saloman.

"It's too rough now," says Anka. "You couldn't row in this."

"But couldn't the bigger boat tow it?"

Per and Anka look at each other.

"It could, I think," says Anka doubtfully.

"How many could it take?"

"Four or five."

There is silence. Four or five of them can go tonight after all. It may be more dangerous. But how to tell, perhaps staying here is more dangerous. Which is it?

Mrs. Saloman says, "We'll go."

Her family turns to look at her in surprise. She looks at her husband. They both turn to the daughters. Hanne and Inge look at each other. Then Mrs. Saloman says again, "We'll go."

Anka says, "Can one of you row out? Do you know how?"

"I'm sure I can do it," says Mr. Saloman.

"I can row," says the teenaged boy, suddenly. Now his parents look surprised.

"Can you?" Anka asks. "The boat will be heavy, and there's a lot of chop."

"Yes, I can." To his parents he says, "I'll wait for you in Helsingborg."

"Where?"

"I'll go to the police till you come," he says. Suddenly he is saying
goodbye to his mother, who has to hold her hands over her mouth to
keep from crying. Then the boy, whose name is Flemming, shakes
hands with the Salomans, and Anka leads them out.

Per waits in the shed with the rest until Anka comes back. She
has signaled the fishing boat with her torch from the little bathing
pier, then watched as the rowboat, riding low, pulled steadily out to
the fishing boat. She has waited to see if the pilot will send them
back, but he doesn't. She has watched from the shore as, instead, the
pilot hands a tarp down to the rowboat, and the Salomans and the
boy snug it down around themselves, for concealment, and protection from the rain. The fisherman, standing in the stern of his boat
with rain pouring down his neck, bends a towline onto the
rowboat's painter, so it won't ride too close to the stern, which
would cause it to swing, maybe even overturn. Then he gives the
order to weigh anchor, hoists his sails, and slips out into the dark
sound, with his rowboat bobbing behind him.

"I am Otto Fischermann," says the teenaged boy's father, in the boat
shed. "This is my wife, Ina." Everyone shakes hands. When Anka
comes in and reports that the boat is away, Per says to the Fischermanns, "You better come stay with us. We'll get you all away together tomorrow night." Again, he must make two trips in the hay
burner, first with the old couple and Tofa and Ditte, then back to get
Anka, Henrik, and the Fischermanns. The second trip is longer, as
Per suddenly drives off the road into a copse of trees when he sees
slits of headlights masked against the blackout coming at them like
angry narrowed eyes. They sit together in the woods with their
hearts firing like muffled guns. The SS staff car sweeps past them in
the darkness, its headlights snooping along the road before it. But it
has missed them. Henrik is deeply grateful for Per's insistence on

driving dark. They climb out and help get the car back onto the road while Anka steers; the mud beneath the wheels is slick and boggy with the rain. Per takes Anka north to the pier where she's left her bicycle, then heads back once again to the Bennike house, to sleep for what remains of the night.

It is now Monday, October 4.

The whole house on Granvænget is on short rations, as no one thought to ask the Salomans for their ration books, and before they left, the Fischermann family gave theirs to the couple who had been hiding them. It's a long quiet day, in which Otto and Ina Fischermann sit together holding hands and praying. For supper, Per comes up from the basement with some tins of food whose labels were soaked off several years before when the storeroom floor flooded.

"No one knows what they are," he says cheerfully. "Could be carrots, could be pudding." They set the table and open the cans. One large one holds stewed tomatoes. A little one has liver paste, one holds olives, two have soup—split pea and barley with vegetables—one lingonberries in syrup, and one some kind of beans. The old couple, fearing the soups have pork in them, eat the olives. Henrik says the liver paste is rather good with the berries. Ina Fischermann says, "Maybe Flemming and the others are in a warm restaurant right now."

"They are probably stuffed with herring and pot roast and potato cakes this minute," said Per. "Skål, Mrs. Fischermann." She smiles and meets his eyes as they raise their glasses of water to each other.

This night, as they gather in the kitchen when it's time to go, they all leave their ration books on the table. "If we get away," Henrik says, "you can use them to take your girl out to dinner." Although they strongly suspect he would use them to feed the next lot of refugees.

"If I had a girl," said Per.

"Not Anka?"

"Anka? No. She's got a fellow."

"We'll introduce him to Nina," says Tofa.

"Our daughter," says Ditte. "You'd like her." The mood is suddenly giddy. This is almost over, they are going. A second later the elation has seeped away. It isn't over, it will never be over, they'll never get away.

Anka comes in. Her nose is red from blowing it, and she needs to wash her hair. All eyes turn to her, tension suddenly ratcheted to the scream point.

"Everything's ready," she says. "You leave at midnight."

"From the same spot?"

"No, there were new tire tracks down to the beach this morning. I think the Germans have been there. You'll leave from Gilleleje. You can wait at the church till it's time to go to the pier. It's a bigger boat tonight. Don't worry, this time it will work."

"It's not the same boat?" Mrs. Fischermann asks, anxious.

"No, he hasn't come back. He probably stayed in Helsingborg to get some sleep."

"So you haven't heard anything?" She means about Flemming and the Salomans. But Anka answers a different question.

"I did hear one thing. There are freight cars in Helsingør that cross to Sweden empty, on the ferry, to bring back ball bearings and such to the Germans. Last night, it didn't cross empty." Her eyes dance with mischief. "They packed it with refugees, and took them all off on the other side before the car was delivered to the loading dock."

Per laughs with delight.

The rest won't be laughing until they are safe on the other side, and see their friends again. The Fischermanns silently take one another's hands.

This time they make the trip to Gilleleje all together in a Falck ambulance Per has arranged. It is long and black, with a white cross sign fixed to the bumper. These are among the few vehicles with permission to be on the streets day and night. How Per knows the driver, they never learn. The driver is a young man with very white teeth, who takes special care to get the old couple settled securely so they won't bucket around in back. They say their goodbyes and thanks to Per and speed off in the night with a total stranger. The driver has his slitted headlamps on bright, and drives fast, as if speeding a heart attack victim to hospital. They pass one SS car going the other way and Henrik's heart is in his mouth, waiting for the stop, the search. They speed on into the dark without mishap, and in fifteen minutes they are in Gilleleje. The church is dark but the door is open. They are shown the ladder to the attic. The old couple approach it timorously.

"She's afraid of heights," her husband says, as if not sure whether to laugh or cry. With her eyes shut, the old lady gets up the ladder. There are many already there waiting, close to a hundred, Henrik thinks. When they are all upstairs, a fisherman's boy comes up behind them and goes among the newcomers, collecting money. The price tonight is only 600 kroner a head. When he leaves with the money, the trapdoor shuts behind him. And trap it could be; what if the boy pockets the money and goes to the police? Why shouldn't he? They sit in the pitch-darkness and wait. There are small round windows set into the attic eaves, so even up here they must not light so much as a match. Somewhere up here there are buckets for toilets, Henrik guesses from the smell, but if you needed them, how would you find them?

It is well past midnight when they hear steps below, then on the ladder. The trapdoor opens again. All eyes are fixed on the square of light it brings—from a torch someone is pointing upward from the floor below—dreading the appearance of a German helmet. The head that appears belongs to the pastor's wife.

"The schooner is in the harbor. You must come very quickly."

The young carry bundles and the old stretch their stiff limbs and all make haste. They move in astonishing quiet. Even the old couple (whom Henrik now has under his protection) get down safely, though the woman misses the last step and hurts her ankle. Outside, in the church garden, helpers are waiting to shepherd them to the pier, where rowboats will ferry them out to the schooner.

The old lady is limping. Her anxious husband tries to hurry her, but her face tightens with pain when she puts the foot down.

"You go ahead," the husband says to Henrik. Tofa and Ditte have started but keep looking back, torn between anxiety at leaving him and fear of delaying.

The fisherman's boy appears from the garden with a wheelbarrow. "It's quite clean," he says cheerfully. The old lady is bundled into it and the boy wheels her along at a trot beside the others.

It takes what seems like forever to get everyone out to the schooner. There are men and women well past youth rowing boats back and forth. Once on board, the refugees are taken down into the cargo hold, packed in tight.

To be locked below in the dark while a ship rocks at anchor is a test for even the steadiest stomachs. A young woman, one of the first aboard, is failing this test. Ditte is crammed next to her. Down in the dark, waiting, they hear at last the rings of the mainsail making a great clatter as the sail is run up the mast. Just as the boat falls off and the sails fill, and the dark hold in which they lie lurches and begins to heel, the young woman begins to vomit.

The boat shapes a course for Sweden (they hope, though it could be for anywhere) and the girl helplessly retches. "I'm so sorry," she whispers. "I don't know what I can do."

"Just what you're doing," says Ditte. She holds her in the rank darkness, smelling of fish and fear and wet wool as the boat rocks through the water. Time seems to stop—it could have been minutes or hours in the inky dark—until the boat turns and stops moving, upright. It has come into the wind. Why? Have they been caught? The hatch doors down to the hold are opened; those nearest can smell the fresh air and see the stars. Appearing in the rectangle of the open hatch is a man in uniform, who calls down, "Welcome to Sweden."

That same evening in Stockholm, this is happening. At ten in the evening, Niels Bohr is finally willing to leave for England. He says goodbye, and when his car is out of sight, Captain Gyth and Dr. Bohr's hosts dismiss the guards and open champagne. Two hours later, when all is quiet in the house, the doorbell rings; Captain Gyth goes to open it. He finds Niels Bohr standing alone on the doorstep. The plane took off but an engine malfunction has forced it back to the airport. Dr. Bohr has taken a taxi back to town.

Captain Gyth spends the night guarding Bohr's bedroom himself. In the dawn, a little keyed up, he hears footsteps approach the front door. He creeps to the door with a pistol in one hand and a candelabrum in the other and comes very near braining the woman who delivers the morning paper.

As the schooner skims out of Gilleleje harbor Monday night, several Gestapo cars arrive at the seaside in time to see it get away. By the time they could summon and send patrol boats in chase, the ship will have reached Swedish waters. Gestapo Juhl has been teased and tricked from here to Helsingør and he badly wants to find a choke point, to cut off the stream of losses.

Tuesday morning, Nina takes a call at home. She has been out of the apartment most of the weekend begging money to help pay for transports; two of her friends collected a million kroner simply by riding their bikes from one estate to the next and knocking on doors. At one rich farm they interrupted a dinner party; they went from guest to guest, asking the ladies to empty their evening bags and the men their pockets to help the Jews escape, and came away with a fortune. Nina herself is so tired and frightened and elated that she has hardly slept since she said goodbye to her parents. In the fury of the first aborted roundup, the Germans hauled off almost anyone in a Jewish household who opened the door. Since then, though, they have announced they will not take half-Jews and have even released some Jews married to Christians. No one knows how long *that* will last . . .

"Nina Moss?" says the voice.

"Who is speaking, please?" she asks after a hesitation. It's a man, the voice not familiar. Her emotions are so unstable at this point she feels for a moment she may faint. There are so many kinds of bad news that could be about to change her world forever.

"It's a friend from the coast. I've just had word that your potatoes arrived."

And she starts to cry.

"Do you understand?" the voice asks.

"Yes, thank you. All of them?"

"Three bushels, all in good order."

"Thank you," she says. She hangs up and leaves the kitchen. She goes to her parents' bedroom and puts on her mother's blue sweater. Then she lies down on their bed with the down quilt over her and cries till she falls asleep in the sunshine.

The caller was Per Bennike. It was a call he needed to make, to give somebody good news, because he himself is feeling raddled with guilt and grief. He who has taken no care of anybody, including himself, for about ten years, is suddenly running lives over his hands and between his fingers like a shower of coins of untold value, and he has just had his first lesson in what the price of this may be to him. The rowboat bearing the Saloman family and Flemming Fischermann was run down in the dark by a Swedish patrol boat. All five of them are presumed drowned, although only Hanne's body has come ashore. He feels it is his fault. He doesn't know how it could be, but he feels this anyway.

When Nina wakes, the phone is ringing again.

Another male voice. "Hello! Is that Nina Moss, please?"

"Who is speaking?" This time she is not frightened. The voice is familiar, though she doesn't place it at once. Her parents and aunt are safe. She has no fears for herself, at least not yet.

"It's Mogens Wessel here. Is that you, Nina?"

"Mr. Wessel!" The father of the children she cared for in Jutland for two summers.

"Are your parents at home?"

"They—no, they are not. Are you here? In Copenhagen?"

"Quite close by. I'm sorry to miss your parents, but may I come to tea?"

"Of course!"

"I'll be bringing some friends. We'll see you soon."

Mogens Wessel arrives with a family of six named Katz, a young couple and four children, including a baby of six months.

"These are our neighbors in Haderslev. There was no safe place for them there," he says to her briefly, as they greet each other. "May they stay with you?"

Nina feels that he wouldn't ask this of her if it were not right and necessary. She says, "Certainly."

"Thank you. Mrs. Wessel sends you this." He hands her a small soft package wrapped in fabric with a ribbon tied around it. Mrs. Wessel has a special gift for making even the simplest things look pretty. Nina opens the bundle and finds about a handful of fragrant dried black tea leaves.

"She says it is your favorite blend. The children miss you."

Nina inhales the spicy bergamot smell of Earl Grey, and thinks of drinking tea and playing dominoes with Mrs. Wessel while the children have their naps. She fears she may cry for the second time today.

"Now—if you're all right here, I must go down to Christianshavn to see what can be arranged."

In Helsingborg, Sweden, Henrik and Ditte have been taken to the home of two ladies, schoolteachers. They have had a hot breakfast and a long nap. The first thing they do when they have bathed and dressed is to go to a bank to change their Danish kroner for Swedish. The second is to go to the post office to send a telegram.

Laurus is at his desk in Baker Street. He knows about the *Wartheland*, he knows Adolf Eichmann is in Copenhagen. How many Danish Jews have been caught he does not know but he knows it is in the hundreds. They have had coded messages from their radio men on Zealand and Fyn, and they have heard from Resistance leaders in Stockholm that there are escapes across the sound every night, but nobody knows how many have come or how many more are in hiding with no way to cross. He is reading a newsy letter from Sydney about the baby's teeth, when the phone rings.

"Moss speaking," he says.

"An international cable for you, sir."

Sydney, he thinks.

"Go ahead."

"Dateline: Helsingborg, Sweden."

Suddenly he is near tears. Please, God, good news ... please, please, please.

"Message: 'Mama Tofa and I all safe. Going to Stockholm tonight. Address to follow. Love, Papa.'"


They will live to see their grandchild. Grandchildren, Laurus hopes. Suddenly he is overwhelmed with missing his family. He wants to kiss his wife and hold his daughter, he wants to put his hand on the bald spot on the back of his father's curly head, he wants to hear Mama and Tofa tease each other while playing duets. For a while after this message he simply sits at his desk, awash in gratitude and longing.

In Helsingborg, Henrik and Ditte decide to go into a restaurant for lunch, to celebrate. (Tofa is staying with a family outside town but will meet Henrik and Ditte at the train.) They explain to the café owner why they have no Swedish ration books. He brings them lunch and will take no money. Instead he brings a bottle of *akvavit* to the table and pours three glasses. Skål, he says. And again, the words that sound like a blessing: "Ni är välkomna till Sverige." Welcome to Sweden.

After lunch they go to the police station to ask what they should do about making themselves legal. The officer does not know anything about Flemming Fischermann. But he was not on duty the day before.

By ten o'clock that night they are in Stockholm, met at the station by the violinist Lindemann and his wife, with smiles and embraces. As they are arriving, an RAF Mosquito is once again leaving Stockholm with Niels Bohr in the bomb bay instead of a bomb. To Captain Gyth's relief, Bohr is now the responsibility of the British. Every minute of the flight it is in danger, especially as it crosses the Kattegat and occupied Denmark. When at last the pilots come to earth at the closest possible point, a base in Scotland, they learn that either Bohr's mask malfunctioned or he was too nervous to remember how to use it right; in any case their precious cargo has been out cold from lack of oxygen most of the flight. The pilots picture having to report to Mr. Churchill, "We got him here—we lowered his IQ a hundred points, though. Is that okay?"

In the small hours of that night, Nina Moss is hiding with the Katz family in a darkened warehouse on Wilder Square, in the south harbor of Copenhagen. Crouching with her in the dark are two other families wearing their overcoats, clutching small bundles, waiting. Mrs. Katz is so tense that she upsets the baby when she holds him, so Nina has taken him. When Nina rocks him and softly hums into the sweet-smelling downy top of his head, he quiets. She feels something move in her heart, as if the simple act of holding a baby has released a mothering urge. She suddenly knows that the next stage of life, if there is one for her, must be to have a baby of her own. For now, Hans Katz is her baby. She feels she has aged ten years in the space of a weekend.

There are four children in the warehouse in addition to the Katzes', mostly puzzled and frightened. A little boy keeps saying that they have to go to the boat now, he can't wait any longer. His mother tells him he must. But he can't, he says simply. A little girl cries because she has to use the bucket in the corner and she can't with all these people.

A young woman comes in with an older man. She comes to where Nina sits with the Katzes. "This doctor has medicine for the little ones, so they won't cry."

"I don't—" Mr. Katz begins.

"I'm sorry, we must. Any noise could endanger everyone. It is quite safe," the girl says. Actually, neither she nor the doctor know for sure that it is safe, but they know that the alternative is not. The doctor starts with the smallest, Nina's baby. He prepares a needle and delivers an injection into the fat little arm. The baby struggles as Nina comforts him. His cries are not loud, even when he is really trying to make a big noise. He is so small. The doctor moves quickly to the next youngest two. They take their medicine well and are praised. When he comes to the eight-year-old, the girl in charge says, "This is your child too?" The Katzes simply look at her. "One child per adult, no more," says the girl. "She'll have to wait. We'll try to send her tomorrow night."

Mrs. Katz had been told this earlier, but she hoped it would go away. "Please . . ." whispers her husband, helplessly.

Mrs. Katz pleads, "She'll be quiet. She understands." The little girl stares, with huge eyes. It is impossible to tell if she does understand, or is old enough to control herself. But the girl in charge, who is not much older than Nina, is not taking these risks because she enjoys playing the villain. She relents.

By the time all the small children have had their shots, Nina's baby seems to be dead. His body is slack and heavy and his eyes, which are partly open, have rolled back in his head. Nina wants to cry, this frightens her so much, and she is suddenly, fiercely, personally, angry at the Germans.

The girl in charge is watching the street now. Outside the quai is brightly lit and patrolled by two German soldiers. The boat they must get to is only a few yards away, across the quai, but the officers in their green uniforms march up and down like inhuman things. They start from opposite ends of the quai, one at the landing, the other out in the harbor, and march impassively toward each other. When they meet in the middle they turn smartly on their heels, stand back to back, and march apart again. This turning maneuver takes place almost directly before the door of the warehouse.

The girl turns to Nina and the Katzes. *"Two minutes,"* she says softly. Each parent lifts an unconscious child, and the girl takes the eight-year-old by the hand. They all move to the door, Nina with them with her dead-feeling baby in her arms. Her heart is stuck in her throat, beating there. How can they go out with those soldiers? How could the doctor tell how much drug to give a tiny baby, what if he's killed him?

The soldiers outside the door come face-to-face. Mechanically they turn on their heels and march apart again. When they are about ten yards away, the girl in charge whispers, "Now. Run!," and leading the eight-year-old she darts across the quai and down the hatch into the waiting boat. As soundlessly as possible they follow, one by one, lugging their heavy unconscious children. Nina's heart goes like a hammer as she reaches the deck, the hatch, the gangway, the hold. The rest come piling across and down, quickly, quietly, so frightened . . . and they've done it . . . they've all gotten on board. (How can it be? Could they really have been so quiet?) The soldiers march stolidly, eyes front, never turning, until they reach the ends of the quai. Stamp. Swish—they wheel around and start back. As they march between the warehouse on one side and the boat on the other, Nina puts her lips to the warm head of her baby. Mrs. Katz shifts the small unconscious child from her arms to those of her husband, who sits now with two bodies on his lap, and the eight-year-old pressed beside him. Mrs. Katz takes the tiny one from Nina, then impulsively kisses Nina's cheek. A few feet away, the marching feet come toward them from two directions. Tramp, tramp tramp, stomp. Stomp. And the feet march away again. The girl in charge touches Nina's shoulder. Then she's up and out of the hold, and away. In a flash Nina follows, across the quai and into the warehouse.

They look at each other in the darkness. Then the girl in charge puts her hands together before her in a position of prayer. Nina matches the gesture and they look into each other's eyes. Each sees in the other the helplessness, the fear they both feel for the souls now trapped in the little boat. Now they have only prayers with which to help them.

They wait and watch. Just after dawn, the crew of the boat, four seamen, come up the quai to make ready for the day's trip out to the Dragør lighthouse. One of them cocks his head toward the warehouse, and the girl with Nina gives him a sign. The men pile lines and gear on top of the hatch over the hold, and when a German soldier arrives to inspect the boat before it sails, they greet him with jokes and offer a "good morning" beer. The soldier drinks, with his foot on the rail, and Nina prays, watching him.

When the German leaves, the sailors cast off and the boat glides in the morning light out onto the canal that will take them toward the Øresund. When the guards on duty change, Nina and the other girl leave a couple of minutes apart. The Germans pay them no attention.

At Kaj's hospital, the wards are full of Jews. So are the chapel, the basement corridors, and the nurses' quarters. Sunday, students found some forty people, too frightened to stay at home but with nowhere else to go, hiding in Ørsted Park in the rain. (This is terrifying in itself; Ørsted Park is not large and there is not enough cover there for a good game of hide-and-seek.) They had them brought in by ambulance. But the word has spread that the hospitals are safe havens, and now more Jews arrive in groups, throughout each day, carrying flowers as if to visit a patient. For several nights they have been taken in Falck vehicles and taxis to Christianshavn, where there are several different escape routes set up. A girl in a red beret runs a rescue transport out of the North Harbor. Another is the Dragør lighthouse boat. Another has been set up leaving Dragør itself, just to the south, and there are more down the coast sailing from Køge and Strøby and various beaches in Stevns, to Malmö in Sweden.

But someone has told the Germans about the hospitals, and since last night, Kaj's is surrounded by Wehrmacht soldiers. The doctors meet in an anxious huddle; they are all in danger now if a search is begun, as they are sure it will be. Someone has an idea. Very early in the morning, before the officials can arrive for the day at Dagmarhus and order Gestapo troops to the hospital, a funeral cortege leaves the grounds. The hearse is packed with Jews, as are the thirty hired cars that follow in stately order. The "mourners" clutch their bunches of flowers and pass unchecked through the line of soldiers. They drive to Lyngby, a northern suburb, where by now there is a group ready to house them and feed them until boats can be found to take them across.

Several more hospitals use the funeral trick that day and the next. But in Gilleleje, Gestapo Juhl has sealed the harbor. The Jews who have heard of the schooner and come to that village are smuggled out to the countryside to hide in barns and farmyards as Gestapo men arrive to search the town. When the Germans have gone and night falls, the Jews are brought back and hidden again in the church attic and in the parish hall; no one knows what else to do. It's cold in the attic. Someone delivers soup and meat but it's so dark they can't distribute the food or eat it without talking. The pastor comes up to pray with them and bless them, but he is free afterward to go back to his house. When the trapdoor opens again at last, it shows them the thing they fear most. German helmets.

A Gestapo man, with another right behind him, pushes head and shoulders into the attic space, holding a lantern aloft. The light finds the uneaten food, and the buckets, and the eighty pairs of frightened eyes.

Gestapo Juhl claims he found the hiding place himself, but in the village it is said that he had help from a Danish woman whose boyfriend is a German. Instead of a schooner to freedom, the captured are loaded into vans and taken to Horserød prison. Within a week they will be on their way to Theresienstadt, in Czechoslovakia.

It is said that no two children have the same parents. Certainly Eleanor Moss got the best of her mother during the war years, when it was just the two of them and they were young together. It was a beautiful October in New York in 1943. Sydney had a seat put on the back of her bicycle and on weekends would ride with Eleanor all the way up Sixth Avenue to Central Park. They went to the zoo, they went to the carousel, they watched people flying kites on the Sheep Meadow and rowing boats on the lake. It was an idyll.

On weekday afternoons, if it was warm enough, Sydney would take the baby to Washington Square to the sandbox, or to the charming vest-pocket park at Abingdon Square. There she would chat with the other mothers while babies sat, planted on their bottoms, and did things to sand. She was at the park one afternoon soon after she got back from Cleveland, knitting away while Eleanor slept in her pram, when one of the other mothers passed her a page of the *New York Times*.

"Look—your husband is Danish, isn't he?"

## SCIENTIST REACHES LONDON
### DR. N.H.D. BOHR, DANE, HAS
### A NEW ATOMIC BLAST INVENTION.

*London, October 8 (AP)—Dr. Niels H. D. Bohr, refugee Danish scientist and Nobel Prize winner for atomic research, reached London from Sweden today bearing what a Dane in Stockholm said were plans for a new invention involving atomic explosions.*

"I wonder if Laurus knows him," Sydney said. "I bet he does, he's a musician. He's met everyone. And, I mean, it's a small country."

In point of fact, Laurus was the person from SOE detailed to greet Bohr at Croydon Airport and install him at the Savoy Hotel. He escorted him to his meetings with King Haakon of Norway, and with Christmas Møller. But in his letters home, Laurus wrote only of his health, of performances, of his hopes for them all for after the war. He liked keeping Sydney as innocent of the war as he could. It was good, he thought, that someone be innocent.

Kaj Moss never intended to join the Resistance. But by the third week of October, there are few at the hospitals uninvolved. One senior surgeon on Kaj's service and one of the ambulance drivers have already had to flee to Sweden, after refugees they'd driven to Humlebaek were betrayed. A pediatrician was sent to Vestre prison when the Gestapo discovered that the patients on his ward were middle-aged and the men were circumcised. Things are uglier and angrier every day, as Berlin sends more Gestapo police to do the jobs the Wehrmacht seem to do without efficiency here. (It is alarming—that a climate of refusal to yield to one's own worst instincts, such as the Danes were displaying, could infect good German soldiers . . . Berlin has assumed that infection would always spread the other way.)

The captured Danish Jews, it is now known, are together at Theresienstadt in Czechoslovakia, a brutal place with four crematoria. It is for many a station on the way to even worse places, but none of Denmark's Jews are sent onward. From the first, the Danes, including the king, have mounted a campaign of vigilance, letting the Germans know that their captured Jews are out of sight but not out of mind. They have gone to the homes of those who were taken and gathered clothes to send to them. Soon a staff of thirty-five is employed full-time sending food, cigarettes, soap, and medicines to Danes, Jewish and Christian, in concentration camps. Jews from other countries arrive at Theresienstadt and then disappear again, but the Danish Jews stay where they are, and are the envy of the camp, as the steady stream of packages from home gives them life-saving comfort and courage. It is common for camp officials to steal packages sent to prisoners, but the Danes attach a duplicate form with proof of receipt to return to the senders. It is thought the Germans cannot resist filling out official forms and, having filled them out, cannot disregard them.

Danish saboteurs and Resistance fighters are not so privileged as the Danish Jews. If caught they are often tortured unless or until they betray their comrades. And when they are sent into Germany and east, it is to hard-labor and death camps. For these reasons, the more Jews who are rescued, the more dangerous things become for those who rescue them. The more escape routes, codes, and hiding places must be changed. And yet more and more Danes who started resisting by helping the Jews will stay in the underground, smuggling out other helpers of the Jews, or Allied airmen shot down over Denmark, or saboteurs who have been compromised and must get out of the country.

Kaj does not know much about Nina's work because it is safer if he doesn't. He stays at the hospital. This frees a bedroom at the apartment, and Nina has use for it. Hers is the place where families wait for transport from Christianshavn. When a family has more small children than adults traveling with them, a child can stay with Nina until an adult is crossing who can carry the little one. Nina has learned how to comfort the parents, to amuse the children, to make it seem a great adventure. She has learned to turn her own fear to the best possible use, being brave for others.

Early one afternoon, when Nina is at home, deep asleep, having been up all night at the warehouse on Wilder Square, she dreams there is a knocking at the door, and wakes up at the same time as she sits up, to find herself clammy with fear sweat.

There *is* a knocking at the door. It is not, however, a pounding as in her dream, but a light tapping. Tap tap. Tap tap. Then a long pause. She listens to hear if the knocker has walked away, but the tapping comes again.

She goes to the door in her bare feet. She listens, trying to intuit what is on the other side. Finally she says, "Who is there, please?"

"Is that Nina Moss?" This frightens her more. Who would answer a question with a question but someone trying to trick her?

She doesn't answer and there is silence from the other side as well. After a moment or two, a paper is slipped under the door. It says, "I am Per Bennike. Please let me in."

She opens the door. A lanky man with broad shoulders and large knobby wrists and hands steps in quickly. She shuts the door again and locks it.

"I didn't want to say my name in the hall."

"Are you wanted?"

The Gestapo now publishes posters, with pictures, of known Resistance fighters.

"How do you do," says Per.

"Sorry." She shakes his offered hand.

"I am wanted, but they don't know yet where to look for me."

"It was you who called me? To say my parents were safe?"

"Yes."

"You are very welcome here. Come in."

She leads him toward the kitchen.

"I won't stay long. If I can help it."

"Tell me what's happened."

"Last night when we took our guests to the loading point, a Gestapo car was waiting on the beach. It might have been coincidence, but I don't think so. We sent a man across two nights ago who didn't seem quite right to me."

"How did you get away?"

"We ditched the car before they saw us. We scattered into the woods . . . I don't know if the others were caught. I got to Helsingør, walking, in time for the early train. There were Wehrmacht guards in the station, but no Gestapo. I pretended to sleep, and kept my hat over my face on the train."

"Do your people know you are here?"

"Yes, I called. When my father heard my voice, he said, 'I'm sorry, he isn't here and we really don't expect him,' so I knew Gestapo were there, or had been. After that I stayed out of sight until I thought of you."

"Are you hungry?"

"Starving!" He smiles, and Nina can't help smiling back. Together they scavenge a meal, which they eat together sitting in the chairs her parents always use when they have their meals in this kitchen. When the kettle boils, Nina takes the little package of Earl Grey down from the best sugar bowl in the pantry. She carefully warms the pot with boiling water and empties it again, then measures out enough precious tea for them both. When the hot water hits the leaves and the scent of bergamot suddenly plumes up from the pot, Per straightens like a dog that's heard a whistle too high for human ears.

"I'm hallucinating," he says.

She sets a tray with pretty cups and cross-stitched napkins. She even has enough milk for a little pitcher. When she pours his cup, he lifts it in both hands and holds it to his face, breathing.

"I'm not going to ask you where you got this. I don't care if you killed someone." The flavor of that tea, the shimmering pleasure of safety and of hunger satisfied, make the moment dreamlike. The little room is warm with the steam and drifting smoke of the cigarettes she puts on the table between them.

"Thank you," Per says.

"You are most welcome," says Nina. For saving my parents. He understands, and she knows he does; to say it aloud would embarrass them both.

"The last time I saw your parents, they said they were going to introduce me to you, after the war," says Per.

Nina blushes and looks at her plate. When she looks up, Per is smiling at her; he's never seen a girl do that before.

"I guess they already have," says Nina.

She has an intense moment of wishing she were going to Sweden with him. She would see her parents. Luck comes in strange forms sometimes. He can't stay, and she can't go. She stands up.

"You're going to be asleep with your eyes open soon," she says. "Go to bed. I'll go see what can be arranged."

Nina shows Per to her parents' bedroom, then goes out to talk to the people she knows. The Dragør lighthouse boat is full for tonight and tomorrow. But there is a group at Rockefeller Institute arranging passages from the south coast.

Laurus will hear all about his escape from Per, after the war. How Nina told him to go to a particular bar and order a drink with a strange name. How a man then joined him and made an odd remark, to which Per made the correct rejoinder. How he was taken to a van waiting in an alley, and shut in the back with three other people, one a fisherman, and one an English parachutist with a bullet wound in his shoulder. How they drove through the night in pitch-darkness, they could not tell in what direction, they did not know for how long. How in Strøby he and the others were taken aboard a fishing smack and each nailed into a herring crate in a fetal position. How his heart nearly stopped when he felt the boat come into the wind and stop moving, and he heard the sound of footsteps pacing back and forth on the deck. He believed, too, he could hear German voices, although from where he lay, it could have been something else, a Swedish dialect . . . How at last the boat was under way again, how the minutes passed, unless they were hours, until someone came with a hammer to open the crate in which he lay, cramped and aching. About the Danish voice saying, Welcome to Sweden, and hearing the pop of a champagne cork. How, as they sailed the rest of the way into Malmö, with Per standing on the deck under the stars, smiling so hard his face hurt, one of the "sailors," a Danish Resistance fighter, explained that they were often stopped now by German patrols and that often, as on this night, the Nazis brought police dogs aboard. But a Dane in Malmö had invented a powder made of human blood and cocaine. The "sailors" carried it in handkerchiefs and, when they were stopped, scattered it on the decks so in a moment the noses of the excited dogs were completely useless. After the war they will laugh, that the Germans never did figure out why the dogs couldn't tell a saboteur from a salmon.

What Per does not tell Laurus, nor Ditte and Henrik, when he sees them, was that by the time the arrangements were made, he could hardly bear to go. There he was, a displaced person again when he finally didn't want to be. He had changed a great deal since the first of October. And just as he understood that, he walked through Nina's door, and she gave him a cup of real Earl Grey tea as if she'd been saving it for him. She fed him and made him laugh and gave him the first cigarette he'd had in a day, and suddenly it seemed that everything he wanted for the rest of his life was in that apartment. Beauty. Civility. Gentleness. Courage. Purpose.

When he woke in the near dark in her parents' bedroom that first night, she was sitting on the edge of the bed.

"Have you been here long?" he asked her.

"I couldn't bear to wake you."

It was so much what he had just been dreaming, that he sat up and kissed her, as if they'd been together for years instead of hours, and she kissed him back. When he finally left, he took the thought of her with him, and carried it around for the rest of the war, and for years afterward.


When Nina is betrayed, it is late November.

Resistance in Denmark has reached critical mass at last, and cooperation is flowing between partisans and SOE the way Laurus has hoped for three years that it would. Codes, reception points, safe houses, and escape routes are established. The codes in Denmark all have to do with the table. Agents are Jam, or Napkin, or Mustard or Gossip or Tennis. A signal that the moon, wind, and weather are right for a scheduled drop is called a "kettle." It's a particular predetermined sentence spoken during the nightly BBC broadcast. The partisans have shortwave radios, but the more agents and materiel are safely dropped, the more sabotage increases, and the more danger there is in using them. The kettle is the safest way to communicate to a whole reception team at once.

The more sabotage increases, the more Werner Best forbids any mention of it in Danish papers. He doesn't want Berlin reading about exploding armament factories or rail lines in a press he controls. In fact, Best has a rather antic view of the truth, as if by controlling the news he controls what is happening. He has actually announced with pride that Denmark is finally "Judenrein." It is, but only because seven thousand Danish Jews are now in Sweden.

On a certain night, the kettle has been broadcast, and a circle of people wait in a dark pasture on an estate in Northern Jutland, near Randers. When a circling plane appears overhead, the correct signal is given by electric torch. Two men appear in the night sky dangling from parachutes, and huge canisters of materiel drift after them. As sometimes happens, one of the men, a former merchant marine, lands far afield and can't be found by the reception team. He sinks his parachute in a pond and hides in a barn until light; then he walks into the nearest town to buy breakfast and arrange to get to Aarhus, to his contact. Unfortunately, he discovers only then that by error he has been given French money instead of Danish. This is enough to attract the interest of the Gestapo officer who comes into the café as he is trying to buy breakfast. The fact that when he is searched it is found that his Danish farm clothes, which have been made for him by SOE, do not have Danish, or any, labels, is enough to indict him. His claim to be the son-in-law of a pig farmer on Fyn is not believed. Even more regrettably, he has failed to shred and swallow a number of slips of paper containing information he should have committed to memory but hadn't. One of them is the address of a safe house in Copenhagen, should he have to leave the country. It is the Moss apartment.


Nina is walking home from class in the early dark. It is cold. She is thinking about the Christmas package her parents will send from

Stockholm. It will be the first Christmas of her life apart from them. She stops on the Strøget to look in a shop window. What can she send to them?

She is surprised to find at her elbow her neighbor, Mrs. Jespersen, who has emerged from the café on the corner, in a hurry apparently; she isn't wearing her hat or gloves.

"Don't go home," Mrs. Jespersen says.

Nina is taken aback.

"They are waiting for you." Mrs. Jespersen is frightened.

"Who?"

"Do you need money?"

"I don't know . . ."

"Here," says Mrs. Jespersen. She slips a hand into Nina's pocket. "That's all I had in the house. Pay me back next time I see you. Don't come any closer." She hurries off down their street. Nina stands in the dark, adjusting. Then she turns back the way she came, and walks very quickly.

There were lists of refugees in her apartment, of moneys paid, of money owed, of boats, and of fishermen. There are names of contacts, addresses, and telephone numbers. They are in the piano bench, in the form of musical notation. It's a pretty simple code; it looks like a student composition, and she hopes to God the men who search the apartment don't try to play it.

She is in the maternity ward at Kaj's hospital, listed as a Mrs. Haxen. One of the nurses has given her a wedding ring. She has been here three days, going a little mad with anxiety and with having to play the patient. The only thing good about what has happened is, she will have Christmas with her parents after all. But the waiting for an escape plan is terrible.

"Your husband is here, Mrs. Haxen," says the nurse on duty this afternoon. Nina looks up to see Harry in the doorway. Behind him, a German soldier passes the door and looks in. Harry is carrying flowers. He comes to her bedside and kisses her.

"Hello, darling," she says, and suddenly thinks of Per Bennike. Perhaps she will see him in Sweden as well.

"Are you feeling better?" Harry is all gentle concern.

"Yes, I'm stronger now."

"We'll have other children," he says.

"I know."

The woman in the next bed, who gave birth this morning, chooses this moment to wake up. She turns over heavily, wincing, and stares at them, not seeming to know where she is. Then closes her eyes again.

Nina and Harry are silent for a bit, each glancing at the woman as if to signal the other. *Be careful.*

"I came to tell you—I'm going to Germany tonight," says Harry. Nina looks startled. "On the midnight train." She stares.

"I thought you were . . . I thought you were going by sea . . ."

"The train will be safer. It will be full of soldiers, after all. I hope nothing happens to it . . ." He waits to see if she is understanding him.

"I do too," she says.

"I'll be fine. I'll sit in the next-to-last car, as I always do. You know, my lucky charm." He smiles, and she nods.

"What will you do if—something *does* happen to the train?"

"I feel sure God has me by the hand." He takes her right hand in his. "I'll trust in Him and wait for a sign." On her wrist, with his finger, he taps: once, then twice, then once. Dum da-da dum.

"All right, then," she says. The nurse, who has taken the flowers, comes back with a vase and the paper they were wrapped in, neatly folded. She gives this to Nina. On the inside, in pencil, there are several bars of musical notations.


At ten minutes before midnight, Nina boards the Berlin train at the Central Station. She speaks German when she buys her ticket, and when she speaks to the conductor, and when she finds a seat in the next-to-last car. The train is quite full, of soldiers who have been celebrating the beginning of their home leave, and of German civilian office workers who serve Werner Best or the Wehrmacht. She is dressed in the woolen skirt and stockings she wore to school four days ago; her blouse and underclothes have been laundered for her by the nurses, and she carries an empty overnight bag. She has money for her passage across the sound and enough to get to Stockholm. She does not know if her parents know she is coming. She does not know if her brothers know where she is. Any contact with Kaj could have endangered him, so she has not seen him since she arrived at the hospital.

Nina sits beside a window. There are two soldiers on the seat beside her, one heavily drunk. An officer sits across from her, and smiles at her when the train begins to move. "We'll be home soon now," he says in German, and she nods. The air smells of beer and sweat and the hot metal of the tracks outside. The noise of the train builds as it gathers speed, and soon they are out of the station and on their way south. There are three others like her in this car, Nina knows, but has no idea which ones they are. She is terrified. And helpless.

The officer across from her reaches into an inside pocket of his coat and brings out something metal. Nina is so tense that she flinches. For a moment she had hallucinated a gun, the man smiling, "We know who you are. You are under arrest."

He is holding out a cigarette case to her, and to cover her spasm of fear she takes a cigarette. The officer lights it for her. He is a handsome man, with dark hair and pale eyes behind heavy glasses. He wears a wedding ring, and she pictures the wife and children waiting for him at home. Two little girls, will it be? No, a girl and a boy, she gives him. They will be tousled with sleep when he reaches them in the morning. Their warm bodies will squirm with happiness at being held by him again. "Vati!" they will cry.

She smokes gratefully; it is much better tobacco than they have had at home. Her face is reflected in the black glass of the night window. How far have they gone now? Ten miles? Fifteen?

As the minutes pass, the officer takes out a German paper and starts to read. The drunk soldier beside her is asleep, but not much quieter than he had been when awake. The second soldier is eating cheese. Her cigarette is finished and she wants another one. How far have they gone now? Twenty miles? What if it just goes on this way mile after mile, until they roll onto the ferry and on to Germany?

There is a tremendous jolt. Suitcases are thrown from the overhead racks, and passengers land in the aisles. Nina finds herself in the officer's lap. The train is stopped. After a stunned moment, the car fills with shouts and babble. "Sabotage," the word spreads through the train. The drunk soldier is on the floor, awake and furious, as are many. One moment they are on their way home, the next they are stopped, stuck, thwarted in the middle of the night, in the middle of Danish nowhere.

Passengers are pouring out of the train now to see what has happened. As instructed, Nina goes with them. The Germans leave their luggage on the train, and she does the same. There is a long drop from the steps to the bank by the tracks below; Nina's shoes were chosen when it was cold but dry. Here in the woods it has begun to snow.

The passengers who have gotten out tromp toward the front of the train, to see what has happened to the engine, to learn how bad the damage is, and will they go on tonight at all. But Nina goes to the back of the train and crosses the track in the dark to the right side. The train has stopped in a place where the woods are close and deep. She slips into them, and waits. Are there other figures doing the same? She senses that there are, but cannot see them in the dark.

A light flashes, very briefly, two times. It is not quite the signal she is waiting for. She watches, and the light flashes again, twice quickly.

That's it, then. It must be. It is cold, her feet are freezing, it is pitch-dark. She goes forward, toward the place where she saw the torchlight. There is a great deal of shouting and hissing steam at the front of the train, but with every step, that is farther behind her. She begins to hear also forest noises. Branches underfoot, animals perhaps, wild night sounds. Finally she can make out a figure before her. A man, tall, standing. She goes toward him. She is listening for footsteps behind her, of the others from the car, but cannot hear them.

"Moss?" says the man softly, when she is close to him, and he can see her.

"Yes."

"Gut," he says in German. "You are under arrest."

$B$y the time Sydney finally met her, the story of Nina's rescue was a family legend.

"She was waiting in a line . . ." cries Ditte, or Henrik, or Tofa.

"I know exactly where I was standing. It was night, and I was in a line . . ." Nina would say. But usually others took up the story again. They had all memorized every detail, every moment of it.

It was April of 1945. Nina was at Ravensbrück. She had spent four months in Vestre prison in Copenhagen refusing to answer questions, and five at Horserød prison in north Zealand. In August, a new prison camp called Frøslev was opened near Padborg, on the German border. Sabotage and unrest had grown much worse in Denmark since the government fell; to try to avoid aggravating it further, the Germans agreed to build a camp inside the country for their Danish prisoners instead of deporting them. Frøslev wasn't so bad, really. They were isolated from their lives, they were bossed around by Gestapo men and put on pointless work details. But there was food, and the sense that as long as they stayed in Denmark, they still in some way led charmed lives, compared with other guests of the Reich. For a month. Then the Germans broke the promise and began shipping people south. No one knew how the choices were made, who stayed and who went. In November of 1944, Nina and seven others were sent to the all-women's concentration camp at Ravensbrück. Such a beautiful name.

On an April night in 1945, Thursday the fifth, she was standing in a line when a guard called her out. "You are going to Sweden," he said to her in German.

You are going to Sweden. She thought it was a new cruel joke. That when they thought of this new way to kill you, whatever it was going to be, they called it "going to Sweden."

But that was wrong. Count Folke Bernadotte of the Swedish Red Cross had made a deal, somehow. He won permission to send Red Cross buses to the camps, to collect the Scandinavian POWs and take them to Sweden so the Germans, seeing defeat coming, wouldn't kill them all first. They would be interned in Sweden, Berlin was told, until the war ended. And presumably, should the Nazis win after all, they could have the prisoners back.

Why would the Germans make a deal like that? Probably hoping for some kind of mercy at the war crime trials to come.

She was taken to the commandant's office. The other Scandinavians from her barracks were already there, and there were two Finns from one of the satellite camps. The group was told they could only leave if they behaved perfectly every minute they remained, if they left their quarters spic-and-span as if they'd been at Girl Scout camp, and if they told everyone on the buses and in Sweden that their time as guests of the Germans had been useful and happy. They agreed to.

Nina's nieces and nephew pressed their cool, untouchable aunt to describe how she felt that last night, knowing she was going.

"Was it like waiting for Christmas?"

"No, not quite like that," Nina would say. (This disappointed them . . . they wanted to share in her joy, and this was the feeling of nearly unbearable anticipation they could recognize. But Faster Nina was juiceless and precise, about this especially.)

"It was not like waiting for Christmas because you *know* that will come, and that it will be very happy. We did not dare hope that. If you let yourself hope that you'd really be leaving, you felt as if your heart might burst . . . or you felt as if electricity were burning up all the nerves in your body, and it hurt . . ." Her nieces and nephew would stare at her, trying to follow this. But failing.

"So what was it like when the buses arrived?" They wanted her to tell this until she told it the way they wanted to hear it. And she tried.

"We couldn't believe it. We'd been tricked and lied to so much. But here they came, just as we were promised, big white buses, clean and bright with big red crosses on them." She would sometimes try here to fit in a little exegesis about the Red Cross, its good works in times of war and other disaster. Sometimes Nurse Cavell even got into it, but the children learned how to get her back on track.

"And *then* did it feel like Christmas?"

"More. But we were still very sad because we were leaving so many others. Two in our bunks were Dutch and one French. They had to stay behind. And one was very ill."

"But the war was almost over, Faster Nina. They would be out in another month or so."

"We didn't know that."

She would tell about how she felt when the buses actually pulled out of the camp. How she was given a cigarette, her first in months and months, and how she saw out the window a child in a farmyard, pulling a little red wooden horse on wheels by a string. How amazing it was, to see life going on, right here, so near. And then, the devastation that war had brought to the German countryside—the people so starved and sad-looking and so much ruin. How they passed a troop of new recruits training for the front. They looked about twelve years old, in uniform, bravely marching. And when they came to bombed-out towns, the Nazi guards on the buses made them pull the shades down, closing out the spring sun they longed for, so they wouldn't see the Germans' humiliation. When they were once again in the countryside they could put the shades back up. Finally the Swedish driver grew irritated and told them to leave the shades up or down, but leave them alone. The Germans left them down. They crossed Brandenburg and then into Holstein and finally

Schleswig without being able to see outside, as if they were traveling in a tunnel. When they reached the Danish border the shades
went up again for good.

"And what happened when you crossed the border?" the children asked happily, because they already knew.

"When we crossed the border, well then . . ." Nina would have
to stop, to keep from crying. She never spoke if her voice might
shake. When she could, she went on calmly. "When we crossed the
border, the road was lined on both sides with people. They were
waiting for us. They were singing, and waving the Dannebrog, and
when we came right to them they were crying out, 'Welcome back,
welcome to Denmark . . .' " Her smile was pinched because her eyes
had filled. It was so much harder to speak calmly of gratitude than of
anger.

"They hadn't forgotten us, you see, that whole long time," she
would go on, finally. "We felt forgotten. Godforsaken. But we were
not. And we cried, and they pushed flowers and chocolate and cigarettes in at the window, and bottles of milk . . . we hadn't seen milk
in such a long time . . ."

"And were you allowed to stop and get out?" They knew
she was.

"We stopped in Padborg, right past the frontier. And the people
of the town—we got out of the buses and they vied with each other
for the chance to take us to their homes, to give us hot food and
water for washing . . ." She had to stop again. "Well. And then the
whole way through Jutland, across Fyn, on to Copenhagen,
people lined the roads, more and more as we approached the city.
At one point we began to sing the Danish national anthem but
the Gestapo men couldn't stand that. They pulled their pistols out
and ordered us to stop. And when we got to Copenhagen,
the streets were filled with people out to welcome us. Filled. The
buses couldn't move. The Gestapo men got mad and they broadcast through loudspeakers, if people didn't be quiet and move away
from the buses, they would turn around and take us back to the
camps."

"What did you do?" they would ask, though they knew the answer.

"We stopped singing and shouting, but we couldn't stop smiling," Nina would say. "We smiled and smiled, on the ferry to Malmö. Although it was hard to have to go right through our country and not stop. It wasn't until we were on dry land in Sweden, and the Gestapo men were on the ferry back to Denmark, that we could shout and cry."

"Did you see Uncle Kaj when you went through Copenhagen?"

"He says he was there and watched us pass, but I couldn't see him. I looked and looked."

"Did Farmor and Farfar meet you at the ferry?"

"They did. They came down from Stockholm, with Auntie Tofa, and Farmor cried so much, because she'd been told I was dead."

"She must have been really happy," Eleanor would say.

"Yes." Though the truth was, it was days before Ditte could stop crying at the sight of Nina. In those days, people had never, even in pictures, seen living people so thin they looked like skeletons, with a terrible parched film of flesh stretched over their bones, teeth falling out of their heads, and their eyes sunk way back in the sockets. The phrase "like something out of a concentration camp" did not exist yet.

The children wanted to know all about what she ate for her first dinner in Sweden, and what she did next, and Nina didn't want to tell them how long it was before she could keep food down without terrible cramps, and how her teeth were loose and her gums bled, and she was so cold, even though it was summer; so she told them about the meals she had dreamed of when she was still in Ravensbrück, how she and her bunkmates used to take turns at night saying what they would be eating if they were at home at that moment.

Then she would tell about how the British marched into Copenhagen in May, and how in June they all left Sweden and went home. And how Moster Tofa's neighbor had taken care of her apartment and watered the plants and fed the cat, how Aunt Tofa said it looked better than when she went away. How Jewish friends came home to find their apartments freshly painted and flowers blooming in the window boxes. Sydney's children loved these stories and asked for them again and again. Apart from stories, they found it hard to spend time with Faster Nina, she was so touchy and reserved, and they knew their mother thought she was basically a pain in the ass.

On April 30, 1945, Adolf Hitler shot himself. On May 4, the German High Command surrendered Denmark to Field Marshal Montgomery. The whole city of Copenhagen rang with joy, as Montgomery was driven, waving from an open car belonging to the king, through streets filled with confetti and Union Jacks. It was no small thing that he reached Denmark before the Russians, or its future would have resembled East Germany's or Czechoslovakia's, not that of the Free West, and Monty didn't beat the Russians by all that much. Christmas Møller came home a national hero for the courage and persistence he had called forth with his passionate broadcasts from London, once the Resistance gathered force and his mission finally clarified. Laurus Moss came home with him.

Laurus was in Copenhagen when his parents and Nina came back from Sweden. There were tears, especially for the marks of suffering Nina wore like a poisoned cloak, which everyone could see but no one talked about. There was a great deal of laughter. It was almost enough to see the comfort Nina drew from simply being again in the completed family circle. Laurus could have stayed for months, revisiting old friends, hearing over and over how this one had escaped, how these others resisted, how the survivors had survived. There were calls to pay on families of those who had not come back. There was so much that was not yet known, just the empty beds, the absence of news from a husband or wife, a son or daughter. Per Bennike came to call more than once, though Nina always withdrew soon after he appeared; Laurus noticed how Per's eyes followed her as she slipped out of the room. And Nina wouldn't talk, to Laurus or anyone, about her time in Germany. "I'm not ready," she would say. Laurus always wondered if he could have helped if he had stayed. If he could have seen signs that others missed that she could start coming back to them, if given the right stone to step to, the right hand to hold for balance. Kaj was so busy with his work and his new girl that he was hardly at home, and Ditte and Henrik were so shattered by the thought of Nina's pain that to them she showed a quiet mask and they all pretended it was her face.

But Laurus couldn't stay in Denmark when he had a wife and child waiting across the ocean. He tore himself away to go back to London, resigned his commission in the Buffs, and managed to book a seat on a Pan Am flight from London to Idlewild on the twentieth of July. He thought about traveling in civilian clothes, but decided that his wife had done without him for four years because he was a soldier; a soldier was what she ought to get back.

The flight, a dreamlike interlude between all that he'd seen and what was to come, took forever. An Englishwoman in the seat next to him was going to Connecticut to retrieve the small son and daughter she'd sent to America at the start of the Blitz. She showed him pictures of the way they looked the last time she saw them, and the pictures her sister in Norwalk had sent a month ago. Laurus showed her a picture of the daughter he'd never seen; Eleanor on the beach at Dundee in her little striped bathing suit. The woman took her shoes off and went to sleep. Laurus dozed, too, and found himself swallowed by a ferocious longing for Sydney, a dream Sydney he'd been inventing and perfecting for four years, for touching and holding her, for the moment they would once again be together as man and wife. It was a longing he had managed to keep tamped down for so long that he felt as if he had opened a door to an empty room and found there a ravening tiger. He had to try to keep himself awake, fearing he might otherwise say in his sleep words that should only be heard by his wife.

When they were finally circling New York, the woman beside him awoke and found that her feet had swollen so that she couldn't get her shoes back on. She began to weep at the thought that she was going to have to greet her children barefoot. The stewardess gave her a pair of bed socks from the first-class cabin, and Laurus convinced her it was funny. His elation at being almost home, almost back in his darling's arms, was so huge, it was like a derangement.

Customs seemed to take forever. As the customs officer handed him his passport and said, "Welcome home, Captain Moss," he turned to wave goodbye to his seatmate. She was putting her shoes on and stuffing the socks into her purse. The delay had done some good.

He walked out into free America with his heart hammering. He heard Sydney before he saw her.

"Laurus!" She was running toward him. He stood by his luggage with his arms stretched wide. She was tan and glowing, taller and thicker than he remembered; then she was in his arms, laughing as they staggered backward a step. Then, a kiss to seal away all that they had missed and to bind them together, lips and tongues and breath. She was finally real, after all those fantasy nights. She smelled delicious, her skin like lemons, her mouth like Dentyne. He was sure he smelled like airline upholstery, stale air and cigarettes, but if she noticed, she didn't care.

He held her at arm's length, at last, so they could look at each other.

"You!" he said.

"You!" she cried. They were giddy.

When they were finally seated in a taxi, with four years of his life stowed in the trunk behind them and the city before them, they looked at each other for long moments, then both began to talk at once.

"When did you—"

"How was the—"

They laughed and subsided. Then they did it again.

"Did you have any—"

"How long did you—"

They looked at each other for another stretch. Finally Laurus said, "Let's just neck." So they did that.

When they got to Perry Street, Sydney paid the taxi, as Laurus had no American currency. When he walked into the apartment he had visited so often in memory, he put down his bags in the middle of the room and stared. Sydney stood to one side, watching him. The living room was smaller than he remembered, the ceiling lower, but the windows were larger. He went toward the kitchen and stood looking in. Sydney had painted it a creamy yellow. There were bright white curtains, and a fan in the open window at the back moved the soft summer air and carried in traffic noise from the next block. He drank all the colors with his eyes. He went in and opened cupboard doors. Then the refrigerator. He stared at the unfamiliar packages, the cleanliness and plenty.

She followed him into their bedroom. The walls had become sky blue in the bedroom, the moldings and ceiling white. There were crisp sheets on the bed and a blue bedspread Sydney had made to match the curtains. He turned to her.

"It's beautiful."

"Thank you."

"*You're* beautiful . . ."

He put his arms around her and whispered into her hair. "All those years, missing this, missing you . . . and you've made it even better than my dreams."

Floating in bliss, he took his wife to bed in the middle of the afternoon. It was fast, it was wild, nearly explosive. Afterward they lay in a tangle.

"Happy?" Sydney whispered.

"You can't imagine how happy." And he fell soundly asleep.

It was dark when he woke. It took him a full minute to realize where he was. Not his bare room in London. Not his bedroom in Copenhagen. At last he came all the way into himself.

He stretched. He felt the temptation to go back to sleep and sleep for a year. He'd had no idea how tired he'd been, couldn't remember when he'd sunk into such an assurance of safety and peace. But he roused himself, pulled on his shorts, and went out to the living room, where he stood in the doorway, watching Sydney sit in lamplight, knitting a sock. She was dressed for the evening, with her hair up in combs or pins, however girls did that.

Something made her look up and she smiled at him. "Welcome home," she said.

"Indeed." He stretched and scratched the back of his neck. "What time is it?"

"Eight-thirty. Are you hungry?"

"Famished."

"They're holding a table for us at Table d'Hôte."

"Perfect."

When he reappeared a half hour later, his hair still wet, he was wearing a suit that had hung in the closet for four years. It was a little tight across the shoulders now, but the pants were loose. He hadn't realized he'd changed.

"You can't imagine what it's like to have an American shower. All that water, as hot as you want it. I thought of staying in forever, but I missed you."

She returned his smile. "You're not going to wear your uniform?"

A moment's pause.

"Do you want me to?"

"It's just the way I pictured it." Her war hero. The heads turning in the restaurant.

"Do you want me to change?"

"Of course not. You must be sick of it."

"It was so nice to open the closet and see these old friends. Look how baggy the pants are."

"Let's go out and fatten you up," said Sydney.

They walked arm in arm up to Hudson Street. "What a gorgeous night," Laurus said. "Isn't it beautiful, the streetlights on, the glow from all the windows." She smiled at the look on his face. He was in love with everything. She'd forgotten that about him, his glorious cheer.

There was a fuss over them at the restaurant. Their special-occasion place. Bruno, the owner, who was Algerian but pretended to be French, welcomed Laurus, held Sydney's chair, was quickly back at their table with the bottle of Veuve Clicquot Sydney had ordered in advance. When the glasses had been filled and the waiter retired, they raised their glasses to each other.

"To us," said Sydney.

"To us. Skål." He looked deep into her eyes and tried to hold them as they drank, but Sydney had forgotten and looked down, smiling, set her glass down, and picked up her menu. Unbidden it brought him a memory he didn't want.

When Sydney had decided what she wanted to eat, she put her menu aside, sighed deeply, and said, "Well. Where shall we begin?"

Laurus began. Once he started talking he felt like a man who'd reached an oasis after years in a desert. He told her about his fear for his family when the roundup of the Jews began. How helpless he felt. He told how he felt when he learned his little sister had been captured, how he schemed to get a message to her, of the terrible day he learned she was no longer at Frøslev. It had taken weeks to find out where she was; thank God for the Red Cross and all they did to protect prisoners of war! He told how he wept when he knew that Folke Bernadotte had succeeded in getting the Scandinavians out, and that Nina was in Sweden with his parents. And finally, seeing them! With his own eyes! To hold each one of them in his arms, to see little Nina, with her skin so dry and thin, to feel her shoulder blades poking out of her fleshless back like folded wings, to see the way she disappeared in front of their eyes, her face going dull, her mind somewhere else . . . What was she seeing? Would they ever get her all the way back? What could he do for her?

He stretched a hand to Sydney, beseeching her help, about to say, Tell me, with your woman's heart, now that you understand, tell me how to heal this damage. And found that his wife was weeping the tears his sister could not. Her cheeks were wet, and when he touched her, she dropped her head and started to sob.

They were back where they'd been when he told her he was going. This restaurant, this wine, practically this same table.

"Darling," he whispered. Appalled. What was it? What had he done, what did she have to tell him? She had some awful disease? She loved somebody else, she was leaving him?

She struggled. He handed her his handkerchief. She mopped and blew and held up a finger to say, Just a second. Just a second.

At last she looked him full in the face. Her eyes were red, her mascara was smeared. "You've been home . . ." She had to pause for a shuddering breath, a diverted sob. "Eight hours."

"Yes . . ."

"You've been home *eight* hours and you haven't asked me one thing about the baby!" She clamped her hands over her mouth and fell to sobbing again. Laurus fell back in his chair.

"You *forgot* me! You just completely forgot me, you forgot what *I've* been through, you forgot we have a baby, who isn't even a baby anymore . . . I want my baby!"

"Where is she?" He was stricken.

"She's at Gudrun's."

"Let's go get her right now." He put his napkin on the table and pushed back his chair, just as the waiter swept in with two plates of hot food and placed them with a flourish.

"No!"

"Yes! Let's go right now. Let's start this evening over—"

"We *can't*. It *happened*. I planned this dinner for you, and I pictured it for four years, and you're goddamn going to eat it! At least *something* will be the way I wanted it." And she began furiously sawing away at her duck à l'orange, putting great chunks of meat into her mouth and chewing while she wept as if she could chew his head off.

THE LEEWAY COTTAGE GUEST BOOK

July 28, 1945

*Home at last,* wrote Laurus. *As we drove into the village this morning, we passed a young black bear on Butter Hill eating blueberries next to the Baptist Church. Everything looks exactly the same. It feels as if I've been on another planet.*

Eleanor had slept on the backseat or sat on Sydney's lap all the way
up from New York. She was adjusting to Laurus slowly. He didn't
know any of her dolls' names, and she wasn't allowed to go in and
get into Mommy's bed anymore when she woke up, and for the first
time she now had to wait to speak until the grown-ups were finished
talking. He preferred to play the piano by himself without any help
from her, although Mommy let her hammer the keyboard at will, and
laughed at the noise she made and told her she was a clever bug. She
kept asking Sydney when he was leaving. If you could have read the
silent thoughts of the three people traveling north in the new station
wagon that morning, you'd have thought they were all on different
planets.

To Sydney, Laurus seemed unnaturally formal. Had he changed,
or was he always like that? When they met she was so young, he
was so grown-up, she'd wanted his approval so badly. She'd wanted
*everyone's* approval so badly. Now she couldn't help noticing that he
never could pin Eleanor's diaper on right, and whenever he pulled
out of a parking lot or gas station she had to yell to keep him from
trying to drive on the wrong side of the road. She had thought he
would be the kind of father her own daddy had been, longing to escape from the bridge game or the dinner party to play hooky with his
little girl. Laurus seemed only to want to escape to the piano.


Laurus had once told Sydney that touring when he was young was
torture, the least musical time of his life, because the only access he
had to his instrument was onstage, and onstage the quartet re-
hearsed and played their one program. In the morning in a new
town, after a late arrival, the string players were all in their hotel
rooms running their scales and refreshing themselves with different
repertoire while he stared out at unfamiliar rooftops and longed for
home.

"You know how you live in the music in your head," he would
say to her. "You're always playing it through, moving around inside
the tempi, suddenly hearing that the alto line should be singing out
over the treble in a particular measure, dying to try it . . ." He didn't

wait for confirmation. She was a musician, too. Of course she understood. Except, she wasn't a musician anymore.


He couldn't explain his longing for hours and hours uninterrupted at
the keyboard. It was an appetite he couldn't control, he had missed it
so much. He longed for certain composers the way a starving man
longs for foods from childhood, except that gorging himself on Schubert after all this time didn't make him sick, it made him more vora-
cious.

He had lost muscle tone in parts of his hands and arms he'd never
known he needed, as he never since early childhood had gone so
long playing so little. He started at the beginning of Hanon and
played his way through the exercises, hours a day, C major, A minor,
F major, D minor, repeated notes in groups of four, detached thirds
and sixths. Sydney watched him from the doorway as he stared past
the music with eyes unfixed, his hands moving along the keyboard
like matched horses in harness, and wondered what was going on in
his brain. He reminded her at those times not of a musician but of a
cuckoo clock. In the evenings his arms ached and he fretted about
wrecking his hands, like Schumann, but he couldn't seem to pace
himself.

But Schumann was a nutcase, Sydney pointed out. Thank God
for Dundee, the high healing sky, and the meadow stretching down
past the garden to the lilac hedge, beauty you could drink like a tonic.
In Dundee she made him promise to stop playing after lunch, to
spend the afternoons with her and Eleanor. He did it, and she
watched him uncoil in the sun, each day a little more, before he went
absent again. Oh, well—she was surrounded by friends in Dundee,
and accustomed to an absent husband.

And then there was the sunny afternoon at the Maitlands' pool,
when Sydney, lying gossiping with Elise, sat up and cocked her sunglasses to look to the shallow end of the pool, to see what was making Eleanor squeal with laughter like that.

Laurus was standing up to his waist in water, while Eleanor
bobbed joyously in her little cork life belt, stretching her chin up to

keep her face above water, her eyes riveted on her father. Laurus picked her up with his hands under her arms. "All right, stay right there," he said. "I'll be right back, don't go away . . ." And he'd take his hands away, dropping her into the water, to screams of delight.

"Do it *again,* Daddy!" Eleanor cried, bobbing and splashing and laughing.

"But I told you not to move!"

"Do again!" And he picked her up, grinning.

"Be careful, honey . . ." Sydney called, not really knowing which one she was talking to. It didn't matter, as neither of them paid her any attention.

"Again, Daddy!" Eleanor gurgled. Sydney looked at their beaming faces, entirely heedless of her, and felt like Candace, sourly watching her husband and daughter cavorting, and didn't like it at all.

"I'm offered an artist in residence post at Mannes," Laurus said, holding up a letter, with a small crow of delight.

It was early October. He'd been out on his new bicycle with the baby seat attached behind the saddle; he'd ridden to Central Park and back with Eleanor, while Sydney labored over a recipe from the newspaper, for some Greek eggplant thing called moussaka that was a lot more trouble than it sounded. The baby was down for her nap now and Laurus was reading his mail at the kitchen table.

"What does that mean?" Sydney was having an inner dialogue with an imaginary Laurus about how much effort she was making to be sure they all learned to eat peculiar new vegetables.

"Eight or ten students. The cream of the crop. Meet with them once or twice a month. I'd have time to perform, to prepare new repertoire. Or whatever I want."

Sydney paused and stared at the grease-spattered recipe again. "Is it worth it?" she asked.

He'd expected congratulations. "I don't understand the question."

"Is it worth it? The time it would take? You don't need the money."

After a surprised silence he said, "That's hardly the point."

"Sorry. What *is* the point?" The eggplant seemed to have absorbed a whole bottle of cooking oil and she was running out of paper towels and places to put the greasy slices.

"It's an honor. And it's refreshing to work with talented students. One needs a structured place in one's professional world."

"*One* does?" She'd begun needling him about Briticisms that had crept into his speech. They reminded her that for four years he'd had a life that had nothing to do with her, made friends and who knows what all with people who had never heard of her.

"I thought you'd be pleased, Sydney. It means I can teach and work without having to travel much. I'm not ready to leave you again, and I didn't think you wanted me to. My music doesn't exist if nobody hears it."

There was a silence. He waited for her to say something, but she turned and opened the refrigerator. She began rooting in the cheese drawer. After a while, when it was clear she wasn't going to answer, he said, "Remind me who these people are who are coming?"

"Anselma Thorne. Dr. Carey's niece. And her new friend Olivia. You'll like them, Olivia plays the flute."

What surprised Laurus about the evening was that he did like Olivia very much, and Anselma quite well enough. Anselma dressed in well-cut trousers and saddle shoes and a man's crisp white shirt. Her hair was short and glossy, her hands beautifully manicured. She had a lovely voice, a cello voice, and a delightful, ready laugh. Olivia was petite and pink with a messy cloud of curly hair. She played the flute like an angel. She'd brought her instrument and some music, and after the moussaka and some retsina, Olivia and Laurus sight-read together. They finished with faces shining from shared pleasure. The women had cooed over Eleanor and brought her a Raggedy Ann. They talked with excitement about the stone farmhouse in northwestern Connecticut they'd just bought. When Sydney mentioned the Mannes offer, in an exploratory way, Olivia turned to Laurus as if he'd won a Nobel prize. When they had gone and Laurus was washing the dishes, Sydney came into the kitchen and kissed the back of his neck.

"I'm so pleased about Mannes," Sydney said.

"I'm very glad," said Laurus, and meant it. "And thank you for a delightful evening."

"Thank *you*. It was fun, wasn't it?"

"Great fun."

THE LEEWAY COTTAGE GUEST BOOK

Tuesday, July 15, 1947

*Papa, Mama, and Nina are here at last! They came by train to Bucksport, where we met them last night. Weather glorious for their arrival. Also, Mr. Brown arrived from Union with our new icebox. Exciting day.*

It was Sydney's handwriting. Laurus and little Eleanor had looked forward to this visit so intensely that it probably couldn't fail to disappoint, and there were already signs that it wouldn't. Fail. Papa Henrik hadn't slept at all well for several days—he hated traveling, apparently. He barely spoke on the drive from Bucksport to Dundee. And Mama Ditte was warm and a dear, of course, but to say her English was rusty was putting it kindly. And Nina . . . well, much as Sydney had looked forward to embracing the sister she'd always wanted, there were early signs that Nina was not what Sydney had had in mind.

Sydney spent the first day of the visit driving her new family from place to place, famous in her legend, so they could get to know her, and all that she had brought to Laurus. They saw the golf course, then the yacht club. Henrik and Ditte exclaimed to each other in Danish in the backseat, and finally Nina translated: "It looks so much like Gilleleje."

"What's Gillal-EYEa?"

There was a little silence. There was too much to say about Gilleleje, and no way to say it right. Their own fear, and that of so many others. The hundreds of Jews who escaped from there, the kindness of strangers, and the worst betrayal of the dark days of the roundup. For a Dane to explain Gilleleje was like an American hav-

ing to explain that sometimes people took honeymoon trips to Nia-
gara Falls.

"It's on the north coast of Zealand," said Nina. Sydney wondered
if they thought she had memorized the map of Denmark. They hadn't
exactly got the map of New England nailed down, she noticed. Ditte
seemed amazed that Dundee was more than an hour from Boston.

By this time the conversation was so far from what Sydney had
planned to tell them, about the Brutal Beasts, and the "O" boats they
raced, about her triumphs on the bay, and the boys she had grown
up with before she chose Laurus, that she just let it go. She drove
them to The Elms without giving Candace any warning, and had the
satisfaction of seeing her mother forced to be less than gracious, as
she already had Bernard in the car on their way to a lunch party
when Sydney's station wagon crunched down the gravel driveway.
After Candace and Bernard left, Sydney showed her guests over the
house, but Papa Henrik stayed in the car, dozing, which offended
her. She cut the tour short and took them home, announcing that no
doubt they all needed naps.

Laurus was so happy to have his family with him, he seemed like
a different person. He was a quiet man, but now he almost chattered.
And they kept forgetting to speak English, in their excitement, in
their joy at each other's presence, so Laurus was constantly having
to stop the party and tell Sydney what they were saying.

"You go ahead, catch up, I'm just happy to sit here and listen," she
said, which was entirely false. She had pictured this visit a whole
other way, the Mosses eager to know all about her, the mother of
their grandchildren, the girl who had made Laurus happy. Instead
they kept talking about how she must come to Denmark, bring the
children, how much she would like this or that. Then they went back
to chattering to each other in Danish. She felt like a pebble thrown
into a rushing stream. She had crashed right through the surface of
the water and sunk to the bottom, while Laurus and his family went
dancing and burbling over and past her, oblivious.

Candace and Bernard invited the elder Mosses to dinner. Sydney
and Laurus were giving a party for the young, to introduce Nina to
their friends. Nina wandered into the big kitchen at about five in the

afternoon. She had had a long nap and a swim and was getting some color in her cheeks.

"May I help you?"

Sydney was mashing potatoes; clouds of steam billowed up from the wide kettle as she pounded with the masher, periodically dumping in more butter, more cream.

Nina hadn't seen such plenty for years. The shortages at home were far worse than they had been during the war. In a sort of reparation for relative wartime comfort compared with the rest of Europe, Denmark had been pressured hard to give disproportionately in the peace to the recovery of Allied countries. Everything was scarce there now, not just food. You couldn't get shoe leather. Some stores carried shoes made of fish skin. They were rather pretty, but they didn't last very long. You couldn't get rubber for tires. Nina's bike at home had rope around the front wheel. Her friend Lars had replaced his ruined tires with little chunks of wood all around the bicycle rim. It was horrible on cobblestones.

Sydney looked up from her work, her face red from effort and steam. Just then baby Monica began to cry upstairs. "Could you get the baby for me?"

Nina simply looked at her, as if she hadn't understood.

"Could you run up and get the baby for me? Just bring her down here with a clean diaper, I'll change her."

"No, I couldn't."

"It's right at the top of the stairs and the diapers are in the . . . Oh, never mind. Here, then do this."

With a flush of irritation, Sydney handed the masher to Nina and left the room. It was easier.

Monica, who was fifteen months old, was standing in her crib with her face red and cheeks wet. She quieted the moment she saw her mother. She was light and wiry, clearly her father's daughter, where Eleanor had been sweetly and calmly plump. Monica was a tense little thing. As Sydney scooped her up, feeling the loaded diaper as she did so, the baby gripped her with her arms and legs as if she were being rescued by a monkey mother from a river full of crocodiles.

"Hushabye. Hushabye, little beezle, Mommy's here. You had a lovely nap, didn't you?" Sydney carried her down to the kitchen where Nina was bumping rather uselessly at the potatoes. Sydney changed the baby on a blanket on the floor beside the woodstove, then retrieved her masher from Nina. She stuck her finger into the potatoes, tasted, threw in another gob of butter and added salt and pepper. She moved now like one who has no more time for idle chat, so Nina drifted out. She was sitting on the porch listening through the window to Laurus playing the piano when the guests arrived. (And Sydney was still in the clothes she had worn all day, having had all the work of the dinner to cook, plus having to feed the babies and give them their baths, all while Nina sat in a rocker on the porch as if she didn't know anyone but Laurus was in the house, and he kept her company.)

## THE LEEWAY COTTAGE GUEST BOOK

Sunday, Aug. 3, 1947

> *Eleanor Wells Moss and Monica Bing Moss were christened today by Mr. Davison. Forty here for luncheon on the porch. We saw a moose in the Peases' field on the way to church—the Mosses feel their American visit is complete. Heavenly weather.*

The christening was in the Congregational Church, whose high cool white sanctuary looked so Scandinavian to the Mosses. Laurus played the music for the service, with a trio of Haydn before morning worship and Bach for the postlude. Mr. Davison preached well, by which Sydney meant briefly. Candace had done the flowers, and they were startling, mostly towering stalks of gladioli from her cutting garden. Eleanor, who was five, looked angelic in a little pink dress from the Women's Exchange, with smocking across the bodice and patent-leather Mary Janes. Gladdy was Eleanor's godmother; Nina was Monica's. After lunch, they had an old-fashioned musicale as had so often been held here on a Sunday, in the old days. Ditte and Laurus played the four-hands *Dolly Suite* of Fauré together, while Sydney passed around the Guest Book, with its entry about the same piece of music played here so long ago, and the whispered exclamations over this only disturbed the musicians a little.

"The longest three weeks of my life," said Sydney to Glad, after she waved her houseguests off on the train. They were sprawled on the bathing beach, slathered in baby oil and smoking Pall Malls while a girl from the village monitored Eleanor and the other children at the water's edge. Monica and tiny Amelia Crane were napping nearby on a blanket in the shade of the changing cabins.

"Houseguests are hard," said Gladdy loyally, though Leeway in her childhood had been filled with houseguests coming and going all summer, her parents' friends and hers and Tommy's all endlessly welcome.

"There are only so many times you can drive to the Jordan Pond House for popovers."

"They did like sailing," Gladdy pointed out.

"It's true, they did. And Nina played badminton. Once."

"Well, they were quiet," said Gladdy, and both of them started to laugh. The Mosses had sat for hours on the porch, reading or simply staring at the bay in the silence, happy to be together and at peace. It made Sydney want to jump out of her skin.

On the other hand, she had rarely known Laurus so utterly happy. His parents would sit at the bathing beach, watching Eleanor and her friends dashing in and out of the water, and it was to them like watching a double exposure, this beach plus another, with other little children, Laurus, Kaj, and Nina, the Hansen children next door, brown with sun and their hair bleached white. Sometimes Ditte would call Monica "Nina," and it gave Sydney the creeps.

The night they finally had the house to themselves again, Sydney felt herself working toward a tantrum, as if now that she could relax, a gate had swung open and in romped disappointment and fatigue and boredom and resentment from where they'd been grazing and nickering and watching from the other side of the fence all week, waiting to get at her. The disappointment seemed, absurdly, to be most of all aimed at Nina. Sydney had somehow thought that here at last would be a female person who would love her and read her mind. Now she felt bereft and foolish, and when she felt things she didn't like to feel, she most often got rid of them by turning them into anger. And there sat Laurus in the next room playing the goddam piano.

When she walked into the room, Laurus turned to her and stopped playing at once. Before she could say a word, he went to her and put his arms around her, and whatever words were in her mouth melted.

"Thank you for one of the happiest weeks of my life," he said.

She felt tears start, and to her own utter astonishment, said, "You're welcome."

"Let's go down to the Seagull and have dinner together."

"With the girls?"

"No, just us."

She smiled, absurdly pleased, and went off to call a sitter.

In early August, Mr. Maitland came to call on Sydney to ask her to join the yacht club council. "It's time your generation started running things," he said. "We thought you'd be the one to show them how." Sydney accepted without asking Laurus.

They went to Gladdy and Neville's for supper in their little rented cottage down the Neck that Neville called Bug House. Their whole crowd was there, Elise and her young husband, Chris, and Lucie Cochran, who was now married to Elise's brother Ned. Of their whole crowd of childhood friends, only Tommy McClintock had disappeared in the Pacific. Their past did not seem gone, and a happy future, a thousand evenings like this with these old friends laughing together, was before them. They ate spaghetti with home-made sauce around a battle-scarred oak table. The men wore blazers without neckties and the girls were in simple sundresses, which was very daring; their parents still dressed in evening clothes for dinner, even here in Dundee. And spaghetti was daring. They had been raised to think of it as immigrant food, or food from a can for small children. Several of the boys had served in Italy and had brought back some news from the culinary front. Spaghetti made the older generation anxious, as if next their children would start putting grease in their hair and wearing loud ties and cologne. The world was changing.

Among the changes Sydney was pleased about was that she had her next project. The yacht club, hardly ever more than a spacious shed in the first place, had to be torn down to the studs and rebuilt over the winter; it was full of dry rot and carpenter ants. The council had hoped Sydney might chair a fund-raising committee, since she and her mother could, if they wanted, simply donate the whole amount needed. Sydney had accepted; she enjoyed giving money away herself and felt no shyness about telling others to do the same, whether they could do so as painlessly as she could or not, but in this case she had a better idea. She thought they should revive the long-standing tradition in the summer colony of do-it-yourself entertainment and put on a show to raise money. She could sing, and Neville, onetime star of the Princeton Triangle Club, could sing and dance, Chris and Elise could act and they could write, and God knows Laurus could play the piano. "C'mon, guys. It'll be a panic," she boomed. They agreed with wine-fueled enthusiasm over the blueberry grunt, and retired to the living room, for two tables of the game of the summer, a form of gin rummy called Oklahoma.

There are silent movies, in color, of the performance they gave that Labor Day weekend. Sydney is everywhere: dancing a cancan with Gladdy and Elise, and soundlessly singing a duet with Neville Crane, both dressed as lobstermen, in oilskins and beards. Neville Crane appears again with Homer Gantry and some other man, no longer known, shirtless in flower leis and grass skirts over bathing trunks, playing ukuleles and dancing a hula. Eleanor and Monica, in their own middle age, find the film in the attic at Leeway after their parents are dead. "The Yacht Club Follies, 1947" is written on brittle masking tape on the canister in their mother's handwriting. They also unearth a projector, on a shelf in a downstairs cupboard crammed with rackets, board games, stilts, hula hoops, wicker laundry baskets of period clothes, shoes, and costume jewelry for children's dress-up, and a thing called a "one-man band" that Eleanor remembered someone giving their mother as a joke present one summer in the fifties. It has horns and drums and cymbals rigged so that when you pound it on the floor all the noisemakers sound at once.

Amazingly, the projector still works. They have to wipe off cobwebs, and it takes some time for Eleanor to remember how to thread the film; their father had shown her how, but it must have been forty years ago. They watch "The Yacht Club Follies" several times, projected against the lime green wainscot wall in the kitchen, before the bulb in the projector blows out with a pop. An old mimeo'd program inside the canister tells them that the duet their mother is singing with Uncle Neville is "The Lobster's Lament" to the tune of "Always." They make plans to have the film transferred to videotape, so they can give copies to their friends whose parents (and grandparents!) are in the movie, looking younger than any of them can remember them.

What Sydney principally remembered from the winter of '47–'48, apart from being pregnant again, was that for Christmas, she ordered a full-length mink coat from Birger Christensen for her mother-in-law. She didn't tell Laurus she had done it. All through their own festivities, the shopping, the store windows, the decking of the apartment with pine ropes, and the secret wrapping of presents, it was her best secret of all.

Their Christmas Eve telegrams from Copenhagen arrived as always, but Sydney waited, giddy with pleasure, for her letter of thanks. She pictured Ditte speechless with gratitude, sending her the kind of mother love that shone in her face when Ditte looked at her own children. And that had never been seen in Candace's. As the snow whipped up and down the streets of the West Village, as the sun shone on crisp new whiteness when they took the children sledding in Central Park, she looked forward to it.

Laurus read the letter aloud when it came at last, translating, as his mother was shy about writing in English.

" 'Dearest Laurus and Sydney, Eleanor and Monica,

" 'We hope you had the happiest of Christmases, and all here wish you a joyous new year.

" 'First, we must thank you for the big box of treats from the U.S. Maple sugar and blueberry jam are both delicious and remind us of happy mornings with you in your beautiful Maine. We all enjoy the butter of earthnuts—' "

"The what?"

"Oh . . . peanuts, peanut butter. 'We all enjoy the peanut butter and the Boston Brown Bread, even Kaj although he has not yet been to Boston—' "

"They call peanuts 'earthnuts'?"

"They grow in the ground," said Laurus.

"Oh."

" 'And we look forward to having you here with us so we can introduce you to our wienerbrød and smørrebrød and other things we hope you will like as well. And thank you so much for the beautiful . . .' Long socks? Did you send them nylons?"

Sydney smiled, very proud of herself.

" 'That is a very great luxury for me and Nina, and Tofa too!'

" 'Thank you for the photographs of Eleanor and Monica, and of your beautiful home in New York City, which we hope someday to visit.

" 'We had a very nice Christmas here, although we wish you could all have been here. Kaj's girl came to Christmas Eve dinner. Nina got the almond in her rice pudding and got an extra present. (A bar of English soap from before the war! I found it in a dresser drawer.) We all went to midnight service except Aunt Tofa, who has a sore throat. We had dinner Christmas Day with the Bing cousins . . .' Now she has a lot of news about people you haven't met yet . . . then . . . Here. 'Last of all, my dear Sydney, I want to thank you for the beautiful mink coat, which the man from Birger Christensen brought on Christmas Eve—' Sydney! You gave her a fur coat?"

Sydney nodded, beaming.

"You are really something!" He turned back to the letter, now smiling too.

" 'You can't imagine my surprise as I opened it, and tried it on for all to see. I looked like a queen! You flatter me so much with your love and kindness in sending me such a present. I know you will understand that you have done me an even greater kindness than you could have known, which is to ease the worry in a mother's heart. I have been so troubled that our Nina seems never to be warm anymore, summer or winter, and especially in winter she must go out to work in all weathers, while I don't have to go out at all unless I want to. So when I am not using it, I am warmed to the heart to know that my little girl is beautiful and warm in that very, very beautiful coat, and I thank you with all my heart for your kindness to us. As the mother of your own dear little girls, I know you will understand what this means to me.' "

Eleanor and Monica, and even Jimmy, though he rarely paid attention to his mother's rants, were still hearing the story of this Christmas right up until Sydney lost her marbles, of how she gave Farmor the most beautiful mink coat in Copenhagen for Christmas, and Farmor gave it to goddam Nina. Faster Nina, pardon her French. A few years later, when it became possible again to buy new automobiles in Europe, she gave Farmor a brand-new English Ford, and when Ditte gave that to goddam Nina, too, that was it, Sydney was done.

## THE LEEWAY COTTAGE GUEST BOOK

### July 29, 1948

> *Arrived home yesterday, after a delightful jaunt to Denmark and France. It's Jimmy's first summer in Dundee. The birds have gotten most of the raspberries already, but everything else is perfect. Gladdy and Neville had us all to dinner last night and this afternoon we went to Beal Island for a picnic. The last of the old houses out where the town used to be was burned to make way for blueberry barrens. Laurus was with the firemen.*

Many years later when they find the old Guest Book, Eleanor and Monica will note, with tempered amusement, that they hadn't known until then that summer could have a single owner. But if it could and if their mother was in charge, it was no surprise that the owner was Jimmy.

They were late getting to Dundee that summer because Kaj Moss was married in Copenhagen to a plump and sweet-natured girl named Kirsten. The ceremony was at Grundtvig Church in the suburb where Kirsten's family lived, a bizarre-looking thing, Sydney thought, like a nightmare version of a proper Danish church, everything stretched out of proportion. Her neighbor at the wedding lunch, a dazzling older gentleman in a very elegant well-preserved blue suit, a Mr. Bennike (seated with her because of his excellent English) was pleased to discuss it.

No, Mr. Bennike said gravely, the great Grundtvig never saw this church; he died in 1872. The wedding church is a twentieth-century monument. No one outside Denmark knows Grundtvig, do they? Sydney agreed they did not. "Certainly the design is not everybody's taste," said Mr. Bennike. "A Danish version of the architect Gaudi, perhaps—you know the Sagrada Familia in Catalonia?" She didn't, but she smiled and cried, "Aha!" And later, "My friend Neville Crane is an architect. He'll be so interested," she said.

Missing his cue to break off and ask her to tell him all about her interesting friends and her life in the USA, Mr. Bennike then told her at numbing length about some important lectures someone gave about Grundtvig during the war, which sowed the seeds of the Resistance. These lectures woke the sleeping Holger Danske. Which was a mythical giant, apparently, who was supposed to rise up and save Denmark if it was threatened. She didn't really get all of it.

Sydney had enjoyed planning what she would wear to the wedding: now that there was plenty of fabric for clothes again, at least in the States, the New Look was skirts with yards and yards of material swooping around the calves like modern-day hoop skirts. Sydney's was pale lilac with shoes to match. With this she wore an enormous picture hat which blocked her view of almost everything but looked extremely stylish. She finally got tired of not being able to see, though, and took it off at lunch.

It was a hybrid wedding service, with both a minister and a rabbi, and included a part where the groom stepped on a wineglass and broke it on purpose. Eleanor was a flower girl, not that she remembers this but there are pictures to prove it, of her in a sort of dirndl with a wreath of sweet peas on her head. It wasn't a wedding with all the trappings you would have in America. For one thing, there were still many shortages in Denmark, and for another, Danes didn't go in for that sort of thing. The wedding lunch was at the Hotel d'Angleterre, so recently the haunt of the Wehrmacht, and the meal went on and on and *on*, with songs and speeches and endless toasts with champagne and caraway-flavored schnapps, God, was *that* awful stuff. Sydney enjoyed talking with Mr. Bennike, and then with his son Per, who was also very handsome.

"Do you come from a musical family, Mrs. Moss?" Per asked her.

"Sydney. My father was musical, and I sing."

"Delightful. Perhaps you will sing something for us later?"

"I really couldn't," said Sydney. Which Per took gracefully as modesty, though that wasn't what it was. "How about you?"

"Will I sing? You wouldn't like it if I did that."

"No, is your family musical?"

"As listeners only. They are great admirers of your husband's playing." Sydney beamed, and then there was one of those "What now?" pauses.

"So you and Kaj grew up together?" she asked.

"We knew each other. But the families grew closer during the war."

"Oh! Were you in Sweden with Far and Mor?"

"I ended up there, yes."

"Wait! You're the one, aren't you?"

"Possibly." Per smiled.

"I know all about you! You saved them!"

"I did what I could. Many others did more."

"C'mon . . . don't be modest!"

This stopped the conversation for a moment. Per was appalled at the thought of being anything *but* modest. Did Americans think modesty a vice? He had thought only Texas.

"And a man posed as a refugee, and then betrayed you, right?" Sydney had misunderstood his silence.

"Yes," said Per.

"Do you know who he was?"

"Yes."

"What happened to him?"

She expected to be told that no one knew, or that the man had been rewarded by the Nazis and was living in some tropical paradise.

"He was liquidated," Per said.

Sydney was briefly silenced.

"The whole time I was in Sweden I dreamed about killing him," Per said, "but when I returned, it had been done." Sydney was thinking that she couldn't *wait* to get home and be asked how the wedding was. Who would have thought it? These mild, courtly people, a nation of murderers! Later she watched Per talking with Nina, who was wearing a slim and simple dress, looking wanly beautiful. She was thinking so much, though, about how she would tell the story of Per, her Danish hero, that she didn't see the sorrow in his face, the frozen misery in Nina's, as they moved stiffly a little away from the others, talking softly, their bodies not touching.


When the wedding party was finally over Sydney and Laurus went upstairs and slept for hours and it was still broad daylight when they woke up at nine at night, and she never did manage to sleep more than a couple of hours in a row during the whole visit because it was always daylight. It wasn't that the wedding wasn't fun, it was, and Sydney had made a toast at one point inviting everybody there to visit her and Laurus in Dundee, Maine, and welcoming Kirsten to *her* family, too, but just about all the rest of it was in Danish.

After the wedding and the usual round of sights in Copenhagen, they had traveled down to Fyn with Farmor and Farfar and Faster Nina. The little ones loved the ferry across the Storebælt. In Nyborg they slept at the Strand Hotel, but every day after breakfast they walked up the road to the Mosses' cottage on the beach and stayed there until well after supper, just sitting around. Well, there was the beach, and there were trips to market on bicycles, thank God.

They were invited by neighbors for coffee and pastries on several mornings. The neighbors ran American flags up their flagpoles along with the Dannebrog to honor them; every house seemed to have a flagpole, with a crisp red pennant with a white cross flapping in the summer light. Over the pastries everyone made stiff conversation in English, and making it was what it was like, elaborately cobbling at their mental workbenches with their useful little pile of English nails and tiny hammers, all the while smiling their beautiful Danish smiles, until the subject of little Monica's name came up. Then there would be a flurry of rapid Danish, the tone altogether different, in which Sydney came to recognize the words "gudbarn" and "MonicaVickfeld," as Nina explained that her goddaughter was named for the Resistance heroine Baroness Wichfeld, who risked her life of safety and privilege to defy the Nazis, and died in prison in Germany. It had been Laurus's turn to name the baby when Monica was born, and now Sydney was glad. It made her and her children seem less foreign here.

After Denmark, Sydney at last got what she'd wanted all her life, a trip to Paris. Paris in high summer of 1948 with three children in tow, one a four-month-old baby, was perhaps not the Paris of James Brant and Berthe Hanenberger. It was hot and Sydney's French wasn't nearly as good as she had been led to believe at the Hathaway Brown School. By the time she finally got to Dundee, her universe felt not larger but much smaller. She had discovered she was not a citizen of the world, as Laurus was. She was not a musician anymore, and she was fluent in one language, period. Her husband was Danish, her children were half Danish, but she was American. And American was a great thing to be. The best thing to be. There was no reason for her ever to go anywhere where she felt diminished or off balance or bored. She had a great time in Dundee that August, surrounded by people who knew exactly who she was and why it mattered. She enjoyed the surprise and interest she saw in Neville Crane's eyes, when he said, "What did you think of the famous

Grundtvig Church?" And she said, "It's like what's-his-name, Gaudi's, Sagrada Familia. Only Danish." Neville sat with her for a long time that evening, with his handsome face bent toward hers, telling her his theories of sacred architecture. Sydney watched the sunburnt triangle at the open neck of his shirt.

Back in New York that fall, when she'd gone to one too many wine and cheese parties after yet another concert of old chestnuts or tedious new music, and seen the glazed look come into some artiste's eyes when he turned to her and asked, "And what do *you* do?," it all felt a little too much like a wedding in Denmark. Sydney announced that New York City was no place to be raising three children, and they must move to Connecticut.

Everything was in boxes. Boxes going to Connecticut, boxes going to West Eighty-sixth Street. The children were in Dundee, at The Elms, with a nanny and two girls from the village to keep them out of Nana's hair. Sydney, dressed in dungarees with a smear of grime along her chin, paced in and out of emptied rooms waiting for the moving van, while Laurus and two of his students carried boxes of his clothes, piano scores, books, and bedding out to a rented truck. The moving van still hadn't arrived when the boys went out with the last of their load, a large oriental carpet Sydney had given Laurus for their anniversary, and a ficus tree in a terracotta pot. They shoved these into the back of the truck, slammed the back doors shut, climbed into the cab with Laurus, and drove away.

Sydney wandered from room to room, looking at a life that had just days ago been full of colors and curves and softness, now transformed into squared-off heaps of dun-colored cardboard blocks. She couldn't even call the moving company to find out where the van was; the phone had been disconnected. The heat of late June was pillowy and dense. She needed a bath, but all the towels were packed.

*     *     *

It was late afternoon when the boys finished carrying Laurus's boxes in from the elevator on Eighty-sixth Street, thanked Mr. Moss for generous tips, and left to return the truck. The only thing that was where Laurus wanted it was his piano, which two men the size of refrigerators had carried out of Perry Street yesterday and delivered here this morning. He supposed the piano bench was somewhere. Meanwhile boxes of books that belonged in the study were in the bedroom and boxes of clothes were in the Pullman kitchen, and boxes of music were everywhere. There was a sofa in the front room that Sydney hadn't wanted, but he couldn't sit on it; the cushions were packed. He had the beginning of a headache but he had no idea where his wash kit, with the little bottle of aspirin, might be.

To be back in a rented apartment, alone, with his life in boxes and nothing in the refrigerator, reminded him of the night that seemed a world away, when he and Imre Benko drank beer at the oompah joint, and Imre told him there was a voice student at Mannes who would pay an accompanist. He knew Imre had survived the war and was back in Budapest, but he hadn't seen him, and didn't know if he ever would again.

It was possible, barely, to remember Sydney as a girl he had just met. A girl he thought he could see—but they were both so young. He could see her so much more clearly now, recognize that he had taken parts of things for the whole of her. Perhaps it was the same with her. No one had intended to deceive. Very likely all marriages are like that, though if he thought of his parents' marriage, he couldn't see beyond the charmed surface. Did Henrik and Ditte ever quarrel or make each other unhappy? He couldn't imagine it. He thought of his own marriage as if they had been two people on a balance scale, each hovering about level as they studied each other, discovered things that surprised or delighted, as they fell in love. But when he had thrown his marriage vows into Sydney's scale pan, her side had begun to dip. And somewhere during the war years, when his attention was elsewhere, her dish of weights had gotten so full of must and should and want to and can't and won't that it had plunged toward the ground, leaving Laurus's light and amiable dish of can, and have, and why not, swinging in the breeze. She had the money.

She had the three children. She had the moods and the hurts and the big vision of herself that had to be seen by others the way she saw it, or something really bad would happen. Life was full of surprises.

Laurus was stretched out asleep on his half-unrolled carpet, with his sweater for a pillow, when Sydney finally let herself in. He woke at the sound of her key in the lock and sat up, taking in the twilight sky outside.

"*God,* that was boring," said Sydney.

"What time did they finally get there?"

"I don't know, I packed all the clocks."

"I can't find my toothbrush."

"I'm not surprised. They were quite sweet really. They'd gotten lost trying to get into Manhattan from New Jersey. Then they got stopped for driving a truck on the East River Drive—"

"They *were* lost."

"Yes. Who knows if we'll ever see our stuff again, they're probably in Virginia by now, trying to find New England. Did you have a good nap?"

"I'm a little stiff."

"Did you dream?" She always asked him this. Unlike hers, his dreams were so playful.

"No. Yes . . ." He thought a minute. "Yes, as you came in I was just dreaming I'd been crowned Queen of the May."

Sydney roared with laughter, one of Laurus's favorite sounds in the world. She looked around at the mess of half-empty boxes. "Did you get the bed set up?"

"No, I couldn't do it without you. I found the sheets, though."

"That's all we need. Let's go eat, I am faint with hunger."

The thing about the period you grow up in is, you're a child. You have no knowledge that history exists. You think it's the world, you don't know it's the fifties.

Eleanor, Monica, and James Brant Moss lived in a big white clapboard house with fieldstone walls bracing the rolling lawns. They had a small swimming pool, a child-sized wooden roller coaster on the lawn, and a full complement of bicycles, skates, badminton and croquet equipment. A family of boys lived a few minutes' bike ride up the lane, and on evenings and weekends there was always a quorum of kids at the Mosses' house for sardines or kick-the-can or spud. In the winters or on rainy days, they turned over the living room furniture and made blanket forts (the other parents in town were very happy to have this going on at the Mosses' house and not their own).

A lot of their games were war games. One boy had a life-sized dummy German Luger, and everyone had cap guns. But they were all experts at making explosive gun noises with their mouths, so anyone with a thumb and forefinger was armed. They watched *Captain Video* and *Howdy Doody* on a tiny black-and-white television screen in an enormous case, and sent away boxtops for things like secret

decoder rings that glowed green in the dark if you held them under a
lamp first and then wore them into the closet.


All three Moss children studied piano. Eleanor dutifully worked
through her Thompson piano books, with some talent but no interest. As soon as she had done her forty-five minutes after school, she
was off down the lane on her bike in search of company. Monica had
to be nagged all week to practice. "You don't know how lucky you
are," Sydney would announce angrily, as if she had personally carried coal scuttles barefoot through snow in childhood to earn these
luxuries for her daughter. "There are children in China who don't
have enough to *eat,* let alone piano lessons." Monica mostly kept her
head down, her shoulders drawn in, hoping her mother would tire of
prodding an inert substance, so she could go back to *The Black Stal-
lion.* She had learned passive resistance as her only defense the morning that, under the spell of some spunky defiance shown by
Pocahontas or Cherry Ames, Visiting Nurse, in a book she was
reading, she had said, "If you think piano lessons are so great, why
don't *you* take them?" She had to walk into her third-grade classroom
a half hour later with her eyes swollen and a clear red handprint on
her cheek. She learned two lessons that day. First, that challenging
her mother's idées fixes about how her children should live their
lives did not improve matters. Second, that if anyone in this town
thought the Moss children shouldn't be whacked at will, they were
keeping quiet about it. Not a question was asked, nor a word spoken,
about the flaming mark on Monica's face. She wondered if anyone
ever told her father about these and many similar moments in their
childhoods, but to that she never learned the answer. She went on
joylessly with her music lessons until she left for boarding school.
     By contrast, as a toddler, Jimmy used to sit on his father's lap for
hours while Laurus played, feeling the leg muscles flex with the ped-
aling, feeling how the whole body went into making the noise. Before he had language for it, Jimmy was moved by the light and dark
colors of the sounds, the shapes of the floods of music his father produced; it was a river he was born knowing how to swim in. He un-

derstood playing as a motion that started from the center of the body and radiated out of the hands and feet and into the machine of wood and wire and ivory. He saw it as magic and power; he felt about driving that piano the way other little boys felt about trucks or trains. And he was deeply musical. By the time he was four he could repeat, note perfect, pieces he'd heard once, so that it seemed he must be reading, though he wasn't. He couldn't read "Jump, Spot," and he certainly couldn't read *Für Elise.* Sydney was convinced he was another Mozart.

Sydney rejoiced at what her husband was passing on to their children, but she *had* been afraid her hearty and sporty neighbors wouldn't know what to make of Laurus. Not that she wanted a husband who drank too much or chased women or wore loud pants, but she wanted him to fit in. Sydney worked like an animal, as she put it, to join the country club and tennis ladder and volunteer for every possible committee, to make the Mosses a force in this town. So she was thrilled when Peg Barker said one day, "Now your husband, Sydney . . . he's a real man's man."

"It's wonderful, the way he's made a place for himself," chimed in a woman named Marjorie. Meaning, in spite of being arty and foreign, which the women liked, but were surprised that their husbands did too. (They didn't know about the half-Jewish part; they might not have liked that so much.)

"He must miss New York," Peg said. It was during a break in contract bridge; one of the girls in their foursome was extremely gravid and had to answer a sudden call of nature.

"Not at all," said Sydney. "He keeps his apartment in town. He can be there as much as he needs to be. But he says he had enough of being away from home all those years during the war. He says he decided then that what he wanted from life was a happy family."

The war years. The women nodded. The war explained most things they didn't understand about their husbands. It was a mystery box in the back of their mental closets, into which they put all kinds of things. "It must be so interesting, being married to an artist."

"Yes," said Sydney. Being married to an artist meant having a husband who can be looking right at you and yet be a thousand miles away, playing through that moody adagio in his brain while you're talking to him, but there was no point explaining it. Being married to an artist meant having the bedside light go on at two A.M., and when the next morning you read what he has scrawled, hoping for a revealing dream or a reminder to take the car for an oil change, you found "Presto! not Allegro! 3d movement, to the repeat."

"So . . . performing? He just gave that up?" Peg asked.

Was there a needle concealed somewhere in the folds of this question? That she'd been selfish in making her husband move to the country? Sydney could spot criticism of herself the way an X-ray machine sees through flesh.

"He performs more than he wants to," said Sydney, lighting a cigarette. "He prefers the preparation. He's preparing some Lukas Foss right now and he's happy as a clam, even though it sounds like a tray of dishes being dropped down the stairs. And he loves his students here, they're so grateful to work with someone of his caliber. He has a private student right here as good as anyone at Mannes. Your deal, partner," she added to their pregnant companion, who sank back into her chair and took up the deck.

"My husband is going to ask Laurus to join the board of the YMCA," said Peg as the cards were served around. "Don't tell him I told you." Peg's husband was one of those men who was at the center of things no matter where he was. He did something on Wall Street, and practically owned Nantucket.

Sydney, thrilled, rushed home to tell Laurus immediately. She felt she'd won a long and difficult campaign. "When George Barker asks you to join his board, you know you've arrived."

"I'm glad to hear that," Laurus said gravely. "I wouldn't want to fall out of the train before we got to the station."

She looked at him to see if this was a joke, or what. It probably was. Danes were always joking.

When Jimmy was eight, the fact that he still couldn't read "Jump, Spot!" was beginning to be more important than his being a musical prodigy. You could go a long way in this world without playing Rachmaninoff, but you couldn't get far if you couldn't read.

In fact, a strange thing had developed from Jimmy's unusual gift. Rather than making him feel specially blessed, it had made him furious. Music came to him the way water falling over a cliff becomes a waterfall, and it no longer interested Jimmy, any more than the waterfall interests the cliff. He'd rather have been eight feet tall, or strong as Superman, or able to fly. Of course he wanted to be special, he wanted to be admired and feared, but he didn't want to sit all day in goddam school, where even ordinary difficulty in learning new things seemed to him like trudging in lead boots through hot tar. He'd had the experience of being born knowing, and he thought all learning should be like that. At least for him.

"He *is* one of the youngest in the class," said Mr. Blodgett, the headmaster of their little Country Day School. Mr. Blodgett sat behind his big desk and Jimmy's teacher sat on a chair positioned as if she were ready to dive for cover if Mrs. Moss opened fire.

Sydney sat spinning the diamond she wore with her wedding ring around and around her finger. She had not expected ever to be told a child of hers should be held back, and she wasn't pleased. She had just spent the best part of the spring organizing a Parents Talent Show for this school. She'd been in the building every day for weeks, no one could have mentioned there was a problem?

"And he's a little small for his age. We think it would do him good to be a social leader. He'd have an advantage in sports too." Oh, did he need one? He was a spaz as well as a retard? Mr. Blodgett could see That Look in Mrs. Moss's eyes.

"This child is a prodigy," said Sydney, her voice alarmingly soft.

"He certainly is, at the piano. Quite amazing," said Mr. Blodgett. "Maybe we should just go over some of his math and reading home-work, though, to give you an idea."

Laurus looked it all over quietly. He was a source of great curios-ity to the teachers. In the faculty room it was said that Sydney and Laurus Moss were like a tiger and a zebra married to each other. What *were* those two doing together? Did Mr. Moss even know what his wife was like with people who couldn't defend themselves? One of the teachers who had Jimmy in kindergarten had taken to telling homeroom teachers to be sure to keep a raw chicken to toss at her if Mrs. Moss started to pace at parent conferences.

Laurus asked some questions. He noticed that when Jimmy wrote anything at all, he used the space on the page very strangely, cramp-ing his numbers together in odd places instead of on the lines pro-vided, as if the empty sheet looked like a minefield to him and he were forced to compress himself around the edges to avoid some-thing fearful.

Mr. Blodgett agreed it was odd. He had no idea what if anything it meant, except that Jimmy had learned bung-all about arithmetic this year and would be in worse shape if they passed him to the Green Level and he had to do long division.

Sydney and Laurus left this meeting in separate cars, as he had a lesson to give and she had a golf match. As she wound through the leafy byways to the club, rich with the emerald green of early sum-mer and the smell of moist earth, she thought about having to tell all her cheery pals her son had been left back. And Jimmy himself would be shamed and furious, she expected, and have to make all new younger friends. There are no stupid people on Laurus's side, none. I suppose these dumb genes are supposed to be from *my* family. And they probably are, too. Goddam Candace.

That night they broke the news to Jimmy, who looked at his sneakers and said not a word while Sydney cooed the news to him. Then he went down to the playroom and colored all over the pages of Monica's treasured copy of *King of the Wind*. Sydney made all Jimmy's favorite food for supper, as if it were his birthday, lamb chops and mashed potatoes and floating island. Later when Monica appeared in the doorway of the den weeping, with her spoiled book in her hand, Jimmy burst in after her crying angrily, "It was an accident!"

Monica, too enraged to speak, turned the pages, holding the book toward her mother. The Godolphin Arabian's noble eyes, his delicate flared nostrils, had been ferociously scarred with orange and purple attack weapons.

"Oh, leave your brother alone, Monica, he's had a bad day."

A strangling cry for justice rose from her throat.

"I said *leave him alone,* Monica!" Sydney snapped. "Act your age!"

After a stunned moment, both children stomped out of the room. Monica, who had never, that she could remember, been either the oldest or youngest, wanted to kill somebody when she heard that particular phrase. Whatever age she was supposed to act was not ever the age it was convenient to be.

Afterward, left alone together in the pine-paneled den lined with book sets and stacks of *American Heritage* magazine, Sydney saw that Laurus was looking at her, with that mild expression that meant he was thinking things he would rather not say out loud. As if he were wondering, "Who *are* you?"

She did not want to talk about it. She knew it wasn't fair, but when she looked at those two stormy faces, her differently loved children before her, it was as if some vast desire took over her brain and did what it wanted, blotting out reason. It was the way she was, there was no point in revisiting the moment now that it had passed.

"They'll both have forgotten it in the morning," she said, with a dismissive wave of one hand.

## THE LEEWAY COTTAGE GUEST BOOK

July 2, 1956

> *Jimmy and I drove up last night,* wrote Sydney, *and had first-night dinner with the Cranes as always. Gorgeous weather and everything looks the same. Ellen Chatto is living in this year. She is having an ugly divorce and she feels safer here. Eleanor is at summer camp and Laurus has taken Monica to Denmark. Al from Plumbing and Heating tells me that something fell in the well and died, so we're filling jugs from the town pump for drinking water at the moment. Lovely to be here.*

Jimmy stayed home with Ellen the next night while Sydney went to dinner at The Elms. Her mother was in rare form and Bernard was better than he'd been in years. The doctors had made him stop smoking, which he hated. "And he was a beast the whole time," said Candace, spooning her soup. "Weren't you, darling."

"I thought I behaved very well," said Bernard.

"You're lucky you have any friends left at all," said Candace, and the Maitlands laughed. Sydney looked up surprised, and noticed something that had eluded her. Her mother and Bernard actually loved each other. How, she couldn't imagine.

"Now tell us all your news, darling," said Candace. She had a way of turning the attention to Sydney at the exact moment that she had a plate of hot food in front of her and wanted to be left alone to eat. Sydney looked with regret at the delicious-looking pile of lobster Newburg she'd just dumped onto her plate, and rose to the bait.

"Laurus has taken home leave," she said. "Monica went with him, to spend the month at the beach with her grandparents." She deliberately said this as if her children only had *one* proper set of grandparents.

"And Eleanor?"

Bernard's adoration of Eleanor was undimmed by the fact that she was growing pudgy hips and breasts and a fascination with hairstyles.

"She's at *that age*," said Sydney. "Too old for camp really, too young for a job. She'll do one month at camp with her best friend, as CITs, and then they'll both come up for August."

"And Jimmy?"

"Most adorable-*looking* little boy . . ." put in Mrs. Maitland, chewing.

"You know, he was an April baby. One of the youngest in his class and he's small, too. We thought, you know, what *is* the rush here? Let's hold him back for the class he probably should have been in all along, and let him be the oldest and one of the biggest. Fortunately, the school thought we were absolutely right."

A brief silence.

"And is *he* happy about it?"

"Jimmy? Oh sure, he's the Go-along-get-along Kid." Having dispatched the subject with this spectacular piece of misinformation, she addressed herself to her cooling Newburg, which was beginning to look like library paste.

It was Amelia Crane, Gladdy's daughter, who began tearfully referring to Jimmy Moss as "Crash," because his way of barging at the start of a sailing race, or disputing buoy room, was to yell ferociously at the boat he was fouling and ram it if it didn't yield. Other boats protested him race after race, and he usually lost, but it didn't make the other children feel better. Sydney contended he was just learning to be a good, aggressive little competitor, but by the end of July, half the yacht club was referring to her son as "Crash" and she held it against young Amelia. It was said by some that Sydney had in semiprivate remarked that Amelia Crane had always been a whiner. If Gladdy heard it, she never ever treated her friend with anything but steady, cheerful affection. In later years it seemed completely forgotten, but there was a time that summer when there was a certain strain in the friendship.

# THE LEEWAY COTTAGE GUEST BOOK

> *We have had a splendid visit. Barring only the fa-*
> *mous absence of cloudberries, we felt completely at*
> *home. The view from Butter Hill is gorgeous; we look*
> *forward to next year!*
>
> *—Per Bennike*

> *—And we hope you will visit us someday in Hornbæk!*
> *With warmest thanks for a delightful week—*
>
> *—Britt-Marie Bennike*
> *Aug. 16, 1956*

In the margins, Britt-Marie had drawn a beautiful picture of the bald eagle they had seen in flight over the bay while sailing one after-noon. She also drew a little family of harbor seals sunning them-selves on Tide Rock.

Per and Britt-Marie were Sydney's idea of perfect houseguests. They spoke perfect English, they entertained themselves all day, Per sailed expertly, and Britt-Marie played good tennis. Further, they were good company when carried off to a picnic or dinner with a lot of Sydney's lifelong friends who happily laughed and teased and gos-siped among themselves as they had every summer since they were children, treating outsiders exactly as they treated each other, as if guests were bound to enjoy immersion in their own narrow summer world, but also as if they had known these newcomers since child-hood and fully expected to know them for the rest of their lives.

It was not every visitor who enjoyed this treatment. Some felt it skipped several stages of formality that upset the natural order and robbed the shy or reserved of necessary decorum, others that it was bloody boring to be expected to take an interest in who was related to whom and oft-told tales about eccentric characters or comic events from the dim past. But some felt there was nothing more fun than a place at the table where food, affection, high spirits, and good-will abounded and all you needed was enjoyment of a joke and a rea-sonable sense of self-deprecation to be wholly welcome. Per and

Britt-Marie fit right in. Per was handsome with a dry, Laurus-like sense of humor. Britt-Marie won herself many fans by being smart and funny and rather dumpy.

At their first Dundee dinner party, Britt-Marie announced firmly that there was a ghost in the guest wing at Leeway. Sydney denied it; Britt-Marie insisted. It flushed the toilet in the middle of the night when she was in bed and Per was beside her and everyone else was upstairs. It smoked cigars outside her window and it rearranged her books. And it spoke Swedish. It was only the Swedish books that it took an interest in.

"Isn't it scary, though?" asked Lucie Cochran Maitland.

"No, of course it isn't scary. It's not as if it spoke German," she said. There were roars of laughter, and the talk turned, as it so often did, to Dundee history. Someone always told the story of the house around the other side of the bay that had once been out on Beal Island, that had a ghost so angry and frightening that the owners gave it to the Dundee fire department, who burned it down.

"Really! A perfectly good house?"

"Laurus was with them," said Sydney.

"You were?"

"No I wasn't, it was before I joined. But Mutt Dodge was. He swears that when the house was engulfed he saw a figure inside, at the upstairs window, trying to get out. He almost had to quit fire-fighting he was so upset."

"And there was no one there."

"No, of course. They had searched every inch of the house beforehand. And they searched the ashes afterward."

"Ooooo, *creepy,*" someone always said, delighted.

Per and Britt-Marie had met in Stockholm during the war. She teased him charmingly about how it had taken him six years to come courting her. "Holding a torch for someone else, I think . . ." she would say.

"No, just stupid," Per always replied.

Britt-Marie was posted to the Swedish delegation at the U.N.

Per had had two novels published in Denmark and was at work on a third, writing in English. They said they loved New York.

"Americans are so welcoming. Very accepting," Per said.

This delighted the Americans, since it was a nice thing to say and also just what they thought themselves. Sydney insisted on introducing Per as "our friend Per I'm-No-Hero Bennike"; she had told all about the part he'd played in rescuing Laurus's parents, but if anyone mentioned it, he brushed it aside. At a party toward the end of their visit, Ned Maitland called down the table to Per, "All right, you Danes, let's have it, it's time. We want to know how you saved the Jews, without being heroes."

Per looked across the table at Laurus.

"There has to be an answer," said Elise. "What is it about Denmark?"

"There *is* an answer," Britt-Marie said, clearly implying that if the Danes were too modest to talk about it, a *Swede* wasn't.

"Denmark is a small country . . ." said Per, and was surprised when everyone laughed. One of Sydney's routines was that when you asked a Dane anything, he started by saying that Denmark is a small country.

"Well, it is," Laurus put in. "It's small and there are national traits. Danes love peace. And they love comfort, and they'll sacrifice a lot for them. But they cannot enjoy peace and comfort while behaving badly. Also, they have great respect for each other. They trust each other to behave. So when they saw that they had to, they all acted the same way out of simple pride, and assumed their fellow Danes would do the same."

"It was a matter of self-respect. Their sense of their own identity," added Per I'm-No-Hero.

"If *that* isn't the most Danish thing you ever heard in your life . . ." said Sydney.

When Gladdy and Neville were brushing their teeth that night, she said, "Weren't you interested in what Laurus said tonight?" She was wearing an old pair of Neville's pajamas. The bathroom, wainscotted with layers of white paint chipping in places, showing the original ancient blue beneath, smelled of soap.

"I *was*," said Neville. "What did you think?" She rinsed her mouth but did not move away from the basin.

"What I was thinking," Gladdy said, "was that I finally understood that marriage." Their eyes met in the mirror for a moment before she turned, touching him fondly on the butt, as he stepped to the sink and she left the room.

Laurus enjoyed the Bennikes' visit very much. On rainy days, he and Britt-Marie would go through the upstairs shelves and cabinets of Leeway looking for Swedish artifacts left by the Eggerses. They found many works of Emmanuel Swedenborg; someone in the family must have been a devotee. Britt-Marie's favorite uncle was Swedenborgian. The more she talked about it, the more interested Laurus became, and the more (she claimed) the cigar-smoking phantom would leave olfactory signs of his presence, which, she added, was palpably benign. This disappointed young Jimmy of course, who would have preferred blood and guts and rattling chains in the spare rooms.

As a man's man, which Laurus truly was, he also relished having his countryman to talk to. One afternoon when Sydney and Britt-Marie were playing tennis, Per came out to join Laurus in the garage behind the house where he was wrestling with the outboard motor from his dinghy. It hadn't run right all summer, so he and Per had carried it up from the dock, and now Laurus had it clamped to a rain barrel with the screw in the water and the housing off. He was happily puttering.

"Goddag," said Per, and Laurus answered him in Danish, hardly aware that he'd done it. They had taken care to speak English throughout the visit so that Sydney would not feel left out. Laurus gave a mighty pull at the engine's starter cord and it screamed to life, making a piercing racket and churning the barrel to a froth before it coughed and died.

"You cleaned the spark plug?" Per asked.

"Sure."

They peered together into the Evinrude guts. "Must be the timing chain," Laurus said.

"Yes," said Per. And then, as Laurus set to work, Per settled down on a crate and said carefully, "Tell me—how is your sister?"

Laurus looked up at him. "You aren't in touch?"

"Not since we moved to New York."

There was a pause. "Not much has changed. She's got her doctorate. She teaches French."

"At university?"

"Gymnasium, like Papa. She likes the seventeen-, eighteen-year-olds."

"Like herself, before she went away."

"Yes. She goes to France every summer and comes home thinner than when she left. I keep hoping someone will reach her. That she'll meet a man."

Per looked at his shoes. "Has she ever told you what happened to her?"

Laurus shook his head.

There was a pause. "And would it do us any good to know?"

Laurus was still for a moment. It felt different, to be talking of this in his own language, and to someone who (he was pretty sure) had loved Nina once. "I'll tell you what I think," he said. "I think that if God *is* God, and He's also good, His ruling love is curiosity. It would explain so much evil. He *can't* interfere, He can only watch, and love, and wait to see how it comes out. So *He* knows what she saw, and to Him it means something we can't know about."

"It's very hard, not knowing," said Per. "Not being able to help."

"Very."

Per said, "When we go to God, if we do, do we find out finally all the things we didn't understand?"

Laurus said, "That's my theory exactly. Being with God will mean understanding all the things that were hidden."

"Then heaven will be a sad place."

"I don't think so. I think it will bring us peace. It will be like watching the movie of your life but all the stories will have endings."

As Sydney's station wagon crunched into the driveway and parked under the huge oak, Laurus added, "If death didn't bring peace, there'd be a lot more upset ghosts around than your wife's cigar-smoker."

As her door slammed, Sydney called, "Okay, we found you. We know you're in there talking about our bra sizes."

"Actually," said Laurus, "I was just explaining heaven to Per."

"Per already knows about heaven," said Britt-Marie. The two women glowed with recent exertion as they approached. "It's in the shape of the Grand Man."

"No," said Per, "it's in the shape of a movie theater. Laurus says we each get to see our own movie in heaven, and in it we'll see everything that was hidden before."

"Good," said Britt-Marie to Laurus, "then maybe I'll understand how your damn wife managed to beat me in straight sets."

"That's your idea of heaven?" Sydney asked Laurus. "I can't even get you to go to the movies now."

"Well, after the movie there will be dinner and dancing," said Laurus.

"Listen," said Per to Laurus. "If you get to see the movie before I do, will you find a way to let me know how it comes out?"

Sydney saw something pass between them she didn't understand.

"A heavenly postcard?" Laurus suggested.

"Guys, come on," she said. "Let's go fall into a pitcher of gin and tonic." The two women started for the house, and Sydney looked back to be sure the men were coming.

## THE LEEWAY COTTAGE GUEST BOOK

July 15, 1958

*The Bennikes are back! They drove up from Boston last night and got here in time for Ellen's fish chowder and blueberry muffins. They've brought their adorable little twin babies, Hanne and Inge, born on Christmas Day!* Lovely *to have them here.*

"Just adorable," Sydney said, holding baby Inge and pushing her nose against the baby's nose, saying, "Gugugugugah! Are they family names? Hanne and Inge?"

Britt-Marie looked at Per, who answered, "They're named for some girls I met during the war."

"Oh, that's lovely, you know our Monica is named for Monica Wichfield," said Sydney. "AAAaghgugugugugug!" And she wiggled her face down into the baby's. "Are they identical?"

"No," said Britt-Marie.


The Bennike family was in the upstairs guest room this year. This was so they could hear the babies from the dining or living room if they cried, which they could not have done if the babies were off in the guest wing. Also, because Eleanor was fifteen this year and she and her best friend, Janet, were spending their summer in Dundee getting their driver's licenses. Janet and Eleanor had a portable record player and a great many records the grown-ups did not care to hear over and over ("To KnoooowKnoooowKnooow him, is to Luuv-LuuvLuh-uve him . . .") so the guest wing was a far better place for them than upstairs.

Eleanor and Janet were the envy of their friends at home. Maine allowed licenses very young, as many farm children needed to drive tractors and such, sometimes on public roads. The girls already had their learner's permits, and vied with each other to be allowed to drive Laurus or Sydney into town to Abbott's or the drugstore. The rest of the time they lay on the lawn or the beach, slathered in baby oil tinted with iodine, holding batwing reflectors under their chins to accelerate their tans. In the evenings, if they didn't have to babysit, they went with Eleanor's crowd of friends to moonlight picnics on Beal Island, or to the drive-in up in Trenton with the glamorous older crowd (usually with about eight of them in one car), or zipped back and forth across the bay in Eleanor's outboard, to friends' cottages to play poker or spin the bottle or to climb Butter Hill in the dark. On afternoons when there was nothing else to do, they would take the outboard and a stack of *True Romance* magazines out to the middle of the bay and drift around, smoking cigarettes and reading, and roasting marshmallows stuck on pencils over purloined kitchen matches. They came home in the evening burnt, sticky, and stinking of smoke; it was blissful.

They were the envy of Monica because they had freedom and breasts and were developing boyfriends. They were the envy of Jimmy because they had the outboard, and matches, and they didn't have to go to goddam camp all summer. Jimmy and Monica both did have to.

Which it turned out wasn't all bad, as they missed the brunt of the major Sydney firestorm of the summer. Eleanor caught most of it, but just to watch was something Janet never forgot, Sydney savaging Eleanor for something they had done together, as Janet sat on the other bed in their little room staring at her sneakers and listening to invective pelting on Eleanor's head and shoulders. When, late in the summer, some of the boys stole a sign from the French camp down the Neck, and Eleanor and Janet hid it for them under a bed and Sydney found it, she swelled up and raged so terribly that Janet was afraid she might actually beat them, which Eleanor said had been known to happen. But by the next day Sydney smiled and joked as if nothing had happened and she had no idea why they were cowering from her. And maybe she didn't.

The cause of Sydney's hair-trigger emotional state was this. (If you didn't count the fact that Eleanor and Janet had breasts and freedom and maybe boyfriends and Sydney had other things but, except for the breasts, not those, and she'd never had an easy time with people having things she didn't.) Bernard, whom Sydney had in a sarcastic way grown rather fond of, had had a mild stroke in the spring, and he was having trouble with stairs. They had installed a staircase lift in the house in Cleveland, and could easily do that here, too, but had not yet; instead, Bernard's bedroom had been moved downstairs for this summer. Sydney explained all this to the Bennikes as they drove over to pay their duty call at The Elms.

Bernard and Candace were out on the terrace overlooking the bay. They were playing hearts and drinking sun tea when Sydney led her guests in, hallooing.

"Hello, darling, how nice! Hello, Mr. Bennike, Mrs. Bennike, how nice to see you again!" Candace rose (stiffly) to welcome them.

"You'll forgive an old man for not getting up," called Bernard from his chair. "I would, but I can't." His speech slur was almost unnoticeable.

"Of course," and "Of course not," and "So nice to be here, how are you?" were lobbed back and forth for several minutes until all were settled and a bell was rung for more iced tea and a plate of cookies.

"Now, Mother, did you ever see cuter babies in your life?" Sydney was holding Hanne toward her as if she were a stuffed animal. Britt-Marie was right beside her with Inge. "They're twins."

"Oh, aren't they precious? Look at the cunning little fingers! Are they twins?"

"Yes."

"Are they identical?"

"They're identical, aren't they?" Sydney asked Britt-Marie.

"No."

"But so much alike, aren't they too cute?"

Bernard was holding out his arms, his smile almost one of longing, and Britt-Marie handed her bundle to him. The baby settled into his arms and he began talking quiet nonsense to her while Sydney watched, pleased. Wasn't that just typical? It was Bernard, the fussy old bachelor, who truly loved babies, while showing one to her mother was like handing a kitten to someone who hates cats. Such a private pleasure.

They had a very nice visit, filled with an update of the Bennikes' situation, Per's new book, a bigger apartment (Well, I should hope so! With twins!). And Sydney had a lot to tell Candace and Bernard about the Cluett Cup dinner at the yacht club she was running, and about Mrs. Maitland getting cross with Homer Jellison that her dining room chairs had not been recaned in spite of a wait of three years. "Why, Mrs. Maitland, if I had known you were so drove up about them chairs . . ." he had said indignantly.

They took themselves off when Velma tottered in to indicate she was ready to serve Mr. and Mrs. Christie their lunch. They had a lovely sail that afternoon while Eleanor and Janet stayed with the napping babies. When they got home, without even being asked to do it, Eleanor and Janet went off on their bikes to have tea at The Elms. Sydney took deep breaths as if inhaling pleasure as she moved around the Leeway kitchen rattling the end of her cocktail in her glass, and heating the dinner Ellen had left ready.

So it was a thunderstroke when they were together around the dining room table, and Sydney called to Eleanor, "Did you girls have a good visit with Nana?," Eleanor said, "Yes! But we're amazed, of course."

Sydney tried to pretend she knew why they would be amazed. She took a swallow of soup; then curiosity got the better of her.

"Amazed?"

"About The Elms."

"Oh. The elevator."

This was a wild guess. But a good one. It had to be either stair lift or elevator; and the guess was worth it, Sydney hated not knowing or seeming to know all the important news before someone else could tell her.

"No," said Eleanor. "That they're tearing it down."

Even Laurus put his spoon down and looked at Sydney, and after a pause for the flame to travel up the wick and get to her, Sydney detonated.

"They are WHAT?"

Eleanor looked a little worried at this reaction. But a glance from Janet confirmed she *had* heard right . . . They both had.

"They're going to tear down the house and build something all on one floor, that Uncle Bernard can get around in . . ."

The look on her mother's face caused Eleanor to subside, though what she'd wanted to say was how cute Nana and Uncle Bernard were about it, how excited to be planning a big new project together.

"She *can't* tear down that house, that's not *her* house! It's *my* house, it's *yours, and Nika's and Jimmy's.* . . ." Sydney roared. "That's *my* grandmother's house, she *built* it, she left it to *my* father, Candace never would have *heard* of Dundee if it weren't for . . . Oh, for *God's* sake . . ." And she ran out of the room with her face in her napkin. You couldn't tell if she was going to cry or throw up.

Eleanor and Janet looked at each other. Per and Britt-Marie looked helplessly at Laurus. Laurus went on with his soup until he had quietly finished it. Then he put his napkin into his napkin ring and said, "Eleanor, would you clear? You all go ahead." And he left the table.

Sydney was in their bedroom, weeping with deep, wracking sobs. Laurus sat beside her and patted her back as she curled in on herself and cried, for her dead father, her miserable childhood, for her grandmother who had loved her but died, and with rage at her *stupid, selfish, unloving, snobbish, fake Southern belle, nobody from nowhere bitch of a mother.* "She's finally done it, just when I thought there was nothing else she could do to me, she's found the way to completely kill me. I didn't think she could, I didn't think she could, I thought we were past this," she sobbed from somewhere inside the coiled whelk she'd made of herself. Then she'd start it again, *stupid, selfish selfish, coldhearted . . .*

Laurus patted her. There was nothing else he could do. If he said, "I'm sure she does love you," it made her madder, and besides, he wasn't certain it was true. Suddenly Sydney said, "I could stop her, you know. Under my father's will. She has no right to do this."

"But you're never going to want to live in it yourself, are you?" Laurus knew she wasn't. She loved Leeway Cottage; The Elms was her past, not her future.

Sydney was trapped, as usual. She most likely *could* stop her mother, with a raft of lawyers, which Candace had probably forgotten. But if she did, she'd be paid back in the coin of her mother's outrage and her husband's diminished respect, and probably be thought behind her back to be a dog in the manger.

After a while he went back down to the table, and he was pleased when Sydney herself reappeared in time for dessert. Her eyes were swollen but she'd washed her face and put on fresh lipstick. She put her chin in the air, took a deep breath, and said, "Well." And gave everyone a big smile. They ate their sherbet and cookies and then settled down in the living room to play Scrabble, while Eleanor and Janet cleared and washed the dishes. Later, tires were heard to crunch in the doorway and the girls went skittering out the back door, letting it slam behind them. Sydney could tell by the sound the engine made that they were off with that boy from the Neck with the ancient black Ford that the children called the Bomb. Nice boy.

Later, in bed, she cried some more, but this time without words, for her summer childhood, her best memories of her father and grandmother, about to be ripped out of the earth like ancient trees. For the fact that even her own children had so much she had never had, a loving mother, a living and sober father, sisters and brothers, *and* all the money and position that had been her only comfort. Laurus patted her.

After that night, she really did seem to have grown a new depth of scar tissue over her heart where her mother was concerned. She dealt with her evenly, calmly, for the rest of the summer, as if she would lose a life-threatening battle if Candace ever guessed how hurt she was. Which for Laurus was a good thing.

The Elms came down in October, and it seemed that half the town went to work building the replacement, to have it ready for Mrs. Christie the next summer. The village buzzed about the design from November to June; the rooms were all strung out on one level, with huge glass sliding doors overlooking the bay, and a shed roof that was practically flat.

"Hell of a strange-looking thing" was Mutt Dodge's opinion. "Can't decide if it wants to be a freight train or the railroad barn." Al Pease was puzzled over installing a bee-day in the master bathroom. "What do you suppose it's for?" he asked. "That you couldn't do in the flush or the sink?" There were plenty of people not far out of town didn't even have their plumbing indoors yet. Now here was a whole new thing for them not to have one of.

THE LEEWAY COTTAGE GUEST BOOK

July 5, 1959

*Arrived in time for Mother's big housewarming. She wants us to call this new thing The Elms, but it should be The Plywoods. It's enough to make you weep.*

Which was hardly a metaphor, as Sydney had wept plenty over it. It had to be admitted that it wasn't just the loss of the old house, which had been a symbol perhaps of regrettable robber baron excess, sure, but as a house it had been gracious, imposing, and based on the best Old World models. So many such houses had already been lost on this coast in the great Bar Harbor fire of 1947, and now another one was gone for No Reason At All. Her mother's new house was not only not gracious, imposing, or curtsying in the direction of Old Europe, it was a triumph of ugliness. And it was in clear sight of the road, where everyone passing had to look at it eight times a day. It was completely out of scale and style with the vernacular architecture, as if it didn't know where it was, and didn't care. Sydney had learned that phrase, "vernacular architecture," from Neville Crane whom she had cornered in her mother's horrible new "library" and forced to state an opinion. If she had been concerned in her heart of hearts that Candace and Bernard might come up with some new miracle of beauty and convenience that would make her dissatisfied with Leeway (and she had been), her fears were put to rest the minute she set foot in Abbott's on her arrival that summer, before she had even seen the new house herself. The town had seen it, and the town really hated it.

They weren't students of Frank Lloyd Wright, or Prairie Style, or any architectural style but their own, which was simple Greek Revival New England farmhouse. But they didn't need to know a two-dollar name for it to know they hated it. Mind you, the town was also prepared to fight fiercely for your right to build anything you wanted on your own land, it was your land and your home was your castle and they had never, up to now, thought they could be made to see two ways on that subject. This was a twentieth-century village with eighteenth-century politics, things had changed so much more slowly here than in the outside world. The word "zoning" had never even come up in town meeting before. It did in March of 1959, though. If a person could build a house like the Christies', why wouldn't somebody want to put in a Dairy Queen on his front lawn? The meeting grew quite hot on the subject when Kermit Horton made a violent speech about how his great-grandfather had settled on Beal Island in 1832 and from that day to this there had never been any interference in what a man did with his own property as long as he didn't kill anybody or poison the waterways. There was no reason to start sticking their noses into other people's business now. Reuben Jellison stood up without being recognized by the first selectman, and said, "Oh, really? I live right next to the Congregational Church, as Kermit Horton well knows. Is it all right with him if I decide to start strip mining? I think I've probably got some pretty good copper in that front field, right down there by Miss Leaf's garden. I don't think she'll mind the noise much, she's gone so deaf..." They had to adjourn for lunch to get people to stop shouting at each other.

Down at Olive's Lunch, during the break, old Carleton Haskell, who was known to begin the morning with a powerful shot of grain alcohol in his coffee before he started out fishing, kept braying that the house was ugly as tunket but that wasn't the nigger in the woodpile. Carleton himself lived in a trailer that wasn't very beautiful, and he didn't figure that was anybody's business but his. The thing everyone was missing was, this was the first time one of them summer complaints had built a house you could live in all winter. The town had gotten used to having them show up in the spring and stay into the fall, and no one wanted to give up the money they gave to the hospital and the library or the taxes on their shorefront property. Sometimes one of 'em would get old and take to bed to die here, but if it took more than a season, they moved into rented rooms in town for the winter and were carted back to their cottages when the weather warmed up. This kind of a thing, though, they build a thing like that with a cellar and furnace and there was nothing to keep them from staying. Retiring for the duration, if they wanted, didn't look to him as if they knocked themselves out working at much that would keep them away. They could start voting at town meeting, putting their kids in the school... next thing there'd be stoplights. A subway to take you from the bank to the grocery store. How were you geniuses going to like that, then?

Carleton Haskell was mean enough when sober, certainly no one was going to argue with him drunk, or even pay much attention. He was even right, though he wouldn't live to see it. He wouldn't as a matter of fact live to see Christmas. There were rarely any plumbing facilities on a lobster boat, and most fishermen who fell overboard and drowned had their flies open at the time; the percentage was particularly high among those who fished alone and whose breakfast consisted of spiked coffee. Carleton Haskell's trailer was hauled away by spring and the land allowed to revert to meadow. The new Christie house was, however, there to stay.

Nineteen fifty-nine was the year Sydney turned forty. She had never looked better, as she vividly knew. Her health was robust, her golf game was terrific, her elderly relatives were able to care for and amuse themselves, and so, at eleven, fourteen, and going on seventeen, were her children. Eleanor had an au pair job down on the Cape this sum-mer but she and her bunch would all be back by the end of August to spend a week or two falling in and out of love with each other. Mon-ica was having her last year at camp. (Monica loved camp, which made Sydney impatient. The kind of girls in her childhood who loved camp and were good at it were also the kind who had never been nice to *her*.) Jimmy was in Dundee, going to Scamp Camp in the mornings and tutoring with Mr. Jellison from the academy in the afternoons. The Leeway family went to The Plywoods every Sunday for lobster Newburg after church, but that was pretty much the extent of oner-ous family obligations that summer. As the August racing series approached, Sydney and Neville and Gladdy Crane decided one evening, after a lot of wine, to charter the Cochrans' International and race together that season. The boat wasn't very fast, but they had a wonderful time. They sang barbershop harmony during the doldrums. One race Sydney brought a handful of screws and nuts in her pocket and threw them against Ned Maitland's mainsail as the fleet rounded a mark; when they heard stray hardware rattling into the cockpit, Ned and Lucie thought their sail was falling down.

The cockpit of a racing boat is an intimate place. The skipper, or "the nut holding the tiller," as they called her (Gladdy in this case), devotes total attention to the course, the sails, and the maneuvers of

the other boats, trusting her crew to act and react without having to
be asked or told. Sydney and Neville were on the jib, with Neville
letting off sail on one side as Sydney trimmed in on the other, Neville
knowing she needed the winch handle before she had to ask for it,
four hands hauling the same sheet when it was too much for two to
do alone. On spinnaker legs one trimmed the guy, the other the
sheet, standing shoulder to shoulder with eyes never leaving the bal-
loon of sail, lest an edge flutter lead to a curl and then to collapse of
the chute. Rufus Maitland, their young muscle, took care of the
mainsail. When they rounded the leeward mark, as soon as the jib
was hoisted and trimmed, they were crouched together on the floor-
boards, thrown into the curve of the hull by the angle of heel, sometimes with green water coming over the rail and down their necks,
repacking the spinnaker for a second set, pressed close out of
Rufus's way as he rushed to clear and secured the spinnaker halyard,
pole, and sheets, before they tacked and lost something overboard.
Sydney quoted Neville a lot that summer. "The thing about The Plywoods," she would say, at a Country Club dinner, or the race tea, or
at intermission at Ischl Hall on Sunday afternoons, "is, it shows no
respect for the vernacular architecture. You see. Otherwise I
wouldn't mind so much."

The final race of the series, they sailed the entire course in formal
evening dress. Sydney was wearing a gown of her grandmother
Annabelle's, with a capacious pleated bosom and jet buttons. Gladdy
wore the dress she had worn to Elise Maitland's deb party, with an
evening stole, since she could no longer begin to fasten the dress up
the back. Neville wore his tuxedo jacket and ruffled shirt and a
bathing suit, which caused everyone to whistle and clap for his
shapely legs. Beautiful young Rufus Maitland was also wearing an
ancient evening dress of his grandmother's, a flapper job in yellow.
Bess Maitland complained that he looked better in it than she had.
They didn't sail very well, but it was agreed at the tea, they won on
style hands down.

*     *     *

When Sydney walked in the front door of Leeway, leaving a dripping spinnaker bag on the porch and carrying her foul-weather gear
in her arms, her face was streaked with sun and salt; she was still
wearing the bedraggled evening dress. At the same moment, Laurus
was coming in at the back, so streaked with soot he looked like a
coal miner. They met in the living room, and stared at each other.

Sydney explained the costume. "I've wrecked the hem," she said,
looking down sadly. "Maybe the French laundry in New York can
do something with it. It was a panic, though. What are you dressed
as?"

"There was a fire up by the old Burial Ground. Three-alarmer; I'm
surprised you didn't hear the sirens."

"We must have already gone to sea. Was anyone hurt?"

"A horse stepped on Al Pease's foot. Could be broken. We got
all the animals out of the barn, though, and saved the house."

"Whose house?"

They were on their way upstairs, Sydney peeling her finery off
over her head, Laurus taking care not to touch anything with his
blackened clothes.

"Webby Allen's daughter. Too bad—nice young couple."

"That is too bad. You want the shower first?"

"You go ahead. You must be chilled through."

"Thanks."

He sat on the closed lid of the flush to pull off his boots, while
Sydney got the water steaming and stepped into the bathtub. She
pulled the curtain.

Laurus carefully undressed and dropped each garment into the
hamper so he wouldn't get inky soot on the bath mats and towels.
He could tell he smelled like a charred log. In the shower, Sydney
began to sing. Laurus sat naked listening to her. It was one of the
lieder from her student days; she was showing off for him. He was
smiling when she got out of the shower.

When they were both clean and dressed, Sydney said, "Gladdy
and Neville asked us for dinner, her peas are in and they have grilse
in the freezer. Can you?"

"I told Hugh Chamblee I'd help him move a stove." Hugh Chamblee was the new minister at the Congo church. Asking someone to help move a stove was a way a man asked another in for a drink.

Sydney just waited. "But I can tell Hugh another night," said Laurus. Sydney had already told Gladdy they'd be there, so she smiled and went down to give Ellen orders about Jimmy's supper.

In the spring of 1962, Laurus was elected president of the local YMCA board. Also, his prize student won a full scholarship to the Juilliard School in New York, the first of her family to get past high school. "A very talented colored girl," Sydney wrote to her mother. "She's coming to dinner here with her parents next week." (She was only sorry she couldn't be present to watch her mother read the letter.) Eleanor finished her second year at Skidmore College on the dean's list. Monica was at Miss Pratt's, and to her father's satisfaction had an au pair job lined up in Jaderslev, Jutland, working for a married daughter of the Mogens Wessel family, who were so fond of Faster Nina. And Jimmy was expelled from school for the first time.

Jimmy had been in hot water a couple of times already that spring. Laurus was particularly annoyed when Jimmy and his partner in crime since early childhood, who had a real name but was known as Winky, borrowed Laurus's elderly Nash Rambler and drove it down the lane to the cemetery, where, in attempting to learn how to use a stick shift without instruction, they succeeded in stripping out the gears. They left the car in the middle of the cemetery drive, ran home, and tried to establish alibis against the fairly inevitable moment when the car would be found and questions asked.

"I was home! I helped Mom carry the laundry up!"

"He *says* he had nothing to do with it," Sydney added.

Laurus just stared at the two of them.

"And I watered the garden, Mom saw me!"

"So the car drove to the cemetery by itself?"

"Maybe a bum stole it."

There was a long standoff in which Laurus merely looked, mildly but steadily, at Jimmy. If you listened to Sydney you'd have thought that Laurus came and went in an artistic fog, unaware of where the children were or how clean sheets got on the beds or the bills got paid, but now and then, and often at inconvenient moments, one suddenly saw that perhaps this was merely Sydney's version.

"May I ask why you left it in the middle of the road?"

Another long pause. "Winky couldn't get it out of reverse."

Sydney looked at him, surprised. Jimmy had finally dropped his eyes to stare at his sneakers. There was something dark and unpleasant to the shape of his mouth.

"Winky," said Laurus. Silence. "And you didn't think of coming home in reverse?"

"Yes, but we're not that good at backing up."

Sydney had to turn away for fear of laughing, or making Laurus laugh. Although Laurus did not look so tempted.

"And it didn't occur to you to bring the keys with you? You couldn't make it go anymore so who cares if I ever see it again?"

Silence.

"Did it occur to you that you could have had an accident? And you and Winky are underage and unlicensed? And therefore uninsured? Do you know what could have happened to all of us if you had hit someone?"

Silence. It had not, of course, occurred to Jimmy or Winky. After very little more conversation Laurus informed him that he was grounded for two weeks except to go to school, and that if he touched the steering wheel of a car again before he had his learner's permit, he would be even sorrier than he was today. (Jimmy had not mentioned being sorry.) After dinner that night Sydney disappeared with Jimmy into his bedroom, where she listened, murmuring, for a long time to a great deal of complaint.

"You know," she said later to Laurus, "there aren't a lot of thirteen-year-olds who do know about liability insurance."

"Did he know he wasn't allowed to drive?"

"Yes, but—"

She dropped it. And was very satisfactorily appreciated by Jimmy when on Saturday she let him go to the movies in the afternoon, knowing Laurus was in New York and wouldn't be home until Monday. Just their little secret.

On a Monday afternoon in May, Laurus arrived home from a student recital in which two of his pupils had particularly shone. The lilacs were in bloom and the air smelled of sunlight and cut grass. Monica was home for her one weekend allowed away from school. (At Miss Pratt's, weekends ran from Saturday noon to Monday evening. Eleanor claimed this was to keep the girls out of sync with the real world, by which she meant the boys' schools, so there was nothing for Miss Pratt's girls to do for their weekends off *but* come home.) From the driveway he could see Monica and her friend Meg sitting in lawn chairs beside the still-covered swimming pool with Latin textbooks in their laps and their faces turned toward the spring sun. Nika, with her fine-boned face and poreless polished skin, looked more and more like Nina at the same age. It was such a moment in the lives of these girls, full of tension and balance, the moment just before they plunged off into the new elements of whatever was going to happen to them. And could anyone prepare them or protect them? No. All people ever did was prepare for the disasters that have already happened. Who could have protected his beloved broken Nina from whatever it was that happened to her?

He walked across the lawn to them, his footsteps almost silent in the grass.

"I take it this is the meeting of the Classics Club?"

The girls' eyes snapped open. Meg jumped to her feet to shake his hand. "Hi, Mr. Moss."

"Hi, honey, it's nice to see you. Sit down. What's going on here, pussy cat?" he asked Monica, ruffling her short sleek hair. "Latin exam coming?"

"Get your helmet, Dad. Mom's on the warpath."

Laurus glanced toward the house. "Why?"

"Jimmy's been kicked out of school." Monica took no pleasure in delivering this news. There had been such a steady drumbeat of expectation in the household from Sydney (who had not exactly triumphed in the educational arena herself) that they *had* to get good grades, so they could go to the *right* boarding school, so as to get into the *right* colleges, the holy grail in the world according to Sydney . . . this felt terrifying to Monica, as if her brother had fallen off a moving train and would now lie dazed and ruined somewhere forever while his life roared off without him.

"I see. Do we know why?"

"Cheating was mentioned."

Laurus looked up at the sound of the kitchen screen door opening. Sydney was there, waiting for him. Her hair was crimped and stiff from a recent permanent wave and she was dressed in cherry-pink shorts and a cable-knit sweater. He went toward her. She didn't like it when something was afoot and the children got to Laurus before she did.

"Before you get upset," said Sydney, with the portentous air of a ten-star general (at least) who has met the enemy, defeated him single-handed, and completed the mop-up operation while everyone else was still trying to get his boots on. This was a familiar spot on her warpath, though a later one than Monica had apparently crossed. Sydney was perfectly capable of conducting all parts of a family drama herself, and it was just as well, this manner implied.

They had retreated to the den and closed the door. "I'm already upset," said Laurus. "What happened? Where is he?"

"He's upstairs. But before you get upset, I want you to know that it's all taken care of. He can finish the term with a tutor and in the fall he'll go to the Cañada School in California."

"Whoa, whoa, whoa. What the hell is the Cañada School? Let's get Jimmy down here, I want to hear what happened."

"The Cañada School is a very good boarding school in California. He'll be far away from the troublemakers he hangs around with."

"Troublemakers he hangs around with? Winky Sylvester?"

"I called Gladdy and Neville, and Neville knew exactly what to do, and we've both talked to the school and it's taken care of."

"Hold on. Please. You called Gladdy and Neville before you talked to me?"

"I couldn't reach you."

"I was right where I said I'd be."

"I know, but I couldn't interrupt."

They looked at each other steadily. Laurus went out and called up the stairs. "Jimmy?"

It took a long time and a certain sharpness added to his tone before he got an answer.

"Will you come down here, please? Your mother and I want to talk to you."

When Jimmy shambled down, he flopped onto the couch and crossed his arms, his expression hooded and sullen.

"Young man."

No response.

"Young man, look at me, please."

Jimmy's eyes looked all over the room before he could force himself to meet his father's blue gaze.

"Tell me what happened."

"Well, but first, Mr. Blodgett doesn't like me . . ."

"It's true," Sydney said. "Mr. Blodgett has it in for him."

Laurus's gaze never wavered. "And you don't think your own behavior has anything to do with that?"

"NO!"

In the next half hour, Laurus learned that Jimmy had already been suspended for a day in April for cheating on a math quiz. He said he hadn't cheated, it was a coincidence that his wrong answers matched the wrong answers of the boy sitting next to him, and Sydney had supported him. After a girlhood of feeling scorned herself, Sydney was working to protect Jimmy from the disaster that had already happened to *her*, by believing anything he told her as long as he looked straight into her eyes when he told it. And since she believed him, and it was shortly after the Nashcan-in-the-cemetery business, she hadn't wanted Laurus to have a cow.

"So no one thought to mention this to me?"

"You were in New York. You took Carla Thigpen to New York that day to audition," said Sydney.

"A girl, by the way, who works like a Trojan at her music, *and* her schoolwork—"

"I'd work at music if you ever let me play the instrument I wanted," said Jimmy.

"This is news. What instrument is it you want to play?"

"Drums," said Jimmy.

(IN MONICA'S ROUND HANDWRITING)

August 25, 1962

> Dad and I drove up from Boston this afternoon and got here in time for a swim at the Salt Pond. It's great to be back. Everything looks the same. Ellen Chatto has a new boyfriend. Meg is coming tomorrow, hooray! Dinner tonight at The Plywoods for our homecoming. Monica.

Laurus had flown to Denmark to spend two weeks with his parents and bring Monica home. For a week Monica was with him in Nyborg, with Farmor and Farfar and Faster Nina and Tante Tofa. Then they'd gone down to visit Kaj and Kirsten and Monica's little Moss cousins at their seaside house on the south coast of Zealand. Eleanor wasn't coming to Dundee at all that summer. She and two college friends had jobs at a dude ranch in Wyoming.

With everyone gone except Jimmy for so much of August, Laurus worried that Sydney might be in a mood when he got back, but in fact, she was blooming. Her color was high and bright, and she was bubbling with cheer. She even seemed to enjoy their homecoming dinner at The Plywoods, which Candace had so wanted to give, although her cook, Velma, was now about a hundred and seemed to have forgotten how to cook anything *but* lobster Newburg, and Monica and Jimmy were so tired of having it every time they saw their grandmother, they wouldn't eat it anymore.

"It'll be fine," Sydney said brightly to Laurus, meaning, I won't have a tantrum about it. "We can go to Gladdy and Neville's tomorrow night and see all our pals."

Candace and Bernard had some tedious old friend from Cleveland staying with them, a confirmed bachelor named Mr. Ellery. He was dapper and clean, at least, which was more than could always be said about the octogenarians. (What was it about that age that they stopped taking baths? Norris Cummings, Candace's old beau, still looked tidy, but he smelled like a garbage dump, as if decomposing had already begun.) Sydney was in rare form, flirting with Mr. Ellery and laughing at his jokes.

". . . and so the king of Denmark said, 'Very well, if you insist our Jews wear the yellow star, then I, too, will wear the yellow star, and so will all of my subjects.' And he was the first to put on the yellow armband and so did every one of the Danes, and the Germans were *simply* furious . . ." Sydney was telling Mr. Ellery.

"No! Why, that's marvelous," cried Mr. Ellery.

At their end of the table, Monica whispered to her father, "Dad— that didn't happen."

Laurus nodded and chewed intently on his salad without looking up.

"I asked Mr. Wessel *and* Faster Nina. It never happened."

"I know," he said to her softly, and touched her hand, but he kept quietly eating. Monica looked at him, puzzled. His mood had changed since they came home. She thought he might be homesick. She tried to tell if at this moment he was annoyed, or what, but she couldn't read a thing in his expression.

After dinner, when Sydney went into the trailerlike living room to make a fourth at bridge, Laurus took Monica home. He dropped her at Leeway, saying he would be down at the firehouse if there was a hurricane or her hair caught fire. He drove off to join Al Pease and Hugh Chamblee and Dr. Coles and the others at their poker game.

Monica didn't go inside. Instead she walked down the white ribbon of dirt road toward the bathing beach. There was a huge glowing moon low in the sky and silver light pooled on the flat plate of
the bay. Denmark seemed like a distant planet, its smells and tastes
and ways so unknown here. Here, no one seemed to know anything
existed except America. She felt melancholy that there was so much
about the world that was badly arranged, and she was so powerless
to change any of it. And annoyed that on this beautiful quiet night,
there was no point going into the house, which she loved and had
also missed, because Jimmy, who had ridden his bike home the
minute he was allowed to leave the table at Nana's, was upstairs in
the bedroom next to hers, whamming away on his drum set.

September 20, 1962

> *I've had a long stretch of useful solitude, prepar-
> ing for the quiet at home, with all our chicks gone.
> Gladdy drove Amelia down to get her ready for
> school, and Laurus wanted to put Jimmy on the
> plane to California himself, so I bid them all goodbye
> the day after Labor Day. Al Pease came last week to
> see about the heaters. He said I wasn't ever to turn
> them on without having him check the pilot lights, or
> we could all wake up dead. It's quite toasty now in
> the kitchen and my bedroom, though brisk elsewhere.
> Gorgeous red and gold leaves all around make the
> pines look more black than green. So glad I stayed to
> see it—my first time! Played golf yesterday with
> Neville—we're the last of our bunch still here. He
> left this morning and I'll be off this afternoon. Can-
> dace and Bernard are staying until Columbus Day
> this year. Ellen will finish closing Leeway when she
> gets back from her wedding trip, and Al Junior, son
> of Plumbing and Heating, will drain the pipes when
> she's done cleaning. Goodbye, good old house, until
> next year . . .*

*Note for next summer: Find out exact date Lee-way was built; Neville brilliantly suggests we give the old girl a 100th birthday party.*

Laurus was unusually busy that fall and winter. He had three tal-ented students from the high school, and was also teaching the younger brother of Clara Thigpen. Richard was not as talented as Clara, but he worked hard. Laurus had a busy performance schedule, mostly in New England, and he was booked to judge a piano compe-tition in Salzburg and another in Los Angeles. He invited Sydney to go with him to Europe; they could stop in Copenhagen on the way home, as it was quite a while since she'd seen the family. She found that she was too busy for that trip, but she did go with him to Los Angeles. She spent one day with Laurus there, then went on to visit Jimmy at boarding school, where he was homesick and furious, and by great luck while there, she ran into Neville Crane, out visiting his parents in Los Gatos.

Laurus gave Richard Thigpen his piano lessons in a music room in the basement of the junior high school. He had tried teaching Clara at her house, but there was too much going on there, and the younger Thigpens were too taken with the exotic visitor to leave them alone. Richard and little Lorma kept slipping in and sitting on the horsehair couch, silently staring, and it made Clara laugh. Laurus regretted it—the Thigpens' piano was a much better instrument than the school one. Still, Clara had to learn to get music out of all kinds of keyboards, and she had. Now it was Richard arriving in the base-ment room at three-thirty on Thursdays.

They were working on Chopin, the Nocturne in E Minor. As he sometimes did when Richard's whole attention seemed not to be on the work, Laurus closed the music book and said, "Let's have some Pinetop."

Richard tore into "Pinetop's Boogie." Their mother played, and this was the music Richard had grown up with. He could play all his mother's tunes by ear, while Mr. Moss's music he learned by reading, note by note, often astonished when he heard what those notes, all like random black bugs that had died all over the page, connoted as sound. The music he played by ear was spacious and three-dimensional, with structures and rooms like castles of sound, while the Chopin was as flat as a map. The challenge in teaching him, for Laurus, was to figure out why the jazz part of the brain couldn't recognize all those same intervals and patterns and rhythms when he was reading.

When the boogie was finished, Laurus opened the Chopin again, and Richard set off along its creaking paths, as stiffly as ever. What am I going to do here? Laurus was thinking. What can I do for this boy, that I couldn't do for Jimmy? He wants it so badly.

He ended the lesson a few minutes early, and said, "It's almost spring. Our crocuses are up."

"Yes, sir."

"So summer's coming. What do you like best about summer?"

Richard looked down at his hands and shrugged. Was the Good Humor truck the kind of answer Mr. Moss wanted?

"How about swimming? That's my favorite."

Richard shook his head. "I like baseball games on the radio."

"You don't like to swim?"

"Don't know."

"Don't know if you like it? Do you know *how* to swim?"

Richard shook his head.

Uh-huh. Okay, let's drop back and see what we've got here.

"Does Clara know how to swim?"

"I don't think so."

There was a public beach at the lake in the next town, with a life-guard. But did they offer lessons? He didn't know. Could either of Richard's parents spare time from work to take them there? Laurus had only been to the lake once or twice when the children were lit-tle; in high summer they were always away in Dundee. And come to think of it, did you need to buy a residency permit to use the beach?

"You should know how to swim."

"Yes, sir . . ."

"You really should. What if you went to sea and your boat sank?" Richard smiled.

"There are lessons at the Y. It doesn't cost very much. Would you like to take lessons? You and Lorma could take them together."

Richard sat still and then shook his head. No.

"You don't want to learn to swim?"

"No. Yes. I do, but we don't go in there."

There. The Y. We.

Right. Laurus's children didn't go in there much either, because they went to the Country Club instead. He played over images of the events he had observed as a trustee at the Y. Square dances, various courses of sports instruction for the young, and lectures and socials for the old. After-school programs. What had he thought, that the Negroes of the town were off somewhere else at their own separate but equal YMCA? Apparently.

"Do you think your mother would allow it, if you went to the Y with me for swimming lessons?"

"I don't know."

"Well, ask her. And if she says yes, next week bring Lorma and your bathing suits."

Over the weekend, he had planned to discuss this with Sydney. He knew she would feel about it as he did, but thought it only right she be forewarned. However, in the event, Sydney was in a mood that weekend. Touchy, blue, preoccupied. Jumping for the phone every time it rang. He didn't know why and she didn't want to talk, so he left her alone.

The next Thursday, Richard came into the music room with a shy smile, his sister, and a paper bag with two towels sticking out the top of it.

"Splendid," said Laurus. Lorma sat silent and attentive as Richard slogged away at the Chopin. He got through it creditably, and they chose a new piece, Debussy's *Arabesque,* for next week. Then Laurus stood up.

"All right? Let's go have some fun."

*   *   *

Richard put his sister in the front seat of the Nash beside Mr. Moss, shut her door carefully for her, seeing that she didn't crush her fingers or toes, and installed himself in the backseat. Off they went down to Main Street, where they drove past the shops and the drugstore and the movie theater, with the children looking out the windows intently, wondering if anyone was noticing them. They turned up Second Street and past the Tots and Teens shop, then into the driveway of the big brick YMCA. Mr. Moss led them up to the double doors in front and showed them in.

Inside, it was like a big fancy school. The walls were glazed tiles, the floors linoleum. They could hear the echoing ring of basketballs being thrown and dribbled and shot in some nearby unseen court. Through an open door to a stairway they could smell something bleachy, a warm thick watery smell. They crowded up close to Mr. Moss, who was saying to a lady in a little office, with a half-door open at the top into the lobby, "Hello, Rosemary. My friends here would like to join the Y; Christine is going to give them swimming lessons."

"Oh, how nice! I'll just . . ." When he moved aside so the children could come up and speak to her themselves.

For a moment she just looked at them. They looked back at her as if they were statues. Laurus didn't think he'd ever seen children go so long without blinking. Then Rosemary looked at Laurus, spun in her chair to look up at the wall clock (no help there), then she spun back and said, "Yes, then. I'll just type up their cards, we'll start with you, shall we?" She looked at Lorma, as if by hitting the smaller one first she might be able to panic them into running away.

First Lorma, then Richard, told their names and birth dates. The cards were typed (she spoiled one, spelling Lorma "Lorna," and laughed nervously while she did it again). She tore the cards crisply from the typewriter and said, "Now there's just the fee . . ."

"I will take care of that," said Laurus. He handed Rosemary some bills and she went to her cash box and handed some back. He showed the children where they should sign the backs of their cards and said, "All right, then. Thank you, Rosemary," and led them off toward the door where the wet cleaning smell came from. As soon as they were out of sight, Rosemary dove for the telephone.

As the children clattered down the stairs behind Mr. Moss the air grew softer and thicker, almost as if it should have its own color. Then they stepped out into a big room with a floor made of water, like a field of bright blue, dancing and reflecting on the ceiling. They never imagined you could have so much water inside a building. There were straight lines, dark blue, on the bottom of the pool; you could see through to the bottom, which you couldn't in a river or a pond. There was a lady in the pool in a white bathing cap cutting through the water like a porpoise with pink windmill arms. Richard listened to the sounds echoing from the walls, smelled the fat soft air, and thought the only place he'd ever seen even vaguely like this was church.

The lady came to the end of her lap and pulled up. She stood in water up to her hips, turned the corners of the cap up to expose her ears, and tipped her head toward her left shoulder, bumping the side of her head with her right hand. Richard was too astonished to ask what she was doing. Mr. Moss started walking along the edge of the water field to the end where the wet lady was. The children stood stock-still, awaiting instruction. The edge you walk on looked wet and it would be bad to slip and fall in before they learned how to swim.

"Hello, Christine."

"Hi, Mr. Moss! I was just doing my wind sprints."

"I saw. I brought my friends for their lesson."

Christine nodded. Laurus discovered that the children were not behind him but standing where he had left them. Christine turned to follow his gaze, and there was a moment of stopped time. She looked at the children in surprise, and they at her, waiting.

Christine woke up, as it seemed, from the little momentary standing coma she had entered, and smiled and waved. She pulled herself out of the pool and took off her cap. The children had now made their way gingerly along the edge of the water field to where she was, and Laurus performed introductions. Richard shook hands and Lorma curtsied. Christine's smile grew warmer.

"Would you show Lorma where to change? Richard, we go this way."

Laurus took Richard to the men's dressing room. Richard looked solemnly at the lockers, the row of big shower stalls, the other plumbing, the small collection of toiletries to be used for free on the table by the sinks, talcum powder and spray deodorant and other things he didn't understand.

Laurus helped him choose a locker, and with his pocketknife cut the tags off Richard's new bathing suit. Modestly, Richard went off to a toilet stall to change. When he reappeared he carefully stowed his clothes in the open locker.

"I don't have a lock for it." He looked anxiously in at his defenseless shirt and pants, his shoes and socks, his paper bag.

"It will be all right," Laurus said.

When they went back out to the pool, Lorma hurried to him and whispered, "I don't have a bathing cap. Mama didn't get me one. The sign said I have to." She seemed certain that that would end the adventure right now, something was bound to and here it was.

"Christine, she won't need a cap for today, will she?"

"No, not at all. She won't have her head in much. Come on, ducks, into the pool."

The look on Lorma's face of surprise, fear, delight, and excitement as she walked step by step down into the pool and felt the water come up to her knees, then her hips, then almost to her shoulders, was unforgettable. It took Laurus back himself to his first forays into the water on the beach at Fyn, with his mother holding his hand, and the shock of the first touch of it, the feel of hot sand under his feet and then the cold between his toes. Then the amazing fact of adjusting to the temperature, of moving into this new medium, of Ditte smiling her delight, so it was unthinkable that he find it anything but delightful. Suddenly he even remembered his first bathing suit, a tiny white and blue knit one (although mostly at home small children didn't bother with bathing clothes). Where was that bathing suit now?

He sat on the bench and watched as Christine showed the children how to breathe while swimming, their faces down in the water blowing bubbles, then turning the head to the side to inhale. She led them in prancing around and bouncing up and down to get the feeling of the water and warm up. She showed them how to take a deep breath and hold it, then go all the way under the water. She showed them they could open their eyes underwater, which was front-page news to them. Lorma couldn't make herself do it, but Richard managed, on the second try. On the count of three he and Christine submerged themselves and shook hands underwater, then came exploding back up, Richard crowing with triumph. They learned to hold on to the side with their whole bodies stretched out on the water, doing the flutter kick. Laurus sat on a bench for an hour and smiled.

By the next week, there were three more students in the class, a friend of Lorma's and two boy cousins. Christine said five was as many beginners as she could safely teach. When more wanted to come, she found a friend with Red Cross training to join her, and the class grew to ten.


It's not that there weren't repercussions. If you advertised in the local weekly for domestic help in this part of the world, there was still a "Whites Only" category in the classifieds, for those who didn't want coloreds in the house. There were plenty who had read the Constitution at some point, who still didn't want a Negro dental hygienist to put her fingers into their mouths, and plenty who did not want Negro children dipping their bodies into the same swimming water as they, or changing their clothes in the same locker room. There were hot phone calls and secret meetings. No one could think of what to do. There was certainly nothing in the YMCA charter that allowed for exclusion of a class of people from membership. You didn't have to be young, or male, or Christian to join. Normally you depended on everyone involved to understand where they did and did not belong. These were well-brought-up people, their Negroes. When Mrs. Delafield had said to her cook back in 1952 that she supposed she would be voting for Mr. Stevenson, her Lizzie had said, "Mrs. D., I was rocked in a Republican cradle."

If a newcomer did something out of place at the Y, or the club, or the country day school, you would normally send the president of the board to solve it quietly, but Mr. Moss *was* the president of the

board. There were two who tested the waters as to impeaching him
or whatever you would do to remove him, but there were not nearly
the votes on the board to do it; too many people respected and admired Laurus Moss. And thought that, whether they liked what he
had done or not, if he thought it was the right thing, well, maybe it
was. And besides, what reason could they give for challenging him?
That you could say out loud?

Finally it was felt that if it could be solved, it would have to be
through outside channels. Meaning, turn it over to the wives.

When Sydney's tennis group finished their matches on a Tuesday in late March, Marjorie Culbertson and Peg Barker invited her
to join them for lunch. Sydney had been planning to go into the city
that afternoon, but it was nothing pressing; she was pleased to be
asked, especially by these two, whom she had found to be rather
tough nuts to crack, socially. When she had showered and dressed
and joined them in the dining room, she was surprised to find two
other ladies already there and waiting with them, older ladies who
had important husbands.

All through the mock turtle soup and the Crab Louis salads, Sydney thought the lunch was social and was terribly pleased. In fact,
she was enjoying herself so much Marjie and Peg were having trouble coming to the point, although the older ladies began to cast
glances at them and finger their pearls. They had ordered their coffee
by the time Peg leaned into Sydney and said, "You know, dearie, we
were wondering if we could talk to you about something."

"Sure," said Sydney, with a sudden irrational lightning strike of
fear jolting her innards. What? What had they heard? What could
they want to talk to her about?

She looked at them pleasantly.

"I think you can guess what it's about."

Four sets of eyes were fixed on her. Four pleasant faces with
carefully cared-for skin and just a dash of light lipstick on, four pairs
of hands with Tiffany-set diamond rings and rows of sapphire ring
guards, the only jewelry besides pearls one would wear in the day-
time. I can guess what it's about. I can guess what it's about? She
couldn't even make her tongue move.

When she only looked at them blankly, Peg for one was surprised. She hadn't exactly given Sydney credit for being that, well, subtle.

"About the Y," said Marjie.

Sydney was still looking blank. Was it possible she actually *didn't* know? No one ever thought of Sydney as being especially well informed, hard as she tried, but could she actually not know *this*? Where had she been?

"The changes at the YMCA," said Peg. "Thank you, Martha." They fell silent as the waitress, who had been serving most of them since they were children, delivered their coffees and packets of Sweet'n Low and took herself out of earshot. "I'm not saying it's bad or wrong, but, you know, this is a sleepy old town. When things happen too fast, and maybe aren't even the best things to happen, but even if they are, if it . . . it up*sets* people. You know the older generation. It's hard for them to get used to new things, and we hate to upset them. When things change, you know, with no warning."

This was unbelievable. Sydney was still looking absolutely blank. They had pictured her stepping up to the plate way before this, giving them some clue where she stood.

At last Sydney said, "I have to say, I'm sorry, but I really don't know what we're talking about here." She was about to go into total gimbal lock, this so completely had the feeling of something she'd been through a thousand times with her mother, she was bad, she was wrong, she'd disappointed everyone, and in her panic she couldn't tell which way to jump to protect herself, since she didn't know what they were on to her about.

Marjorie stepped in. She didn't know if Sydney was playing them or if she really had no idea, but in her view, there was no more point in beating about the bush.

"Your husband. You understand, we're all crazy about him but . . . he's invited some colored children into the YMCA. It started with two, a few weeks ago, at the swimming pool, and it's just—well, it's mushroomed."

There was a time delay tripped in Sydney's head; it honestly took her several seconds to hear and understand this. While she cranked

her paralyzed brain, trying to get the engine to turn over, her mouth
said, "He did what?"

One of the grande dames spoke up. "He took several little colored children into the Y and bought them memberships and swimming lessons . . ."

"My God," said Sydney, "I think that's *marvelous.*" She slapped
the table and a grin spread across her face. But no one else was smiling. There was, therefore, nothing further for her to say, except,
"Thank you so much for lunch, ladies." And she got up, pushed in
her chair, and disappeared. By the time she'd gotten her raincoat on
and reached the front door, she was actually laughing aloud. They
could hear her.

LAURUS'S HAND:

June 20, 1963

> *We came up early, as Sydney is trying to shake a
> flu or something—thought Dundee air would be
> good for her. Ellen's new husband, Ray Gott, did
> the gardens this year and they look wonderful.
> Neville and Gladdy not here yet, so our welcome
> dinner will be chowder and blueberry muffins by the
> fire. Can't think of a nicer way to start a summer. Al
> Pease thinks we need a big new hot-water heater; the
> old one let go all over the pantry floor when he
> started her up. Looks as if we'll have to redo that
> floor as well. A shame, it was only eighty years
> old . . .*

Sydney had not been sleeping well for several months, and she'd
been hard to live with. She snubbed people in the village at home,
because she fancied they'd snubbed her. It was true, some *were* snub-
bing her, annoyed about the Y, but not nearly as many as she
thought. The first week in Dundee was not a great deal better; she

got very shirty with Al's wife, Cressida Pease, who was not at the HairCare when Sydney showed up for her appointment.

"Maybe I could take care of you," said Ronnie, whose last name was also Pease, but whom Sydney referred to as Ronnie HairCare.

"No, you *can't* take care of me . . . Cressida has my formula. Everyone else does it wrong."

Ronnie picked up the telephone and dialed her sister-in-law.

"Cressida—Mrs. Moss is here."

There was an exasperated silence. Then Cressida said, "*Now?* I'm in the middle of my baking."

Ronnie said nothing.

"All right, I'll be right there. Give her a magazine."

Sydney gave Cressida a thorough dressing-down for her trouble when she arrived.

"The girl was very snippy when I called for my appointment. I've been supporting this shop for *years.* There are very good people over in Northeast Harbor, you know. I bring my business here out of loyalty."

"It was me, Mrs. Moss." Cressida dabbed thick foul-smelling eggplant-colored goo into Sydney's wet hair.

"She said she couldn't find a place for me until today. I pointed out I'd come at ten every second Tuesday since the year one—"

"It was me you talked to, Mrs. Moss. I keep the appointment book." Gently, Cressida dabbed and combed the wet hair, resisting an urge to spin the comb until she had a good snarl and then yank it out. "I told you, I have your usual time blocked out for you for the whole summer. You never come up this early before . . ."

"I can't believe you couldn't find me an earlier time than today."

"I did, Mrs. Moss."

"*Excuse* me . . ."

"I did find an earlier time."

"Then what am I doing here on a Friday, when I should be at a meeting at the yacht club—rather important, by the way?"

"I don't know, Mrs. Moss. Your appointment was for yesterday. The twenty-fourth. Ronnie heard me say it."

Sydney, who was at this point a plastic sheet in a chair with a neck and head sticking out the top, stared up at Cressida in the mirror. Cressida was a big woman and her family had lived in this village for seven generations. She wasn't easily cowed. When Sydney simply sat, as if she didn't believe her, like somebody's Last Duchess but with her hair all full of purple slime, Cressida put down her dye brush and went to get the appointment book.

Silently she held it under Sydney's nose and pointed. Thursday, 10 A.M., there were heavy erasure marks and *Mrs. Moss—color and set* was written in over whatever appointment had been rescheduled to make room for her. When Sydney still didn't say anything, Cressida turned the pages of the book, to show her that the hour and a half, from 10 to 11:30, was blocked out with her name written in every second Tuesday through the summer. Cressida carried the book back to the telephone desk and went back to work on Sydney's head.

Sydney didn't say another word through the whole appointment. When she was dried and finished, she paid Cressida, leaving exactly the same tip as usual, and bustled out to her car with an air that seemed to say, Nobody knows how busy I am and how many urgent matters are waiting for me to attend to them.

Cressida went over to her partner and said dramatically, "Why, Cressida, I am *so* sorry I made such a mistake, I hope I haven't inconvenienced *you . . .*" Ronnie Pease and her customer, Susan Coles, both rolled their eyes.

"Takes all kinds," said Ronnie.

"I gotta go home now and start my baking over," Cressida said, taking off her smock. "If my two o'clock is on time, can you start her?"

" 'Course, dear."

Jimmy, home from boarding school, was supposed to be doing landscape work for Mr. Dodge this summer, but three days in a row now, he'd slept through his alarm and come down for breakfast about the time Ellen Gott was washing the luncheon dishes.

"Well, hello, sleeping beauty," Ellen said as he sloped into the kitchen.

"What time is it?"

He was shirtless and barefoot. He wandered to the refrigerator, opened the door, and stood staring in as if he had gone back to sleep on his feet.

Ellen looked up at the clock on the wall and didn't bother to answer. Her own son, Dennis, had been up since four-thirty that morning, out lobstering with Merle Pert. She heard him go out the door every morning from her bed. She herself had been here in the kitchen at Leeway in a crisp white uniform at seven.

Jimmy took a container of leftover lamb stew to the kitchen table, took a fork from the drawer, and sat down to eat it cold, hunched over the Tupperware with both elbows on the table as if he had to protect the food from the packs of ravening dogs that might surge through the kitchen at any moment.

"What's for dinner?" he asked with his mouth full.

"Lamb stew," said Ellen.

Jimmy stopped eating and looked into the plastic tub. Lamb stew? *This* lamb stew? "Really?"

"No," said Ellen. "I'm roasting chickens."

"Oh." A joke. He resumed eating.

"Where's Dad?"

"He went out after breakfast, he didn't say where. Ischl, I assume."

"Where's Mom?"

"She just went to play golf."

"What kinda mood's she in?"

"Pretty much like spit on a griddle."

Jimmy nodded and went on chewing. He watched Ellen take two piecrusts out of the oven.

"You making strawberry pie?"

"Yes."

"Good. Are people coming for dinner?"

"The Cranes."

"I didn't know they were here."

"They're coming today."

"Is Amelia coming?"

"Don't know. I was told four Cranes."

Four. That probably meant Amelia *and* bugle-butt Toby, the mad farter. Jimmy found the younger Cranes completely annoying.

In the event, the guests were Gladdy, Amelia, and two houseguests, a Philadelphia couple making their first visit to Dundee. It was a very gay party. Afterward the houseguests signed the guest book, thanking Sydney for everything from the meal and the company to the beauty of the landscape, as if she had personally arranged for both the glaciers and the end of the Ice Age.

When the guests had gone, Laurus said, "Well, that was a great success. I missed Neville, though. When is he coming?" Sydney looked suddenly exhausted, as if she had lost the power of speech.

"You're tired, aren't you?" he said. She nodded. "You work hard at these parties. I appreciate it. Go to bed," he said. She nodded, touched his shoulder in thanks, and went upstairs. Laurus went into the kitchen to pay the young Coles girl who had served and was washing up. Then he went to have a talk with Jimmy about his non-appearance at work, but Jimmy was already gone, into town no doubt to look for trouble. Although it didn't seem to Laurus that Jimmy had to look very hard; trouble seemed to be looking for him.

Laurus was having a cup of soup at Olive's Lunch and reading the *Bangor Daily* when Mutt Dodge came in the next Friday. He sat down at Laurus's table. "Thought I might find you here." Olive's Lunch was on Main Street, and you could tell who was inside by the cars that were parked out front as you went by.

Their waitress, one of Max Abbott's granddaughters, came over to see what was wanted.

"Just a Tab, please," Mutt said. "No, what the hell, I better have a lobster roll, too. Thanks, Polly."

"I think I can guess what you want to say," said Laurus.

Mutt was grateful for the opening. "I can't keep your boy on, Laurus. He missed three days' work this week and was late the other two. And it was prime outdoor weather. It's not fair to the rest of the crew."

Polly brought Mutt his food and offered Laurus a refill on his coffee.

"Have you told him yet?" he asked Mutt.

"No. Wanted to tell you first. Don't think it will come as a surprise, though."

There was a silence as Mutt chewed, and Laurus stared into his coffee cup.

"I'm awful sorry about it," Mutt added.

"Don't be. Mutt—if he were your boy, what would you do? I can't let him lie around doing nothing. He's too young for the army."

"If he was my boy, I'd get him up every morning at four and throw him in a lobster boat with Tom Crocker. Tom needs a stern man bad. Once he's out at sea there's not a lot of slacking he can do. Tom Crocker ain't a man you want to disappoint. You know Tom?"

"To speak to. I'd have to haul Jimmy out of bed myself and carry him to the boat."

"Yeah, I know. Raising kids is fun, isn't it?"

"But you'd do that?"

"I've *done* it. My boy Augie went through a patch where we were ready to have him locked up. A summer out lobstering can be real good for the character."

"Would Tom take Jimmy?"

"Yeah. He'd take him. He's not young as he used to be and he drinks a little. Has some trouble keeping good help. 'Course, you might have to pay the boy's salary yourself."

"It'd be cheap at the price."

"Yeah, it would."

Mutt put some money on the table for his lunch, gave Laurus a pat on the arm, and went out.

\* \* \*

When Laurus came home after the afternoon rehearsal, Jimmy's bike was sprawled in the driveway. Laurus had to get out of the car to move it in order to get his car up to the kitchen door. There was no one in the kitchen when he went in; there was a tablet on the counter with Ellen's instructions about what she'd left and how to get it ready for the table. He walked through the dining room and living room. Still nobody.

He found Sydney in the little study at the end of the porch. She was sitting at her desk with her back to the door. Her head was bowed over arms folded on the desk, and her body was shaking with silent weeping.

"Sweetheart," he said. She jumped, as if she'd forgotten someone else lived here. She turned to him, her eyes and nose streaming. She made a pathetic attempt at a smile, then groped for Kleenex.

Laurus went to sit in the chair next to her desk. What on earth was happening here? Had someone died? Who? Whom did she love enough to mourn so much, besides Jimmy? He'd known her to weep with anger, but this was different, this was devastation.

Finally he put his hand on her arm and said softly, "Tell me. What's happened." She shook her head and covered her face with the tissue she was holding, and lost control again.

"It's not any of the children, is it? The girls?"

She shook her head.

"Your mother?"

Sydney shook her head.

Finally she managed, "I'm sorry to frighten you. Everyone's all right."

Then what was this? Certainly a death of some kind, if it wasn't the beginning of some really terrible emotional sea change.

She stood up suddenly. Her eyes were magnified behind a sheen of tears. She looked at him, direct to the point of nakedness, and said, "Would you hug me?"

He stood quickly and enfolded her. She cried more, she wiped her nose, she grew slowly calmer. He murmured and rocked her from one foot to the other.

"I'm sorry," she said, when she was a little calmer. "I know I must be scaring you."

"Don't be sorry. Tell me how I can help."

She shook her head, and stepped away from him. "You can't."

"Are you sure?"

"I think I'll go upstairs and take a hot bath."

"That's a fine idea," Laurus said.

He watched her go, still mystified. He listened as she crossed the great living room to the stairs. Laurus sat down again. He looked at the flowers in a vase on the desk, one of the beautiful things that Sydney did all summer, bringing the garden into every room. A square blue envelope facedown on the blotter. A library copy of *Anthony Adverse* open over the arm of the couch where Sydney usually sat. The big terra-cotta pot of geraniums outside the door on the porch, now in afternoon sun, and the thunderheads beyond darkening the sky over the bay. What had happened? What just happened?

Suddenly Sydney was back in the room. She was naked except for her wrapper. She came in quickly, and sat down opposite him. She said, "There *is* something you can do for me."

"Tell me."

"I don't want to be here now. I don't want to be here. Take me somewhere else."

"You don't want to be in Dundee?" Dundee was the only place she ever wanted to be in summer. Probably the only place she wanted to be, ever.

"Not right now."

There was a pause as he thought about his commitments. About the problem of Jimmy. Then he thought of the beautiful summer places of Europe he hadn't been to in so long, or ever. Brahms's own Ischl retreat. Baden-Baden. Capri. Was there really anything to prevent their going?

"All right. Go have your bath. In fact, take your book and get into bed. I'll bring our supper up on a tray." He knew this was not an evening to devote to Jimmy's sulks and self-justifications. He had decided what to do about Jimmy.

Sydney looked as if a huge weight had been lifted from her heart. She picked up her book and stood up. She picked up the blue envelope from her desk and slipped it into the book as a place mark. She went out. Laurus went on sitting where he was, as the late-afternoon light began to leak out of the room.

When Jimmy got home he found his father waiting for him in the kitchen. He took a Coke from the refrigerator without speaking and was about to stroll on to the dining room and about his business when his father's voice stopped him like a hand on the back of his collar.

"Young man, sit down."

Jimmy turned and looked, trying to gauge what his chances were of ignoring this summons. Nil, he decided resentfully. He walked back, every step a grudge, and flopped down across the kitchen table from his father. He took out his expensive pocketknife, opened his Coke with one of the many blades, and took a deep swig from the bottle. Finally he put the drink down, leaned his elbows on the table, and said, "So?"

"Mutt Dodge tells me he had to fire you."

"Fire? Is that what he called it? I'd say I quit."

"And you're proud of being a quitter?"

"Don't call me names, Dad. It's my life. I don't want to spend it digging holes for rich people's rosebushes, so sue me."

"I've got news for you. It's not your life yet."

"Whose is it, then?" Jimmy was startled and contemptuous.

"You are a child of this house, beholden for every mouthful you eat and every pop you drink, and as long as you are under my roof, you will behave as if you have some character."

Jimmy was amazed. He had come to assume, given his mother's power and her adulation of himself, that his father was more or less afraid of him. He said rudely, "It's Mom's roof."

Laurus remained utterly calm. "There are a great many things you do not understand, and that statement reveals one of them."

"There's a lot I *do* understand, though. That you *don't*," Jimmy said aggressively, and his gaze met his father's.

"I doubt that," said Laurus. "But if it's true, believe me, I don't want to hear about it from you."

Jimmy was surprised that every time he thought he'd landed a knockout punch, he found his father still out of reach, and moving faster than he was. Since he'd never seen him fight, he didn't know that he *could*.

"God, you're smug," he said finally.

"You are welcome to think so. Think whatever you want. But as long as you're under this roof, you will behave like a gentleman." Then he described to Jimmy how he was to spend the rest of the summer.

And for the rest of the summer, Jimmy entertained his new townie friends with renditions of this speech. Whenever they got enough beer in them, they called for him to "do the Great Dane." Jimmy was a wicked mimic, and when he was finished with declaiming, "You *will* be*have* like a *gentle*man," in his father's accent, he would swing into Winston Churchill. "We will fight them on the beaches! On the rooftops! We will fling our pots and pans!" *Their* war. *Their* heroism. *Their* Brave New World. They thought they knew *everything*.

The third Tuesday in July, Cressida Pease, in her pink uniform and white Hush Puppies, had Mrs. Moss's formula all mixed up in a purple paste. It was ten past ten.

In the mirror, Ronnie saw her glance at the clock. She was herself working on Mrs. Christie, who liked her hair rinsed a shade of blue that approached indigo.

"Your daughter's late for her appointment," Ronnie shouted at her cheerfully. Candace had taken her hearing aids out for her shampoo.

"What? My daughter?"

"Yes. She must be running late."

"You're expecting her?"

"Yes."

"Well, she's in Greece."

Cressida loomed up beside Ronnie to make sure she had heard that right. She and Ronnie held a long glance in the mirror.

"Greece, is she!" Ronnie shouted pleasantly. "Why, she was just here a week ago, I thought she was here for the summer."

"I know! So did I! But they upsidoodle changed their plans, and went off to Greece."

"Doesn't that sound nice," shouted Ronnie, looking hard at Mrs. Christie's blue head so as not to look at Cressida.

"With their boy, Jimmy?" Cressida asked. She knew from Sue Dodge that Mutt had had to fire him, after giving him the job in the first place when there were local boys who needed the money. If she learned he'd been rewarded with a trip to the Aegean, she thought she might have to shoot somebody.

"Why, Jimmy is living with Ellen Chatto and her new husband. He has a job fishing with Mr. Crocker. I offered to have him stay with us, but I really don't think Mr. Christie would have liked it. He's not used to having people going in and out at four in the morning . . ." She waved her hands to indicate that this was of course impossible, nobody could actually put up with that.

Cressida was now shoveling purple goo into the trash basket. Then she went to the phone.

"Is Mrs. Cluett in? Well, could you give her this message? It's Cressida Pease at HairCare. I know she was hoping for a morning appointment and one just opened up. Yes. You can tell her I can take her every other Tuesday at ten. Yes. Starting next week. I'll expect her then unless I hear from her. You're welcome."


Down at Olive's Lunch, on a Friday in early August, Tom Crocker came in for his dinner after he'd stowed the day's catch. His clothes were soaked with sea salt and sweat. He stumped through to the washroom in the back to clean his hands and face before he sat down at the counter.

Mutt Dodge was there, finishing his coffee.

"Tom."

"Mutt."

"You look like you're getting around a little easier."

"Yuh. Believe I am. Been a warm summer, that oils the joints some."

"It has been warm. How you making out with that Moss boy?"

Polly Abbott brought Tom a plate of fried scallops and a cup of coffee without being asked. Tom looked at his plate, as if trying to recognize what was on it, then said, "Well. I hate him, but I've decided not to kill him."

"That's good, Tom. That's probably the right decision."

"He needs killing, quite a bit, but at least he's getting a little faster at the work. And he doesn't talk. That's in his favor."

Tom was famous for his hatred of the summer people, and he hated them twice as much when they chattered.

"He getting to work on time?"

"Yuh. Ellen's boy drops him on the dock every morning at four-thirty sharp. Some mornings he's even conscious."

August 18, 1963

> *So glad to be back. We've had a beautiful sail through the Greek Isles and the coast of Turkey. Both brown as berries. Eleanor and her young man arrive tomorrow. Monica comes the end of the week. Per and Britt-Marie were here with the twins for a week while we were gone, and Ellen says they had a grand time. (Didn't sign guest book, as no one could find it.)*

Jimmy wasn't allowed to come home even when his parents were back at Leeway. No one wanted to have to get him up and drive him to work. This was hard on Sydney, but she didn't complain much. Laurus settled with Mr. Crocker that Jimmy would finish work the weekend before Labor Day and be allowed to move home for a week of vacation with the family. But it didn't take Eleanor and Monica long on the ground to figure out why they weren't hearing wails of complaint from Jimmy about this. Unable to keep the hours of the summer kids, not that he was so crazy about most of those assholes anyway, Jimmy had gone native. He was in with the year-round kids who worked raking blueberries and waiting on tables, went to the local academy and planned to go to Husson College in Bangor after high school, if they went to college at all. Monica heard he even had a girlfriend, a wild child named Frannie Ober, who could drive.

\*    \*    \*

Monica, Eleanor, and Bobby Applegate, Eleanor's beau who was having his first look at Dundee and Dundee at him, took a picnic out to the south end of Beal Island, to try to find where the village used to be. Everyone said there were ghosts out there if you found the right cellar hole. Also there was a beautiful island graveyard up on the ridge, but you needed local knowledge to get to it, and that was rarely shared with the summer people. They never found it, but they'd had a fine time plunging around in the underbrush, eating blueberries, and gathering mussels from the tidal flats to take home for supper. After they ate the sandwiches and fruit Ellen Gott had packed for them, they went skinny-dipping, their sun-heated flesh fairly shrieking at the chill of the water; there was nothing to do but plunge in headlong, which they did, squealing. Seagulls wheeled overhead and the deep August sky arched over them, sporting high streaks of cloud.

"Mare's tails," said Bobby, treading water violently to keep warm.

"What kind of weather does that mean?"

"I have no idea."

The three of them lay naked in the sun afterward, drying off, sheltered from the view of passing fishing boats and yachtsmen by a boulder that sat across from the nub as if it were a beach ball a giant had bounced down to the water's edge and then lost interest in. They were waiting for the tide to come back up and float the outboard, which lay on its side on the wet sand. They could have carried it, if they all heaved together, but why bother?

"Got to see a man about a dog," said Bobby. He roused himself and started up the beach toward the alder scrub, brushing sand from his blue-white backside. After a few high steps, the shells and stones biting into his feet, he came back and put on his sneakers and marched off again, naked from the ankles up.

"Watch out for bears," said Monica.

After a moment, Eleanor sat up groggy with sun and started to look around, for her clothes.

"I hate putting on underwear in mixed company," she said. Monica sat up, too, and decided it would be odd for her to remain naked if Eleanor was dressing; after all, Bobby was *her* boyfriend. She found and pulled on her underpants and shorts. She used her T-shirt to brush the sand off her feet before putting her sneakers on, but they were full of sand anyway.

"Do you think Big Syd is on something? Drugs?" Eleanor asked.

"Like what?"

"I don't know. Her pupils are all tiny little pinpricks."

"She might be. She hasn't said anything horrible to me since I got back."

"Me either. Or to Bobby."

"Though she does keep calling him 'Mr. Applegate.' " They both laughed.

"She's young for the change of life, isn't she?"

Bobby was making his way down the beach toward them.

"Uh-oh . . . *Déjeuner sur l'herbe* reversed."

"And minus the grass," said Eleanor. Bobby was shaking the sand out of his boxers, which he then tried to put on without taking off his sneakers, which involved a lot of undignified hopping on one foot when the shoe got stuck.

"That's the way they do it in the Mr. Universe contest, I'm pretty sure," he said when the girls stopped laughing.

"You're *my* Mr. Universe, honey," said Eleanor.

"Oh, mine, *too,*" said Monica.

Well now, thought Monica in the bow of the boat on the way home across the bay, that's what love should be like. Easy. Friendly. Fun.

Distinctly unlike the marriage they'd grown up observing. Lucky Eleanor.


On Labor Day weekend, Elise Maitland Henneberry gave a fiftieth birthday party for her husband at her parents' boathouse. The party was called for noon, so that people could sail over, or come by canoe if they liked, and so the older folk, Bess and Gordon, Candace and

Bernard, Miss Holmes who was at least a thousand years old, would enjoy themselves and not worry about dinner being served too late or getting to bed after nine o'clock. There were kegs of beer and laundry tubs full of ice, with wine bottles and cold soda ever replenished. The volunteer fire department was cooking the lobsters on the beach in exchange for a large contribution to their budget from the senior Maitlands.

In the Maitlands' cove, the yachts were dressed with pennants up the headstays from the bow to the tops of the masts and down the backstays to the afterdecks. The children were down playing at the water's edge; the teenagers and college kids swam off the end of the dock or played capture the flag on the vast sloping lawn. In the boathouse, the main room was set with tables for the blue-hairs. Everyone said it was the best Labor Day weather they'd had in years.

Laurus was on the beach with Al Pease and Mutt Dodge and the others, stoking the fires beneath huge iron grills made years ago by old Bowdoin Leach. They were heating mammoth pots of water for steamers and lobster and corn on the cob. Up in the boathouse kitchen, the firemen's wives were preparing Ronnie Dodge's cornbread for crisping, and making huge bowls of coleslaw.

Monica, sitting on the seawall quietly observing, noticed her mother in the boathouse by herself, looking a little lost. She was on her way to keep Sydney company when she saw Cressida come out of the kitchen with a huge tray of shucked corn, intersecting Sydney's meander.

"CressEYEda! How *are* you, sweetie? I missed you!" cried Sydney. Her tone was loving, little girlish, certainly no tone Monica had ever heard her use with the help before.

Cressida missed a beat or two, before replying neutrally, "Welcome back, Mrs. Moss. Did you have a good vacation?"

"It was lovely! Have you been to Greece?"

Cressida, who didn't actually get to Bangor that often, looked at her.

"No," she said.

"You can't imagine how clear the water is! It's *turquoise*. You should make Al take you. Of course I didn't let anyone touch my hair while I was away, I couldn't trust anyone but you. Look at those roots, I look like a skunk."

This remark left Cressida nearly speechless. Finally she managed, "Well, give us a jingle, we'll get you fixed up," and escaped with laden tray.

Monica told her sister that the look on Cressida's face as she went down the stairs was like someone who had just been told that Martians were talking to her through her fillings.

When Mrs. Dodge had set out gallons of homemade blueberry ice cream, Elise's children came out of the kitchen with a sheet cake blazing with candles, and everyone sang. Bobby stood with his arm around Eleanor. "This is amazing," Bobby whispered to her. "Everyone's so happy. It's like a wedding with no strangers to be polite to."

"Except you," said Eleanor.

"The whole place is a summer romance." Ah good, Eleanor thought. He has passed this test. She couldn't imagine not marrying Bobby, but she also couldn't imagine marrying someone who didn't get the point of Dundee.

Elise Maitland's brother Ned read a long and affectionate poem in dactylic hexameter. Gladdy and Neville Crane sang "The Old Mill Stream" in barbershop harmony: "Christo, you old salt-i-i-ine, When we first . . . met . . . yooouuu, You were twen-ty-twooo, Now it's pruunes . . . for . . . you . . ."

They had their words copied out on matching sheets of blue letter paper. Neville had to hold his at arm's length in order to read it, while Gladdy had hers in near her nose.

"Who are they?" Bobby asked.

"Amelia Crane's parents. My mother's closest friends. They're who I want to be when I grow up."

"Now that's a recommendation."

"Come, I'll introduce you."

\*    \*    \*

Monica saw her father drive the station wagon down the lawn about ten minutes later to collect Candace and Bernard, so they didn't have to trudge back up to the big house. (It was not clear that Uncle Bernard even *could* walk that far.) She was surprised when her mother got into the car with them and went home, too. Neither of her parents came back to the party, which was probably just as well, because Jimmy and his townie friends showed up toward sunset, and by the time Monica left, he and his mad bad girlfriend were so drunk they could barely stand up. As she walked away Jimmy was surrounded by admiring cronies, yelling in a British accent: "We will fight them in the outhouse . . . we will smite them with our brollies . . ."

For Laurus, the most uncomfortable moment in that whole difficult summer was the dinner party Candace gave at The Plywoods on Labor Day itself. There was the inevitable lobster Newburg, and then bridge, four tables of young and old. Toward the end of the evening, he and Sydney were playing Neville and Gladdy. Sydney's mood was dispiriting to him. She was angry again, hurt, sad, likely to behave like a cat in a bath at any moment. She'd been fine all evening, and then suddenly she was hissing and scratching. At poor Gladdy, of all people.

It wasn't anything that was said. It was the crackle of current around the table, a feeling like the punishing treble of a too-bright piano. Laurus was dummy. Sydney, unusually for her, had gone on drinking after dinner, her father's late-night tipple, whiskey and soda. She moved in staccato, throwing down cards, snatching up tricks. At one point she laughed unkindly when she trumped an ace from Gladdy. The worst moment came when Sydney threw down her hand and said, "The rest are mine." She was reaching to sweep up the deck when Neville said gently, "I think you've miscounted."

"Oh, *do* you," she said, as if he had slapped her. "Fine. Let's play it out."

They did, and Neville was right. When the last trick fell to Neville, Sydney looked stricken. No one spoke for what seemed like minutes. Then Sydney said to Laurus with effort, and a very forced smile, "Sorry, partner."

"No harm done," said Laurus, "we're still killing them." And the deal passed to Gladdy. As she was shuffling, Sydney rose suddenly and left the table.

When Sydney didn't come back, the other three sat in silence.

"Do you suppose she's ill?" Laurus asked. The Cranes said nothing, and did not look at each other.

Finally, Neville said, "She seemed all right at dinner."

"Gladdy . . . could you see? Would you mind? If she's sick, she'd rather have you than a man . . ."

When Gladdy still didn't say anything, Laurus seemed about to say more. Gladdy stood up. "Of course," she said.

Now that the two men were alone at the table, there was another silence, until Laurus said conversationally, "I'm sorry we didn't get to Egypt. What do you know about the Library of Alexandria?"

Gladdy found Sydney in the guest room at the far end of the house. She was sitting on the blue-flowered bedspread sobbing as if her insides would come out. She stopped and looked up when the door opened; Gladdy saw a hope in her eyes that was almost desperate, but it fled the instant she saw who it was who had come. With a flip of her hand that expressed despair, she turned away from the door and her weeping resumed. She held a handkerchief in her lap, and she twisted and twisted it.

Gladdy closed the door behind her and went to a chair in the corner of the room. She sat up straight, not comfortably, and she looked at Sydney. She said nothing, and made no move to come closer.

"You shouldn't be here," Sydney said, finally.

"I know. But your husband asked me to come."

Sydney mopped at her eyes and held the handkerchief against her lips. She was trying to stifle her tears and hold her sobs in; it seemed important to her to show some self-mastery now. Gladdy sat quietly. She watched Sydney as if with curiosity.

Finally Sydney raised her ruined face to address her friend. The lens of tears made her eyes seem enormous.

"I don't under*stand,"* she said, "why it's always like this. Why am I *always* the one in tears?" There was a bitter edge to these last words and she looked at Gladdy as if she expected an answer. Gladdy said nothing.

"I don't understand, why he wouldn't . . . when I wanted . . ." She stopped again because she could hear that her voice now held anger, and she knew from long experience not to show that card when others might hold better ones.

Finally Gladdy said, almost gently, "You have much more money than I have, and you are much more beautiful. You always have been. But I am better at loving, and being loved."

As the words hung in the air between them there was, most unwelcome, a tap on the door. Gladdy called, "Yes?"

"Oh, are you . . . ?"

"We'll be out in a minute . . ."

Sydney looked at Gladdy and said, "I can't. I can't go out there."

"I'm sorry," said Gladdy, "but you have to." She got up and slipped out the door, closing it behind her.

In the hall, waiting, was old Mrs. Maitland. "I'm so sorry, are the other loos full of people?"

"The other one I know how to find is full of my husband." Mrs. Maitland smiled.

"Sydney will be out in a second."

"Thank you."

Gladdy went back to the card table where the men were talking about the Valley of the Kings, and when Sydney rejoined them, surprisingly composed, Gladdy dealt the next hand.

In the spring of 1964, Monica, a glorious senior, was sunbathing by the pool in Connecticut with three friends from boarding school on a Sunday afternoon. They had slept until noon, and now were eating peanut brittle and smoking Kools. Monica heard the back door slam, and looked up to see her mother stalking across the lawn toward them. She sat up and pulled up her bathing suit straps.

Sydney stood over the girls, drawn up to her full height with her nostrils all pinched and flutey, a demeanor Monica perfectly recognized. Sydney waited for maximum attention, like a headmistress who refuses to speak until there is deathly quiet in the auditorium.

"Your sister," Sydney finally announced in her grandest manner, "has cheated you out of a wedding."

Monica couldn't understand the sentence.

"Eleanor?"

"Your sister *Eleanor*. Has *eloped* with Bobby Applegate."

The other girls were now sitting up, attention riveted.

"Really? Cool!"

"Monica, *try* to speak English," said Sydney, furious.

"What happened? Where are they now?"

"They were married in New York, yesterday, and I have no idea where they are now. On their way back to school, I suppose. She won't even be able to graduate as Eleanor Moss, you know. She won't even have her *real* name on her diploma."

"Did you talk to her?"

"I did *not* talk to her. I talked to Bobby's father, who apparently was their witness. He *aided* and *abetted* the whole thing. I suppose he wanted to get out of paying for the rehearsal dinner."

Monica made a successful effort to look grave. This preference for Bobby's parents over her own, after the circus of bride's magazines and wedding plans Sydney had already begun, though the young couple had not even announced an engagement, would be insanely wounding to her mother. Finally Sydney said, "I have to find your father," and swept off.

When the kitchen door slammed, Monica began to laugh.

"What? What? Do you think she's pregnant?"

"Cheated *me* out of a wedding! Oh, God, isn't it wonderful?"

But her friends didn't quite understand it; only Eleanor would.


There was no celebration when Eleanor graduated from Skidmore, or as Jimmy (who was not in attendance) called it, Skidmarks. Monica wasn't allowed to leave school so close to her own graduation; at Miss Pratt's the weekends after May 15 were closed for seniors. So only Sydney and Laurus went. Eleanor had had to move out of the college dorm for the last few weeks of class, since it was thought unwholesome for a married woman, with her dangerous carnal knowledge, to live among innocents, but she'd found a very nice room in a boardinghouse which Mr. Applegate was paying for, until Sydney found out and insisted on paying instead. The Applegates senior attended the graduation with Bobby; Sydney kept introducing Eleanor as "my daughter, Mrs. Applegate," to other girls' parents. Twice in Eleanor's hearing Sydney said loudly to relative strangers, "They eloped last month, and she isn't even pregnant! Isn't it ro*man*tic?"

Sydney set to work trying to make Bobby Applegate's mother into her new best friend, but she found it slow going. "So the king said, 'Very *well*, my Jews will wear the yellow star, but so will I and so will *all* my subjects,'" Eleanor heard her shout. Mrs. Applegate murmured and smiled. Shortly after the graduation lunch, all the Applegates, including of course Eleanor, drove away, en route to Georgetown for Bobby's graduation.

Monica's graduation from Miss Pratt's was the following Thursday. The weather was fair, and Monica, in a white dress and a crown of flowers, was one of the honor guards of the Daisy Chain. There was sentimental weeping, and singing in the garden, and a Justice of the Supreme Court gave the commencement address. Monica tried her best to make everything perfect for her mother, since that was the niche in the family ecology that seemed available to her, but it was all for nothing. The night before the event, her parents, tracked by phone to the Wayside Inn, were informed that Jimmy had been expelled from school again.

Actually, he had been expelled after the fact, the fact being that he had disappeared entirely. The whole day of her graduation, Monica kept looking around for her parents, as she accepted the French prize, as she marched in the garden with her white crooked staff, beside the slowly marching white-clad girls bearing the long heavy rope of white daisies with yellow centers. Her parents were off somewhere, on telephones, her mother alternating between fury at the school, which had waited several days before admitting Jimmy was gone, and fear for Jimmy (where *was* he?). Her father was trying to keep his wife calm and take sensible actions. Laurus called the police to report a missing person while Sydney stood outside the booth whimpering and shouting instructions to him as to what to say. He had a long talk with Jimmy's dorm master, and another with the headmaster, while Sydney stood next to him and then made him repeat every word from the other end.

Monica had her trunk and suitcases packed, her pennants and stuffed animals all given to younger girls, her roommates helped to their parents' cars and kissed goodbye for the hundredth time. She was alone in an empty room when her parents finally reappeared. She and her father heaved the luggage down the stairs in several trips. They drove away from the school, with only a chemistry teacher Monica had never studied with happening by to wave as she departed. In the backseat, Monica lit a cigarette before they crossed the town line, to see if that would get a rise out of them, but it didn't.

When they got home, the cook (a new one, colored and ancient) said that yes, there had been messages. Many. She showed them the notepad where she had laboriously written them. Jimmy's school had called. Jimmy had called, to say he was all right. "Did he say where he was?" Sydney demanded, but the cook said no, and of course she didn't ask. Why would they need to know that? He was at some boarding school, as she understood it. She'd never met him. And Ellingod had called.

Sydney and Laurus looked at each other. Is this someone you know? each look asked the other.

"Ellen Gott," said Monica.

"Yes," said the cook, "that's what it says."

Sydney dove for the phone on the wall.

"Oh, hello, Mrs. Moss," said Ellen's big cheerful voice.

"Ellen, have you heard from Jimmy?"

"I've got him right here. I've been calling to see what you want me to do with him."

"Oh, thank *God,*" Sydney breathed, and mouthed to the other two, He's there. Nodding her head. Yes. He's there.

"Is he all right?"

"Seems to be."

"How did he get there?"

"Hitchhiked."

"And walked," Jimmy was heard to prompt from the background.

"And walked some."

Laurus took the phone, and Sydney sat down at the kitchen table, where Monica was eating a cup of yogurt and thinking about what else was in the refrigerator that she could eat whenever she wanted, freed finally from the confines of formal meals at school.

Sydney said, "I could *kill* your brother," in a tone that Monica knew meant that she loved Jimmy more than any creature on earth and was already in her mind turning this into a comic story, another of Jimmy's winning escapades.

"Be my guest," said Monica.

Laurus drove to Dundee to collect the reprobate. The drive home was long and quiet. Around New Hampshire, Laurus asked Jimmy what he thought should happen now.

"There's a school in Vermont I could go to."

"What kind of school?"

"It's like a farm, school, thing."

"I'm not getting the picture."

"It's this farm, and you grow your own food, all the vegetables and wheat and stuff. And you can eat meat if you want, but if you do, you have to raise the animals and slaughter them yourself. If you don't want to do that, you don't eat meat and you don't even wear leather, no shoes or belts or anything."

"Is academic work included in this plan?"

"Oh, yeah. All that stuff. I assume. You rotate through the barns and the kitchen and learn to do all the jobs. It's, like, school about how the world works. Really."

"And you think that would suit you?"

"Yeah," Jimmy said. "It would be real."

"What was not real about the very expensive school you just ran away from?"

"California?"

"Is that your answer? California was not real?"

Jimmy shifted unhappily and looked out the window.

"It was all right."

"Then why did you run away?"

"I didn't want to be there."

Several miles passed in silence.

"But you would want to be at this farm school? Does it have a name?"

Jimmy told him the name and said he would, yeah. He really would. He thought so.

"Do people go on to college from this school?"

"Is that so important?" Jimmy asked angrily.

"It is to your mother."

"It's not her life."

"I'm aware of that. Do you have an interest in farming as a career?"

"I like being outdoors."

"But not digging holes for rich people's rosebushes."

Jimmy shot his father a look. More silent miles.

"May one inquire how you heard about this school?"

"A friend of mine goes there."

"Which friend?"

"You don't know her."

"But what's her name?"

"Frannie."

For once, Sydney got no chance to muddy the waters. Monica didn't see it happen, she never heard a raised voice or a charged conversation between her parents that June. They did spend a good many quiet evenings in the upstairs sitting room instead of coming down to the den for cocktails, while Jimmy sulked in his tent and Monica and her friends sat on the terrace in the heat-swollen evenings, watching fireflies and talking about their future lives. Dinners were pleasant and normal, served every night at seven-fifteen in the dining

room, the cook passing the overcooked vegetables, and everyone
drinking milk. Monica was away a lot, as many of her friends were
having debutante parties. Candace had urged giving one for Eleanor,
when she was that age: "Eleanor would love all that." Sydney had
known Eleanor *would* love all that, but refused. So naturally she
wouldn't do it for Monica either. Which was fine, Monica would really *not* have loved all that, being the center of attention, though it
was fun going to house parties and meeting her friends' friends, and
all that dancing. However it was worked out, by the time the parents
left for Dundee, Jimmy had been packed off to Denmark. Jimmy had
made the mistake of letting his father know which briar patch he actually wished to be thrown into, and in his quiet way Laurus had remained adamant. His plan included keeping Jimmy away from
Dundee for an entire year.

August 24, 1964

> *Young Mr. and Mrs. Applegate arrived last night*
> *after a harrowing drive from Boston in rain and hail*
> *(flights to Bangor all canceled). They are blooming;*
> *lovely to have them both here. Bobby's parents will be*
> *here tomorrow, weather permitting. Such fun to have*
> *the house full.*

Candace and Uncle Bernard, whose special love for Eleanor, "his"
baby, had never wavered, were giving a huge party for the newlyweds, with a tent on the lawn and a dance band, exactly like a wedding reception, and Sydney was furious about it. For one thing, she
had *told* them, there was no reason to reward bad behavior in this
way, but Bernard said, "Nonsense—she's married a wonderful
young man and it's a cause for celebration." (As if it were *his* business.) Kaj and Kirsten and two of their children were coming from
Copenhagen, also goddam Nina, and Sydney was having all the
work of feeding and entertaining them all and none of the fun of
planning the party and being Queen of the Hop. Eleanor knew her
mother would booby-trap things if she could, but remained unrepen-
tant and pleased. She was in some way more Sydney-proof than

Monica. She had Laurus's sunny steady temperament, which protected her from feeling her mother's attacks so deeply, and also, she had had those years alone with her mother during the war.

The day after the dance, Gladdy and Amelia Crane gave a lunch party for the young Applegates and the Danish cousins. Sydney was off escorting the senior Applegates and Kaj and Kirsten to Mount Desert where they would see Thunder Hole and have tea with popovers at the Jordan Pond House; Sydney had made a face with her tongue out at them behind their backs for Monica's benefit as she announced this. Nina had elected to stay home with Laurus. They were sitting on the porch, reading, when Laurus noticed an unfamiliar car come slowly up the lane and pause, just past the Leeway Cottage driveway. The driver peered up at the house, then crept off. In a moment the car was back, going in the other direction, and this time it turned timidly into the drive and came right up to the porch steps.

Laurus went to the top of the stairs and watched the driver dismount, a woman of about his age in a shirtwaist dress, nylons, and clean white sneakers. Not a Country Club girl, nor yet from any of the old year-round families, that he knew, anyway. Probably raising money for Ischl or the hospital.

"Good afternoon," he said.

"Are you Mr. Moss?"

"I am. Are you where you mean to be?"

She smiled. "I am."

"Please come up, then."

The woman climbed the stairs and gave him her hand. "I'm Hannah Ober," she said.

"Laurus Moss. This is my sister, Nina Moss."

Laurus was still waiting for the shoe to drop.

"I'm Frannie's mother," she said.

"Please," said Laurus. "Sit down."

The three of them sat and looked at each other. "I think you may know my husband Harold. From church," said Hannah.

"This is the mother of Jimmy's girl," said Laurus to Nina, who murmured and nodded.

Ellen appeared at the door from inside. "Oh, hello, Hannah!"

"Ellen, how are you?"

"I came to see if your company needed anything, Mr. Moss."

"Could we have some iced tea, do you think? Will you have iced tea?" he asked Mrs. Ober. The atmosphere was distressingly polite. What had she come to say, that she demanded he keep his badly raised, unpleasant son away from her daughter? Who could blame her?

When Ellen had gone, Hannah Ober smoothed her skirt over her knees and asked, "Have you met Frannie?"

"No. My daughters have. But Jimmy is away this summer."

"I know," said Hannah. "Believe me." And smiled. Her hair was graying and she wore no makeup, but when she smiled she was beautiful.

"Is Frannie here in Dundee?"

"She was. My husband took her back to Boston when he went down. My mother came for a visit and I didn't think I could handle them both at the same time."

"Where do you live?"

"We have a camp up by Third Pond."

"How old is Frannie?" Nina asked.

"Seventeen, just."

"Ah. An older woman."

"Yes."

Ellen was back with the tea in tall glasses, with mint from the garden, and a plate of cookies. She gave them each a paper napkin with LEEWAY COTTAGE printed on it in navy blue. When Ellen had gone, Hannah said, "I like Jimmy very much."

"*Do* you?" Laurus knew that his son had his good points but was hard-pressed to know how others could recognize them.

"Yes, but I should add, I've always been a sucker for the bad boys."

"And so is your daughter."

"Oh, indeed. But don't tell *her* she and I have anything in common.

I'm glad I remember giving birth to her or I'd swear she'd been left on the doorstep by wolves." Laurus laughed and Nina smiled.

"No wonder she and Jimmy are soul mates."

"I teach that age," said Nina.

"On purpose?"

"Yes. They are a great deal of trouble to themselves, and of course *we* know nothing." Her voice was unexpectedly warm with affection.

"We know *nothing*. Frannie's father and I are both heartless poops who never loved and won't lift a finger to fix what's wrong with the world. Frannie is furious about Vietnam, and apparently it's my fault."

"Yours personally?" Nina asked, smiling.

"Yes."

"I congratulate you," said Laurus. "I would be pleased if Jimmy were angry about the state of the world, instead of his many personal complaints."

"Wait until he's draft age," said Hannah. "I understand he's in Denmark?"

"Yes. Working on a pig farm."

Hannah smiled and drained her iced tea glass. "That's rather inspired."

"Thank you," said Laurus.

"But it won't last forever."

"No."

"Thank you for seeing me," she said, rising. "Whatever happens next, I thought it would be wise if we'd met."

"I agree."

"If you'll give me a paper and pencil, I'll leave our telephone numbers here, and in Boston." Laurus got a pad, and they exchanged numbers. "Frannie has one more year of boarding school."

"Which she likes, I understand."

"Yes, thank God she likes *something*. You notice there isn't an inch of leather on my person . . . We continue to eat the dear lambies and moo cows, though. It makes mealtimes with her a treat."

"I wonder how she handles Jimmy's cheeseburger habit."

"Is he going back to California?"

"No, we're keeping him at home. He'll go to the public high school."

"And we shall see what we shall see."

When she had gone, Nina said, "Nice woman."

"Yes."

"What if they *are* soul mates, Jimmy and her daughter?"

"Do you believe in soul mates?" Laurus asked.

"I think I do," said Nina. And suddenly there were two big questions yawning between them, that neither would ask and neither should answer.

Nina stood and gathered the tea things. As she bent over the tray, Laurus noticed how thin she was. Suddenly he could see her as the children must, not a slightly faded version of the lovely girl she had been, but a bony older lady who always needed a sweater, even in August. He watched her open the door and slip into the dark house, and then sat by himself looking down the lawn to the bay. Sydney had run the Danish flag up the flagpole along with the Stars and Stripes, to honor the houseguests. They stood out smartly in the afternoon breeze. Very picturesque.

In the winter of 1965, Eleanor was pregnant; she and Bobby spent Christmas with the Applegates. Supposedly to fill in the gap made by Eleanor's absence, Nina Moss was invited to come for Christmas in Connecticut. Laurus was so pleased with this plan that Sydney had to pretend to rejoice (in spite of the fact that Nina stepped off the plane wearing *the* mink coat, and never once seemed to think that this was anything to do with Sydney).

It wasn't anything Nina did that you could object to. She was pleasant, she agreed to anything you planned for her, she brought thoughtful presents for everyone. It was just all so *measured,* so *chilly,* as if she expected any minute you would step in something smelly and walk around with it on your shoe. To everyone except Laurus it was as if she were behind an invisible shield, or under a bell jar. No matter what hubbub swirled around her, and with Jimmy and his new friends slamming in and out, playing pool downstairs, having constantly to be asked to turn the music down, there was plenty, Faster Nina sat quietly in the wing chair in the living room reading Camus, in French.

"She teaches French, you see. In Copenhagen," Sydney would

say when explaining her to other guests at Christmas parties. Sydney could just picture her, with her pencil-slim skirt and her snobby posture and sleek little head and a little pince-nez on the end of her nose. (Not that Nina wore glasses.)

The part of this visit Sydney remembered longest was the night they played a game called Careers that someone had gotten for Christmas. Jimmy was out "at a dance," he had said (smoking pot in somebody's poolhouse was more like it, Monica thought), but Monica was at home. In this game, each player had to decide in advance what proportion of Happiness, Fame, and Fortune she required for a successful life, then try to acquire it. Monica had played before and explained the rules. "Why do they say fortune, when they mean money?" Laurus asked. He and his sister glanced at each other at the same moment, wearing the same smile.

"What's the difference?" asked Sydney. It was always like this when Nina was around, there was a secret current running between brother and sister. Sydney felt left out, and it made her mad.

"Why fame?" asked Nina. "Why fame instead of love?"

"If you have fame, you can get all the other things," said Monica, without irony. She was home for her first vacation from college.

"I see," said Nina, smiling.

As they played, Sydney began to tell Nina what a lovely visit they'd had this summer with Per Bennike and his delightful wife and children, how she really ought to go see them when she was in New York. Nina sat quietly looking at the game board. Later Sydney couldn't have told you when or how Laurus seized the wheel from her, but suddenly she found they were right out of the strait of Delightful Times the Family Had Shared with Scandinavians Not Including Nina, and into the wide and pacific bay of Emanuel Swedenborg.

Monica was quite interested, as she'd had a formidable teacher at Miss Pratt's who was Swedenborgian. They talked about heaven in the shape of the Grand Man, about how everyone's masks and dodges would fall away and they would become their essential selves, entirely composed of what on earth had been their ruling loves. And there would be work in heaven, and sex. (Monica couldn't wait to tell her friends about that.) There would be hell, too, but the people who were in it wouldn't experience it as hell, they would experience it as what they had always thought was the truth about how the world worked.

Laurus rolled and landed on "Climb Famous Peak" and earned six Happiness hearts.

"Unfair!" said Monica. "Look how many hearts you already have!"

"But that's the way the world works," said Nina. "Those with great happiness always get more. Oh, look, lucky me, I can start farming!" She paid $1,000 in scrip for the privilege. That was as close as Nina got to gaiety.

"Do people from Swedenborg's heaven get to visit hell?" Monica wanted to know.

"Would you want to?" asked Laurus.

"I would, very much," said Nina.

*Scary,* Sydney thought. She could picture Nina behind a one-way mirror in a heavenly viewing box over a pungent dark red sea of the damned, as in the hidden observation room in the children's nursery school where teachers and parents could watch how the children behaved when they felt unobserved. Sydney had thought it rather mean and unfair, especially the time they made her spend the morning watching little Jimmy.

"Does Swedenborg believe in reincarnation?" Monica asked.

"I do," said Sydney. "I'm sure I've lived before." She rolled the dice.

"You *are*?"

Sydney counted out her steps to a square that said "Lunch with Royalty, Draw 2 Opportunity Cards." "Absolutely. I have dreams where I know things I couldn't have seen. Or I'll come to a new place, and know I've been there before."

"Like when?" said Monica.

Sydney appraised her Opportunity cards, and said, "The first time it happened I was your age. It was in Egypt. Think about it, why *wouldn't* God want to give you more than one chance to get it right?"

"You think God cares?" Nina asked.

"Well, it would make all the difference, if the world isn't really as unfair as it looks."

Nina thought about this gravely and then gave Sydney a sweet smile.

Laurus said, "The thing that's so hard about being human is the not knowing how to do right, not knowing what the grand scheme is. In Swedenborg's heaven you know exactly where you fit in the Great Body. You know what your job is. It's un-knowing that makes you feel far from God."

Monica was looking skeptical. At nineteen, she felt far more certainty about many things than her father apparently did. "Does Faster Nina know about seeing your movie in heaven?"

"No, I don't," Nina said. "Tell me."

"Daddy says, in heaven you get to see the movie of your life, with all the mysteries explained. You get to see all the scenes you missed and the parts you never understood."

"Like what?" Nina turned to Laurus.

Because he didn't want to say, he answered lightly. "Everything. Where you lost your favorite pen. Where all your missing socks went. Curiosity is the great underestimated passion." He smiled, so Nina couldn't tell if he was serious or not.

"But Daddy, once you've seen your movie, then what?" Monica asked. "Do you get born again?"

"Then you're content. You can be done with life and go on."

"To what?"

"To being part of God. Being filled with Knowing."

"But . . . what will *happen*?"

He passed Monica the dice. "I guess that curiosity will be satisfied, too." Monica looked as though being filled with Knowing didn't sound like much of a payoff. She wanted to know if she could come back another time as Nefertiti, or a dolphin. And whether she got to choose.

But after that Laurus talked more often, cheerfully, of how he was looking forward to Seeing His Movie. And Sydney, finally paying attention, wondered what it was he wanted to see. She knew it would be about her, and she was afraid she knew which scene.

Most of the family's milestones were to be seen in the Leeway Cottage Guest Book. Eleanor and Bobby brought Annabel Applegate, the first of the Mosses' grandchildren, to Dundee in 1966. Monica's wedding in 1971, which Sydney was allowed to design and manage from stem to stern, was recorded as the most perfect thing that ever happened, although a number of the key players had memories that substantially contradicted that report. Jimmy's passage through the late sixties and early seventies, which included several colleges, a great many drugs, and mercifully only one motorcycle crash, was largely unremarked in the Guest Book, though it was writ large in the family annals elsewhere. Frannie Ober's wedding was in the Guest Book; Jimmy, Laurus, and Sydney were all invited, and Laurus and Sydney went. By the time Jimmy sobered up, cut his hair, took a bath, and looked around wondering where ten years had gone, Frannie was serving her first term in Augusta as state congresswoman.

Candace's death was recorded in the Guest Book, in the sense that Bernard's first (and last) summer alone at The Plywoods was remarked. Candace had bought burial plots for herself and Bernard in the New Cemetery at the head of the bay in Dundee, and there she

was laid in the early spring of 1975. No one records that on that occasion Sydney threatened to have her father and Berthe Hanenberger dug up and moved there from Cleveland, where no one was
left to care about them. She was persuaded not to, for reasons of
seemliness and also by the fact that the New Cemetery, opened in
1848, was running out of plots. Also unmentioned was the fact that
in Candace's will the famous Annabelle pearls were left not to Sydney but to Eleanor, to hold for baby Annabel. Eleanor loved the
pearls and wore them constantly until her Annie came of age, but
never in her mother's presence.

There was note of Ditte Moss's death, as the family had to pack
up and fly to Copenhagen in the middle of an August, but not of
Henrik's, since he died in winter. Summer after summer had been
filled with houseguests from Connecticut, and rotating visits from
the grown children and growing grandchildren, and occasional ap-
pearances of Kirsten and Kaj, and Danish cousins, and infrequently
and briefly goddam Nina. House and equipment repairs and replace-
ments were noted, and in 1986, the centennial party was held for the
house itself, as suggested by Neville Crane all those years ago.

By 1986, it was possible to see what the end would be. Not how it
would happen, or what it would mean, but what it would look like.

June 30, 1986 (In Sydney's hand)

> Arrived last night. Few flowers in garden yet—a
> cold wet June. House looks very well, with reshin-
> gling finished and a new 52 gall. hot-water heater in
> the guest wing. Ellen Gott has retired, replaced by
> Shirley Eaton, and a college gal as 2d maid. Few
> flowers in garden yet.

Laurus's enduring pleasure those years were his Thursday-night
poker games. They were no longer at the firehouse, where the active
volunteers were now younger men, though Al Pease was still fire
chief. They most often met at Mutt Dodge's house; Sue Dodge liked

to have them. They'd have been welcome at Hugh Chamblee's as well, but gambling at the manse . . . well, there could have been talk.

They were playing seven-card stud, deuces wild. As he dealt, Al said, "You get much of a turnout for Tommy Hobbes, Hugh?"

"Quite a good house. The young were fond of him. They dedicated the academy yearbook to him last year, did you know that?"

"Tommy Hobbes hung up his boots?" said Laurus, as he raised the ante. He'd been in Boston the past five days.

"He did."

"When?"

"Tuesday. Went to bed Monday night and woke up dead."

"Well, *that's* the right way to go," said Laurus.

"In' it. See and raise." Tommy was a World War II vet who had come back from the war all right, but all wrong. He'd been an only child of an English couple who'd come to the village in service in one of the big cottages, and stayed. Both parents had been dead for years, and Tommy lived on in a ramshackle house in the woods, with a great many cats. He was always to be seen around the town at a loose end, happy to carry your groceries or help pull your car out of a snowbank. In summer he found work on the road crews, holding the sign that told cars when they must stop and wait, and when they might proceed. He always smiled his bug-eyed smile.

"I call," said Laurus. The hands were laid down and Laurus took the pot. The deal passed to Hugh, who shuffled and said, "Five-card draw, nothing wild."

"So what's Tommy going to want to know when he gets to heaven?"

"Prob'ly why Cressida turned him down," said Mutt. "Poor bugger never got over that."

"Poor bugger never got over the Battle of the Bulge," said Laurus. "Of course, according to Swedenborg, he may not know he's dead yet. He's probably standing around with his parents and some angels trying to get the hang of that. Oh ho, what have we here?" he added, as he looked at the cards he'd drawn.

There was a round of betting.

"Are we talking about angels with wings?" asked Mutt.

"I don't think so. I don't know where they get their clothes, but they're thick around us, looking pretty human."

"I'm having trouble with the idea of Tommy Hobbes as an angel," said Al. "To tell the truth, I was looking forward to not having to deal with Tommy Hobbes at all in my afterlife."

They all laughed.

"But in heaven, you might like him. Just think, with all the mask and outer shell stripped away, and nothing left but the pure Tommy, you might be crazy about him."

"With all that stripped away, he'll smell better."

"He won't smell at all. Without bodies, we only have sight and hearing."

"I thought you told us there would be marriage and sex in heaven."

"Yes, there will be. It'll be different, but it'll be great."

"Cressida's looking forward to that," said Al Pease.

The deal passed to Andy Coles, who called for a hand of Texas Hold'em.

"How do you know all these peculiar games, Andy?" Mutt asked.

"Misspent youth. Did you ante, Laurus?" The way they pronounced it, it sounded like Lars.

"What? Sorry." He pushed some chips into the center.

"I wish more of my patients could go like Tommy," said Andy. "I hate when they're suffering, and it goes on and on. I had a patient this winter, eighty-eight, in a coma, no living will. I had to send him up to Bangor. They kept doing things to him, when the family was begging them not to. Finally took off one of his legs and by the time he died the bill was thick as the Boston phone book. None of it did a damn bit of good. And all the money he thought he'd put by for his grandkid's college . . . gone."

They played out the hand.

Al said, "I don't know why everyone thinks this should be left to doctors. Any plumber worth his salt can arrange to have everyone in the house wake up dead."

"Is *that* what you all talk about when you go to the Plumber's Ball?" crowed Mutt. Al and Cressida had once gotten all dolled up and gone down to Portland for a Plumber's Ball, and no one in Dundee had ever let Al forget it.

"Listen, Al," said Laurus.

"What are we playing?"

"Blackjack. Al, I want you to promise that when my time comes, you keep Andy away from me. I'm looking forward to heaven and I'm announcing here and now I want you to take care of it."

"I'll be happy to. What's a friend for?"

"All right, you're all my witnesses. Mutt?"

"Hit me."

Laurus dealt around the table.

Faster Nina died in the winter of 1992. Laurus and Monica went over to Copenhagen for the funeral. It was small and quiet. Everyone agreed there was no point asking Sydney to go; she was increasingly made anxious by unfamiliar surroundings and she wouldn't understand the Danish service anyway. Nina had left careful instructions for her final arrangements: what hymns she wanted, a request for cremation, what clothes she wanted to wear, even a little doll she wanted to take with her. Her careful planning was just what one would have expected. But everyone was surprised by two things in Nina's will: one request for each brother. Nina had left a small bequest to someone they'd never heard of named Hans Katz, about whom she said only that he was born in Jutland in about March of 1943 and had emigrated to Israel with his family in 1958. She asked Kaj to find him and send him a sum of money and her blessing. The other was that Laurus scatter her ashes on the bay at Dundee.

"Why, I wonder?" Kaj and Kirsten had supposed she would go into the churchyard with Papa and Mama.

"She always said she was so at peace out on the water there," Laurus said, but he was as surprised as they were.

Laurus knew, too, that the request was a measure of how close Nina felt to him, and was both glad for her forgiving love and bitterly sad that he hadn't seen more of her over the years, had her to stay longer, and more often. But. Well.

He and Monica flew home with Faster Nina's ashes in an urn wrapped in brown paper. Kaj's wife and daughters had taken care of finding the doll she had mentioned, and the final costume, all thoughtfully collected in a corner of the closet. That part was over by the time Laurus and Monica got there.

"What was the doll like?" Monica asked her cousin. She pictured a beloved memento from Nina's childhood, or maybe something she had hoped one day to give to a daughter of her own. Wouldn't that be sad.

"It was a scary little thing. More like a fetish than a doll. It had little stick limbs, with clogs and a babushka."

Monica kept her godmother's ashes for the rest of the winter and brought them up to Dundee at the end of July.

In those days, Eleanor and Bobby rented a house down on the Salt Pond in Dundee and were there for most of the summer. The whole Applegate family came each week to Sunday supper at Leeway as once Leeway had gone to The Elms, and later to The Plywoods. Jimmy and his wife and children spent several weeks in July at Leeway and overlapped for a necessarily brief time when Monica and her children came for August. The Guest Book was kept in Laurus's hand or Monica's in these years.

August 2, 1992

*On this beautiful summer day, we took Faster Nina to the middle of Great Spruce Bay and said goodbye to her. Jimmy, all the Applegates, Mother and Dad and I, and Mr. Chamblee went with her. Mr. Chamblee read the 121st Psalm, and Dad read a poem by Robert Frost: "Nothing Gold Can Stay." The Lord shall preserve thy going out, Nina, and*

*thy coming in, from this time forth, for evermore.*
(Monica)

That night they had family dinner at Eleanor's, and told stories about
Nina, trying to fix her in their children's minds. How she shopped so
carefully for each child's Christmas present. How she always had a
book in French somewhere about her. How she loved Paris and was
so grieved when the Jeu de Paume, her favorite museum, was closed.
How she would sit on the porch at Leeway and look out over the
gardens and the bay. How modest she was; how they never would
have known about the brave things she did in the war if Per Bennike
hadn't told them. It didn't feel as if she had left much behind, for a
life of seventy years. The young blamed her smoking for a death that
came too early. Laurus felt, but did not express, a very different
sense of his sister's loss; that sometime during the war her essential
self had been murdered, and she'd had to struggle on from there as a
husk, without dreams or hope. Seventy years of that seemed to him
quite long enough.

"Monica," said Eleanor that summer, "do you think Syd Vicious
should be driving?"

The sisters were playing golf together, content in the late-
summer sunshine to see so many people around them on the tees and
greens whom they knew and in many cases loved.

"Why, just because she keeps turning on the windshield wipers
instead of her turn signal?"

"One of these days she's going to step on the gas when she meant
the brake. We'll be lucky if all she does is kill her*self*."

"Have you talked to Dad about it?"

"I brought it up."

"What'd he say?"

"He said she doesn't drive very fast."

They both laughed, and paused while Eleanor located her ball in
the blueberry scrub.

When they were on the tee of the fourth hole, their friend

Amelia came bowling up the Point Road in her little death trap, a restored Corvair convertible from her teenage years, kept on the road by ingenious substitutions of body parts her husband scavenged from an auto graveyard north of Bangor. The car lived in a decaying barn in the winter and was only driven on sunny summer days, as the top had long since disintegrated.

They waved and Amelia pulled off the road and left her car tucked in among some pines. She joined them on the tee.

"Who's winning?" she asked.

"We have no idea. Here, you're up." Eleanor handed her a driver and Monica gave her some tees and a ball. When they were all safely over the road and wandering down the fairway, Eleanor said, "We're trying to figure out how to stop Big Syd from driving. I'm afraid she'll run over one of the children."

"Uncle Laurus can't stop her?"

"Can't or won't. You know how they are. If you don't talk about it, it isn't happening."

"They're very sweet together," said Amelia. "I saw them having lunch here yesterday, talking about what it is they like to eat. Your mother couldn't remember the word for salmon."

"Usually they just look up trustingly at the waitress and say, 'that fish that we like, that's pink.' "

"Your father's got most of his marbles, though."

"Thank heaven."

"Syd Vicious can't remember the names of her grandchildren but she can sure hit a golf ball," said Eleanor.

"Yes, but then she hates her grandchildren. She likes golf."

"She couldn't hate her grandchildren," said Amelia.

Eleanor and Monica looked at each other.

"Amelia—you've led a sheltered life."

"She hates them. They interfere with her children paying their undivided attention to *her.*"

"Come on, you beastly ball, go in go in go in. Oh! Rats."

"The Gantrys have stopped driving," Amelia said.

"Really! How did Georgie manage that?"

"Well, of course her mother's blind, but it was the three-martini

lunches that really worried her. She and the boys discussed an inter-
vention. But the more they talked about it, the more they said, 'You
know what? They're in their eighties, they've been drinking like this
all their lives, if you took it away from them, what would they do
with themselves? Take up brain surgery? Join the Peace Corps?' So
they took away their licenses, and hired a driver."

Amelia played one more hole with them, then ran back to her car
and went on to wherever she had been going.

"Do you think Dr. Coles could help us?" Eleanor asked Monica.

"Yes, maybe."

"Loser of this hole has to call him."


On the eighth hole, Eleanor suddenly asked, for reasons of her own
that Monica would understand only later, "Do you think Dad was always faithful to Big Syd?"

"Why? Don't you?"

"I don't know. He traveled so much. He must have been
tempted."

They both thought about how different their father seemed from
men their own age. So formal. So courtly. So unbuffeted by emotion.
Could that have been true, or was it just his manner? His manners?

"You know," said Monica. "Once when we were sailing, just the
two of us, he talked about a girl he knew in London during the war.
A nurse from Oklahoma. She sang 'White Christmas' in April, because someone asked her to. He thought that was priceless."

"Really," said Eleanor. "And why did that come up all of a sudden?"

"That's what I couldn't figure out. It just seemed to please him to
talk about her."

"Did he ever see her again?"

"Yes, he did. Maybe that's what brought it up . . . no, that can't be
it, it must have been way earlier, because it was the summer he got
the—"

"Monica!"

"Sorry. What he said was, he was in Chicago, decades later, with the Chicago symphony. Some big donors were giving a party for him, the way they do, and he walked into the house and there she was. She was the hostess. She was married and had about five children."

"Yes? And?"

"And I don't know. How could I ask?"

"Did she know he was . . . you know, the person she knew in London?"

"Oh, yes. She'd been waiting for him. She was waiting for him to recognize her."

"And he did right away?"

"Apparently. He said she looked just the same. He said, 'It's you!' and asked her if she still sang 'White Christmas,' and she said no, but she was still a hell of a dancer."

Monica's ball had gotten in under the cedar trees, with no room for a backswing.

"You can drop out," Eleanor said.

"No, I'll drive out with my putter." She did so.

As they walked toward the green, Eleanor said, "Would we like it if we thought he . . . if they . . . ?"

"I don't know. I think we really would, don't you?"


There was another car incident late in the summer, when Sydney went to call on Gladdy. Amelia's daughter Barbara was staying with her grandparents, as the little cottage her parents rented was full. She heard a car honking at the back door, then Grandma Gladdy calling from the back porch, "Sydney? Is that you in there?"

"Yes, I'm—"

Silence.

"I didn't recognize the car," Gladdy called.

"No. It's rented," Barbara heard Mrs. Moss yell from inside the car. "I got a bung in mine and it went to the shop. This is rented."

"Well, come on in, I'm making iced tea."

"I will but I . . . I can't figure out how the door unlocks."

"Wait till I get my shoes on, I'll come help."

"No, never mind. I've got the window down, I'll just climb out."

At this point, young Barbara cried from the upstairs window, "Mrs. Moss! It's Barbara, just wait one second, I'm coming down," and Sydney subsided and waited.

"I don't wonder you were troubled, Mrs. Moss," Barbara said kindly as she opened the door for Sydney. Her feet were bare and her hair was wet from the shower.

"I kept pushing the—"

"Oh, I know. These Japanese ones are *so* different."

"Well, thank you . . . dear."

"Barbara. Amelia's daughter."

"Yes, of course you are," said Sydney. Barbara was perfectly sure she didn't know who she *or* Amelia was. As Sydney climbed to the kitchen, Barbara tried to keep from laughing out loud at her mental picture of Mrs. Moss getting halfway out the window in her big Bermuda shorts and then plunging headfirst onto the driveway. Which would probably break her neck and not be at all funny, but still . . .

In the early summer of 1993, Sydney was notified by the DMV that she would have to come in to Union to requalify for her license. Laurus drove her over and sat with his straw hat on his knees while she went out in the Oldsmobile with the young man in brown, to demonstrate her ability to weave between orange cones, properly observe lights and street signs, and parallel park. This last had terrified her, because the arthritis in her neck made it hard for her to turn her head enough. Laurus had gone into town in the evening with her and coached her while she practiced and practiced in the empty parking lot of the Consolidated School.

She was beaming when she came in from her road test. Laurus raised both fists and shook them, a gesture of triumph. Submissively Sydney was then led into the back of the building to take her written test and have her eyes examined. When she came out, her license to drive had been canceled.

"I'm sorry," said the nice young man in brown. Sydney was so mortified and angry she wouldn't look at anybody. Laurus put his straw hat on his head and his hand under Sydney's elbow, which she shook off. The young man in brown watched from the steps of the building as they drove off, just to be sure it was Laurus at the wheel.

\*    \*    \*

Jimmy arranged for Tom Crocker's grandson Marlon York to come to work at Leeway Cottage, in theory as yardman, but in fact to drive Sydney wherever she wanted to go. Marlon drove slowly, which was fine with everybody. Also he didn't drink, having had a violent case of hepatitis when a boy, so he could drive in the evenings as well. The first summer Sydney submitted to this regime with bad grace, but by the following year, she had forgotten whatever point of pride the arrangement had wounded. She was glad, if mildly surprised, to see Marlon every morning, and came to enjoy going into the garden with him and teaching him things. Marlon was hopeless with the flowers and never learned, but as Sydney did not remember having already taught him what to do about rose hips, or staking the dahlias, she didn't realize she was explaining for the fifth or ninth time. She got respectful attention, and he got a patient teacher.

Laurus had turned eighty that year, and had some angina. The children began to worry about him sailing *The Rolling Stone* with only Sydney for company. *The Rolling Stone* was a graceful little sloop, with a comfortable head and four berths below and a dinghy called *No Moss.* (Sydney's sense of humor.) He had hoped Sydney would learn to like cruising, as nothing made him happier than to be anchored for the night in some wild harbor with only the sky and the gulls for company. She had tried, too, but she had never overcome her conviction that fascinating things were happening at home and she was missing them. He gave up, and enjoyed himself taking his grandchildren out exploring Frenchman's Bay and beyond, until they in turn grew too sophisticated to be missing the action onshore. Nowadays, he loved to go out on picnics, and to watch the August racing. He and Sydney had bought a new fiberglass International for the grandchildren, and rain or shine, Sydney was out there on deck with her binoculars trained on the racers, muttering "get it up get it up, get your damn spinnaker pulling . . ." and so forth, as if she were manning every position herself. Laurus ignored the fact that she was often watching the wrong boat.

"Pop's fine," Jimmy said scornfully to Eleanor.

"I know he's fine. But what if he had a heart attack or a stroke? Or fell overboard? Mother wouldn't know how to get home, she couldn't use the ship-to-shore, they'd be off to the Azores."

"Hey, look, I took care of the Marlon deal. Over to you."

Eleanor waited for Monica to arrive in Dundee, and they faced their father together.

He listened to them quietly. Then they all stared at each other. Finally he said, "Thank you, girls. I appreciate your concern."

There was another pause.

"But?"

"But what?"

"You appreciate it, but what are you going to do?"

"Think about it," he said. And he got up and went upstairs.

Next Eleanor and Monica took their husbands out to dinner and explained their fears. The husbands looked at each other.

"What do you want us to do?"

"Talk to him. You have penises and deep male voices."

"I wouldn't want my children telling me what I can and can't do," said Bobby.

"I wouldn't, either, but we've probably all got a lot of things in front of us we aren't going to like."

"What if they—"

"Okay," said Bobby. "When he wants to go out, I'll go with him."

Eleanor and Monica looked at each other. Neither one of them had thought of this, and it wasn't what they'd planned at all. It meant Bobby would be off attending to Laurus and Sydney at all kinds of moments when they would rather he were doing things *they* wanted him to do. Or else he wouldn't really do it, and Laurus would fall overboard and their mother would be found weeks later on the high seas in a horrible state and they'd be criticized. And they'd be sad about their father. "Nonsense," said the husbands. "He'd be delighted to go that way."

June 30, 1996

*The attic hot-water heater tank leaked and flooded into the blue guest room. Total renovation has been supervised by Shirley and Marlon. New wallpaper and furniture (Eleanor chose) are all in place, and all was covered by insurance. New tiles in the bathroom very fancy.* (Laurus's hand.)

"Welcome back, Mr. Moss," said Shirley Eaton. She was standing in her white uniform on the back porch of Leeway as the station wagon pulled in, loaded with all the strange gear the Mosses were accustomed to drag back and forth with them, framed pictures and waffle irons and doormats and you never knew what. Marlon York had gone down by bus to drive them to Dundee. Not that Mr. Moss couldn't, he drove everywhere at home; it just seemed better, even to him, that he not drive such a long way.

Laurus seemed to have shrunk over the winter. He was always a lean man but now he seemed actually diminutive. But spry and cheerful. Sydney was plump and her hair had gone white. She looked up the porch steps at Shirley and smiled and waved. She inhaled the air and looked around her as if she'd been in a time machine or space capsule and emerged to find herself in the most beloved place in the world. It pleased Shirley to see it.

Mrs. Moss greeted Shirley with a hug and kiss, then Laurus led her up to view the new arrangements where the flood had been. Shirley knew that in the old days there would have been an explosion right about the time she reached the top of the stairs. Paint not right, wallpaper imperfectly hung, tiles not the shade she liked. But instead she came downstairs beaming, after a thorough inspection, and said it was just lovely, how lucky she was, how thankful that they had taken it all in hand. Everything was perfect.

Eleanor came over as soon as Shirley called to say they'd arrived. She stopped in the kitchen to discuss the situation with Shirley, whom her children referred to as "the white army."

"Drive went all right?"

"Seems so."

"How'd she like the upstairs?"

"Seemed pleased as punch," said Shirley. "I've never known her so cheerful." Shirley, like anyone who had worked for Sydney, had had her share of fang marks to show for her trouble.

"Yeah, well. They may have finally gotten her meds right," said Eleanor.

July 2, 1998

> *We made very good time getting here. Shirley and her helpers have everything ready and Sydney has gone straight down to the garden to commune with nature. Porch has been repainted. Everything else is the same. Glad to be here.* (Laurus's hand. A little more spidery than formerly.)

Sydney *had* gone straight down to the garden, marveling. The colors and shapes of the flowers seemed like exotic jewels, surprising and new, and yet also, somehow, like very old friends. She no longer remembered how many thousands of hours she'd spent in these rows, pruning and cutting and weeding, giving orders in the fall for things to be separated, fed, or rooted out, cutting flowers for the house in midsummer, arranging them at her worktable on the side porch. But she found the residual feelings from those hours waiting for her, of peace and pleasure and usefulness and belonging. Unfortunately, after reveling in these, she forgot to come back up to the house. Shirley realized it before Mr. Moss, and went down to find her, which wasn't as easy as it sounds, as Sydney had sat down on the grass path between the iris beds to wait for the situation to clarify. She smiled sweetly when Shirley appeared. The new gardener had watered that morning, and Mrs. Moss's skirt was quite wet, which she didn't seem to mind or notice. It was something of a job to get her onto her feet. Shirley was glad it wasn't Mr. Moss trying to lift her.

As they made their way back to the house, Sydney heard Laurus playing the piano and knew to go toward that.

Laurus looked up as they came into the great room. "The piano is in beautiful tune, Shirley. Thank you for having it done."

"I know it pains you if it isn't right. Now, I think Mrs. Moss may want to change her . . ."

He got up and came to them. "Yes, I see. I'll take care of it. Thank you."

Eleanor and Bobby drove up while the elder Mosses were up-stairs. They went in through the kitchen to talk with Shirley, who told about the excursion to the garden. "No harm done, but . . ."

"We'll talk to Daddy," said Eleanor. At home, the cook lived in the house, but in Dundee no one had done this since the year Ellen Chatto was getting divorced. Shirley thought it wasn't right for the Mosses to be alone in the house at night. It worried Eleanor, too, al-though she recognized that in Connecticut, in case of fire or flood, Laurus would have to rescue Sydney *and* the cook, who was almost as old as he was and in far worse shape.

Her parents came down, bathed and polished and dressed for the evening, her mother in bright nautical red, white, and blue and a string of white beads—she had started wearing costume jewelry years ago when she traveled, and had gradually forgotten she had anything else. Laurus was wearing a blazer and an ancient pink oxford-cloth shirt which he left here in his summer closet, spotless white slacks, and a pair of boating shoes that had to be forty years old. Eleanor felt a rush of love for them both, as they stood there all shiny and pleased, looking forward to the evening and the summer.

They all said good night to Shirley and went out through the kitchen and gingerly down the back stairs to where the station wagon was waiting. Marlon had unpacked it and swept it out and taken it into the village to fill the gas tank before the station closed for the evening. Mr. Moss liked to keep the tank topped up. (In case of what? Indian attack?) He took very good care of his belongings, disliking change or fecklessness or lack of method. He polished his own shoes, sewed on his own buttons, and put name tapes in his clothes, as he had begun doing during his war. He meticulously met every service recommendation for his cars, his lawnmower, his boat, and his pianos. He loved taking care of things.

On this beautiful lavender evening, smelling of fir trees and wood smoke, Eleanor and Bobby Applegate, both over fifty, climbed into the backseat of the station wagon like children while Laurus installed Sydney in the front, fastened her seat belt, walked around the rear of the car (as he had taught them to do as children, so as not to be run over should the car suddenly start up), got himself in behind the wheel, and fastened his own seat belt. He adjusted the seat, adjusted the mirrors, and finally, as if enjoying every familiar gesture and action, ceremoniously started the engine and inched off down the familiar driveway, on the way to yet another welcome dinner with their best friends, at the start of yet another Dundee summer.

"How are they?" asked Monica on the phone. She was not coming until August and then it would have to be for a short visit, as her widowed mother-in-law was having a health crisis, and Monica's husband was an only child. There was no one but themselves to see to her, and they'd been at it all spring with no end in sight.

"It's like living underwater," said Eleanor. "They—do—every—thing—like—this . . ." She spoke at the retarded speed at which her parents seemed to her to move. "You take them to the club for lunch, you run up the stairs to get them a porch table, you move it into the shade, you get a pillow for Mother's chair, you go to the loo, you run back out to see if they're coming, and they're still getting out of the car." Far away, Monica laughed.

*The Rolling Stone* was in the water, on its usual mooring. One of Eleanor's sons was the designated boat boy, whose summer job, not that Laurus knew it, was to make sure that Granddad never went out alone. The boy would telephone Leeway every morning and confer with Laurus about the weather. Once in a while they'd agree that it would be a fine day to run down to Camden to look at the hills, or do what Laurus called "going to look for buffalo," which meant just puttering along the coast, poking into little harbors, and nosing about deserted islands. More often they would agree that for one reason or another, the day was not auspicious for boating after all. They'd usually go out in the dinghy anyway and spend a little time aboard, polishing the fittings or fooling with the charts, plotting the best courses for cruises they would take when the time was right. Which it never would be.

On Thursday nights, when Laurus went to his poker game, Eleanor had her mother to dinner. In past years this had been very hard on her children, since Mommy Syd asked the same questions over and over; but sometimes her mother would surprise Eleanor with a story she'd never heard before, a memory that emerged undamaged by long submersion and uncorrupted by retelling. (Sydney, like so many others, believed implicitly in the last version of any story she'd told. Once she'd started telling it a certain way, not to mention embroidering for better effect, she had no idea what parts she knew and which she'd invented.) This year the dinners were actually easier, since Sydney had stopped using language much at all. Instead she hummed in a musical approximation of the rhythms of speech. It was rather comforting.

"Your halo is bright in heaven," said Monica on the phone, when Eleanor described it.

"Well, Daddy needs the break," said Eleanor.

"Don't I know it. I suppose Jimmy has been very very helpful?"

"Oh, please." Jimmy was living near San Jose, very involved with a software gaming company that was just inches, he said, *inches,* from going public and making his fortune. He didn't think he could get east this summer at all.

Bobby, who was a venture-capital guy, had been shown the beta version of the company's flagship product. He said, "Trust Jimmy to find a way to make hay out of ten years on psychedelic drugs."

"He called me the other day," said Monica.

"Jimmy?"

"To explain that he doesn't call Mother more often because when he does, Shirley lectures him about not calling enough."

"What'd you say?"

"Get over it."

It was hard to make Eleanor even cross, let alone angry, but she did resent Jimmy's inattention, especially to their mother. It was pathetic, the worshipful way Sydney lit up when she heard from him. Or even *of* him. Still, it wasn't Sydney who worried them these days. It was their father's inexplicable (to them) insistence on doing so much—really, everything—with Sydney and for her. He was eighty-four himself and should have been relishing the time on earth that he had left, not living like a prisoner.

On a Thursday morning in August, Monica and Eleanor sent their mother off to the hair parlor with Marlon at the wheel, and cornered their father in the study where he was paying bills.

He beamed when they came in and, ever courtly, left the desk and sat down in a chair facing them.

"Well, it's so nice to see you."

"You, too."

"What are your plans for the day?" he asked happily. "Would you like to get out on the water? We could take a picnic."

"That sounds lovely, but Dad, could we talk about something?"

Suddenly wary, he said, "All right," and sat looking at them.

The two women looked at each other. You go. No, you.

Eleanor started. "We're worried about you and Mother. We're worried about how much you have to do for her . . ."

"I am doing exactly what I want to do," he said, his voice and face both quiet and neutrally pleasant.

"We understand that."

"And we love that you want to do it."

"But we're worried about what could happen."

"Like what?"

There was a little silence.

"Suppose somebody broke into the house. What would you do?"

"I'd do exactly what you'd do. Call the police."

"A fire, then," said Monica, knowing this wasn't what she meant at all.

"Dad, what if you fell. Or had a heart attack, or . . . you know. What if the two of you were alone and something happened to you?"

"Why don't you tell me what you're driving at?"

"We'd feel better if someone was in the house with you at night."

"Or if you'd consider—"

"No."

This stopped them. They were prepared for questions, they had plans in mind. They hadn't anticipated flat refusal.

"I do not care to discuss this any further. If you'll excuse me, I have things to do here." And he got up and sat back down at his desk. He sat there perfectly still with his back to them until they left the room.

Neither sister spoke until they were out of the house.

"I guess we're not going on a picnic," said Monica. They were both so upset that they went and told Bobby. He took them into the village where a new bistro had opened in the former blacksmith shop, and made them drink wine with lunch.

"Well, that's over," said Jimmy on the phone. Eleanor and Monica were on separate phones at Eleanor's house.

"Oh, come on, Jimmy. This isn't safe. If something happened to him, Mother wouldn't know what to do—"

"Why is this our business?"

"Jimmy! Use your head."

"Monica! Don't lecture me!"

"Could we stick to the point here?" This was Eleanor.

Silence.

"All right, Jimmy. You tell us. What should we do?"

"Nothing."

"You know, Uncle Neville and Aunt Gladdy are totally happy in that what-d'you-call-it—"

"Death camp," said Jimmy.

"—Rosemont place. Totally happy. They have their own apartment, their own furniture, there's tennis and bridge, they like the food, they have new friends, they have buses to take them to concerts and movies—"

"Eleanor."

"What?"

"It sounds lovely. If you want to move there, you move there. But this is not your life."

"I *know* that! I'm just—" Suddenly Eleanor was very near tears.

"Did you like it when you were engaged to Bobby and Big Syd thought it was her wedding?"

"I wasn't even engaged and she—"

"Did you like it?"

"No."

"How is this different?"

"You know how it's different!"

"No I don't," said Jimmy.

By this time Monica, who was on the cordless phone from the kitchen, had come up to Eleanor's bedroom and was sitting on the bed beside her, holding the receiver to her ear.

"The difference," said Monica, "is that they're old. They're fragile—"

"Not that fragile. They're both in good health. Dad's of sound mind. He's perfectly able to choose what risks he wants to run."

"Jimmy, you're saying that because you don't want to have to come here and help us deal with it."

"Monica, someday you are going to be sorry you said that."

"I'm sorry already," she said, and began to cry.

"I can't take much more of this," said Eleanor.

"Neither can I," said Jimmy.

The three sat for about a minute, just breathing into their telephones. Finally Jimmy said, "I know what you're afraid of. But if Dad isn't afraid of it, then you'll just have to live with it. It isn't your life."

"But it is. It affects us all."

"I didn't say it doesn't affect us. But it's his choice."

"What about Mother? She can't choose."

"She has chosen. She wants what he wants."

"You don't think Dad would mind if he fell down a flight of stairs and lay there all night? Or died?"

"You may be afraid of his death. But he isn't. I think he gets up in the morning and says, 'This is the day the Lord has made,' and if it's his last, well then he's looking forward to seeing his movie."

"I can't talk about this anymore," said Monica.

"I'm sorry, but it's what I think," said Jimmy.

"I can't either," said Eleanor.

"Goodbye, then," said Jimmy.

When they had hung up, Eleanor looked at Monica and said, "Jimmy's right. I'm afraid of his death. I'm afraid he'll die, and there won't be any movie." She began to cry.

Bobby appeared in the doorway holding a pair of large, full martini glasses with salt around the rims.

"Ladies, I have made margaritas."

"You're a saint," said Monica. She took the glasses and held them while Eleanor wiped her eyes and blew her nose.

"I thought you would like to know that your father just dropped your mother off for dinner. He's gone to play poker."

"Great," said Eleanor.

Laurus was out on *The Rolling Stone* watching the International racing, when he came so near hitting a buoy that his grandson was alarmed.

"Granddad? Did you see that?"

He had to wait a moment or two for his answer. They were under power, luckily, as the boy could not have handled the sails single-handed, any more than his grandfather could.

"Would you take the wheel for just a minute?" Laurus finally said.

"Granddad?"

"I'm all right."

"But what is it?" The boy had the helm.

"I have a headache."

"Should we go in?"

There was a pause, in which the boy felt panic rise so high in his throat he could taste it.

"I think maybe we should. Go in."

The boy kicked up the speed and set a course for the committee boat, grateful that the racing fleet was behind him in something close to doldrums. He steered close and the captain of the race committee came on deck without his having to blow the foghorn, which made a terrifying noise. He put the *Stone* in neutral and dropped the engine noise.

"Everything all right?" called Rufus Maitland, noting that old Mr. Moss was sitting down and looking odd.

"We're going in. Would you call my mom and tell her?"

"Righto," said Rufus, heading below to radio the club to relay the message by telephone.

By the time the boy brought the boat into the yacht club dock, a landing he and his grandfather had practiced at tedious length for which he was now extravagantly grateful, Eleanor was pulling into the club driveway. She met them on the dock.

"Oh, hello, honey," her father said when he looked up and saw her.

"Hi."

"Are you giving the tea?" Laurus asked.

"No, I just thought I'd see how you were getting along." She could see the pain in his face but knew it would be fatal to start fussing.

"Well . . . I have a headache."

"Where?"

He touched the side of his head. "And I think . . . something with that eye." Eleanor and her son looked at each other.

"Why don't I run you in to see Dr. Coles?"

The fact that he didn't refuse instantly told her that something was really wrong.

"I hate to run out on my sidekick here . . ."

"I'll be fine, Granddad."

Laurus let the dock boy give him a hand stepping down from the boat rail to the dock, another bad sign.

Three days later, at the Seacoast Medical Center in Union, Eleanor was on the phone to Dr. Coles in Dundee. Outside in the corridor, Bobby sat with her father, who had dressed himself in the clothes he'd been wearing when he was brought in, and announced to them when they appeared that he was glad to see them, because he was checking out and they could drive him home.

"I'd be happier if he'd go to Bangor for an MRI," said Dr. Coles, "but I have to admit, I can't make him. There isn't any reason to keep him in the hospital if he wants to leave."

"But he's had a stroke."

"He's had a stroke. But the first twenty-four hours make all the difference and he came back pretty completely."

"But Dr. Hayes said it could happen again, he wanted to watch him—"

"It *could* happen again. On the other hand, it might not happen for years, or ever. His vision is normal, I examined him last night and didn't see any residual impairment. And I'm told he had a disturbed night because he wanted to be at home. That's not good for him."

"Is that your medical opinion?"

"Yes, Eleanor, it is."

She thanked him and hung up. She felt that the doctors were in cahoots with her father against her. Even the nurse in charge of the floor had fallen for Laurus when she asked him if he knew who was president of the United States, and Laurus said stubbornly, "I may not know his name, but I know I didn't vote for him."

Laurus did *not* like being in the hospital. And today he did know the president's name, and anything else they could ask him.

"You take care now, Mr. Moss," said the nurse as Laurus walked to the elevator, with Bobby and Eleanor trailing behind, carrying his newspapers and books in a paper bag, and the geranium Gladdy had brought him, and his little duffel bag with his pajamas and slippers. "Enjoy your poker game . . ."

"You're not planning to play poker tonight," said Eleanor in the elevator.

"Yes I am. It's Thursday."

"Do you want to end up right back in the hospital?"

"I do not. I do not ever want to go to the hospital again."

They emerged into the daylight. Bobby persuaded Laurus to stand at the door in the shade and let him bring the car, but just barely. They installed Laurus in the front seat and Eleanor behind with the belongings. As they drove down the main street of Union, the sidewalks busy with summer tourists in shorts and sandals (although by far the greater number of tourists would be up at the mall on High Street), Laurus said, "Look, they're doing *The Mikado* at the Opera House. I think your mother would like that. Don't you?"

Eleanor leaned forward so her head was nearly between her husband's and her father's.

"Dad, you tell me. You won't consider having someone live in the house with you."

"I would if it were necessary. But it's not."

"You won't even talk about moving somewhere where you could have help taking care of Mother, and yourself if you should ever need it . . ."

"No I will not, and I don't want you and your sister trying to go behind our backs. We've made our own bed, without help from you, and we intend to lie in it."

Eleanor was quiet for about a half mile, trying to figure out what exactly that meant. And how did he know not to include Jimmy in this?

"All right, tell me this. You won't go for an MRI."

"I do not want any more hospital."

"Tell me why not. What happened at the hospital that was so bad?"

"I'm old. I've had a very interesting life, but I have no intention of living forever and I don't want strangers doing things to me I don't want."

"All right. What if something happens to you so you aren't dead and you can't live as you do now? What am I supposed to do? Will you tell me? Do you want us to build you a platform in the woods like the Indians and drive off and leave you? That will look wonderful in the papers."

"Five-card stud," said Al.

"So what'd you say?" Hugh Chamblee asked Laurus.

"I told her I'd made arrangements with Al to take care of it." The men laughed.

"But that won't help you if you're in Connecticut," said Hugh. "You better find a plumber there who makes house calls."

"Maybe I better not leave Dundee."

They played the hand out, and the deal passed to Al.


Mutt Dodge and Hugh Chamblee were having lunch at Olive's.

"What do you make of Laurus?" Mutt asked. "I gotta admit, I see this from the daughters' point of view. My father's ninety-three and I can't do a thing with him. Lives alone and likes it, shovels his own walk, won't have a generator . . ."

"How'd he make out in the ice storm, then?" The region had had a bad one the past winter, with power out for days.

"Just fine. He lit a fire in the woodstove and got in bed with the dog. The two of them ate Ritz crackers for two days and then they got their power back."

"Ours was out for six days."

"I remember," said Mutt.

OhnoOhNoOhNoOhNo.
Oh . . . wherewherewherewhere?
Now. How. Ohno. Ohno.
Mmmm. Huhuhuh.
Honey . . . honey . . .
Hm. Hm. Huhuhuhuh . . .

The phone rang in Cressida Pease's kitchen. She had just come down from the fair. Everyone else was up there waiting for the fireworks. Cressida had seen fireworks in her time and she hadn't taken a heavy sweater. The evening had turned nippy.

"Hello?"

"Yes!"

"Hello?"

"Uuuuuuhhh . . . here . . ."

Cressida held the receiver away from her ear and looked at it in annoyance. Then she hung up before the voice on the other end could ask her if she had Prince Albert in a can.

Shirley found them.

It was Sunday morning of Labor Day weekend. She didn't usually work on Sundays, but she'd promised Eleanor she'd come in, as she'd have most of the week off and Eleanor couldn't be there herself. The Applegates had gone to Rhode Island to a godchild's wedding. Jimmy was in California and Monica was at home nursing her mother-in-law.

Marlon was supposed to drive Sydney and Laurus to Connecticut Tuesday after the worst of the holiday traffic. Shirley had plenty to do before then, baking blueberry muffins and Mr. Moss's favorite butterscotch cookies for them to take home in freezer bags for the winter. She had all the laundry to do so the water could be turned off and the pipes drained before frost. After they'd gone, she had to pack up all the liquids in the house from kitchen and bathrooms and laundry and carry them home in cartons to keep in her own warm basement, where they wouldn't freeze and burst.

She'd let herself in the kitchen door and had the coffee made and the orange juice squeezed, and was setting the dining room table for breakfast, when she noticed it was time Mr. Moss was down, and she didn't hear anything. She stopped and listened for the creaking of footsteps crossing the bedroom floor above, of water running in the bathroom. All was quiet. She made the batter for blueberry pancakes. When there was still no stirring, she thought she better just run up and see if everything was all right.

"Mr. Moss?" she called, from the foot of the stairs.

Nothing.

She called again. The grandfather clock in the living room struck the half hour. He was always up by seven-thirty.

Stopping on the landing, she began to taste the air. There wasn't so much a smell, as something you could feel in the back of your mouth. She didn't want to go farther, but she did.

The bedroom door was shut; no one answered when she knocked. She opened it, and the smell was like a pillow against her face. She went straight to open the windows. Then she turned to take in the scene.

A lamp was turned on beside the bed, though it was bright daylight. The bedclothes where pulled back. Mr. and Mrs. Moss had both *been* in the bed, but they weren't there now. The bathroom door was open, and that light, too, was on.

It took her a minute to get herself moving toward the door, not wanting to find what she knew she would find.

They were lying together on the tiled floor. Mr. Moss was in an awkward pile, with one arm crumpled under him. It looked painful. He had a pillow under his head, though, and the blue and white overshot counterpane from the bed was bunched over him. He was still and his face was a bad color.

Mrs. Moss, in her pink nightgown, was lying on her side on the bath mat beside him. She had one arm around his shoulders, as if she were trying to keep him warm. With her other hand, she held his hand. Her skin was a waxy yellow, and one eye was open, unmoving.

Shirley went out to the bedroom again, and turned on the overhead light. She looked carefully at the scene. A cordless phone was on the floor. A glass of water on Mrs. Moss's side of the bed had been knocked over. She looked at the space heater; the dial was turned up, but it sure wasn't giving any heat. She turned the gas off, then went out, closing the door behind her.

In the kitchen, she sat down at the table and had a quiet cry. What if they had suffered? What if they'd been frightened? Then she blew her nose and tried to think whom she should call. They didn't have 911 in Dundee. This wasn't a case for an ambulance. She guessed she might as well call the fire department.

"Hullo?"

Who was that? Oh. "Al? Is that you? I'm calling the fire department."

"What's on fire?"

"Nothing."

"Good. Is that Shirley?"

"Yes . . ."

"I set the phone at the firehouse to ring through to home last night so everyone could go to the fair," said Al. "What's the trouble?"

Shirley told him.

In the Pease kitchen, Cressida saw Al go still. He hung up abruptly, without saying goodbye. Sitting at the kitchen table in her pink quilted bathrobe, Cressida watched his mouth work in a way she knew. Trouble.

"Who was the fella said be careful what you wish for?" Al asked presently.

Cressida didn't know. "What'd you wish for?"

"Not me. Laurus Moss. He's gone."

Cressida moved in her chair, relieved it wasn't one of their own. "I'm sorry," she said. She knew Al had been truly fond of Laurus Moss. "He was a real gentleman."

"Yuh," said Al, surprised at how upset he was. He paused. "I better get over there." Instead he sat down at the table with her and picked up his mug of coffee. Cressida watched him, wondering what he would do with these feelings, since expressing them was out of the question.

"Want me to heat that up?"

Al shook his head. He took a long swallow. Then he said, "I hope he's seeing his movie."

Privately Cressida thought the only thing Laurus Moss needed to see a movie about was how he happened to marry that awful wife, but this wasn't the time to say it. "We'll never know," she said, and stood up to clear the breakfast plates.

Nina is in Frøslev prison camp on October 2, 1944, her birthday. She turns twenty-two. The prisoners' barracks here are set in a semicircle like beams radiating from the sun, the role of the sun being played by the central guard tower. Barriers of barbed wire extend straight out from the tower on either side, bisecting the camp, captives on one side, captors on the other. The Germans' quarters are similar to the prisoners' barracks but there are important differences. The Gestapo men eat, drink, and smoke as they like. They come and go. They have no machine guns trained on them. The only route from the prisoners' side of the camp to the Germans' is a narrow choke point, the hallway through the base of the central watchtower itself.

Frøslev camp is run by the Gestapo, under SS General Pancke. General Pancke reports not to Dr. Best but directly to Berlin. Nina arrived at Frøslev in early September, in a van from Horserød prison near Helsingør, where she'd been sent after the SS in Copenhagen got tired of questioning her. Like all prisons in German-occupied territory, Horserød was growing crowded with resisters, Communists, and other thorns in the Third Reich's side, as well as its original population of criminals. Nina was among some twenty prisoners scooped up from Horserød without explanation and sent south. Others included an elderly Lutheran minister who had been caught hiding Jews in his crypt, and a half-dozen "asocials," thugs who were not part of the Resistance except insofar as there was a profit in it or an opportunity for violence.

The asocials wear a thick stripe of hair running down the middle of their otherwise shaved skulls from forehead to nape, a style they call "Red Indian." In the van they spat and made crude jokes throughout the journey, or sat in a row and stared at Nina in silence until her discomfort made them laugh. She was the youngest person in the van and easily the prettiest. There were older prisoners who would have intervened if they could, but it had been all too clear that the Gestapo men guarding them enjoyed the game as much as the asocials.

On arrival at Frøslev, an officer explained that they would be deloused as a sign of the Germans' care for them. As long as the men and women were to experience this care separately, Nina felt it would be easier to bear than the trip had been.

The women prisoners are all in barracks H-16. There are fifteen bunks to a room; she has an upper one. Each barrack is run by Danes appointed by the Gestapo. It saves the Germans trouble, as the Danes are very good at organization. It is also very good for the prisoners, who, Nina finds, have managed to "organize" all sorts of things not dreamt of in General Pancke's view of prison life. There is a gymnasium headmistress in Nina's room named Ulla, who has "organized" a complete set of art materials with which she makes forbidden pictures of camp life. She also conducts courses for the younger women, to keep their spirits up. There is nothing so cheering as learning new things. When Nina joins them, the course in progress is medieval history. On her birthday Ulla makes a beautiful card for Nina, which is signed by all the women in their room. It helps, in prison, to develop a prison "family," and though Ulla has many acolytes in the camp, she responds to something in Nina, her intelligence, her wide frightened eyes, her gentleness. Nina is deeply grateful for Ulla's protection.

The women prisoners work in the laundry, doing the wash for the inmates and their warders as well. The workshops are also run by Danes, so the work is hard but not crushing. It will be worse in the last months of the war, when the population at Frøslev has swollen from the 1,500 it was designed for, to 5,500. But it will never be the murderous slave labor found in the south. Also, in early autumn of '44 the food is still adequate, as it will not be much longer, even here.

The women cross into the men's area of Frøslev only when they go to the dining hall. The men call this "the hormone hour." Much information is exchanged at the hormone hour. At least two radios, illegal anywhere in Denmark if not set to the official government station, and especially inside a prison camp, have been organized. They are hidden under bunks, beneath trapdoors, the antennae concealed behind now a picture, now a shaving mirror. The radios come out for the BBC broadcasts after the Gestapo men and women have gone through the choke hole in the watchtower for their dinners on the other side. Maps of Europe have been drawn from memory, and the Allies' progress is marked every night, the news quickly spreading from barracks to barracks. Dieppe is liberated. Brussels is liberated. The Allies have broken the Gothic Line in Italy. The British are in Greece. The British are in Athens and Rommel is dead.

Prisoners make calendars marking each day they survive, and look ahead to the still blank squares of November, January, March, wondering on which they will mark VICTORY—on which will they mark FREEDOM. If at all. If they live.

They have made tiny chess sets out of contraband, they have manufactured decks of playing cards. There is even one camera, with smuggled film, making a secret record of prison life. They are lucky to be here.

Nina misses home and her parents desperately. She saw Kaj twice when she was in Vestre prison in Copenhagen, and once, to her joy, got a tiny message from Laurus, which had been rolled up and hidden in a cigarette lighter in the compartment meant for flints. It was handed to her by a man she passed on grim echoing stairs as she was taken down from her cell for transport to Dagmarhus for more questioning. It meant more to her than anything could have, short of a personal visit from the king. Though the lighter was soon confiscated, she managed to keep the scrap of paper with her like a fetish until the delousing at Frøslev. The loss of it frightened her badly.

She has not been tortured; she doesn't know why, except that it seems that many of the Germans in Denmark are lonely, and actually want the approval of the Danes, who are so beautiful, so Aryan, so like themselves. She has been asked over and over why she doesn't admire the Reich and its dream of strength and order stretching into the future for a thousand years. They never give up the hope that she will decide she has been misled by the bullying British and tell them who her contacts were, how the transports work, what codes she knows. Always they would start her interrogations by putting an open pack of Chesterfield cigarettes on the table in front of her. If she picked it up, she was theirs. There was more than one moment when, tired, scared, and longing for comfort, with the craving for nicotine singing in her nerves, she thought she would do it. Once, her hand moved out onto the table on its own, like a swimmer on a cold morning, putting a toe into the water. She could smell the tobacco, even the paper. She could feel already the hot smoke moving into her chest, the feeling of relief and calm it would bring, the sting in her nose as she exhaled. Her questioner, in his handsome black uniform, started to smile. Nina's brain deserted her hand and returned to her head; instead of grasping the pack, she flicked it with her finger and spun it off the table. It pleased her to see her inquisitor dive to the floor to retrieve it—no one under the peace and plenty of the Reich of 1944 was prepared to waste a pack of American cigarettes.

She didn't know why they gave up and sent her to Horserød, except that the Resistance had grown far more active and violent since her capture, and the Germans had their hands full. Trains and their tracks kept blowing up. German ships were blown up by mines attached to their hulls below the waterline, by partisans swimming at night in the inky water of blacked-out Danish harbors. In Odense a warship was given its official launching photographs, taken with smiling Nazis in crisp uniforms posed alongside the Danish workmen, and then blown up by a bomb left in a worker's lunchbox while the launching party went for schnapps and smørrebrød.

There were, too, accelerated retaliations for this sabotage. The beloved poet-preacher, Kaj Munk, had been murdered in January. The photograph of his corpse, on its back in a ditch, eyes closed and mouth open as if crying out, lived in Danish memories for decades. Through the spring of '44, in payment for bombings of things the Germans needed, there were bombings of things the Danes loved, carried out by the Danish Nazis of the Schalburg Corps. "Schalburtage," it was called. In June, patriots managed to blow up the heavily guarded Globus plant, which made replacement parts for German warplanes. Two weeks later they succeeded again, this time destroying the Dansk Riffelsyndikat, which supplied the Germans with small arms and artillery. In retaliation the Schalburg Corps burned down the Royal Danish Porcelain factory, and destroyed the student union at the University of Copenhagen. In late June the Tivoli Gardens themselves were bombed, a devastating wreckage the Germans said was necessary to stop good Aryan young people from dancing like Negroes in the dance halls of the place. Widespread striking and civil disobedience flared throughout the summer. On September 19 the Germans, finally provoked past endurance by its hindrance, inaction, and apparent inability to keep partisan prisoners from "escaping" out the back doors, attempted to arrest the entire Danish police force. Nina and the women watch from the windows of the laundry when several hundred policemen are brought into Frøslev, smiling and singing. And they watch when they are taken away again, bound for Buchenwald.

You can write one letter a month from Frøslev. You are allowed to write twenty lines, of not more than sixteen syllables each. Nina writes to Kaj. You are supposed to be allowed one visit a month, of ten minutes' duration, with an interpreter present. On the day Kaj is to be with her, all visits are suddenly canceled, no explanation given. Nina learns after the war that Kaj waited in Padborg for two days hoping to be allowed in, but at last had to give up and go back to Copenhagen. Travel is very difficult, the trains crowded and unreliable, being subject to sudden stops and searches, long delays, and of course, sabotage. By the time Kaj can come again, Nina is gone.

In Frøslev you can receive a Red Cross package every six weeks. Nina gets hers the day before her birthday. It is a wonderful day. She washes with real soap, she shares her sausage with Ulla and the women in her room. On that same day, during the hormone hour, one of the girls is passed a copy of a song someone has written, the words set to music known to them all from the songbooks that are in every Danish household. After supper they sing it lustily, and can hear that in other barracks the men are singing, too. It wakens deep and soul-feeding memories of singing this melody with parents, with classmates, around bonfires on midsummer nights, or snugged in from the deep winter around parlor pianos, and in cafés and bars. Having known these songs by heart from childhood is part of what makes them all Danes together. Another part is that if you are German and do not perfectly understand the Danish sense of humor, it sounds respectful, and sweet, even about their German brothers. If you know, however, to listen only for every second line, the song is very rude indeed.

One day in late October, Ulla is taken out of the laundry during work detail, and she disappears. Nina is agitated until Ulla is with them again. She reappears in a fierce mood.

"What happened?" Nina asks when she can.

"Stupid questions," says Ulla.

"Who was it?"

"The fat one with the walleye. I don't think he enjoyed it much."

"No?"

"No—I corrected his grammar. His German grammar."

Nina laughs aloud.

"Poor Germany," says Ulla. "In the hands of furious bricklayers and washerwomen."

There is a new officer from General Pancke's staff in the camp. Day after day, people are pulled out of work, out of meals, even out of bed, taken to the central watchtower house, and questioned. The week after Nina's birthday, suddenly, several dozen of the men are seen standing in the cold, each with one bundle or valise, being loaded onto a bus. Then they are gone.

A week later, Nina, Ulla, and five other women in the laundry are called out one afternoon and told to pack their things. Nina is so frightened her bowels start to rumble. They are loaded into the back of a truck equipped with wooden benches; it is already full of men with their overcoats on and their bundles between their feet. They sit in this truck under armed guard, without moving, for several hours, getting colder and colder, and Nina thinks maybe this is some witty new form of torture. Maybe in the end they will all pile out again and greet their friends and have supper.

Then a second man with a machine gun swings into the truck with them and pulls the gate shut behind him. He knocks on the back of the cab. The engine starts. The truck pulls out of the yard and stops at the gate. The gate opens, and the truck moves through. Nina feels the gears shift. Craning her neck to look out over the tailgate as they gather speed, she sees the gate to the prison yard being swung back in place and relocked, closing them out. In a matter of minutes they cross the border into Germany.

Hours later, in the blackness of a rail yard in Hamburg, they are ordered out of the truck. The men are formed up and marched away into darkness. The women are loaded into a freight car waiting on a siding, already crowded with women from prisons in France and stinking from the one inadequate half-drum in the corner that is serving them all as a toilet. When the door of the car slides closed, they are left in a darkness like a dirty black sock pulled over the face. It is hard to breathe, it is so dark, and there is no room to sit or lie down. Nina has lost Ulla. Around her, strangers stand stock-still, packed together, and wait. The women smell of sweat and rotting gums. Some swear, some weep, some pray aloud. One keeps keening "ma petite . . . ma belle, ma petite . . ." until someone tells her to shut up. Then they lurch like drunken livestock when the car begins to move. Nina can feel the breasts of the woman behind her push against her back, and the hard bony butt of the woman in front of her shoved against her ribs. The woman in front is well over six feet tall; it is hard to believe she is a woman at all. Where is Ulla? In the rattle and racket, someone close by her in the crushing dark snakes a hand into the pocket of Nina's coat. Nina angrily jabs an elbow into the press of bodies. By accident she also steps hard on someone's foot who cries out in turn. She doesn't know if she has found the thief or hurt someone as bewildered as she, but the hand withdraws.

Her legs ache and she is woozy with headache and hunger when the car stops and the door is opened again. A faint gray light is beginning to show in the night sky. Outside standing on the frosted ground there are SS men, and some female overseers, two with large dogs. Nina is among the first to reach the door, moving along in the pack which is like one sorrowing beast with hundreds of legs. At the edge of the car, the beast breaks apart as it goes over the ledge and drops to earth. As she shuffles forward, through the open door she can see pine trees in the dim morning. They are in the country. What country? Where are her father and mother, which direction? What would they feel if they knew where she was?

She drops to the ground and her frozen feet feel as if they have shattered on the impact. Trying not to stagger, she obeys the order, barked in German, that they fall into formation, five abreast. "Weiter! Rasch! Rasch! Los! Los!" From her rank in one of the first rows, she hungrily breathes in the scent of pine and the gray light after the long odiferous blackness. She sees Ulla come to the door of the car. Ulla looks old, her skin gray. This night has been hard on her. Ulla looks down at the drop and hesitates. "Rasch!" yells the overseer. She jumps, crumples, and disappears from view. The SS men shout at the women who move to help her up, but in a moment Nina sees Ulla standing on her own.

When all who can have left the car, two guards climb into it and throw out the corpses left behind. Nina watches them land on the frozen ground, their eyes staring, their arms and legs at painful angles. "Marsch!" yells the young woman with the biggest dog. Not all of the women understand German, so their progress is ragged at first. The women who are confused are shouted at to obey; the women who try to translate for them are shouted at to shut up. As they march away from the railway into the silent village, Nina looks back to see the name on the front of the station. FÜRSTENBURG says the sign. They are still in Germany.

As they march through the silent village, it is stunning, after all these months, to be so near to people sleeping on sheets in their own beds, people who will wake to the sounds of the bells from their own church, and the voices of their own loved ones. Who are they? If they knew we were out here, would they try to help us?

They soon leave the village behind and walk into the countryside. There is a hole in Nina's shoe and stones have gotten in. She is very cold. But the air smells of snow, and fir balsam; then there is a lake, lovely in the autumn morning. The walking is beginning to warm her. Nina watches the pale mauve colors of dawn on the slate gray water, and admires the little summer cottages standing shuttered here and there in the woods. And then, there are the walls of the camp. They are high and smooth, and there is barbed wire stretched along the tops. "Rasch!" bark the guards. Before them, the gates open. Their first view of Ravensbrück.

Inside, suddenly in a new world with only treetops visible beyond the walls, the women stand at the edge of what they will come to know as the Appelplatz, the roll-call place.

Roll call is in progress. Thousands of prisoners, all women, stand in ranks, ten abreast, eyes forward. Most wear striped prison dresses, but some wear oddly assorted street clothes. They are all ages and shapes and sizes. As the newcomers watch, the guards and trusties pace around the prisoners, counting, shouting, calling names. An old woman not far from them falls over and lies in the dirt. No one else moves. Very few eyes even shift to her when she falls. Nina gathers that the head counts are not right, that people are missing. For hours—how many, two?—the prisoners stand in silence, eyes forward, amid shouting and snarling, with trusties and guards going to the barracks and back, looking for the missing, until an order is given and the ranks break up into work details and are marched away.

Still, the newcomers stand where they are. Separated from them by a ribbon of barbed wire is a low building through whose windows they can see SS men and women eating, smoking, drinking coffee. Off to the left is the main "street" of the camp, flanked by rows of barracks. Across the Appelplatz Nina can see and smell what she correctly assumes to be the kitchen. It has been full daylight for many hours, and they have been told nothing, and given nothing to eat. The overseers come and go, and no one speaks to them, except to tell them to shut up and stand still. A woman near Nina with a hard cold snuffles and hawks and wipes her dripping nose with her hand. Finally a woman in SS uniform arrives and impatiently, as if they had kept her waiting, orders them to take off all their clothes.

SS men continue to come and go as the women obey. Soon Nina stands naked in the pale autumn sunlight with her belongings at her feet, angry and ashamed. For some of the older women it is even worse; they have not been naked in daylight before even closest family members since they were children. Let alone outdoors before strangers. She thinks of how her mother would feel. Plump maiden Faster Tofa, who plays the violin so gracefully.

Ulla stands in the row behind Nina, her bearing straight, her eyes still and focused far away. Her gray body hair is sparse, and her flesh hangs loose. She does not meet anyone's eyes.

An SS woman looks them over and orders them to move in single file into the building before them, leaving belongings behind. They will never see these again, except in rare cases on the backs of more privileged prisoners. A scrap of pencil Nina brought from Frøslev, and her birthday card from her friends there, and a warm pair of socks from her last Red Cross bundle, all disappear. They are on their way to the "showers." Showers. There have been rumors about these showers. In they march, their feet bare against wet scummy floors. There are rows of showerheads along a concrete wall. They crowd underneath them as ordered, and wait for water or death.

The water is actually warm, and while the soap is harsh, made with little fat and mostly lye, it is a surprise and relief to wash at all. When the water stops, they are herded off, still wet, to be inspected for lice, while new arrivals take their places under the showers.

The lice inspectors are prisoners. They wear uniform striped dresses, aprons, kerchiefs, wooden shoes, and lavender triangles. Their prison numbers are in three digits; they have been here a long, long time. They are German Jehovah's Witnesses, who could have gone home years before if they would only hail the Führer. They will not, because their Jehovah forbids acknowledging false gods, but this doesn't mean they are gentle.

The lice hunters' hands are horny, with dirty fingernails. Methodically they pick through each woman's hair, on her head, in her armpits, at the crotch. If nits or bites are found, the woman's head and body hair is shaved. When this happens, Nina can't look in the direction of the weirdly bald creature, stripped and stripped, she is so filled with dread and horror. She waits for her turn, as already more dripping-wet naked women come from the showers. These women are speaking something Nina doesn't understand, Czech or Hungarian, and some have children with them. Naked young boys and girls, bug-eyed with fear.

Nina holds her mind blank as a big stale-smelling woman with a goiter on her neck paws through the hair on her head and body. The woman wheezes as she works, as if some sort of untuned stringed instrument is stuck in her throat. Nina can hardly believe her relief when the inspector woman pushes her to move, get out of the way. She is done, and she still has hair. She follows the others out the door to the roll-call grounds again, where they stand naked, waiting for the doctor.

Nina passes the time watching brightly lit clouds form into mansions or cotton balls or piles of white peonies in the sky. There must be a lot of wind up there in the crystal blue; the clouds move fast across the dome of heaven. She makes bets with herself as to how long it will take a particular cloud to hit the sun, and counts out the seconds until the eye of the world blinks out. Then the seconds until it blinks on again.

They don't own anything except their bodies at this juncture. There is not a rag, a towel, or a hairpin among them. Nina and Ulla and a woman from Fyn called Søsti huddle together. They are not allowed to talk. Time has turned into an alien substance, sluggish and punitive.

The SS doctor arrives at last with a detail of guards, and the women are ordered to walk, on parade, past these men who study their figures, their gaits. It is not, in this instance, an advantage to understand German. The coarseness and contempt that is felt for them as captives, and as women, is revolting.

Nina notices that a teenaged girl, not yet starved enough to have stopped her menses, is bleeding down her leg. She is pointlessly trying to screen her pubic area with her hands, but the blood smears between her thighs like bright paint. Two of the guards point and nudge each other. Nina can imagine the sticky feel of it. It's been months since she bled; how many? In Vestre prison, must have been the last time. She doesn't remember having to organize or wash rags in Horserød or Frøslev.

When they have all been stared at, walking, some with heads high, most with eyes on the packed dirt beneath their bare feet, they are once again lined up at a door to go in to the doctor. Nina thinks she has never been so cold.

The line is moving like a worm a hundred feet long, into a room and out the other side, with a brief pause by each worm segment at the examining table. Through the door as she waits her turn, Nina can see the doctor. He has curly red hair and thick glasses. His method is practiced, his manner bored. With each woman he lifts her arms, then her breasts, to be sure she isn't concealing deformities or contraband. He bends her over and searches her anal cavity. Then he orders her onto a bare table on her back. He stands between her raised knees and jams a cold steel speculum into her to hold her vagina open. He settles his ample buttocks on a stool and with angled mirrors on metal stalks, has a good look around inside her. There is a light stand on little black wheels in the corner, but it must be broken. Instead, for light, a guard standing beside the doctor holds an electric torch trained on the woman's most private parts. The only conversation is between these two, about where the doctor wants the torch aimed. It doesn't take long, but it's much more like a search and seizure than a medical exam. Most are weeping by the time they are done.

The doctor rarely shows any reaction to what he is looking at, or to the gasps of shock or pain or the tears coming from the other end of the body on the table. He makes no attempt to sterilize his instruments between uses. He just sticks them into woman after woman. Nina feels fear like nausea creeping on her as she moves toward him. Sweat is pricking her armpits. She tries to steel herself, tries not to look, tries to take herself mentally elsewhere. But when it is her turn and she feels those hard fingers in her rectum, followed by the legs roughly spread, and the cold and slimy metal pushing in, she is so horribly present and alive simultaneously to what it feels like and what it must look like, that she feels she will never again be completely human.

The doctor adds a fillip to her examination. When she gets off the table, he stands, too, and puts his moist hands up to her face. He curls her lips back with his thick fingers and examines her teeth. He says something to an SS man lounging nearby, and a note is made.

They are outside again. Nina can't help herself; she spits on the ground. She wants to do it again and again but a guard steps toward her, threatening. Now Ulla is beside Nina, and Søsti is coming out the door. A large cloud has blotted out the sun and the afternoon is colder than the morning. It's been more than twenty-four hours since they had anything to eat.

They are ordered into lines, for their final processing. On long tables before them are piles of civilian clothing. The Reich has run out of striped uniforms. One by one each woman is handed a dress, a coat, a pair of shoes, some underdrawers. There is no attempt to give them clothes that fit; if anything, the opposite is the order of the day. Slight skinny Nina gets a fat lady's summer dress of flowered georgette and a coat of navy poplin with the buttons missing in place of her own winter clothes. Ulla gets a dress with a tight bodice she can't possibly close. Søsti gets shoes she can only get her feet halfway into. The clothes all have big $X$'s painted on the back, in case anyone thinks she can get away and melt into the surrounding country unnoticed. There are hundreds of dead lice in the seams of the coats. And their owners are . . . where?

They are given numbers in the high five digits, and one by one assigned to categories. The Danes are all Politicals but they get no red triangles to wear, as the Reich is out of those, too. At last, they march off to the admissions block where they will be quarantined.

The quarantine is hardest for those who have not come from other prisons. They are homesick and shocked, like houseplants stuck into freezing cold ground with no chance to harden off. Although they are healthier coming into the camps, they die much faster. They fail to heed warnings from more experienced prisoners; they don't yet believe they are here. A Jewish girl from Liguria who had been living aboveground, passing as Christian, has her coat stolen immediately. She has to stand in a thin dress in the winter morning at roll call with her head and arms bare and blue; roll call takes six hours that particular day as an unusual number who have died during the night fail to appear, and all are punished.

They are given typhoid shots from fat blunt needles. The doses are much too strong and Nina grows hot and ill from hers, but she is lucky. She has Ulla and Søsti to bring her food and water and to see she isn't robbed as she sleeps. The Italian girl is dead in four days. The Frenchwoman who shared her bed points this out to the Block senior so the body can be carried off to the funeral parlor crematorium in Fürstenburg and the rest of them won't be punished at roll call.

The Block senior is Polish. The Poles as a group are the intellectuals of the camp, the best linguists and best educated generally; so many Block seniors in the camp are Polish that all the seniors are known as Blockovas. This Blockova is in charge of teaching them the camp rules while they are in quarantine. How to make their beds, how to wear their kerchiefs, how to address superiors. She gives all instruction in German only. Some new arrivals don't know what's happening or why for weeks, if they live that long.

The Blockova tells them that if they are strong enough, they should volunteer for work outside the camp walls. It is physically grueling, but there is a chance there in the gardens or forests to dig a potato or gather mushrooms, and unlike those inside, you get a noon meal. This Blockova is reasonably kind, though not to the point of compromising the special deals she has organized to benefit her favorites and herself.

Quarantine is expected to last two or three weeks, but the sudden arrival of hundreds of Jewish women from the Budapest ghetto swamps the admissions block after a week and a half, and the Danes are moved out to a barracks that is now a mixture of cultures and languages, the most common being Ukrainian. The new Blockova is another Pole, a pharmacist in her old life. Here they sleep three to a "bunk," really just a wooden platform, the platforms stacked three high. Ulla, Nina, and Søsti are assigned a bottom bunk, which they think is good luck; it means Ulla won't have to climb up and down, which is hard for her, as the cold and her fall from the freight car has aggravated an injury to her shoulder.

They are wrong about the luck, as they learn the second night, when a woman in the bunk above them suffers an explosive bout of the shits. It runs down over the edge of her bunk and onto the inside edge of theirs. Søsti yells as she finds it in her hair. In the bunk above, the sufferer weeps and apologizes (they infer from her tone, though they don't know her language) while her bunkmates shout angrily at Søsti. Most of the toilets in their barracks, of which there are only twelve for hundreds of women, are broken. Eventually the sufferer is led by her bunkmates outside to the "chicken roost," a long row of seats braced above a pit, entirely exposed. The smell of shit and lime from these pits is one that will never entirely leave Nina's sense memory. It appears on the wind at unexpected times until she is an old lady.

The woman is still helplessly evacuating during roll call at five the next morning. Watery shit runs down her legs, into her shoes, and onto the ground. Women to whom this happens are called "Schmuckstücke," piece of jewelry, as in "what a gem she is." When they are finally released from roll call, about eight o'clock this particular morning, the Schmuckstücke is told to stay where she is, wet and stinking. They never see her again; she has been transferred to the diarrhea barracks, known inevitably as "the Shit Block," where conditions are so vile as to be indescribable.

Ulla has learned that their Blockova teaches classics in the underground camp university. Ulla asks her, in Latin, to be allowed to move with Nina and Søsti to a top bunk. When they come back from work detail at the end of the day, it has been done.

They have acquired bowls by now, and wooden spoons. Ulla brought a bowl from quarantine and shared it with Nina. Søsti had to save half her bread ration to barter for a bowl from a woman who had two, as her bunkmate had recently died. Nina does the same, and on their first Sunday in the barracks, the only day of freedom now (work shifts now run eleven hours a day, six days a week), Ulla sews for them pouches in which they can keep their belongings always with them; their bowls and spoons hang from their waists.

They eat in their barracks. At 4 A.M., when the first siren sounds, panicky activity explodes from the quiet bunks. Women run to line up for the toilets. Others make the beds in the precise way ordered. The table seniors and their helpers go to the kitchen and carry the food back to be doled out by the room seniors. In the morning, it's "coffee" (a brown liquid the Blockova claims has sedative in it, probably bromide) and the day's bread ration. At 5 A.M., the siren sounds for roll call. The morning roll call is shorter than the evening, often not even two hours long, as the SS wants the work details on the job as soon as possible.

Ulla and Nina are assigned to the textile factories, working yarn-spinning machines alongside mostly Soviet army women. Ulla is older and much less physically strong than most of the workers. One who works at Ulla's bench, a Slavic girl with big bones and most of her teeth missing, is struck by Ulla's pale blue eyes, with their yellow lights around the pupils. She tells Ulla whom she is missing, who it is in her life who has eyes like that, but they have no common language. Still, the girl protects Ulla; she and Nina know they could have drawn much worse work. Standing at the machines over ten hours a day is painful. Also the light is bad, and the air is filled with fibers that make their eyes and noses burn. But the SS men who oversee this shop are older and calmer than the ones in the sewing and fur shops, who stride up and down between the aisles of the machines yelling "Your quotas! Your quotas!" and punching women who fall behind. The workers who can keep the pace are paid half a reichsmark a day, which they can spend at the canteen for such luxuries as a paper of salt. Workers who miss their quotas have their pay docked, and the pay is in any case a tenth of what the work would have fetched outside the camps. Himmler, who set up the camp system, is getting rich. Lucky him. It may be true that there is sedative in the "coffee." In any case, those who will survive this experience have the trick of narrowing their brain functions to a pinhole, as an alligator in winter goes for hours without breathing and drops her heart rate to almost stopped.

Søsti is in the furrier's factory, where the air smells all day of blood and tanning acid. Skilled furriers are sewing the skins of angora rabbits, raised in the camp for the purpose, into the lining of hats, and larger pieces of fur into winter coats for SS officers "in the east." The "larger pieces of fur" is where Søsti's bench comes in. Fur coats, they are told, are turned in by patriotic Germans to aid the cause of the mighty Reich. But it is perfectly clear that in fact almost all of them have been stolen from Jews. The workers are watched as if they were deceitful rodents scavenging for nuts, as they unstitch the linings, sometimes silk and satin, often monogrammed, from these coats. Usually the coats have been stored in SS warehouses for who knows how long, and are full of fleas and lice. But sometimes there will be a handkerchief in a pocket, still smelling of lavender or cloves. Once the woman across from Søsti found a cough drop and managed to unwrap and eat it before she was seen. Once Søsti found a green suede glove. She held it to her nose and tears started in her eyes. The next thing she knew, a guard had clubbed her in the back of the head. He stood over her, yelling in German, as she got up from the floor and delivered the glove to him. (Why? What did the Reich need with one glove smelling of lily of the valley . . . ?) The saddest was when they found bank-notes or jewelry sewn into the linings to pay for escape and a new life.

When the furs had been stripped of embellishments, they ripped out the seams of the garment. You had to work very fast, with your face close to the dust- and bug-filled pelts, to be sure to cut only the threads that held them together. Søsti hated it; she couldn't stop wondering what the owners were thinking when they first put on this coat or jacket of mink, of beaver, of fox fur or Persian lamb, feeling loved and warm and lucky, looking forward to a dinner party or a night at the opera. She was with them in the hopefulness of sewing valuables into secret pockets, picturing themselves at safe harbor in Cuba, Brazil, the United States. She cried at night and threatened to accept the offer made to her and Nina, to go to work in the whorehouses at Buchen-wald or Sachsenhausen.

"You get your own room; you can sleep all day and work only two hours a night. And they let you go after six months," she wept to Nina. This was in the hour before lights-out at 9 P.M. Søsti lay with her head in Nina's lap, while Nina patiently picked out lice nits from her hair and crushed them with her fingernails.

"Liebchen," says the Frenchwoman in the bunk below them, "if they let you go after six months, we'd all do it. They work you until you get syphilis or the clap, then they send you back here. Stop crying."

In early November, hundreds of skeletal women arrive in Ravensbrück from Auschwitz, where the gas chambers have been closed as the Soviet army approached. The result was overcrowding. The governors of Auschwitz solve this problem by sending it to Ravensbrück. In the "slum" barracks, where the Danes are, there are suddenly four and five to some bunks, and the overflow women sleep on the floor. Even the elite barracks, the Polish and the Jehovah's Witness blocks, lose their day rooms; everyone eats her "coffee" or soup standing up. The hundreds for whom there is still no room are put into "Block 25." Block 25 is a tent.

The tent had been set up as auxiliary admissions but by this last winter it is permanent housing for Jews, Gypsies, and the weakest from Auschwitz. There are no toilets or washing facilities except a ditch outside. There is little light. It is literally freezing inside, and the savage, starving women lie in their own shit in wet icy straw. There are no work assignments for them. The seniors of Block 25, who would ordinarily dole out the food to the inmates, are afraid to go inside, so they put the food through the flap, and those strong enough to get to it first, eat. The rest lie in their filth and starve to death. Practically all the Auschwitz women assigned to the tent will die there, and the screams and stink from inside are with everyone else day and night. Guards patrol the outside, to keep the tent dwellers in and the other prisoners out. When some of the Communists, the best-organized group in camp, manage to steal ten-gallon vats of watery soup and smuggle them into the tent, the women inside lunge, fighting, for the stockpots and overturn them all.

There is now a sickening greasy smoke in the air, coming from right outside the front walls of the camp. The crematoria in Fürstenburg cannot dispose of the bodies fast enough anymore, and the camp has built its own ovens. Nevertheless, in all the blocks, the dead pile up faster than they can be burned. They are stacked now in the washrooms overnight, and Søsti hears that in some of the blocks when the bodies are carted out in the morning, they bear marks showing people have tried to eat them.

Nina, Ulla, and Søsti are allowed to keep their bunk to themselves, because Ulla is a favorite of the Blockova. This means, too, that when the room senior dishes up their soup at night, she dips to the bottom of the pot, so they get bits of potato peel or other solids. But the degradation of conditions all over camp has created a new problem. There are more and more orphaned children. The children in the tent whose mothers die simply starve to death. But when children from the barracks lose their mothers, other women adopt them, hide them and feed them and share with them whatever they have. A week before Christmas, Ulla brings a small Hungarian girl home with her from evening roll call.

The Blockova doesn't like it. The room senior doesn't like it. The girl is small, she looks unhealthy, she may be Gypsy. The Frenchwoman in the bunk below vehemently doesn't like it and says things Ulla is glad the child can't understand. They think her name is Zsuzsa; anyway, that's what they call her. Now they sleep in the bunk with Søsti's and Nina's heads at one end, Ulla's and Zsuzsa's at the other. They teach the child Danish words for "please," "thank you," and "water." When they are at work during the day, she stays in the block and plays very quietly with a doll someone has made for her out of straw.

Astonishingly, some women from the elite blocks get permission from

the Head Overseer to put on a Christmas party for the camp children. (The
Head Overseer is, after all, a woman, too.) They are allowed to build and paint
a set for a puppet theater. There is a Christmas tree. A choir sings "O Tannenbaum," and many in the audience, prisoners and guards, cry, thinking of
home. The puppet theater falls flat—the younger children are frightened of
the talking horses and sheep; the only animals they've ever seen are guard
dogs. But the Christmas Man puts presents under all the children's pillows
that night. Zsuzsa gets a tiny doll, a stick dressed in a striped prison uniform
dress and a kerchief. It's more like a fetish than a doll, but it must remind
Zsuzsa of her dead mother, for she is never without it after that.

On the second day of March, Nina is braiding Zsuzsa's hair in the hour
before bed when an overseer appears and orders the Blockova to summon
Fräulein Nina Moss. Ulla and Søsti reach to touch her, hold her back. After a
stunned pause Nina climbs down from their bunk and goes to the overseer.
She can feel her friends' eyes on her back as she walks away from them
through the babble of bodies and voices on the bunks and floors. With the
overseer, she disappears outside.

The overseer, a tall blond girl in a skirt, thick stockings, a warm black coat,
and boots, marches Nina between the rows of barracks to the administration
building. She is shown into a room, where an officer is waiting for her. He
does not rise when she comes in. He has a sheaf of papers on his desk he pretends to study, while filling and lighting his pipe. Upside down, she can read
her name on the folder.

"Miss Moss," he says at last, in German. Nina bobs her head. "I am told
you have been very modest about your war work."

Nina says nothing. Adrenaline jolts her like a seizure.

"Others, though, have told us a good deal. We have found new work for
you that will be familiar. We think you will be good at it."

"Danke," says Nina automatically.

"Oh, you are most welcome," says the SS man. He is about forty, fleshy
and quite handsome, with pink cheeks and blue eyes. "Overseer Bauer will
show you the way."

Nina is walking now under the low winter sky with the girl in the boots. Is
she a draftee or a volunteer, this young woman? Was she taken from her parents' apartment or farm perhaps, and required to join the war effort so her
family could eat? Or is she enjoying this?

The woman doesn't talk. They are going toward the gate to the outside of the camp, where one of the endless construction projects has been going on all month. What is it this time? Garages, kennels, new hutches for the rabbits? They can build kennels, but they can't build a barracks for the people in the tent.

Nina is outside the gates. Bright lights shine on the frozen earth around them. A men's work crew from one of the satellite camps is hauling a cart, loaded high with sand, through the rutted and frozen mud. One of the men wears a woman's overcoat, with a pinched waist and padded shoulders. The men don't even look in her direction.

Nina has worked a whole day in the spinning shop, and now she is apparently to work a night shift, too? The workers on night shift suffer even more than the rest, as they have to get what sleep they can in the noisy barracks during the day, while the life and death of the camp goes on around them.

They are approaching a fence two meters high around the new structures, which are just over the wall from the undressing barracks where her own clothes were taken away from her. Above the fence she can see a smokestack; this is the building they have been smelling for many weeks. The young overseer opens a door in the wall and follows Nina through.

Here is a squat concrete block with a tall smokestack belching greasy smoke with a rotten sweetish odor. Beside it is an even newer building. In fact, it is not entirely finished: it lacks a necessary step up to reach the door. A block of loose bricks must be used for now. Like the other, this new building has no windows, just a door and a vent pipe on the roof.

The overseer points to this door, and orders Nina to go in.

She is in a room lit from above by a single bulb. The room is crowded with women, hollowed out and gaunt, who turn to stare at her. Their eyes are avid. Who is she? Has she come to join their fate, or to make it worse in some way? Nina doesn't know the answer. She feels like vomiting.

They have all been brought here under cover of darkness. Is this a deportation station? Are they to be marched off to another camp? Lately women have been disappearing, officially to a new "rest camp" in the north called Mittwerda. But the people who go there are the ones who are too weak to work but too strong to die, and no news has ever come back from any of them.

This room smells of urine and shit and sweat and vomit, all of which the women have brought in on their clothes. The overseer orders a group of them to move aside, and when they do, Nina sees that behind them, there are children.

Three boys and five girls. It is hard to guess their ages, as they are starving, and thus small, with big peony heads on thin neck stalks. They look up at her, or don't bother. Two girls seem to be sisters; the others are palpably alone, although they are bunched together.

"You are to help with the children," says the guard in German. "Keep them calm, get them ready for their journey, as you did in Denmark." She goes out, locking the door behind her.

Nina and the other women look at each other. Yes, all right, she will help with the children. But these other prisoners could help, too. She believes she can see that they want to—it makes you feel less subhuman if you care for a child, or in some way comfort somebody else.

Nina goes to the children and kneels down to them. The two older girls look at each other. Nina reaches out to a small boy, but he doesn't know her. He cringes.

The outer door opens, and more women, a half dozen, are marched in by someone who closes the door and locks it behind them. One of the new women stares at the children, puts her hand to her mouth, and begins to weep. She stretches her hand toward one of the girls. They shrink from her. The woman is deranged. The outdoor lock tumbles and chucks again and a guard comes in.

"All you women, take off your clothes."

This is it. This is the way it ends. Nina thinks of her mother—what will she say, when she learns how it was for her? Will she ever learn? Or will all trace of her disappear in oily smoke? She reaches for the buttons on her dress.

"Not you, moron," says the guard to her. All the women's heads turn to Nina. Not her? Why not her?

Now all the women save Nina are standing naked, their last belongings on the floor in piles. Some seem hairless because they are old and their hair is sparse and white. Some have swollen bellies and breasts that hang like emptied sacks and stick arms and legs like an insect's. There is a Rabbit among them, Nina sees now. She hasn't seen one for months. They are Polish Resistance fighters on whom the doctors did medical experiments here in the first years of the war, transplanting bones, rubbing dirt and gangrene into gunshot wounds (to test new drugs under "battlefield conditions"), or cutting muscles and shattering bones with hammers (a regeneration study). When the experiments ended, the ones left alive were returned to the barracks, but known as Night and Fog prisoners; it was understood that they could give evidence in any war trial, and thus must disappear before they left Ravensbrück alive. When the Germans began killing them this winter, they fled their barracks and disappeared into hiding places all over the camp. Some had even been sheltered by the miserable inhabitants of the tent. This woman, whose face must once have been quite beautiful, is missing a foot and most of her shin, and has a crippled arm besides. She is unable to stand by herself but the guard allows another woman to brace her up. Most of them stand still and silent. A few look at Nina as if to say Do something! Help us!

An interior door opens, revealing another room beyond the one where they stand. From her corner, Nina can see only the light from inside it and a glimpse of blank wall. A guard and a prison senior, a man, come into the room. The guard orders the women to go through the door, and one by one, they go. The Rabbit, who had survived so much, goes in last, with her human crutch. The door is shut behind them, and locked from outside. The men go out and Nina is alone with the children when the screams and pleas begin from inside the room.

It doesn't take long. By the time there is silence, the children have drawn close to each other and several are crying quietly, as Nina is herself, though she doesn't know it. The little boy who first shrank from her lets Nina take him into her lap.

Time ticks on. The ticking sound is in Nina's imagination; somewhere in the world there are still clocks. Somewhere in the world free people know what time it is. Somewhere there is a world where no one knows this is happening.

When the outside door opens again, the guard and the trusty come back in. Their skin is pinched and colored from the cold outside. The trusty has a gas mask on his chest, dangling from the strap around his neck.

"Make them take their clothes off," says the guard to Nina.

It's not exactly that she didn't know this was coming. It's more that she's slowed down the ticking of the absent clocks so that the moment wouldn't arrive. Tick.

She turns to the children and says to them gently, in Danish, "Take off your clothes, now, little ones."

They stare at her. No one moves.

She tries again in German, then French. At last, the twin girls let go of each other's hands and untie the belts around their thin dresses. Nina nods and praises them, knowing she is betraying them utterly. She turns to the others and says, "Good. See?," and the others look. Two more who understand begin to undress. The rest are too young, too stunned; they stand like dead dolls.

Nina takes off the shoes of the little boy she is holding. He looks up at her. Does he have any memory of loving hands doing this, before his evening bath? She has no idea. He would have been born in wartime; perhaps he's never known the animal pleasure of warm soapy water after a good supper, before lullabies and bed.

The little boy's underpants are a dirty gray rag. The guard indicates she can leave those on him. Of what use to the Reich are torn and shitty baby underpants?

The strangest thing about this room now is the quiet. Nobody speaks, nobody weeps. The children stand like little naked wraiths. When the last kerchief and shoe are removed, the guard says, "Good. Line them up over here." Nina somehow herds the children toward the interior door, where they move instinctively into a line; they have already been in so many. The little boy in Nina's arms doesn't move, however; he won't or can't stand on his own, so she carries him and stands in the line with him in her arms. The guard opens the door before them. Nina can see most of the room beyond; a blank concrete square, empty. There's one lightbulb burning inside. The guard orders the line to move forward and Nina repeats him in French. The two oldest girls walk forward, and the rest follow. Nina thinks, Now we die.

When she reaches the door, the guard takes the boy from her arms and carries him into the room. He sets him down with surprising gentleness. Then he comes back out and pulls the door closed. The small faces of the figures huddled in the middle of the floor stare out at her until the door cuts the link between them. Maybe I'm already dead, Nina thinks.

There are only a few puzzled yips from inside this time. Nina stands with the guard, waiting for silence. Then silence is there, and they stand waiting

some more. Nina wonders if it's crazy that all she can think of is a clock ticking somewhere. The clock on the kitchen wall at home. Is it ticking?

The guard says a word, and goes to the outside door, indicating she
should follow. Nina notices she is fully dressed, wearing her coat, her kerchief, everything, as she was in the bunk a million years ago, before she was
called. You aren't allowed to wear coats or extra stockings to bed, but until
bed, in this winter cold, they wear all they've got, all the time. The guard leads
her outside, back into the rotten smoke smell, and takes her around to the
back of the building. They have to pick their way around a ladder leaning on
the roof. Only years later, surrounded by peacetime pleasures, will Nina remember that ladder and think, Oh. Of course . . . that's how they got the
poison gas in, canisters, pellets, down the flue. She'd been wondering how it
was done.

At the door in the back, they stand and wait. The winter wind ruffles
Nina's hair; there are big crows, maybe ravens, coming and going over the
high brick walls of the camp.

The trusty reappears, wearing the goggles and snout of the gas mask on
top of his head. He puts the mask on his face, transforming himself into
something like a nightmare pig. He opens the door, and Nina is looking into
the room the children disappeared into. No one inside is standing. The trusty
goes in. In a moment he is back, carrying Nina's boy. The guard orders her forward; what, is she asleep? The trusty holds out the body and her response is
instinctive; she takes it. You cannot drop a child.

The boy is limp, his body cooling. His eyes are open and there are tears on
the lashes. He has died crying. The guard leads her away while the trusty
starts carrying the bigger bodies out and dumping them into a cart like the
ones she saw being used to haul sand. He leads her into the crematorium
building, right up to the open furnace door, and she throws her boy in. Then
she is taken back to the gas chamber building where more children are waiting for her care.


Nina does this job for two weeks. Ulla has gotten sick, probably with pneumonia. Nina doesn't really care. Or if she cares, the caring seems to be outside
her, on the moon, somewhere she can know about with her brain but not

begin to feel. She sleeps as she can during the day, when Søsti and the others are at work. At night she goes to her job carrying children to their deaths. Ulla dies. The next day a white bus with the big red cross arrives, with packages for the Danish prisoners. When Nina's is handed to her (they have to wake her up for this), she sees the handwriting of a person in Copenhagen who has packed this box for her, and written her name on it, and then at the end of the day walked through the familiar streets, or ridden a bus, or a bicycle, home to a Danish supper. She looks around for Zsuzsa to share her package with, but Zsuzsa is off somewhere.

That night, of course, when her children are brought in to her, Zsuzsa is among them. She is so relieved to see Nina. She says, "Water, please, Nina," in Danish. "Later," says Nina. When she tells the children in Danish to take off their clothes, Zsuzsa understands and obeys. Her small prisoner doll in its striped uniform is tucked in her belt inside her clothes. She gives it to Nina to hold for her when their little line is ordered forward into the inside room.

Nina lies in a sort of altered state most of the next day on their foul-smelling mattress, a sack stuffed with straw, shocked to realize that she is a human being, with a name, who is remembered at home. She sleeps for an hour or two in the afternoon, finally at peace, and after supper, when the overseer comes for her, she says that she will not have anything more to do with the children. She expects to be killed at once.

She is sent instead into the sewing factory for the night shift. She is much weaker than she was when she arrived, and she doesn't learn the work very fast. She never sees Søsti anymore except for minutes at roll calls. She has lost her camp family. She knows what will happen next. She takes to carrying a small bar of soap from her Red Cross package around in her pocket.

One night, a woman comes into the sewing shop as Nina's shift is beginning. She is a prisoner, but her job is like the job of hall monitor children prized at school, the person who keeps the others in line and quiet, as they pass from classroom to assemblies or to music or art studios. This woman has a list. She gives it to the foreman of the floor and he calls out the numbers. Some fifteen women lay down their tools. Nina is among them.

They are lined up. They are marched downstairs. They are walked outside into the night air. The weather is mild and there are puffs of cloud in the starry night. The trusty woman walks up and down their line, waiting for a guard to escort the women to the building outside the gates. Nina catches her eye.

"I have soap," she says to her in French.

The woman looks up and down the street between the barracks. No one is near.

"Show me."

Nina slips the soap out of her pocket and cups it in her palm. Real soap is incredibly rare here.

"Donnez-le-moi," says the woman, and Nina slips it into her hand. The woman pockets it and jerks her head. Get out of here. Nina steps out of line and walks quickly back into the factory and up the stairs. The factory foreman gives her a look of surprise as she comes back, but does nothing further. Nina sits back down to her work.

A week later, Nina is standing with a group from the factory waiting to be taken back to their barracks when a shoving match breaks out among two prisoners from Yugoslavia. She doesn't understand what they yell, or what it's about. Two SS men arrive quickly and quell the disturbance by knocking one of the girls on the head. Then as she lies on the ground, with her eyes rolled back and her mouth open, he seems to realize that now someone is going to have to either carry her to the infirmary or wait with her until she regains consciousness. They decide they don't care to do either, so the second guard shoots her. Now they can leave her there and send someone with a cart from the crematorium.

Then, almost as an afterthought, he orders the rest of them marched not back to their barracks, but forward toward the front gate, to the building with the fence around it. This is done.

When they get there, there is a wait until someone can come unlock the gate. There are always waits. Nina has a packet of Danish tobacco in her pocket. She catches the guard's eye, and tells her this. The guard makes a face and walks away. But as the wait lengthens, she thinks better of it. She comes back and holds out her hand for it. Then she says in German, "Go." Nina walks off quickly toward her barracks. Behind her she can hear the guard respond to a question. "A mistake," she hears her say.

Nina is now out of everything from her Red Cross package except a tiny piece of chocolate. She knows that if she has nothing left to trade, her life is over. But one afternoon, unable to sleep, as she lies in the bunk holding Zsuzsa's doll, there is a surprising shock of flavor on her tongue, and she realizes she has unwrapped the last piece of chocolate and eaten it. It is the thirty-first of March.

Five nights later, she is once again just inside the walls, waiting for the front gate to be opened. She is standing in a line.

Al Pease got to Leeway first, followed by Dr. Coles. After looking things over, they sat in the kitchen with Shirley, drinking the Mosses' breakfast coffee, and waited for someone to come from the sheriff's office in Union.

"You shouldn't really have touched anything," said the officer when he finally drove in. He was new to the area. He looked as if he weren't used to shaving yet, or else needed a sharper blade. He was big and young. He had his revolver in his holster and the handcuffs on his belt, and he clanked when he walked up the stairs.

"Well, the house was full of gas," said Al. "She didn't have much choice if she didn't want to be blown up."

The officer conceded this. He stood at the bathroom door and looked at the bodies. Then he wandered around the bedroom and spent a minute or so staring at the heater.

"Nothing wrong with it," said Al. "It's just old. They knew never to turn it on without calling me to put it in order."

"Sydney wouldn't have remembered that," said Dr. Coles.

"He must have fallen," said Al.

"Looks like she was trying to keep him warm." Neither of them wants to look into the bathroom again.

"I'm surprised she remembered there *was* a heater," said Andy.

"It's a real sorry way to go," said the officer, wondering why no-body had been taking care of these sweet old people, if everyone knew they were so dotty.

"Oh, I don't know about that," said Al.

The officer looked at him. He looked at the heater. He said, "Why wouldn't they put in a furnace, if they were going to stay here in the cold."

"The house is on ledge. You couldn't use it far into the fall; the pipes would freeze."

"They liked things the way they were."

"What do we do now?" Shirley asked.

"Start calling the children, I guess."

Shirley went into the study where Mrs. Moss kept the family telephone numbers written, in very big numbers, on a piece of paper attached to the blotter with yellowing Scotch tape. She began to dial.

Eleanor, Jimmy, and Monica are sitting in the dining room with the photograph albums and scrapbooks, stacks of clippings, letters, snapshots, and grocery lists that have emerged from drawers, bookcases, and the cupboard behind the chimney. It's time to lock up the house and go, but none of them is ready to leave it. Eleanor picks up an old address book. It is bound in fabric with appliquéd felt golf balls and tees, and so stuffed with extraneous papers that a rubber band holds it closed. Eleanor found it back in the drawer of Sydney's bedside table. At one touch, the brittle rubber snaps. She starts turning the pages.

Monica looks up when she hears her sister say, "Oh, my God."

Lying before her on the table are a blue envelope and a matching sheet of letter paper.

"What is it?"

On the back of the envelope, in pencil, their mother had written "7/19/63." Eleanor hands the paper across the table to Monica. It reads:

*I loved you, even now I may confess,*

*Some embers of my love their fire retain;*

But do not let it cause you more distress,

I do not want to sadden you again.

Hopelessly and tongue-tied, yet I loved you dearly

With pangs the jealous and the timid know;

So tenderly I love you, so sincerely,

I pray God grant another love you so.

N.

Jimmy takes it and reads it quietly as Monica says to Eleanor, "It's Uncle Neville's writing." Which they all recognize. That architects' printing.

After a pause, Jimmy says, "You didn't know?"

His sisters turn together to him. "You *did*?"

"It went on for years," Jimmy says, with no pleasure. He is thinking of the year he was kicked out of Country Day. The long phone calls behind closed doors. Their mother's volatile moods that year, to which he was so attuned. The summer only he was at Leeway with Sydney, and she sang and laughed all the time. And the next summer, when she had herself taken away.

"Uncle Neville." Eleanor and Monica were looking at each other. "And they had to go on seeing each other every day all summer, year after year . . ."

"How could she do that to Gladdy?" asks Monica.

"Did Dad know?" Eleanor asks.

"I couldn't tell," says Jimmy. "Gladdy did."

"How do you know *that*?"

"She caught me watching Mom and Uncle Neville at a yacht club party. I was fourteen. They were dancing together, and suddenly while I was watching *them*, I saw Aunt Gladdy was watching *me*. She gave me this very steady look, and then she turned away from the dancers and began talking to somebody. So I did, too."

"She *adores* Uncle Neville," says Monica, trying to take it in.

"And she forgave them," says Eleanor, puzzled. "She forgave them both. I wonder how."

After a long silence, Monica says, "Come on, orphans. We're going to freeze in here. Let's lock it up and go get dinner."

# ACKNOWLEDGMENTS

Sanna Borge Feirstein has given me priceless support throughout the research and writing of this book, sharing impossible-to-find books from her family's library, and introducing me to the people and re-sources of the Scandinavia House in New York, where lectures and the library also proved invaluable. Sanna introduced me to Stig Høst, whose memories, writings, and advice were riches in them-selves, as well as keys unlocking further doors. In Copenhagen, Hen-rik Glahn and Inge Bonnerup and Lars and Charlotte Lindeberg were extraordinarily generous, sharing memories, answering ques-tions, lending an armload of books unavailable in English, not to mention supplying coffee and wienerbrød so delicious that we're still wistful about them. Jim Colias has been unfailingly generous, not to mention charming, with his knowledge and contacts. Aase van Dyke spent hours with me translating, answering questions, and illuminating cross-cultural mysteries, and has continued to be so helpful with books, information, and resources that I'll never be able to thank her properly. Vebe Borge, pursuing a parallel project of his own, seemed sent from heaven as I was discovering exactly how hard it was going to be to get an accurate picture of life at Ravens-brück. John Hargraves introduced me to the Danish-American film-maker Alexandra Moltke Isles, whose documentary *The Power of Conscience: The Danish Resistance and the Rescue of the Jews* is a marvel of concision and who graciously shared resources and family stories that helped immensely. Jerri Witt was my rod and my staff when it came to Laurus's professional life and repertoire. Christina McHenry, Elvira Bass, Tom Richardson, Anne Johnson, and Bobby

Patri all lent or pointed me to books I would otherwise have missed that contributed to my understanding of some aspect of my characters' lives. Neal Johnston shared his vast knowledge of things musical, and even came up with an incredible rarity, a book in English on how Bulgaria saved *her* Jews, which had nothing directly to do with my subject but satisfied a by then rampaging curiosity. Lars Lindeberg, China Neury, and Philip Armour IV gave generous help on Swedish matters. Lucie Semler, Robin Clements, Sanna Feirstein, Jerri Witt, Joy Richardson, Shery and Breene Kerr, Susan Richardson, David Gutcheon, Alison Rogers, Angelica Baird, and Lars Lindeberg each read the manuscript in various stages of its evolution and provided notes and comments for which I am forever grateful. And, as always, I am grateful to my agent, Wendy Weil, for her support, her judgment, her humor, and her lifelong friendship, and to Meaghan Dowling, my wonderful editor, for much the same.

For those wishing to know more about the historical underpinnings of this novel, a selected bibliography is available at *www.beth gutcheon.com*.

## About the author

## About the book

## Read on

Insights,
Interviews
& More . . .

# Meet Beth Gutcheon

© 2005 by Nancy Crampton

BETH GUTCHEON grew up in western Pennsylvania. She has spent most of her adult life in New York City, except for sojourns in San Francisco and on the coast of Maine. In 1978, she wrote the narration for a feature-length documentary on the Kirov ballet school, *The Children of Theatre Street,* which was nominated for an Academy Award; since then she has made her living as a fulltime storyteller (novelist and sometime screenwriter). Her novels have been translated into fourteen languages, if you count the pirated Chinese edition of *Still Missing,* plus large-print and audio formats. *Still Missing* was made into a feature film called *Without a Trace,* and was also published in a *Reader's Digest* condensed version, which particularly pleased her mother. ༄

# A Conversation with Beth Gutcheon

*Leeway Cottage is your seventh novel, and the second to have a historical element. Can you tell us how it evolved?*

My father, who spent his boyhood summers on the coast of Maine with his cousins, kept a guest book from a summer house that no longer exists called Fagerheim (pronounced FOGgerhime). The house had been built by a Norwegian musician in the 1880s, then sold to another musical family whom my grandparents used to visit at the turn of the twentieth century. The guest book is full of sketches and doggerel by, in many cases, the grandparents or great-grandparents of people who still summer in that colony today. I always wished it were possible to know what lay behind those entries. What did the people mentioned in its pages look like, what were they wearing, who was in love with whom, who feuding with whom, what made them laugh, and what exactly did they do all day? Since I couldn't make the Fagerheim guestbook talk, I started thinking about a novel that would take place in such a summer colony, with the guestbook of a particular house as the spine of it.

I wanted to examine a certain kind of twentieth-century American marriage, in which the husband and wife, as they have grown and as life has changed them, appear by midlife to be so different as people that outsiders (or insiders—their own children) ▶

> " I wanted to examine a certain kind of twentieth-century American marriage. "

**A Conversation with Beth Gutcheon**
*(continued)*

can't understand how they chose each other in the first place. And yet in their generation, born right before or right after the First World War, oddly matched couples usually stayed together, kept their promises (or appeared to), and even appeared devoted to each other. Theirs was the last generation to be pretty much untouched by Freud, by the psychologically examined life, for good or ill. For some of both, probably. I wanted to try to fully imagine what such a couple each thinks they are seeing in the other when they fall in love, and when they marry, and how they handle the surprises to come as they grow to understand what it is they have actually chosen.

*Did the idea of making Laurus a Scandinavian musician come from the house, Fagerheim?*

Well, it was an obvious and useful narrative shorthand for the differences between Laurus and Sydney: Laurus is European and an artist, and Sydney a rich and provincial American with no idea of what she doesn't know. The fact that Laurus is specifically Danish has a different source. It made sense that he be from a small country with a history and culture not as familiar to American readers as perhaps France's or Italy's, because it would be more interesting both for me and for the reader. That said, Denmark was the obvious choice for me because I had fallen for it the first

66 Denmark was the obvious choice for me because I had fallen for it the first time I went to Europe when I was seventeen, and had subsequently spent a summer there as a pathetically ill-equipped au pair. 99

time I went to Europe when I was seventeen, and had subsequently spent a summer there as a pathetically ill-equipped au pair. During that summer, I learned something of the Danish Resistance during World War Two, though how much I really understood of it I can't tell you, having now lived with my research so long that the chickens and eggs are all in a heap together in my brain. As that part of the story began to evolve for me, the shape of it was at first very different from what it became.

### In what way?

I first thought I would tell it from the point of view of a Jewish family, in fear and jeopardy, and the drama of their rescue. The easiest books to find on the subject dealt in most detail with the stories of the Jews who were saved. Their stories were riveting, but once the refugees got to Sweden, as the very great majority did, their story from the novelist's point of view is effectively over. While for my characters the trauma and drama continued. As I delved deeper into the subject I came to see that the less well-known story is of the Danish partisans. It is true that almost all the Danish Jews survived. But a tremendous price was paid by many of the Danes who saved them, those who lived and the many who didn't, and the Danes as a people are so modest and self-deprecating that they weren't talking about it. So Laurus's sister ▶

> 66 It is true that almost all the Danish Jews survived. But a tremendous price was paid by many of the Danes who saved them ... and the Danes as a people are so modest and self-deprecating that they weren't talking about it. 99

### A Conversation with Beth Gutcheon
*(continued)*

and brother became partisans, like so many young Danes of sixty years ago, and that took me where it took me. What happened to Nina helped tell the real story of Sydney and Laurus's marriage. As a safe, lucky American, there was so much Sydney never understood about what it was like for Laurus: what he remembered, what he regretted, what he mourned for, even after she had lived with him for sixty years.

*Do you see Sydney and Laurus as metaphors for their countries? Or for the United States and Europe?*

Of course.

*Can you say more about that?*

I'd rather not.

I will say, though I don't much want to talk about this either, that I live six blocks north of what we used to call the World Trade Center, and that I was standing on the roof of my building looking south when the top of the south tower slumped sideways and fell off, followed by the disappearance of the rest of it. Being in the presence of so many souls streaming into the ether at once certainly made for a paradigm shift, for me and so many others, and was certainly with me as I wrote the proposal for this novel the following spring.

*Leeway Cottage* is a story. It is *about*

> **Leeway Cottage** is a story. It is *about* something, for me, but its job is to be a story about specific people, as true as it can be about its own time and place.

something, for me, but its job is to be a story about specific people, as true as it can be about its own time and place. Sydney is as much shaped by the fact that she has a monster mother, that she is an only child, that her father died when she was young, and by her simultaneously deprived and overprivileged upbringing, as by being American. Similarly, young Laurus, whose parents and siblings are cheerful, optimistic, humorous, and emotionally generous, thinks that's what family life is always like, because he comes from that kind of family, not because he comes from Denmark. Even if he sees signs that Sydney lacks some of those qualities, he doesn't read the signs because he doesn't expect them to be there. Many readers of *Leeway Cottage* go through the same process with Sydney. When she's a little girl, they sympathize with her, as we usually do with children, and they expect her to grow up to be a heroine because they were rooting for her in the early chapters. In fact, there are a lot of signals in those early chapters that Sydney may be socially tone-deaf, that her loneliness in childhood could just as easily leave her inept or unable to imagine other people's realities as make her sensitive or sympathetic. And especially, that being simultaneously deprived and overprivileged could make her angry without good inner controls over her anger, and vain about the wrong things in life, just as likely as it could have made her flexible and loving. The fact that a person has been ▶

badly hurt in childhood does not necessarily lead to kindly adulthoods; we know this in life, but apparently don't expect it in fiction. Dickens may have a lot to answer for here.

*Does it concern you that some readers seem taken by surprise by the kind of wife and mother Sydney becomes?*

No. The seeds are there, to the extent I can fairly sow them, given that I believe in free will. It was never predetermined that Sydney would turn out as she did. If she and Laurus hadn't been apart for those long years of the war, she and the marriage might have been quite different. If she'd had only sons, she might have been a different kind of mother. If she'd kept up with her music, and taken herself seriously in some way other than as a big fish in a small pond, things might have been different. For her in childhood, many outcomes were possible. But as we all know, every major choice we make closes off other options. She tended to make choices based on impulse, and in reaction to emotions she hadn't much understanding of, while Laurus, who has much more discipline, both intellectual and emotional, tended to make decisions out of principle. That worked out well for Sydney, to the extent that anything did.

*You've written about daughters with difficult or "monster" mothers before. Can you talk about that?*

66 It was never predetermined that Sydney would turn out as she did. 99

8

It's just one more way of looking at the mystery of personality. The subject could just as easily be fathers and sons, except I'm not a man and would more likely get details wrong. I believe that most children of difficult parents have a special fear of becoming like those parents when raising their own children. Some do anyway though, some don't, and some split the difference. I have a novelist friend who says that he never puts his hand into his mother's cage without its coming out bloody. There was something about the wives of that mid-century generation, at least those who had a certain level of privilege—it could have been caused by a hundred things, and I have my theories and readers will have theirs—but in a way that you don't often find represented in song and story and American myth, a significant sample of them seemed to hate their daughters, or their sons, or their grandchildren. Why? Were they jealous, were they angry about restrictions in their lives that didn't exist for their daughters? It seems worth trying to understand.

*Since you brought up Dickens, who are your influences?*

Dickens, of course. We read *David Copperfield* in eighth grade and I never stopped. At Harvard back in the day, one of your four major courses junior year was a small or even individual tutorial (as I recall it) in whatever area of your major you most wanted to ▶

> 66 I have a novelist friend who says that he never puts his hand into his mother's cage without it coming out bloody. 99

9

**A Conversation with Beth Gutcheon**
*(continued)*

study in depth. Esther Purpel and I wanted to read Dickens and there was only one instructor in the department who was willing to take us on, Donald Doub, God bless him. The rest were all trying to write their own doctoral theses, or striving to publish not perish, and far preferred you read something they already knew, like Shakespeare, or something there wasn't much of, like Austen. With Dr. Doub we read comic literature, in translation if necessary, the first term, from Gil Blas and Don Quixote through Fielding and Smollett, and in the second term, all of Dickens's fiction. All. It was an absolute feast. For the rest, if influences mean what you read over and over again, Austen, Evelyn Waugh, Scott Fitzgerald, and Willa Cather.

*What are you working on now?*

I'm a long way from the writing stage of what I'm working on, but I know where I'm going. When you work in a long form you have to have, or develop, a long attention span, but at least in my case the concomitant of that is you don't do well with interruptions. So I can't really settle into the next book until I can lock the doors and turn off the phone and stay that way for about two years. I'm still seeing *Leeway Cottage* along its course toward open water, which still feels like part of the working on it. But from the beginning, my editor and I have known that the novel after *Leeway Cottage* would be about what happens when

> 66 I can't really settle into the next book until I can lock the doors and turn off the phone and stay that way for about two years. 99

Sydney and Laurus's children inherit the house together. My grandmother apparently used to say that you don't know what kind of parent you've been until you see your grandchildren. Similarly, I won't have finished looking at Sydney and Laurus's marriage until I see what becomes of their children. So I'm working, in the sense of reading and thinking, on who they grow up to be. And collecting stories of the family politics of inheritance. And I've structured the Moss family's time frame such that the two daughters of Sydney and Laurus go to the same boarding school, in the same years, as the characters from my first novel, *The New Girls.* Maybe I'll use that and maybe I won't, but it's fun knowing it's there. ❧

# Spotlight on
# *More Than You Know*

**A *Los Angeles Times* Best Book of the Year**

"Combines the chilling tension of a murder mystery with the most tender elements of youthful romance. In this tale, haunting in every sense, Gutcheon uses her well-honed insights into human passion and her remarkable skills as a storyteller. . . . Gutcheon is a wonderful writer. *More Than You Know* is a triumph, ghost and all."
—*Boston Herald*

*Below is an excerpt from chapter one of* More Than You Know. *In a small town called Dundee on the coast of Maine, an old woman named Hannah Gray begins her story by saying, "Somebody said 'true love is like ghosts, which everyone talks about and few have seen.' I've seen both and I don't know how to tell you which is worse." Hannah has decided, finally, to leave a record of the passionate and anguished long-ago summer in Dundee when she met Conary Crocker, the town's bad boy and love of her life. This spare, piercing, and unforgettable novel bridges two centuries and two intense love stories as Hannah and Conary's fate is interwoven with the tale of a marriage that took place in Dundee a hundred years earlier.* More Than You Know *is now available in trade paperback from Harper Perennial.*

MY CHILDREN THINK I'M MAD to come up here in winter, but this is the only place I could tell this story. They think the weather is too cold for me, and the light is so short this time of year. It's true this isn't a story I want to tell in darkness. It isn't a story I want to tell at all, but neither do I want to take it with me.

If you approach Dundee, Maine, from inland by daylight, you see that you're traveling through wide reaches of pasture strewn with boulders, some of them great gray hulks as big as a house. You can feel the action of some vast mass of glacier scraping and gouging across the land, scarring it and littering it with granite detritus. The thought of all that ice pressing against the land makes you understand the earth as warm, living, and indestructible. Changeable, certainly. It was certainly changed by the ice. But it's the ice that's gone, and grass blows around the boulders, and lichens, green and silver, grow on them somehow like warm vegetable skin over the rock. Even rock, cold compared to earth, is warm and living, compared to the ice.

For miles and miles, the nearer you draw to the sea, the more the road climbs; I always think it must have been hard on the horses. Finally you reach the shoulder of Butter Hill, and then you are tipped suddenly down the far slope into the town. My heart moves every time I see that tiny brave and lovely cluster of bare white houses against the blue of the bay.

The earliest settlers in Dundee didn't come from inland; they came from the sea. It was far easier to sail downwind, even along that drowned coastline of mountains, whose ▶

66 It's true this isn't a story I want to tell in darkness. It isn't a story I want to tell at all, but neither do I want to take it with me. 99

peaks form the islands and ledges where boats land or founder, than to make your way by land. In many parts of the coast the islands were settled well before the mainland. This was particularly true of Great Spruce Bay, where Beal Island lies, a long tear-shaped mass in the middle of the bay, and where Dundee sits at the head of the innermost harbor.

Not much is known about the first settlement on Beal Island, except that a seventeenth-century hermit named Beal either chose it or was cast away there, and trapped and fished alone near the south end until, one winter, he broke his leg and died. Later, several families took root on the island and a tiny community grew near March Cove. Around 1760 a man named Crocker moved his wife and children from Beal onto the main to build a sawmill where the stream flows into the bay. The settlement there flourished and was sometimes called Crocker's Cove, or sometimes Friends' Cove, or Roundyville, after the early families who lived there. In the 1790s, the town elected to call the place Sunbury, and proudly sent Jacob Roundy down to Boston to file papers of incorporation (as Maine was then a territory of Massachusetts). When he got back, Roundy explained that the whole long way south on muleback he'd had a hymn tune in his head. The tune was Dundee and he'd decided this was a sign from God. "God moves in a mysterious way, his wonders to perform: He plants his footsteps in the sea, and rides upon the storm" went the first verse. The sentiment

66 Not much is known about the first settlement on Beal Island, except that a seventeenth-century hermit named Beal either chose it or was cast away there. 99

was hard to quarrel with, though there were those who were spitting mad, especially Abner Crocker, who had to paint out the word SUNBURY on the sign he had made to mark the town line, and for years and years faint ghosts of the earlier letters showed through behind the word DUNDEE. ◕

# Have You Read?
## More by Beth Gutcheon

**DOMESTIC PLEASURES**

After her ex-husband dies in a plane crash, Martha Gaver is horrified to learn that the executor of Raymond's estate is Charlie, the conservative, insufferable lawyer who represented Raymond in their bitter divorce. Yet soon after they reenter one another's lives, Martha, Charlie, and their teenage children find they have more in common than they imagined as they struggle to rebuild their lives . . . and that opposites really do attract.

"There is a world of entertainment in *Domestic Pleasures*."
—*New York Times Book Review*

"This is the novel as we used to know it, with laughter, tears, true-to-life details, and a must-know-what-happens-next story line." —Penelope Fitzgerald

FIVE FORTUNES

*a novel*

Beth Gutcheon

AUTHOR OF *More Than You Know*
AND *Leeway Cottage*

## FIVE FORTUNES

Witty, wise, and hope-filled, *Five Fortunes* is a bighearted tale of five vivid and unforgettable women who know where they've been but have no idea where they're going. A lively octogenarian, a private investigator, a mother and daughter with an unresolved past, and a recently widowed politician's wife have little else in common, except for a thirst for new dreams, but after a week at the luxurious health spa known as "Fat Chance," their lives will be intertwined in ways they couldn't have imagined. At a place where doctors, lawyers, spoiled housewives, movie stars, and captains of industry are stripped of the social markers that keep them from really seeing one another, unexpected friendships emerge, reminding us of the close links between rich and poor, fortune and misfortune, and the alchemy of chance.

"[Gutcheon] has absolutely perfect pitch when it comes to capturing the voices of these remarkable women. I loved it."

—Anne Rivers Siddons

## SAYING GRACE

A powerfully moving novel about Rue Shaw, a woman who has everything worth having— a much loved daughter, a solid marriage, and a job she loves—plus one great failing: she wants things to stay the same. Set in the close-knit world of a country day school on California's gold coast, *Saying Grace* captures a clash of values and cultures that profoundly shakes the entire community, especially the life of Rue Shaw, who heads the school.

"Deliciously readable."

—*San Francisco Chronicle*